Emma Darwin was born in 1964. [...] first novel, was acclaimed in nine countries; *A Secret Alchemy* is her second. She lives in London.

Praise for *The Mathematics of Love*:

'A daring debut novel ... Emma Darwin's prose is golden and convincing. Addictive' *Daily Express*

'Convincing and involving ... a book to lose yourself in' *Daily Mail*

'The reader is spellbound ... electrifying' *Independent*

'This sweeping tale of nineteenth-century war and courtship and twentieth-century teenage rebellion has a real flavour of its own that will grip you to the end ... an accomplished, vividly realised debut' *Marie Claire*

'Absorbing ... will fit comfortably beside *Birdsong* or *Captain Corelli's Mandolin*' *Tatler*

'A beautifully written, intelligent book ... as historically graphic and passionately romantic as Sebastian Faulks's *Birdsong*' *Waterstone's Books Quarterly*

'Fascinating ... If you're in a book club torn between lovers of nineteenth-century and modern fiction, *The Mathematics of Love* may be just the thing to square the circle ... hauntingly beautiful' *Washington Post*

By Emma Darwin and available from Headline Review

The Mathematics of Love
A Secret Alchemy

A Secret Alchemy

Emma Darwin

headline
review

First published in Great Britain in 2008
by HEADLINE REVIEW
An imprint of HEADLINE PUBLISHING GROUP

First published in paperback in Great Britain in 2009
by HEADLINE REVIEW
An imprint of HEADLINE PUBLISHING GROUP

I

Cataloguing in Publication Data is available from the British Library

ISBN 978 0 7553 3067 6 (B-format)
ISBN 978 0 7553 4974 6 (A-format)

Typeset in Centaur by Avon DataSet Ltd, Bidford-on-Avon, Warwickshire

Printed and bound in Great Britain by Clays Ltd, St Ives plc

Headline's policy is to use papers that are natural, renewable and recyclable
products and made from wood grown in sustainable forests. The logging and
manufacturing processes are expected to conform to the environmental
regulations of the country of origin.

HEADLINE PUBLISHING GROUP
An Hachette UK Company
338 Euston Road
London NW1 3BH

www.headline.co.uk
www.hachette.co.uk

In memory of my father

The Woodvilles

Jacquetta de St Pol, Duchess of Bedford *1416?-1472*
= 1) John, Duke of Bedford *1389-1435*, uncle to Henry VI   = 2) **Richard Woodville**, 1st Earl Rivers *1405?-killed 1469*

Anne *1438?-1489*	Mary *1443?-before 1481*	**Sir John** *1445?-executed 1469*
Margaret Lady Maltravers, later Countess of Arundel *1439?-1490*	**Sir Edward** *1447?-killed 1488*	Thomas *1449?-?*

Elizabeth *1437?-1492*
= 1) **Sir John Grey of Groby** *1432?-killed 1461*

— **Sir Edward Grey** *d. 1547* = **Elizabeth, Lady Ferrars** *d. 1483*

2) Edward IV (see *The House of York*)

Jacquetta *1444?-1509*

Lionel Bishop of Salisbury *1446?-1484*

Richard 3rd Earl Rivers *1448?-1491*

John *(died young)*

Lewis *(died young)*

Martha *1453?-?*

Eleanor *1454?-?*

Katherine Duchess of Buckingham and later of Bedford *1452?-before 1513*

Anthony 2nd Earl Rivers *1442?-executed 1483*

Thomas Grey Marquess of Dorset *1455?-1501* 'Tom'

Sir Richard Grey *1460?-executed 1483* 'Dickon' in Parts One and Two

= 1) Elizabeth, Lady Scales *1436?-1473 (no issue)*

= 2) Mary Fitz-Lewes *(no issue)*

illegitimate issue by Gwentlian Stradling: Margaret Stradling

> Names in **bold** are characters who appear in the novel, with the title which they are most often given

The House of Lancaster

Margaret Beaufort *1443-1509*
= 2) Edmund Tudor *1430?-1456*

Henry Tudor
Earl of Richmond, later **Henry VII** *1457-1509*
= **Elizabeth of York** *(see The House of York)*

Henry VI
1421-killed 1471
'Henry of Lancaster',
= **Margaret** *1429-1482*
'Marguerite of Anjou'

Edward
Prince of Wales
1453-killed 1471
'Edward of Lancaster'
= **Anne Neville**
(see The Nevilles)

Arthur
1486-1502

Margaret
1489-1541

Henry VIII
1491-1547

Elizabeth
1492-1495

Mary
1495-1533

Edmund, Edward, Katherine
(all died young)

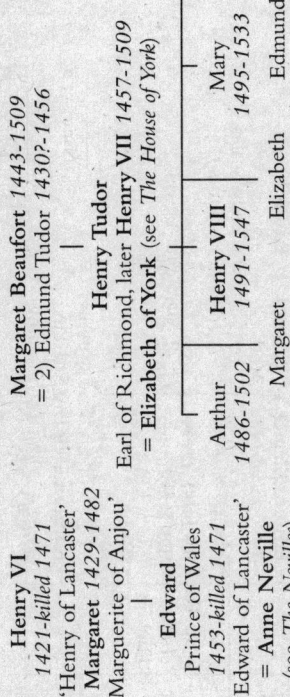

The Nevilles

Richard Neville, Earl of Warwick
1428-killed 1471, 'the Kingmaker'
= Anne de Beauchamp

John Neville
Marquess of Montagu
1429?-killed 1471

Richard, Duke of Gloucester
later **Richard III** *1452-killed 1485*
(see The House of York)
= **Anne Neville**
Duchess of Gloucester,
later Queen Consort *1456-1485*

George Neville
Archbishop of York
1432-1476

and
six more
siblings

George, Duke of Clarence
1449-executed 1478
(see The House of York)
= **Isobel Neville**
Duchess of Clarence *1451-1476*

Anne
(died young)

Margaret
1473-
executed 1541

Edward
1475-
executed 1499

Richard
(died young)

Edward
Prince of Wales
1473-1484
'Edward of Middleham'

illegitimate
issue by
various
mothers

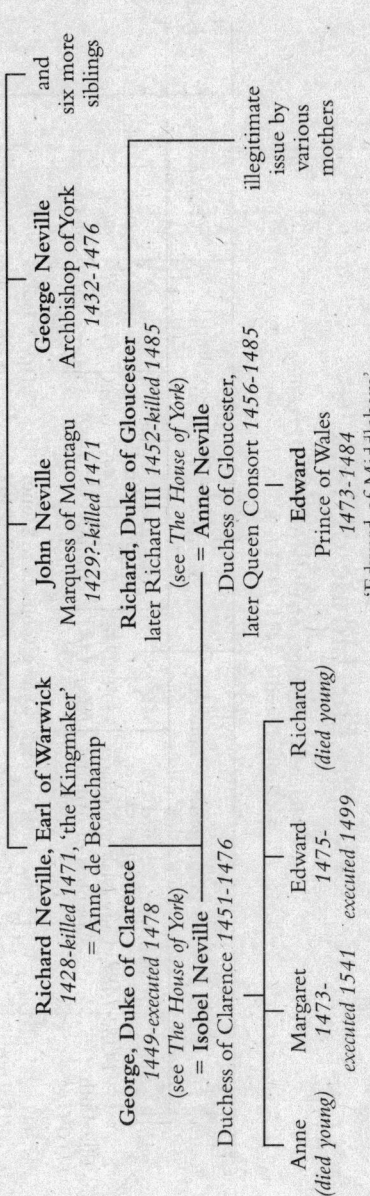

The House of York

Richard Plantagenet, Duke of York *1411-1460*
= Cicely Neville *1415-1495 (see also The Nevilles)*

Joan *(died young)*

Henry *(died young)*

Anne *1439-1476*

Edward Plantagenet formerly Earl of March, later **Edward IV** *1442-1483* = Elizabeth Woodville *(see The Woodvilles)*

Elizabeth of York, Queen Consort to Henry VII *1466-1503 (see The House of Lancaster)* 'Bess'

Mary *1467-1482*

Cecily *1469-1507*

Edward, Prince of Wales, later **Edward V** *1470-killed 1483?* 'Ned'

Margaret *(died young)*

Richard, **Duke of York** *1473-killed 1483?* 'Dickon' in parts Three and Four

Anne *1475-1513*

George *1477-1479*

Katherine *1479-1511*

Bridget *1480-before 1513*

Edmund *1443-killed 1460*

Elizabeth *1444-1503/4*

Margaret Duchess of Burgundy *1446-1503* 'Margaret of York'

William *(died young)*

John *(died young)*

George, Duke of Clarence *1449-executed 1478* = Isobel Neville Duchess of Clarence *1451-1476 (see The Nevilles)*

Thomas *(died young)*

Ursula *(died young)*

Richard, Duke of Gloucester later **Richard III** *1452-killed 1485* = **Anne Neville** Duchess of Gloucester, later Queen Consort *1456-1485 (see The Nevilles)*

Names in **bold** are characters who appear in the novel, with the title which they are most often given

illegitimate issue including, by Elizabeth Lucy: Arthur Plantagenet, Viscount Lisle *1461-1542*

The type is cast in a mould that can be opened and shut very quickly. The metal, which is ladled into it, consists of lead, arsenic and regulus of antimony. At the same time as the metal enters the mould . . . a rapid movement is made by the hand holding the mould, which increases the pressure on the bottom where the actual letter is formed.

R. R. Angerstein on Baskerville's type foundry

Prologue

What I have known, I shall not set down. My habit is silence, and it is a habit that has served me well. Words set on paper are dangerous. Wise men will write no more than is needful, and give it into the hand of their most trusted messenger. No more, that is, than gains the messenger stabling for his horse and safe conduct into the hall, and a privy hearing with its lord. All else is a tale for the messenger to tell: arms and allegiances, open war and secret plans, love and hate and the safety of the realm. So it is with me. After a lifetime of such tales there is no house so safe they may be told within it, no castle so strong it may not be breached at the turn of Fortune's wheel. At the hour of my death my memories, my tales, will die with me. The great men and their masters, whom I have served with so much diligence and secrecy, expect it.

There are men, and women too, who have witnessed these events and others that I have not. Like pilgrims we have travelled the same road, stumbled over the same stones, knelt at the same shrines, yet each one of us has made a different journey and met a different end. And what our journey truly was, what story each has to tell, none can discern until all journeying is done.

Even the one I loved above all others did not know everything that I have known. He was spared that much sorrow. I sang the 'Chanson de Roland' and he spoke of Gawain. I held him in my arms while he wept for his father's murder, and side by side we shed the blood of traitors and the infidel. We rejoiced in our love: body and soul together. Though seas and mountains and the enmities of princes kept us apart, there was no distance between our hearts. That I could do nothing for him when his boy was taken is the great bitterness of my long life. That he is dead is my great grief.

But my greatest secret he cannot know, and that is a mercy for which I thank God. For I know what came to his boy, and the younger one too. I know as few others do, for few others could have found it out. I could not tell my love, so I told the woman he loved most in the world, as he would have wished. She is wise, and discreet, and lives retired. She will not speak of it.

No human creature knows all. That is the power of God alone, and to God alone shall my story be told.

Louis de Bretaylles

Part One

Beginning

MATERIA PRIMA is that which has been stripped of every form by putrefaction, so that a new form can be introduced.

Sir Isaac Newton, *Index Chemicus*

I

Elysabeth — the 31st yr of the reign of King Henry the Sixth

The road home to Grafton was always a merry one. That it was the custom of families of our degree to send their children away, the better to learn the skills and lessons proper to their estate, did not make my childhood's exile from Grafton to Groby any easier. Sir Edward Grey of Groby was kindly enough, but his wife Lady Ferrars was not. Besides, what girl of seven or eight would not miss her home and her sisters? Nor is the promise of a good marriage much comfort to such a child. When my sister Margaret joined me at Groby it was better, and as I grew older I learnt discretion, so that Lady Ferrars could find no fault with my words or my duties, still less in my seeming submission to her in all things.

That year we lay for a night at Harborough, for Sir Edward Grey's man that rode home with us from Groby said that with the snow threatening as it was, it would be folly to press on further and perhaps find ourselves stranded at nightfall. As ever when journeying I slept ill, as much from the joy of being headed for home – and for the whole of Christmastide – as from the weariness and aching cold that seemed to have seeped into my bones with the ride and not let go. Our bed was warm, but more than once Margaret protested in a whisper that I had woken her with my restlessness. At last Mal, sleeping beyond her, was roused by her sighs. She propped herself on one elbow. 'Are you sick, Mistress Ysa?'

'Yes, sister, are you sick?' said Margaret, poking me in the side. She was ever one of those who is always either wide awake or dead asleep. 'Or do you just wish to keep us all from our rest?'

'If I could sleep, I would, sister,' I said. 'And, no, I'm not sick. But it's not given to us all to snore like a pig in shit as soon as our heads hit the pillow.'

'Mistress Ysa, if Her Grace your mother could hear you she would give you a box on the ear,' said Mal.

'Yes, but she can't.'

'Have you said *Paternoster* and *Ave?*'

'Yes, Mal, many times.' Had I not said them wholeheartedly enough, or was God not listening tonight? I wondered. Mal would say that the words were enough, which set my sleeplessness at God's door, but such a blasphemy mercifully stuck in my throat before I had uttered it, so that my penance would be that much less at confession.

The bed wobbled as Mal sat up and swung her feet to

the floor. 'I'll make us all a posset. There's some ale still in the jug, and the fire's well enough.' She pulled her cap tight down about her ears, put on her shawl and pushed her feet into her shoes, for even with the fire still alive it was very chill. I kept my shoulders well under the covers, so that only the tip of my nose was cold, while she shuffled to and fro, kindling a taper at the fire to light the candle, then stirring up the coals and putting the poker into them. She swilled our cups out with washing-water and tipped it into the chamber pot. We had thought this inn a slovenly place, for no servant had come to clear the dishes after we had supped, but now we could be glad of that carelessness. Honey and camomile and cinnamon Mal conjured from somewhere in her baggage, and spooned into the ale jug.

Margaret rolled over and got out of bed to piss, complaining about the draughts as she sat on the pot. She got back in, with much uncalled-for flapping of the covers, and moved across so that the linen of her smock touched me like a cold hand, and she put her elbow on the plait of my hair, then protested when I pushed her off it.

Mal straightened up with the poker in her hand. For a moment I saw it, white-hot against the dim cold of the chamber, and then she put it into the jug as if it were a knife and she killing some beast. The crackle as it struck the ale made a little thrill run down my spine as it always did, and after a moment the scent of hot ale threaded through the cold air to warm my nose. I sat up and put my pillow behind me.

Mal gave Margaret and me each a cup, blew out the candle and got back into bed with her own. The cups were wooden and no more than warm in the hand, but the ale was almost too hot to sip and rather than cool it by blowing I breathed in the fumes of honey and herbs and spice.

'Will Master Antony be at Grafton, Mistress Ysa?' asked Mal. 'Oh, Mistress Margaret, your feet are like ice.'

'Yes, I think so. I hope so. I haven't seen him for an age.'

'He said he would be,' said Margaret. 'He told me so.'

'And what do you know of it?' I said. 'In his last letter he was not so certain he would be let come home.'

'And what of Sir Edward and Master Grey?' said Mal, in the over-calm voice that seeks to dispel an argument. 'It is said they come to Grafton for Twelfth Night, and we know what that means.'

'So you *are* to be married to John Grey, then?' said Margaret, before I could decide how to answer Mal, for I did not understand what I felt about the matter, still less what I was prepared to say. 'Ooo, Ysa! What will it be like to be bedded by him? Will you like it?'

'Well, I shan't tell *you* anything about it, you nasty, inquisitive brat! It's my affair, not yours.' The ale had cooled a little, and it tasted like summer, sweet and heady.

'But such a match will be arranged for me in my time,'

said Margaret. 'I have a right to know!' Had we not both held our cups, I would have swatted at her as I would a wasp, more in irritation at her buzzing than in any hope of quieting her.

'Now, now,' said Mal, 'there's no need for you to be worrying about that yet, Mistress Margaret. Could Mistress Ysa not have been married two or three years ago, with her the most beautiful girl in all England like her ma before her? If your father had wished they could have sealed the bargain long since. She could be a mother herself. But no, they've waited till now. Sixteen's a good age for wedding, and no doubt they'll do the same with you. Now, you both drink up, and I'll set the cups down and we can all go off to sleep. We've a long ride in the morning, and the snow thick too, like as not.'

We did as we were told, and snuggled down again. Mal leant over and set the cups on the floor, then pulled up the covers over all three of us. The ale and the camomile together were making me sleepy, and Margaret too, I thought.

What would it be like? I wondered. I knew John, of course; when I came to Groby he was as kind to a home-sick brat of seven as a grown young man of twelve will trouble to be, far kinder than Lady Ferrars, who had only ceased to call me a tiresome, froward child when Margaret arrived and played the part better than I ever could. Once John mended a toy that Margaret had broken, and sometimes he would let me watch him as he tried the paces of a new horse in the paddock, and when I stumbled and lost my place in a song, he would cease piping and start again at the beginning without a sigh. Lately he had lived at Astley Manor, which his father had given him, and I saw even less of him, for it was thirty or forty miles away. We both knew, though it was unspoken, that we were to be wed. But I could not really believe it would happen.

'Mal, what's it like?' said Margaret.

'What's what like?'

'Being bedded by a man. By your husband. What was it like for you?'

'That's nothing you need to know about yet, Mistress Margaret, and I'm not going to tell you. 'Tis private, between a man and his wife. Have you never seen such things on the farm?'

'But it's different for people, you know it is.' Margaret's voice was slurring. 'And Ysa needs to know, only she'll never ask.'

There were times when I was almost grateful for Margaret's shamelessness. She was right, I did want to know, and here was a better time to find out than most, in the warm dark where my face could not be seen, and told by Mal, who had been wed, and borne a child that died of a fever. Her man was killed by falling in the mill-stream not long after.

'Well . . .' said Mal, slowly, as if she was considering what to say. She dropped her voice as she used to when we were little and she was telling us tales at bedtime of Robin Hood or St Francis or Queen Mab. 'Of course, your father will pay for a Mass. You'll go into church after the wedding, not like me and my man. Or maybe it'll be private, in the chapel. And then you'll have the feast. It'll be a fine one your father'll give for his oldest daughter's wedding, you mark my words. And then the women will take you to your wedding chamber and help you to undress and put you to bed. And then his friends will bring him to you, with singing and pipe and tabor, and leave you together.'

She ceased speaking just where my mind always ceased to be able to imagine it. By my ear, Margaret heaved a big sigh that ended in a snore, and I knew that she slept.

Mal heard it too, and only then went on speaking, more softly still: 'And then he undresses too, and gets into bed. And you kiss and hold each other and he touches you all over, wherever feels good to him. And it feels good to you too, you'll see. And then when he's ready, he lies on you and you open your legs and he puts his thing in you.'

I knew where she meant in me, for a faint, fearful excitement trembled there when I thought of such matters and made me run my hands secretly over my breasts and waist and thighs. 'Does . . . How does he?'

'Oh, Mistress Ysa! He's hard, you see, with all the kissing and the touching. And – and it hurts a little. That's your maidenhead breaking. There's blood like when you get your monthlies, only just a little if he's kind, and I'm sure such a fine gentleman as Master John will be very kind . . . And then you're truly man and wife, till death takes one of you, and again in Heaven, so they say. I'm sure my man's waiting for me . . . Now, we must both be off to sleep.'

Soon she, too, slept, but I lay awake for some time until I could help it no longer, but tried to feel through my smock what Master John would feel. The fear and excitement grew, though for a while I dared do nothing in case I woke the others. But I longed for more, and at last had to rub myself until I trembled all over as if at the edge of some abyss, then fell hot and sore into it, and slept at last.

~

It had indeed snowed in the night, we found, but by dawn it had stopped, and the wind had dropped too, so that although there was no sun the ride from Harborough was more pleasant than we had expected. Still, it was slow enough going, Sir Edward's man having Mal behind him, that we decided not to break our journey in Northampton to hear Mass, though it was the feast of St Thomas the Apostle. The horses clopped over the bridge into Far Cotton. We were nearly home, telling the villages as we passed through: Blacky More, Collingtree, Roade, the turns to Ashton and Stoke Bruerne, the bridge, the turn to Alderton, and then the road lifting away from the river in fading light until we could just see the church and the roofs of the Hall.

At last we turned off the high road, at last we turned into the gate, and there was Jacquetta running through the yard. She had grown, I thought, but her face was red and tear-stained. At the sound of horses she turned and saw us. 'Ysa! Margaret! John and Lionel took my poppet! They're going to burn her!'

I rode towards the mounting block to get down, but Margaret kicked her foot free of the stirrup and slid down in the middle of the yard. Jacquetta seized my hand and dragged us to the rough ground by the muck-heap behind the stables. The boys had built a bonfire of sticks too green to do much more than smoulder and, sure enough, Jacquetta's poppet Igraine, that had once been mine, was perched on top.

I boxed John's ears. 'Take her off now, you bad boy! And never do that again!' He'd grown too, but he was still too short to reach Igraine with the fire burning even a little. I looked round, and saw a branch they hadn't put on. 'Margaret, hold my gown.'

She kilted up my skirts and held them clear of the fire as I leant forward with the branch and managed to knock Igraine off the top. She rolled down among the sticks and I snatched her up and gave her to Jacquetta, who cradled her and kissed her. Margaret grabbed Lionel by the shoulder and cuffed him soundly. He tried to shake himself free. 'We were only playing the witch Jeanne d'Arc and Duke John of Bedford!' he said. 'Jacquetta's too old for poppets. I heard my lady mother say so! She's going away soon.'

'None of your business!' I said. Lionel always heard more than he should. 'How dare you take great Duke John's name to be unkind to Jacquetta?' I looked round. Jacquetta was holding Margaret's hand and sniffing into Igraine's cap. 'Now be off with you, before I decide to tell my lady mother.' The boys took to their heels and disappeared through a gap in the hedge, for all it was almost dark.

'Mistress Ysa!' It was Mal, calling from the yard. 'Where are you?'

I shook out my skirts and straightened my back against the weariness of a long day's ride. 'Coming, Mal! Margaret, you've got ash on your nose.'

'Well, your hands are sooty, and the bottom of your gown, too,' she said over her shoulder, jogging towards the yard.

I followed. 'Wash first or greet first?'

'Ask Mal,' said Margaret, rounding the corner.

Mal was standing at the top of the steps and by the light of the cresset at the door I could see she was tired and cross. 'Hurry now. Her Grace is in the Great Chamber.'

'How is she?' I said, when I had caught my breath.

'Her belly's so great now, she looks as if she doesn't sleep so well.'

Margaret and I glanced at each other, and spoke at once. 'Wash first.'

My lady mother was sitting at the table in the Great Chamber with the account books spread out before her, and Master Wooton the clerk hovering at her shoulder. 'We cannot hope that the revenues from France will recover . . .' she was saying, as we entered.

We knelt in the doorway, the draught making the candles on the table flicker. She heaved herself to her feet and, peeping upwards though my head was still bowed in proper obeisance, I saw that the frown cleared from her brow.

'Welcome home, daughters.'

'Madam, I greet you well,' I said.

'And I,' said Margaret.

My mother walked so heavy and slow that Margaret was swaying on her knees with weariness before she had reached us and we had each kissed her hand.

'*Levez-vous, mes filles,*' she said, and when we did I found that my eyes were level with hers. She kissed my cheek. 'You've grown, Ysa,' she said. 'Is all well at Groby?'

'Yes, madam. Lady Ferrars greets you well, and says that, so please you, Sir Edward and Master Grey will be with us on St John's Day, God willing, or the day after.'

She nodded, and when she went to raise Margaret, Margaret stumbled and almost toppled over. My mother kissed her. 'You're weary, daughter. Off to bed with you. Ysa, stay, and we will talk. Mal, will you have wine sent

15

up, please? And Master Wooton, I think we must speak further tomorrow.'

He piled up the books and papers and balanced the inkpot on top. Mal shepherded Margaret out, but not before Margaret had made a face that was meant to show Master Grey kissing me.

'Be so good as to pull my chair to the fire,' said my mother, 'and a stool for yourself.' I was glad to do it, for we had washed in cold water for speed's sake, and I was shivering still.

She lowered herself into her chair and waved that I should sit too, but kept her eyes fixed on the fire. At last, she said, 'You know with what purpose Sir Edward and Master Grey will come to Grafton?'

'Yes, madam,' I said. Even in my weariness I felt again a little shiver of fear and heat.

'And you are content?'

'Yes, madam.'

'We are alone, Ysa, you may speak freely. Truly, are you willing to be married to him? It is not ... You know Master Grey quite well, of course. And he will have his mother's title in time. He's not ill-looking, either, though one could wish him taller. But are you sure that he will be a good husband?'

'I think so. But how can I be sure when I have never had a husband before, nor he a wife?'

'It's a good match for both families, but your father and I want you to be happy, too. When I was wed for the first time . . . Well, His Grace of Bedford was a very kind man as well as a very great one. But it is never easy, the business of becoming a wife.'

I wanted to ask, 'Was it not easy for you after, when you became my father's wife?' but did not dare. It could not have been like the marriage they set before me, that was sure. They had loved each other so much, Mal said one evening, when Sir Edward and Lady Ferrars were away and we were sitting over the fire at Groby. They had loved so powerfully that they endured scandal and poverty by being married in secret without asking the King's permission. 'For though he was His Grace of Bedford's seneschal in Normandy, and a knight, he was not more,' Mal had gone on, whisking the next chestnut out of the fire and tossing it to me. 'While your lady mother was the second lady of England. And so newly a widow.' I had almost burnt my fingers, peeling off the chestnut's blackened skin. Inside, the flesh was hot and sweet and tasted faintly of burning.

'Yes, madam, I know,' I said now to my mother. 'But I shall have you to advise me, and though she would like to, Lady Ferrars has trouble finding fault with how I do my duties or my lessons.'

She reached down and stroked my head. '*C'est bon, ma chère fille!* I am glad to hear it.' I was not sure what of my words had made her glad: that I should do my work well, or that Lady Ferrars was annoyed by it. 'We might bespeak a hanging from the sisters at Lincoln,' she went on. 'Melusina, perhaps, for your ancestry, as well as for good fortune in childbed ... But, daughter, if you have any doubts – any matters that you would like to be settled before the contracts are drawn up – you must tell your father, or me, and we will arrange things as best we can.'

I had not thought she would consult my wishes thus. True, provided it was made with due courtesy, my mother listened to any request or complaint that even the lowliest of the household had to make. But on so great a matter of family business as an eldest daughter's marriage? I had not expected this, and had no answer ready. And yet, did I truly have no concerns in the matter of my own future? I stared into the flames until my cheeks felt scorched, and realised that I did, but that my doubts were not ones that I could have spoken of to my lady mother, or dictated to a clerk to be written into my marriage deeds.

Una – Monday

There's scarcely a house's depth between Narrow Street and the river: the back of mine hangs over the water. I let myself in and dump my bags in the hall. It all looks clean enough, though it smells of tenants: fag smoke, takeaways, and the cheap furniture that Uncle Gareth let us have from the Chantry so that we could take our own things with us to Sydney. But still, underlying it, I can smell the Thames: wet and cool and slightly rotten. It's high tide, and in the sitting room the midsummer light is liquid, with sun-struck scraps of silver dancing over the ceiling in the way that Adam loved.

Two years is not long enough to have acquired equanimity. For a while the fog closes in on me, grey and suffocating.

When I can breathe again I stare across the river, trying to find something impersonal to hold on to, something that won't remind me of Adam, nor yet remind me that he's dead.

From here there's little indication of the passing of time, except for the moon-drawn rise and fall of the river. At low tide there are a few yards of rubbish-strewn shingle; at high tide the water runs perhaps six feet below my study window. Rotherhithe on the far bank is too distant to be real; we watched what was renamed Docklands as one might a strange colony of insects. First the sturdy cranes began to rust and the fog-blackened warehouses emptied. Next they were tramp-haunted shells. Then they sprouted spindly builders' hoists that vanished as suddenly as they had come, leaving smart little flats and restaurants garnished with industrial chic, the warehouse pulleys shiny and unturning. Now the millennium is only five years away. I never thought I'd see it in without Adam.

When I'm steady I haul my bags upstairs and start unpacking. It was winter at home, and I've brought too many sweaters even for an English summer. I unlock the tenant-proof cupboard, find our own clean sheets and make up the bed. My jet-lagged flesh aches to lie down, and I mustn't: I'm only in England for a week, and there's a lot to do.

This isn't a professional trip: I haven't got time for archives and seminars and working lunches. I've brought plenty of work, nonetheless. On the plane I picked my way through Charles Ross on Edward IV, and compared him with Michael Hicks on Richard III, though I must get down to primary sources soon. Just after Dubai I dropped a photocopy of a learned paper that I foolishly hadn't stapled, and was still apologising and retrieving pages of references from under people's feet over Cyprus. No, this isn't a work trip: it's to sell the house and see the family. It's to sign away the last of my English life, and go home.

'It'll be lovely to see you,' said my cousin Izzy on the phone two weeks ago when, late one evening and two whiskies down, I finally decided to do it, that there was no reason to delay. When we bought the house in Narrow Street it wasn't a Queen Anne Residence Convenient for the City, it was a tenement, in a slum. You could almost smell Sherlock Holmes's opium dens, see the lascars and hear the drunken sailors. Not any more. There's every reason to put the house Adam and I bought when we married – to share for the lifetime that we thought our marriage would be – into the hands of a sharp-suited, slavering estate agent. 'And it's good timing from the practical point of view,' Izzy said. 'There's a bit of paperwork to do with the Chantry. You know the house is going to be sold?'

I hadn't. Even with Australia no further away than reaching for the phone, even though Izzy and Lionel are all the brother and sister I have, sometimes news takes a long time to get to me.

'*Sold?* When was that decided?'

'Only last week. I was about to write to you. And it's not the workshop, not for the moment, just the house. The Press will carry on,' Izzy said, the echo of her brisk, working morning booming off the satellites towards me. 'It would be hard to think of the Solmani Press not existing, wouldn't it? Though I'm afraid it won't be long. Uncle Gareth's not getting any younger. If you ring when you get here, shall we have supper? I can fill you in properly then, and we can have a good old catch-up. Lionel's around: I know he'd love to see you. D'you want me to tell him? Save you the phone call? And Uncle Gareth, of course, he'll be so pleased. Anyway, have a good flight.'

And now I'm here, and due at Izzy's at seven. I want to see her, but why must it be like this? Why can't it be her coming to us? Stupidly, I can't believe I'll never be 'us' in this house again: Adam's medics, hard-drinking and funny; my historians, dryer and quieter; Joe and David, the couple next door; someone over from America for a conference; Izzy, perhaps, or even Uncle Gareth. Perhaps

I'd had time to cook a big casserole or maybe pasta, perhaps Adam led a foraging expedition to fetch food from the Indian restaurant: they didn't speak much English there, but it didn't matter because we were usually the only English customers; they made no concessions with the spicing. There were evenings when hospital pagers went off as regularly as clocks, others when we'd gather at the sitting-room windows in silence to watch the moon and its reflection moving over the waters, or noisily to cheer the fireworks of half a dozen Guy Fawkes displays; once we held a Midsummer's Eve party, and watched the sun rise, spreading silver-gilt across a mother-of-pearl morning.

It's Midsummer's Eve any day now. Like a child I want to cry at the smashing of my world, and then at my own impotent petulance. And when I've mastered myself I realise just how much I ache, ache with dreariness, deadness almost. There's always the fog of missing Adam that fills my head, and hangs between me and everything else, but now all the trains and tubes, airports and aeroplanes seem to have laid a grubby, sterile carapace over my skin. I haul off my shoes, strip off my jeans and T-shirt and get into the shower. The water's scalding and fierce, cracking the carapace, bouncing off the bones of my shoulders and running through the roots of my hair like hot fingers. I tip my head back so it streams over my face and fills my ears till all I can hear is water. I want to stay like this for ever.

I can't. I open my eyes and reach for the shower gel, which does hair as well. Someone gave some to Adam for Christmas, ages ago, and I liked the smell so much, and the straightforwardness of it, that I took to using it too. Neck, chest, arms warm and slippery with eucalyptus and mint. When I'm clean I take some more gel and try to find all the twinges and aches of travelling: shoulder muscles tight under my fingers, sides and lower back so stiff that when I dig my thumbs in it's as sharp as pinching myself. Even the soles of my feet seem to have knots in them. But at last I must get out, get dry and dressed, must find my England Admin notebook and ring the estate agent, then make appointments with banks, solicitors, accountants and stockbrokers.

I pull on sweatpants and a top and go down to the corner shop with the air threading coldly through my still damp hair. Last time we were here the shop never seemed to have much more than UHT milk and sliced white, but it's changed hands. I come back with an expensive bagful of organic salad, wholegrain bread and free-range eggs; the wine's much better. But I'm suddenly so impossibly weary that I don't want to eat anything, or even have a drink. 'Grief is exhausting,' I remember Adam saying of someone else, some patient's wife or husband. 'It's like having a permanent leak in your vital systems.' I can do nothing but go to bed, defying travellers' wisdom and medical sense, and I dream, as always, of Adam.

~

I don't remember Izzy's block of flats being as tall, dark red and unrelievedly Edwardian as it looks to me in the yellowing evening light. She herself has narrowed and neatened inside her well-cut black sweater and trousers that make my jeans and T-shirt seem too casual; her hair is short and sharp, more silvery than dark but, then, she is five years older than me. We hug.

'Una, it's so good to see you. You're looking well. How are you? How are things?'

'Fine, thanks. Busy, you know. Sorting out the house and so on.'

She takes my statement at face value. 'Of course. Still, it shouldn't be hard to sell.' And then, like a satellite delay, what I haven't said reaches her, and she answers it with another hug of my shoulders. 'I'm so sorry. But I'm sure it's the right thing to do. You must say if I can help.'

Izzy flew out to me when Adam died. There's nothing else she needs to say. 'Of course I will,' I say.

Her studio's at the back. I stare down into the communal garden, where a blackbird is standing in the now violet light, his ebony head cocked and his yellow beak ready to stab into the earth. To the left of the great, north-facing window is her Ballets Russes shawl, framed in dark wood and hanging on the wall. The fringes are combed and pressed straight, and the light from the window lies on the glass and makes it hard to see the silky curls of orange and scarlet and peacock blue. Evidently she doesn't wear it any more. I remember her trailing around in it at Chantry studio parties. Even the smell of her studio is the same as it was then: the familiar creamy-sharp smell of paper and ink overlies the faint spice of seasoning box and pear-wood blocks. For a moment I'm wholly, head-spinningly, back in my childhood, watching the way she moved, laughed, talked, and wondering if I'd ever have that ease with all these people, that grown-up kind of belonging.

There are a couple of photographs of Izzy's daughter Fay, and a charming wood engraving – Izzy's work – of her digging in the sand at the seaside. But on the workbench I see that Izzy's sandbag has no half-sketched-out block waiting, and she's set aside the big lens on its stand.

'You know the Chantry archive's going to San Diego now I've finished cataloguing Grandpapa's letters?' says Izzy to me. 'I've only got to get it all together now, and it'll be ready for shipping. They're going to put everything on microfilm for anyone to look at. Even on a computer. I'm going to get as much publicity as I can when the archive transfers. San Diego are good at that. There might even be enough interest to persuade someone to republish *At the Sign of the Sun and Moon*. Perhaps even a *Collected Letters*. There's so much interest in fine printing, these days. I get an enquiry from a researcher every few weeks. Red or white?'

I'm familiar enough with publishers to know that her thinking is almost certainly wishful. And those research enquiries don't sound enough to fill her days. How does she fill them? Once, she had three projects running most of the time: one in the clean light of early morning, research and reading in the bright, dull light of noon, and another as the sun slanted, picking out the grain and curve of every stone and blade of grass. I can't see any sign of such things now. Is being the family historian, as she calls it, the only life left to her?

There are prints on the walls. I can see four that were published as headings to a nicely produced anthology of poems about the seasons. A few years ago I found a copy secondhand in a Sydney bookshop, and gave it to Adam for some small anniversary. 'Autumn' is the best, I think now; the foreground is a dried leaf, exquisitely curled, with every vein and rib as exactly and gloriously necessary as the arches of a Gothic window. But though the studio isn't specially tidy, there's no sign of fresh ink on the stained central table or any cutting tools or knives or fragments of wood or lino that would suggest work in progress. I wonder how much work she's getting these days. Most of my childhood drawing and story-writing was on the back of her declared failures. When I was little at the Chantry, and everyone was busy, I used to crawl under her workbench in the studio, and find the tiny scraps lying on the floor, as secret as treasure. The wood ones were impossibly pale and fragile, no more than grains of gold and silver still magically clinging together, while the curls of lino were thicker and browner, reticulated like little caterpillars, still faintly smelling of warm linseed. I'd look up and see Izzy's legs in their darned stockings and lace-up shoes hitched round the stool's legs, and hear her heavy breathing. She never minded my being there, unless things were going wrong. Then she'd suddenly tell me to go, not unkindly, but without leaving any room for argument, and I'd crawl out and stand up, picking more debris from where it had stuck into my bare knees, and comforting myself with a hope that there'd be a new cake for tea or that Uncle Gareth would help me with my history prep.

'Red or white?' asks Izzy, again.

'Oh, red, please.'

She heads for the kitchen. 'Shan't be a moment.' I see a copy of *At the Sign of the Sun and Moon* on the shelf.

The roundel again on the title page, and a quotation I know by heart because it appears, set small, in every book the Press has ever issued. 'As the *Edda* tells it, in the land of the giants lived a man named Mundilfoeri and he had two children: his daughter Sol was the sun, and his son Mani the moon.'

I riffle through the pages.

In 1936 Kay Pryor graduated from the Slade, and decided that the development of his painting would be best served by moving to Paris. He had never been as deeply concerned with the day-to-day work of the Solmani Press as his younger brother, Gareth, and his departure made little difference to the running of it. But, as William wrote in a letter to Beatrice Webb,

> With Kay gone, the house is quieter, but we realise how much his work as a painter has kept all us craftsmen up to the aesthetic mark: as he used to say, in the dramatic manner of the young, he had no allegiance to anything but art. Gareth in particular misses him; he has looked up to him since they were boys, and it is always he, when some question of design comes up, who says, 'What would Kay think? He'd know the answer.' But Kay's leaving does ease one private fear of my own. Ever since the day, all those years ago, when Maud and I first saw the Chantry chapel among what were then orchards and fields, and knew that we must make it the soul of our house and workshop, the soul even of our family itself, I've feared that one day Kay and Gareth — so different in temperament — might not be able to agree over the running of the Press. Elaine is married to Robert Butler — had you heard? — and if she has a son the problem might yet be compounded, or indeed resolved. Who knows? But for now, at least, I may take pleasure in news of Kay's successes abroad and Gareth's passion for the Press at home, and know that no rivalry troubles our family.

Having, as he said in a letter to his mother, '[g]ot what there was to be got,' from Paris, in 1938 Kay moved to New York. There he joined circles that included such up-and-coming *painters as Ben Shahn and Charles Demuth, and in such works as* Battery Park, Nightfall *(1938, Museum of Modern Art, New York) and* The Dock at East Egg *(1939, Private Collection) he was quickly recognised as having brought a uniquely English sensibility to a circle otherwise much concerned with industrialism and its aesthetics. At the outbreak of war William took on the full burden of running the Press again so that Gareth could volunteer for the Royal Engineers; he was taken prisoner at Tobruk and repatriated in 1945. On a visit to London in 1941 Kay received his call-up papers and joined the 8th Royal Fusiliers: he was wounded at Coriano during the Italian campaign, and the war ended before he recovered. He returned to New York, where in 1946 his mistress Lucie Lefevre, an artist's model whom he had known before the war, gave birth to a daughter, Una Maud Pryor. In the following year Kay and Lucie were killed in California when their car ran off the Coastal Highway at the Bixby Gorge, and baby Una came to the Chantry, to be brought up with Elaine and Robert's children, Isode and Lionel.*

It's beautiful letterpress: Plantin, pressed richly into fine paper by one of William's most gifted heirs, sitting well in the hand, the jacket heavy matt paper with a roundel of Izzy's engraving of the Solmani Press sign, which hung above the workshop, festooned with ivy. The roundel is blocked in gold on the boards too. It's Izzy's history, the official version, the story of record; I notice she even refers to herself in the third person. It's my history, and not my history.

She finished the story with the death of our grand-father, and when it was published I read it quickly, always with only one eye while eating breakfast or on a bus or somewhere else distracting. Then I put it away, and since then I've only opened my copy – first edition, personally inscribed 'To dear Una with all love from Izzy' – when there was nowhere else I could check a necessary reference.

I put the book back and move round the room. Here's the big group portrait: *The Solmani Press, Silver Jubilee, 1936,* the brass plate says, shiny and faintly green round the edges with polishing. Grandpapa – William Pryor – standing beside Grandmama in the basket chair. And their three children: my father Kay on his right with a palette was a quicker, darker, wirier version of Uncle Gareth, the portrait tells me. I wouldn't know. Uncle Gareth himself in the doorway to the workshop, with the current apprentices to one side of it – very little younger than him, but somehow so clearly not sons of the house – and Aunt Elaine slightly separate, with an apron and a trugful of carrots.

Izzy returns.

'Don't they look proper to us, these days, all wearing suits and ties?' I say.

'It was usually shirtsleeves and aprons in the workshop. This was a formal portrait. I don't know why he insisted on Mummy wearing an apron. It makes her look as if she wasn't part of the Press. I've left it to the

San Diego collection in my will. It's a particularly nice portrait of Uncle Gareth, I think.' It's true, though he's younger than I ever knew him, standing with one long-fingered hand on the frame of the doorway, and that look on his face that I never thought about then, but now I read as kind, amused and always welcoming.

'Tell me how Uncle Gareth is. I'm going down to Eltham tomorrow.'

'Come into the kitchen while I deal with the food,' says Izzy. The kitchen's narrow and dark, as they always are in these mansion flats that were built for a world with servants, and the view is of drainpipes and blind bathroom windows. 'Well, he is seventy-eight, so I suppose it's only to be expected. But you'll notice a big difference.'

I pick up the handful of cutlery that Izzy's put on the table and lay it out. 'He was spry enough at Aunt Elaine's funeral.'

'I know. It's since then, I think. I suspect he doesn't eat properly, with Mummy not doing the cooking, and I live in terror of hearing that he's hurt himself on one of the big presses. Imagine if the motor on the Vandercook was going.' After a career of studying printing presses, I can imagine only too well. 'He's living in the workshop, did you know? And very short of money. He's had to let out the whole of the Chantry house. That's why it's got to go, sad though it is. It's impossible for him to cope with. It's full of students and fly-by-night types. Goodness knows what they get up to. I don't think he ever gets round to going upstairs and seeing. Lionel's begged him time and again to get a management company to deal with it, the way you have in Narrow Street. References and proper tenancies and everything. But he just says that the Chantry always *has* been a haven for people who don't fit elsewhere, and he's not going to change now.'

'Well, that's true enough. Was there ever a time when there wasn't some defecting Hungarian painter in one of the attics? Remember Theo Besnyö? Or one of Aunt Elaine's friends running away from a bad marriage. Or me, even.'

'But you were family,' says Izzy, bending to get supper out of the oven. 'Sorry, hope you don't mind it's only shepherd's pie. I remember Mummy lying in bed with flu and explaining it to me, when Uncle Gareth went to America to fetch you home. She said it would be like having a little sister of my own. I remember she was worried that Uncle Gareth wouldn't be able to manage; she felt terribly guilty that she'd been too ill to go. "Babies are hard work," she said, "even once they're walking. I'll need your help." And then you arrived. Funny little thing, you were — what were you? Fourteen months or so? I think I thought you'd be like Lionel, always shouting and running about, only you were so solemn and quiet, holding on to Uncle Gareth with one hand and Smokey Bear with the other. You'd only just learnt to walk. Mummy thought of you as her third child till the day she died.'

It's true, she did. With Aunt Elaine it didn't matter that I had no parents of my own, that no one had been able to find out much about my mother, that my parents hadn't been married. There was Aunt Elaine's husband Uncle Robert, but for all practical purposes she and Uncle Gareth were my parents. They were my parents just as Izzy's my sister and Lionel my brother. 'I know,' I say, and I don't have to say any more because Izzy understands, and gives my hand a squeeze before starting to dish the shepherd's pie out of its carton. But perhaps the old ache kindles something else old in my memory, because I add suddenly, 'And then there was Mark.'

'There was, wasn't there? He must have been one of the longest-standing ones. I wonder what happened to him.'

'I suppose we'll never know now.'

'Funny he never got back in touch. For a reference, if nothing else.'

'Maybe he wasn't going for skilled jobs,' I say casually. 'He was very practical all round. Then he'd only need ordinary references from whatever his last job was.'

'A fully trained fine printer, taught by William and Gareth Pryor, being a caretaker or something? Why would he do that?'

'I don't know. I never did . . .' Perhaps it's because my grief for Adam never sleeps that such an old bewilderment can still make my throat ache. 'It's sad to think of the Chantry going out of the family at last, after all the times when Uncle Gareth managed to rescue it.'

'I know. But he ought to be retiring, not coping with tenants. He's not going to be able to go on with the Press for much longer either. And what *matters* will be safe at San Diego: the archive, the proof prints, all the rest of it. And the history in the book. There's so much interest in the fine presses of the past.'

'The Solmani Press isn't in the past.'

'Well, technically, no.' She spoons peas into a dish. 'You would have got in touch, if you'd needed to know anything about it for your own work, wouldn't you?'

'Of course. Though it isn't really my period, twentieth-century fine presses. I'm more about early-modern European printing. Gutenberg's heirs, the rise of individual piety in the the late medieval period. Presses and typography, of course, but reception history as well.'

'What history?'

'Horrible word, I know, but interesting subject. What people actually bought, how the industry worked. Readers as well as writers and printers, if you like.'

'So what are you working on now?' Izzy sits down. 'Do help yourself to peas. Only frozen, I'm afraid.'

'Well, I've only just started thinking about it. But I want to spread out from pure bibliography. I want to write about people . . . It's still very easy in bibliography to forget that books are something real people buy and read and lend and lose, and they're not always the fine books, the grand ones, the innovative ones. I want to make a different kind of shape out of books, the shape of people's lives. All those colophons and presses, all that paper and iron and ink, I've had enough. I want to know someone – really know them – by their books. I ... Well, I've decided to write about Anthony and Elizabeth Woodville, but in terms of their books.'

'Who? Oh – yes – hang on ... Wars of the Roses? Didn't she marry someone?'

'Yes. They were brother and sister. Elizabeth was married to Edward IV. She was married to Sir John Grey before, though, and had two sons. He was killed in battle, and she married Edward. And Anthony was the first writer that Caxton printed in England.' The shepherd's pie is very hot; I have to drink some water before I can go on. 'It's about what books they owned – what Anthony wrote – and what they might have read, and what that tells us about them. And what it tells us about their world, their cultural background, about how the book trade worked.'

'You'll be on home ground in Eltham tomorrow, at the Chantry, with the Palace up the road. Do you remember how we used to bike past and see Army officers some-times, and wonder if they were spies? Even though we knew it was only really a staff college?'

'I'd forgotten that ...' I can almost smell the hot tarmac. 'There's been good research on her books, but nothing on his. And no one's pulled it all together into a narrative. Elizabeth had two more sons by Edward, and Anthony brought up the older one, Prince Edward, the way they all used to, having their children brought up by someone else.' She tops up my wine glass. 'When Edward IV died, his younger brother Richard, Duke of Gloucester, seized the throne and put the two boys in the Tower. And he imprisoned Anthony in Yorkshire. Anthony didn't have any sons himself, and his things were scattered. It's a struggle to find enough material to put flesh on the bones . . . Did you say that Eltham Palace was being restored?'

'Yes, English Heritage have just taken it over, Lionel says. It should be very fine when they've finished. All that art deco, and Edward IV's Great Hall. Pity they wouldn't be interested in the Chantry, with so little of the chapel left.' She laughs. 'Maybe we should blame Hitler for demolishing that and only leaving the house. That's in a bad state, too, now. I think you'll be pretty horrified. Do help yourself to more wine.'

As we eat I ask after Fay, Izzy's daughter. Her husband works for Shell; Izzy shakes her head, puzzled almost to the point of disapproving. 'She hates Bogotá, but other than that she seems quite happy drifting along in his wake. I think she does occasionally use her anthropology degree, but only as a hobby.' She reaches behind her to take a postcard down that's stuck on the fridge. It's of a tapestry of some sort, with brilliantly coloured squared-off characters: *The Marriage of the Sun and Moon*, according to the back. 'Her father was out there, and they went up into the Highlands, looking for folk traditions. This was from some little local museum. He rang me, said she's fine.' Izzy and Paul divorced years ago, and though there was another woman involved, I got the feeling she was a symptom more than a cause; she's certainly not on the scene now. Izzy went back to calling herself Isode Butler, as she always had for work.

We've finished the wine rather quickly, and the jet-lag fog's creeping over me again. 'You said there are things for me to sign, to do with selling the Chantry?'

'Lionel's got all the documents, though there's some complication with his share of the freehold so he may not have them ready yet after all. Apparently he passed it on to Fergus: some tax thing. It may all have to go off to him – to Fergus, I mean.'

'How is Fergus?' I ask, getting up. 'I'm sorry, I'm horribly jet-lagged. I'd better go home before I fall asleep.'

'Of course, poor you. He went up north after he'd finished his sculpture Master's. Goodness knows why – you'd think once you'd been at the Royal College you'd want to stay in London. Somewhere near York, I think. His girlfriend came from up there, but they've just split up. When did you say you're seeing Lionel?'

'Day after tomorrow. He's invited me for the night.'

'That's good. We should be able to get going, then. I've done my best with the archive, but what with the stuff I've got, and what's still at the Chantry, and a bunch of the Press accounts books and records lodged at St Bride's Printing Library, it's all a bit of a muddle. I'm spending this week sorting it out before it goes to California. Doing an inventory and so on. When do you go back?'

'A week today, I couldn't manage to get away for longer. It should be enough, if Lionel's got ready the things he needs me to sign. And . . . apart from catching up with you and Lionel and Uncle Gareth, I don't want to linger over – over all the sorting out.'

'I know.' She kisses me. 'Dear Una, it's so good to see you, and looking so well all – all things considered.'

'Yes,' is all I say, but again she hears what I haven't.

'Poor old Una. I'm sorry. It'll take a while, Adam and all. Especially . . . Well, he was so *right* for you. I used to envy you, it all coming right in the end.'

I know what she means. Funny how fifteen years of, well, unsatisfactory relationships can come so right, so quickly. It occurs to me that Izzy's own married life worked in reverse – a good-looking marriage that wasn't so good after all – and for all my grief I suddenly don't envy her that, but I don't quite know how to say it. She was always the one who did things well. I was the little sister who didn't know how to go about doing the same.

'I know how busy you are,' Izzy's saying, 'but shall we meet up again this week? Go out for a drink or something? How are you getting home?'

'I came by tube, but I thought I'd get a cab back. Will there be enough black cabs around for me to hail one?'

'I don't know.' Perhaps black cabs are a luxury she can't usually afford. But she produces a mini-cab number, and after the usual awkward wait for it to arrive, I clamber in and am driven away.

Jet-lag loosens the moorings of your everyday mind. I'm thinking about the ruins that are all I've ever known of the chapel at the Chantry, the thick stumps of flint and stubby buttresses that were once walls; the tarry beams and props supporting the wall of the house that once joined it; the tiled floor, with the white harts and fleurs-de-lys still visible, though the grass creeps over them. Once I dug some tiles up in search of buried treasure, and found only earth and worms.

In that memory the tiles are quite big so I must have been small. I imagined a ruby or a diamond or a gold ducat tucked under each one, mine for the finding, though I didn't know what a ducat looked like. I prised up one tile after another with a palette knife I'd borrowed from the studio without asking, scattering white harts and fleurs-de-lys about me and scrabbling in the earth beneath, and I thought about how I would share out the treasure when I found it. Lots of ducats for Aunt Elaine, so she could have a washing-machine in the kitchen instead of the copper in the outhouse, and some of the rubies and diamonds for Izzy to wear with her best frocks, and a few ducats for Lionel because he wanted a camera of his own so much, and all the rest of everything for me so that I could buy my ticket to go on a big ship and a fast train across America to find my father's pictures and bring them home.

Uncle Gareth found me as I was trying not to despair. 'Oh, Una, Una,' he said. 'Did you have to do that?' I must have said I was looking for treasure, because he took out his hanky, which always smelt of the workshop, and wiped the earth and the tears off my face and said he understood, he'd always wondered if the monks had left any treasure when he was my age. But monks didn't have treasure, they took vows of poverty. Or if they *were* given any, they spent it on helping people, or making the chapel beautiful, just the way Grandpapa had, so I mustn't spoil it by digging things up.

'But I need the treasure!' I said, and told him what I needed it for.

Uncle Gareth scooped me on to his lap, and didn't say anything for a long time. 'I know,' he said at last. 'Poor old thing. I understand. I miss him too, you know. Very much.'

'Will I ever see his pictures?'

'I'm sure you will, old girl. But they're very grand — very special pictures — and they're safe in San Francisco in a big gallery. One day we'll go and find them, shall we?' Even Uncle Gareth's smell made me know he meant it, and we would go. 'One day, when you're older. And when we dock in New York we'll ride up and down in the lifts in the Empire State Building.'

He gave me another hug, and helped me put the tiles back so that no one would know what I'd done, and then asked if I'd help him with a very important job in the workshop. So that by the time Aunt Elaine came looking for me to give me my supper, I was covered with oil and ink and the glory of having put the Chandler & Price press back together all by myself, with only a little help from Uncle Gareth, he said, and only with the hardest bits.

Even in the Chantry house you couldn't help thinking there was something more in the world under your feet. The thick smell of damp, stone and earth when you first went down to the undercroft beneath the house seemed to breathe it, as if the dark was older and fuller of history, even, than the stones of the walls all round you: as old as the earth itself.

Actually, the walls of the undercroft were only as old as Grandpapa. I knew because he'd told me: he'd made the undercroft when he built the house. And when they dug it out, he said, he found a beer bottle from the Great Exhibition, and a coin from the American War of Independence, and lots of those clay pipes with long thin stems, and bits of blue and white china from the days of Queen Anne, like in *The Tailor of Gloucester*. He had to put the stones in to keep the earth back and build the house above it. But maybe if he'd dug more, he said, he'd have found a gold cross and candlesticks. Maybe a statue of Mary and baby Jesus that the monks had buried in a hurry to keep them safe from King Henry's soldiers. Maybe silver coins or jewels, or secret maps of treasure islands and magical rivers, or goblins' teeth, or the bones of other monks from even longer ago, when the chapel was new and everyone believed. I wouldn't mind the bones if Mark was there, I thought but didn't say, or the goblins. He and I could tunnel deep enough, long enough, for a year and a day, through thirteen waxes and thirteen wanings of the moon. And there'd be an underground river, and I'd use seven of the monks' gold coins to pay the ferryman, and when we landed we'd walk down an aisle like a church's, and there'd be another undercroft, like this one only much, much bigger, wide with pillars as tall as trees, a hall so high you could hardly see the roof. There'd be a great fire in the middle, the light leaping and licking into every corner so there was no dark left. Lying around it on bearskins and piles of silvery straw, with their swords and their armour shining in the firelight, would be the knights. And with them, on a bed made of ivory and gold like an altar and heaped with furs and silks, would lie King Arthur and Queen Guinevere, hand in hand, waiting to be woken.

～

All the way home in the stale-air-and-diesel grumbling of the mini-cab I think of Adam, because that's what I do when I'm too tired to stop myself, though what I think of is nothing I could draw, or speak of, or write about. I can't hear his voice or feel his touch, but what fills me is too real, too whole, to call memory or even remembrance.

The mini-cab drops me at my front door in Narrow

Street, and all is quiet. But if it's late enough, if the fog's closing in, if you're sad enough, jet-lag makes you hallucinate. When I walk into the sitting room I see a figure standing by the window, looking out over the dark water. I dig my fingernails into my arm to wake myself up, and walk forward. He's not there.

It isn't Adam who's not there, though. It's Mark.

Antony — Matins

I do not sleep so well, these days, and wake early. This morning I stood watching the sun rise over the Fosse and Sheriff Hutton village, and listening to more noise of business from below than I have been accustomed to hear so early in these long days.

When the sun had risen in all its blind glory, I turned away.

It is said that a chamber such as this is all that the soul requires. Four paces wide, and six deep. It is the same at both sides, I know, for I have measured them. Four well-made walls of pale grey stone, a high window to admit God's light and air, the timber under my feet and above me as straight and seasoned as the door.

My old friend Mallorie, and the Duke of Orleans: it was enough for them. They even wrote great works in their imprisonment. Is it enough for me? Here I have all that a man's body requires: food, shelter, clothes. The sun and the moon shed light for me, and I have my book of hours. I would I had Cicero or Boccaccio, or better yet Boethius in my hand, but perhaps to have them in my head and heart – as I do – is enough.

I have my rosary, and I have that which I could not have hoped for: the Jason ring. I pray that Louis is safe, and have some hope of it for he, of all men, will know how to slip through Richard of Gloucester's net. It were no true love that could wish him prisoned, but such is my love that even as I thank God he is not, my heart aches with wishing that he were with me.

'If wishes were horses, beggars would ride,' Mal used to say, when we children pestered her to bring us fairings from the market: gilt gingerbread, whip-tops, ballads, ribbons for the girls. I said it in my turn to Ned, for even the wishes of a prince may not be granted if the good of the kingdom, or his soul, says them nay. Ned is not held thus, is he? A child of twelve summers, not yet a man to offer them any threat. Can it be God's will to hurt such a good, such an innocent prince? I will not believe it. Ned is no enemy to Richard of Gloucester. He has Ned close, and thus has no cause to do him greater harm. I know it to be true – I *know* it to be true.

And yet my spirit requires a consolation I cannot have.

To face all that Fortune brings with steadiness and faith is the highest virtue a man may seek, whether he be the meanest or the most worshipful in the world. That is what the philosophers say, and what I have written many times. When I was first taken, I thought they would make away with me privily. I feared that I would not know the hour of my death, so I tried to keep my soul in readiness for the end.

Each time I heard the bolts drawn back I would pray, *Deo, in mano tuo*. It was weeks before I realised that it would not be thus. For an hour or two I hoped. And then I understood that I would still die, and that it no longer mattered if it were known, for there was no man with the power or the will to protest, or to do Prince Richard, Duke of Gloucester, harm in revenge.

And now I know the hour of my death. We ride today from Sheriff Hutton, south and west, to the great castle at Pontefract, and there, on the morrow, I am to die.

I have made my will. I shall not see Louis again in this world. There is nothing left to me, either of duty, or of love, except for God.

When there is nothing left, there is always prayer.

Beyond the door I hear the sharp stamp and clatter of men called to attention. The bolts are drawn back, and the well-oiled lock turns like Fortune's wheel.

II

Antony — Prime

This midsummer dawn is so early that the world seems barely to have slept. I pull on my gloves, for my hands are still cold: the leather presses the Jason ring into my skin as if Louis himself touches me. Even the horses, dozing in the chill mist, hang their heads as if exhausted, with none of the scuffles and nips that horses do, as men do, to find out who is master this morning. It is sixty miles to Pontefract. We will ride it in one of these days, almost without end, that are bringing me so swiftly to my own.

The Constable has given me his word that at Pontefract lie Elysabeth's boy Richard Grey, and my cousin Haute, and good old Vaughan. They were taken because they were doing their duty, and under my command. God send that I am allowed to see them. God send them courage.

When most of the men are horsed and ranged about me, I mount too. They are never insolent, rarely even surly, yet I feel their presence about me as I would a steel chain. The Constable has a pouch of dispatches for Anderson, who commands the troop; they say a few words.

It is the horses as ever who know before we do that the time has come. They are suddenly alert, shifting and tossing their heads, then orders are spoken, the dark bulk of the main gate cracks open, and we ride over the drawbridge and through the bailey, on to the open road.

I look about, for we were muffled in darkness when they brought me to Sheriff Hutton, and I have not been in this country for many years, though once I reconnoitred it as carefully as any commander must. It is flat, quiet land, seamed with innumerable streams that the men call becks. Could it be — could one of my crazed hopes be granted — that deep in the trees I shall see a shadow that is Louis? I must not hope it, for neither safety nor fortune can come to him here in Richard of Gloucester's country. Ahead the forest begins, and the warming sun breathes the smell of pines towards us, above the peat-scented mist that lies over the marsh and breaks into wisps about the horses' legs. The road lifts to a bridge over the Fosse itself where Whitecarr Beck joins it, and as we clatter across a heron turns its head to gauge this new threat, then shakes out its wings and, with a few, quick steps, rises into the air.

The body has its own memory. My left hand shortens the reins before my mind knows it, and my right arm aches with remembering the shift and grip of my goshawk's weight. She was big, even for a goshawk, and her name was Juno. When she bated on her block in the mews her wings were the best part of four feet from primary to primary, and my care for her, that summer, was such that any day I could have told her weight down to the nearest ounce and grain. 'Goshawks are delicate,' Wat the austringer would say. 'They'll not take much lightening, but if you overfeed her by so much as a fieldmouse, Master Antony, she'll rake away and never come back.' My belly would quake at the thought of losing her. Even now I remember the steely blue-grey gloss of her back as if I could touch it, the soft, white speckled chest-feathers that she would let me rub when her mood was good, her long, strong legs that took possession of my fist like a conqueror.

'She sees every feather of that heron,' Wat said, 'even your young eyes, master, they're nothing to hers. Now, gently off with her hood. Let her see it first. You'll feel when she wants to fly.' I unhooded her and unknotted her leash, and she shifted her talons, loosing her wings at the shoulder as if she readied her sword in its scabbard. She turned her black-capped head, her gaze fixing on each part of her new surroundings in turn, like a bowman on guard duty.

My father sat still on his horse in the water-meadow's morning light, and Wat nodded to me as the heron's flight steadied, high above and before us. I did my best to throw Juno into the air. My arm was puny against the weight and power of her surge and my hand clenched tighter before I realised and opened it to let the jesses go.

Up she rose, not in pursuit but surveying the ground; the sun was behind us as we watched. Then, after what seemed little more than a breath, she fixed on the heron and went after it.

I was a boy then, twelve years old and home for the harvest. Home, perhaps, for good. Only the night before my father had declared it more fitting that I be brought up in my own inheritance than in that of another.

But of him I dare not think.

The eye of my mind can still see how the birds flew, raptor and prey, Juno streaming after the heron, the heron's steady wing-beats quickening at some sign or sound of danger that we humans could not read, thrusting through the air. But Juno had more speed and soon was close enough to rise up high above her prey, and pause for a moment of suspended time, before stooping like some sleek and taloned cannonball. Down and down she stooped, and the heron tried to twist and double back, its head weaving, its great wings clumsy in such unaccustomed need. Then Juno reached forward and, with a surge of power, seized the heron's neck and bore it, struggling, to the ground among the reeds. All we could see was a puff of feathers floating downwards against the sky.

By the time we cantered up, Juno had killed the heron and was beginning to plume it. Wat walked forward and took her off, at which she bated angrily before she would jump to my fist and be hooded. Wat gave the heron to one of the men who, with a flick of his fingers, tied its feet and slung it on his belt.

'She must think she deserves it,' I said.

'She does, son,' said my father. 'But if she eats it, where's our dinner? And she'll not be hungry for more, and will not hunt for us. Or she will eat her feed as well, and sicken.'

'Sire, do you think I would feed her back at the mews, if I knew she'd had so much in the field? Wat has taught me better than that.'

'No, I know you would not. But she's wild, don't forget. She's not a dog, or a man. You cannot teach her loyalty. She has none, and she's no use for yours. You are not her liege lord, nor she your servant to command. She will not work for you now in the hope or certainty of favours or protection later. All she knows is that today she was hungry, and we helped her to her food. Tomorrow? Who knows?'

He was silent, looking over his land — so carefully manured and tilled, coppiced and drained, as it was by his order and with his overseeing — as if it, too, might be lost to him on the morrow.

Then he shortened his reins. 'Come, son. Perhaps we can put up a hare and give the dogs some sport.'

~

In the forest insects hang where the sun's streams warm the air; as we ride through they dart and nip. The horses toss their heads and snort to shake them off, but we trot too fast for all but the biggest flies to stay with us. How it will be when the horses are weary, I do not know. The marshes north of York are low-lying, and agueish even in winter; on a hot summer's day they swarm with gnats and midges.

'Captain Anderson?'

'My lord?'

'Where do we change horses? Or do we not?'

'I have not yet decided.'

I know what I would order in such a case, but this journey is not mine to command. After a moment Anderson says, 'Have no fear, my lord, it is provided for, as are all matters to do with the security and good ordering of His Grace's affairs.'

'I have no doubt,' I say, and indeed I have none. Richard of Gloucester has ever been thus, and thus he commands the allegiance of men as much as does his royal blood and the confidence of his brother whom I have learnt to call *the late* King Edward. Have I not made Richard the chief executor of my will, though he be my captor and my enemy even to death?

Men are not hawks: we have allegiances. It is our nature and our safety, for no man is so strong that he has no need of other men, as liege lord or servant, as confessor or Father or server at the Mass. Then there are those men who become companions by chance or design, whose friendship knows little of command or obeisance, at least till their own allegiances drag them apart. Nor can one who has sisters such as Elysabeth and Margaret, or a mother such as ours, disdain even the companionship of women, though I never found it in my first wife. She was all that is commonly looked for in a wife, but we were not well matched. In my second marriage I had hoped to make amends for my fault in the first. That I failed in love for Mary too, and now have failed in guarding even her bodily safety, is not the least of the things for which I must pray forgiveness.

I have no hope for myself, not for this world, though I hope for forgiveness in the next. Only one small flicker, like a dancing insect, will not quite leave me. Louis may yet be at liberty, and no man is more cunning in dangerous times. This tiny hope should comfort me, and it does. Yet still I fear for him. When there is so much awry among the rulers of the realm, so many secrets that threaten so many men of power and mettle, even one such as Louis may take one step too many in the shadowy world he knows so well, for my sake and for Ned's. Perhaps even now he is fled to Burgundy or his own Gascon lands. Perhaps he has even been taken.

But that I cannot believe easily: he is too clever for that. And if he is fled . . . it will be from policy, not fear.

I comfort myself with knowing that our love has reached further than this, in its time, and endured. I will believe that it endures still, and for ever.

The country now about us is more open, and to the east, through the mist, burns the sun. We ride west, and I may not yield to my desire to turn aside and seek the light. I long for it, even as lovers' souls are drawn to the moon though clouds shadow it. And thus, too, are pilgrims' souls drawn through incense smoke to the great candles of the shrine, where they may at last hope to touch God. My soul is as weary as a pilgrim's. This day, I must believe, is my final earthly pilgrimage, though none can know what will be asked of his soul on the other side of death.

Una — Tuesday

When I turn into the drive from Sparrow's Lane I see that the Chantry window-frames are peeling a little more, and some slates on the roof of the front porch – the pilgrim's porch – have slipped. Higher up, one window has a flag of Che Guevara caught at the top for a curtain; another has underwear and a pair of trainers on the sill. But the bulk of the house looks exactly as it always has: broad and solid in rose-coloured brick, gabled and windowed with deliberate plainness. It was grafted on to the medieval chantry chapel, and my post-Victorian grandfather would have no vulgar improving and reworking of what he'd fallen in love with: the true, pure Gothic of pointed arches, hammer beams, and tracery like stone lace. I don't remember the chapel, only the ruins, and they haven't changed. There are the stumps of the flint walls, now lapped with rank grass so that the tiles are invisible, the tarry pit-props and rusting bolts that hold up the end wall of the house, which was never built to stand on its own.

Here and there I can see rubbish: a rotting sack, beer bottles, cigarette butts. Beyond the bulk of the house, across the garden, is the workshop, long and low and rose-pink too, built to house presses and storerooms and binding machines, and all the paraphernalia of such an ancient trade and craft. It rained last night, and there's a smell of apple trees and earth and even, faintly, of the spindly roses that somehow still straggle up from their beds and through the suffocating grass.

My memories are almost suffocating, too. It had just stopped raining the day Mark came to the Chantry, I remember, and the garden smells were so thick I could almost see them. I was sitting at the front of the house, in the pilgrim's porch, looking at the wreck of my dolls' banquet. Bertie-the-beagle-next-door hadn't wanted to be a noble charger after all — at least, not when I tried to wedge Golly's feet into his collar to ride him and be the King's Coronation Champion. Even Smokey Bear had been knocked flying when Bertie escaped.

I heard a scrunch on the gravel: a boy a bit bigger than

Lionel was pushing his bike up the drive. It wasn't the butcher's or the baker's, and he didn't have a telegraph boy's uniform on.

He cleared his throat hard. 'Excuse me, miss. Could you tell me the way to the Solmani Press?'

I jumped down from the bench, picked up Smokey Bear from the puddle he was lying in, and sat him in the sun to dry. This was interesting. 'I'll show you.'

Visitors came to the pilgrim's porch and jangled the big front-door bell, and tradesmen jogged down the path along the side of the house to the back door and knocked. Family went in and out of any door that wasn't locked, and we children climbed through the windows as often as not. I wasn't sure what to do with this boy, but I knew it would be rude to ask what he was. So instead I said, 'Are you looking for Uncle Gareth?'

'Is that G. Pryor Esquire?' He had a local voice, and his clothes were shabby like Lionel's but not mended, and a bit too big the way mine were because they'd been Izzy's first, and sometimes Lionel's too.

'Yes.' I suddenly realised. 'Are you the advertisement?'

Willing boy wanted for general duties, Uncle Gareth had written on the card he put in the window of the newspaper shop. *Must be conscientious and hardworking. 5s. per week plus dinner, rising to 10s. after 3 months' trial. Half day Saturday. Apply to G. Pryor Esq., The Solmani Press, The Chantry, Sparrow's Lane, New Eltham.*

'Yes.' He bent, still holding his bike, picked up my

golliwog and smoothed his hair where Bertie had chewed it. 'This yours?' I nodded. Golly was still a bit slobbery, but not so bad that Aunt Elaine would notice and want to wash him. I didn't like it when Golly smelt of soap. 'Can you show us the way?' the boy said. 'Don't want to be late.'

'Of course,' I said. But I still didn't know what to do with him. In the end I took him the other way, across the garden.

He looked up at the broken walls I used to think were like the wreck of a ship. 'Was that a church?' he said, in a church voice. None of us family went to church, but Aunt Elaine used to let Annie who helped in the house take me to the children's service sometimes, when she went with her little brothers. I quite liked it, specially the singing. No one sang at home. Uncle Robert said it was because none of us could do anything except croak.

'It was a chapel. It's real medieval. King Arthur mostly,' I said.

He nodded. 'Like Lancelot.'

I led him across the lawn and under the apple trees, with his bike wheels making a snake-trail after us in the wet grass. I pointed out the well, the hen run, the stump on the elm where a branch had broken when Izzy was climbing it, and she fell off and broke her arm too.

In the workshop none of the machines was going and Uncle Gareth heard us talking and came to the door.

'Mark Fisher?' he said, holding out his hand. 'I'm Mr Pryor. Mr Gareth Pryor. How do you do?'

Mark Fisher pulled off his cap, then shook hands. 'How do you do, sir?'

'Put your bike in that shed – there – and I'll show you round. See you later, Una. Thanks for showing Mark the way.'

They disappeared into the workshop. I wasn't allowed in there unless I was asked, though often if I hung around looking hopeful in the doorway Uncle Gareth would declare a tea break, and say I could come in, and one of the assistants would give me a slurp of tea, sugary the way I liked it, and half a biscuit. But today everyone was busy, stacking and wrapping and cleaning and oiling. I went away, but Aunt Elaine spotted me before I could get back to my dolls and I had to help with the laundry.

I was standing on a box hanging up wet tea-towels when Mark Fisher came out of the workshop again, pulling on his cap.

'Hello,' I said, over the tea-towels.

'Hello,' he said, starting to wheel his bike along the path towards the front. 'Look at you, all tall all of a sudden. Did Merlin magic you, then?'

'No. I wish he would.'

He stopped. 'What would you ask him for, if you could?'

I thought, I'd ask for a magic carpet like Aladdin so I could fly round the world and find my father's pictures, but I said my usual answer instead: 'Roast chicken and lots of chocolate cake. And a puppy.'

'A puppy of your own?'

'Yes. Only Aunt Elaine says he'd get under her feet.' I could see he was feeling sorry for me. It was a lie and I didn't really want a puppy, so it was sort of cheating to have him being sorry for me. I said quickly, 'What about you? If there was Merlin.'

'I used to think a job. But I've got that now.'

'Are you going to work for Uncle Gareth?'

He smiled like the sun was coming out. 'Yes.'

'Oh, good. Are you starting now?'

'Monday, eight o'clock.' He touched his cap to me. 'Goodbye till then, Miss Una.'

'Goodbye, Mark. See you on Monday.'

He even knew my name, I thought, and he called me 'Miss' as if I was a grown-up, or nearly grown-up like Izzy. I picked up Smokey Bear and Golly from where they'd been playing Pooh-sticks in the rainwater butt, and went in to see if Aunt Elaine had any bits of apple left over from making the Eve's Pudding.

Now as I approach down the path I can hear the slow waltz of a hand-press, and then it goes quiet. Uncle Gareth appears in the workshop doorway. 'Una! My dear! I saw you from the window. How are you? Good flight?'

There's much less of him to hug than there was five years ago, and underneath the oily resin scent of ink and the cleanness of shaving soap he smells of old age. He was never tall; now he's no taller than me.

'I was so very sorry about Adam, Una, my dear. He was a good man,' he's saying, and I want to scrunch myself into his arms and know that it's all right, that Uncle Gareth's here, that he's always here, that he'll never leave me, that it'll all look better in the morning.

He never did leave me, and neither did Aunt Elaine, until I didn't need her any more.

But I still need Adam, and he didn't want to leave me. He fought every inch of the way, every milligram and bloodcount, every injection and X-ray, every pill and incision and suture. He used to worry that I'd rather know less of it all, but when I said, 'No, it helps to know what they're doing,' I meant it, and he trusted me enough to believe me. As if coming back to the Chantry has opened the channel to other memories, I suddenly see the hospital rooms, the books, the diagrams. Perhaps because Adam was a doctor himself, his own doctors were unusually frank in their Australian voices. They were kind, they knew what it meant to Adam, and to me, but they were brisk and efficient, too, as hard as the steel and plastic and chemicals they pitted against the creeping malformation, hacking back as best they might against the mere fringes of the ancient, brutal wilderness of life's own cells. And they lost, and the metastasising cells, the secondary lesions, the tumours and gangrenes won, and destroyed his body, though never his mind, the body I loved as he loved mine that is still, obstinately, whole.

Uncle Gareth doesn't let go until I've wiped my eyes and blown my nose. Then I look around me. 'Izzy said you were living in here now.'

'Yes, the old storeroom makes a very nice bedroom. And, of course, there was all the plumbing ready in the darkroom to make a little kitchen and bathroom. I do very well.'

The workshop, too, looks much as it always did, though the presses have been shoved closer together on the brick floor at one end to make room at the other for a couple of armchairs that I remember, now standing before a two-bar electric fire. One is much more sat-in than the other, I can see, and on the bookcase next to it is a fleet of photograph frames. There's a small desk covered with slithering piles of paperwork. Is it the furniture of ordinary life that makes the long, low space seem smaller? No, it's a physical contraction. At the other end there's a partition, and beyond it the new storeroom: racks of paper and stacks of books.

'What are you working on at the moment?'

'Come and see.' He takes me over to the hand press. 'Forgive me if I clean it, would you?' he says. 'Bad practice to leave things dirty overnight.'

'I'll do it,' I say, taking the rag and solvent bottle from his hand. 'I haven't forgotten how. You show me what you're doing.'

'Only if you put an apron on over that nice frock,' says

Uncle Gareth, plucking one from a hook. He always did notice clothes, and that was vaguely in the back of my mind when I was getting dressed this morning, though it's Uncle Gareth's habit that calls it a frock, not its own nature, which is Indian-printed cotton. I did get round to ironing it, which I wouldn't have bothered to normally. The smell of solvent is sharp, as potent as Christmas-tree scent. 'It's a children's book,' Uncle Gareth is saying. 'Well, as much for children as for anyone else. *Jason and the Golden Fleece*. Look, this is one I've already folded to see if it works.'

I put the cleaning things to one side. It's not really a book, in fact, it's a concertina of heavy, creamy paper, and it reminds me of the reproduction of the Bayeux Tapestry, which I was allowed to have when I was in bed with a cold, the story unfolding in space as well as in my mind and before my eyes. The pictures are wood engraving with the words set in type below.

> *But King Aietes did not want to give the Golden Fleece back to Jason, because any kingdom which had the Fleece was happy: brother was friends with brother, and that whole realm grew rich and peaceful.*

They're not the cool, marble, long-limbed Greeks we learnt at school, whose heirs they said we were. These rough, chunky figures are like gnarled old olive trees clinging to a barren, rocky gorge, somewhere in Asia

Minor. They play out their story, but the artist really has studied the Bayeux Tapestry. Here, too, like a counterpoint, a figured bass, is, literally, a figured base: along the bottom of the page runs ordinary life, Black Sea style. Goats milked and yoked oxen ploughing, an eagle seizing a lamb, ships built and rigged, and fleeces used to pan for gold. These are things that make sense of the great loves and jealousies and battles that rage above their heads.

'It's wonderful.'

'It is, isn't it? Binder's nightmare, though, I fear. They're already cross with us because it's late. I'm having to work half-press at the moment, not having an assistant. But I've had excellent advance orders, enough to make up for the loss on *News From Nowhere*.'

'Goodness, does anyone still read William Morris?'

'Apparently not . . .' He nods approval of my cleaning of the block in the press. It's like grooming a horse must be, I sometimes think: the block solid and still, the press standing quietly under my hand but always with the possibility of movement. 'Now, tell me your news.'

I tell him a little about what I need to do in this flying visit to London, selling the Narrow Street house and settling everything. And I say more about our – my – house in Sydney, about how the garden slopes down to the cliffs and the steps from there to the beach.

'It must be beautiful. Wish I could see it,' he says.

'Come and visit. Come in November and we'll show

you some sun. They keep telling me I should have a birthday party. Maybe I will.'

He shakes his head. 'I couldn't leave the Press. Not for that long. Or the tenants in the house. They're very well behaved, whatever Izzy says, but still . . .' He peers out of the window. 'Sun's over the yardarm, wouldn't you say? Whisky all right? I'm afraid I haven't got any wine. Can't seem to pick up you young ones' habit of drinking it on its own.'

'It was you who taught me to like whisky,' I say, following him into the kitchen that was the darkroom. It's extremely neat, Uncle Gareth always was, just as his hands were always clean and still are, however inky anyone else got. But the kitchen smells of old dishcloth and it doesn't look as if he ever cooks. The glasses he gets out of a cupboard are smeary with short-sighted washing-up. Discreetly I rinse them under the tap, and dry them with a piece of kitchen roll, rather than the neatly folded but musty-smelling tea-towel.

'Are you sure you couldn't come?' I say, when we're settled in the armchairs. I take a pull at the whisky. 'Is there no one who could mind things for you here? A friend's offered to do a big party for my fiftieth. Come for that.'

'Really, nobody,' he says, shaking his head again, then looking away. The way his head moves so that he can look at the bookcase at his elbow, as if drawn irresistibly, takes my gaze with it. As clearly as if he'd picked it up I see he's looking at a photograph of Mark. It's half obscured by one of Adam's and my wedding, but I think it's an enlargement made from some small part of a lost original. Mark's grainy and insubstantial, as memories are; the harder you look at them, the more they break up into dust, and yet you can't help peering at your memories in the hope that they'll come clearer.

Mark did leave me – us – the Press – and I never knew why, not really. Perhaps it's because we're in the workshop that suddenly, somewhere in the depths of me, the old scar starts to ache.

'Doesn't Adam look handsome in that?' says Gareth, as if neither of us has been looking at Mark. 'And what about work? You said in your letter that you were writing about Anthony Woodville.' I explain. 'He's an attractive character, isn't he?' says Uncle Gareth. 'I remember you telling me what was written on the manuscript of his *Dictes and Sayings*. Not Caxton's printed version, the grand, illuminated manuscript, the one that was presented to the King and Queen.'

'It's marginalia, not contemporary,' I say, and the words swim up from my memory: ' "This Earl was the most learned valiant and honourable knight of the world for his time, yet all was exercised with adverse accidents in his life. At length came to achieve the honour of an undeserved death." His name is scratched out too, everywhere it appears in the copy.'

'Is it really? He must have seemed quite a threat, even

when they'd killed him . . .' Uncle Gareth shakes his head, wonderingly. 'How young they were, to be fighting over a kingdom. I remember being amazed when I discovered that Shakespeare's Crookback Dick, whom I used to have nightmares about, was only thirty-three when he was killed at Bosworth.'

'And that he wasn't crook-backed. At least, the real Richard, Duke of Gloucester, wasn't . . . But you're right. Edward IV was eighteen when he won the battle of Towton, which finished off poor old Henry VI as a king. And he had brothers, and then sons. All those glamorous Yorkist men. Though no one would have put money on *Richard* ending up on the throne. It's people whose main use is as inheritors and rulers of land who have power when they're so young. That's why gentrywomen were married in their teens – twelve or thirteen, sometimes – and the boys the same. That's their value.'

'But such boys had to prove themselves, too. Their value was in what they could do.'

'Of course. It's hard to see it with poor old Henry, mind you. Though going mad was hardly his fault. Not that he was much good before that. Did you know that at the time it was called the Cousins' War?'

'No, I didn't. Makes sense, of course. I suppose no one *asked* Henry if he wanted to be a king. It was the Lancaster family business . . . Do you have a thesis yet? A definite line?'

'No, not yet. It's centred on their books, but I don't

know what they'll tell me. The politics are so huge and complicated, they tend to dominate any account. But I'm sure that's not how it felt at the time. What about all the stuff that was to do with living, having children and day-to-day managing the household? No one's approached them as I'm planning to. There's space for that.'

'How much do we know of the books?'

'Well, there's been good work on what we know of Elizabeth's, which is very little. And we can work out a lot more for Anthony, because of course he translated quite a lot, and so on. And Edward's library is well known. He was a great collector, had special caskets made for his favourite books so he could take them with him from palace to palace. Even on campaign. But no one's brought all that together.'

'And then there's the princes in the Tower. What's your view?'

'Of who killed them? And when? I don't suppose we'll ever know, though I know where I think the weight of probability lies. In a sense, it's not necessary for the kind of bibliographic study I'm doing. It's what it must have been like for them, for Anthony and Elizabeth, never knowing what had happened. Where the boys were. If they were alive or dead . . .' And for the life of me I can't stop myself going on. 'You never heard from Mark, did you?'

'No.'

'Only – only Izzy was wondering what happened to him.'

'Dear Izzy. She keeps telling me to get some help. I – I suppose that's what made her . . . think of Mark.'

'Yes,' I say, respecting his evasion. This is the right moment, though, to ask him about how he isn't managing, but the words stick in my throat.

'She's convinced the Press is going to the dogs, just because one of her pet reviewers didn't think much of *News from Nowhere*. Said it "betrays the spirit of Morris's own Kelmscott Press".' He snaps out the words, as if they really stung.

'Would you mind? It's not as if you *like* Kelmscott work.'

'I don't like Morris's design, but you can't argue with the importance of the Press.' He sighs. 'I suppose if I'm honest he had a point. Some of the registration was a bit off, and the paper was quite transparent, so you could see the two sides didn't match. Very regrettable. It was November – do you remember how gloomy it was?' He grins. 'No, it was summer for you.'

'It was gloomy,' I said, and he gives my shoulder a pat on the way to topping up our glasses.

'It shouldn't have happened. One of the lightbulbs had gone, and I'd run out of spares. It was such horrid weather that I didn't go down to the shop, just put up with the bad light. A mistake, of course. I'd get an assistant if I could. But real printers don't grow on trees, and cost accordingly.

And it's too slow for the young. But other than that, *News from Nowhere* was well up to standard. It's hard to get the paper for letterpress. Even so-called fine presses turn out to be using photo-litho, and computers and so on. And then the paper dealers say there's no demand.'

I'm about to say that I've seen some very good work done by photo-lithography, when rock music bursts into our quiet, loud enough to make me jump.

'Just the tenants, don't worry.'

'Heavens! Don't the neighbours mind?' It's not the real, raw thing of my teenage years, more seventies heavy-metal, but very loud.

'Yes, and they will come and complain to me, instead of them. They're convinced they'll get sworn at if they go to the house, though that only actually happened a couple of times. When did Eltham get so bourgeois?'

'It always was. Grandpapa used to go on about how the semis grew like mushrooms after the Great War. How it used to be orchards and meadows till then.'

'But they weren't bourgeois then, they were homes fit for heroes. And the tenants are very good, really. We have peace for days after I've had a word. There are only two at the moment, though I wouldn't go bail for the girl-friends they import. And they always warn me if they're going to have a party.'

He reaches to pour more whisky, and as the sleeve of his jacket slips back I see a nasty-looking dark patch on his forearm.

'Have you hurt yourself?'

He finishes pouring and the cap jingles as he puts it back on the bottle. 'Oh, that. Just caught my arm on the iron.'

'On the *iron?*'

' "Wash on Monday, iron on Tuesday," ' he says. 'Dear Elaine trained me well.'

'Yes, bless her.'

'Izzy and Lionel want me to sell the Chantry house,' he says suddenly.

'So Izzy told me. What do you want?'

He sighs. 'I suppose it's for the best. Apparently it'll fetch a lot.'

'It's not as if he's living in it any more,' Izzy had said.

'It'll be an awful wrench,' I say, and realise that it will be for me, too, to know that it's gone, even though I'll be back on the other side of the world. Even though compared to Adam's death . . . I swallow. 'But you'll have the workshop. And lots of money. You can do it up. Get help.'

'I told you, you can't get printers any more.'

'I didn't mean that kind of help, if you really can't find it. But a cleaner. A gardener. Grow some vegetables.'

'Now, Una, you know I can't grow things. That was always Elaine's department. But it would be nice.' He looks round. 'Though I don't know . . . I doubt I could find anyone. All the neighbours say you can't find a gardener these days for love or money. And I wouldn't have a cleaner I couldn't trust, not round the Press.'

His arguments for changing nothing emerge with the briskness of someone who doesn't want to be persuaded, for reasons too deep to be uprooted by mere common sense. I look at him, and in the fading light see Mark's photograph behind his shoulder. 'You don't want to sell the house, do you?'

'Una, my dear, I'm seventy-eight, and I'm not getting any younger. I've faced that, you know, just as I've faced everything else. I thought I could face this too.'

'You thought? Not now?'

'Lionel rang up just before you arrived.'

'I'm going to see him tomorrow.'

'So he said. He's looking forward to it so much. But it wasn't about that, it was about selling the house. He says he's been advised that it's not saleable without the workshop. We've got to sell the whole Chantry, not just the house. The workshop, all the garden. Everything.'

'*What?*'

'Something to do with access to the road, and planning permission, because they'll want to build.'

'But—'

'I know. I'd have to move. A flat, or something.'

'Could you –' I swallow hard '– could you not buy somewhere with enough space? Or even have a workshop somewhere separate?'

He shakes his head. 'I'm too old to start again . . . No. If it's all sold, there's no getting away from it: it would be the end of the Solmani Press.'

71

Elysabeth — the 33rd yr of the reign of King Henry the Sixth

In the end, after many months had passed, and with each my courses had brought a disappointment, I determined to go on pilgrimage. John was too busy with the manor, and the endless struggle to keep the King on his throne and the Queen from driving all who wavered in their allegiance to Lancaster into the arms of the Yorkist rebels. But to my joy Antony came with me. He journeyed to seek the grace that he seemed always to yearn for, though I know few boys or men who lacked it less. I travelled all those miles to pray for a son.

Two years married, and I was still barren. I could not understand why it should be so. John took me whenever he was at home, and with a little advice from Mal, I had learnt to please him, and to be pleasured by him in my turn, for to do so, she said, would help a baby to come. Besides, she said, it was hard enough to be a woman, and no need to stint such pleasures as I could find. Such matters were privy to us, or as privy as the lives of the master and mistress of a manor can ever be. But with my belly thin and my breasts dry I was still a poor wife in the eyes of the world, and at each of her many visits to us at Astley, Lady Ferrars looked more sour and was secretly more pleased, for if I had no child the Astley lands would revert to her estate.

Grafton was on my way from Astley to Walsingham, and I spent some happy days playing with the children and taking some of the household cares from my mother's shoulders, for she had but lately been brought to bed with Eleanor, and with each baby, she said, it seemed more weeks before she found her full strength again. I said nothing, but she leant forward and patted my hand. 'All will be well, *ma fille*. Keep faith.'

Then Antony and I set off for Norfolk. We rode by Northampton, Peterborough and Wisbech, and stopped with our Haute cousins at Lynn, to hear the news and give it, and rest the horses and ourselves. Antony wrestled with our cousins and played quoits, while I asked advice of my aunt Haute for the getting of children. Then we rode on, the road thick now with pilgrims: Castle Rising, Flitcham, New Houghton. At Fakenham we left the horses and walked the Pilgrims' Road in the bitter salt wind that comes off the Wash as if it would strip the very clothes from your back. I shivered and pulled my cloak close to my throat. But Antony seemed indifferent to the cold. He was no more than thirteen or fourteen summers, a boy, a little brother whose sins and hopes were trifles, when I was a woman grown and praying for a son. And yet as clearly as if I had reached to touch him I knew that there was no part of him, no step that he took on this pilgrims' road, no glance that he cast that was not part of his pilgrimage, of his offering of this journey to God.

The chapel was a still centre where we knelt as the wind streamed endlessly outside. I fixed my thoughts on our Holy Mother, and my eyes on her image, and prayed that her will be done, and that her will might be to grant me a son, or even a daughter, for then I might hope to get a son in time. The chanting rose and fell, the frankincense so thick in the air that I could fancy it soaking into my flesh, into my still narrow womb, ready to quicken with John's seed. Then I looked sideways.

Antony's eyes were open, gazing on Our Lady, his hands reaching out to hers, and his thin body stretched upwards, almost ready for flight.

~

When John told his mother that I was with child, she had perforce to give us joy, but the sourness lingered in her voice. I got little help from her in the first, sickly weeks, but Mal said that the sickness heralded a boy, and this hope strengthened me to ignore her. By the fourth month I was in better health, and all still seemed to be well.

Thus it was the Monday before Whitsun and only a fortnight before my time when from my bed, late one evening, I heard the scurry and jingle of a horse ridden at full speed into the yard. I sat up too hastily, and my head swam. I had to wait before putting on my nightgown over my smock and going heavily downstairs. When I entered the hall, the messenger – one of John's father's men – had already told all, and been dismissed to wash at the pump, sup in the kitchen and find a bed in the hayloft.

John tossed a scrap of paper on to the table; the few words were scrawled on it, and only begged him to listen to the bearer, then make haste to do as Sir Edward asked.

'What is it, husband? Is your mother ill?'

'My father says that King Henry is bound for Leicester, for the council that's called. But Richard of York is on the road from Ludlow to catch them. We must hasten to join the King, and with as much force as we can muster. Would that your father were not in command at Calais! We have need of every man that's still faithful to the King and the House of Lancaster.'

'I know. But Calais must be held, and he is best fitted to do it. And there are enough men at Grafton still. Has your father sent word there?'

'Aye. We are to meet there. On the London road we will get news of where we may reach the King.'

'But, John, would it not be quicker to ride straight to Leicester?'

'King Henry may not reach Leicester. And if Richard of York catches him ... The King has His Grace of Somerset with him, of course, but few other men of note, and only a handful of troops — an escort, not an army. There's little York doesn't know about moving quickly, and his men learnt their business in the French wars. It's thought the Earl of Warwick will join him. It may come to battle. We must reach the King as soon as we may, and pray that others do too. Else we might as well hang ourselves now, as wait for York to order it.' He patted my shoulder. 'Go to bed, wife. You must get your rest, and I must make ready.'

But I did not go to bed that night, any more than John or most of the household did. There were supplies to be put up for the journey, and food for all before they started. The kitchen maid stirred up a sulky little fire from what was left of yesterday's. Then I sent her off to the storeroom to find bread and meat and cheese while I set porridge on to boil and drew more than one jug of small ale. Twice I was summoned to help in mending jackets and finding gloves, and stayed to persuade a reluctant tenant to join us in protecting His Grace the King, and twice I got back to the kitchen to find the porridge boiled over and the fire all but put out.

They rode before dawn had done more than soften the skies from black to grey, and though Mal insisted I go back to bed, I lay awake till noon. My baby seemed all elbows and knees that morning, first poking out my tight-stretched belly, then pushing up till I could barely breathe, then down so hard and long that I had to get up and call Mal for help that I might piss. And when at last he was still, even then I could not sleep. My mind buzzed: there was new fear for John, and well-worn fear that my baby might be a girl, and puzzlement that I could be both glad and sorry that Antony was not older, and might not also join in riding to protect the King.

Later that very day a packet arrived from my mother, I remember. I asked the man who brought it from Calais what news he had, but he had landed at Ipswich and stopped only at Grafton, and had no knowledge of what passed in London. I would have given him money and food and kept him with us to join the rest, had he been a man of my father's, but he was of the Calais garrison, given leave to go home to Nuneaton to attend to his old mother's affairs.

My mother wrote in English, and enclosed a copy of *Lancelot, ou Le Chevalier de la Charette*. I was touched that she should think less of my education and more of my pleasure.

Daughter, I greet you well and send you God's blessing and mine. I pray that you and all at Astley are well. I sail tomorrow and the Lord providing I shall be with you Saturday the next before Whit Sunday. It is often said that the firstborn wait for the full moon, and I have found it to be so. So tides and winds willing I shall be with you. But my dear daughter should your pains begin before that, pray to our Lady, but fear not. Mal is wise and handy — did she not save my little Martha when she would not breathe? — and God will send you a son, and all will be well, I know. By the same man I have sent to Grafton ordering that Margaret may come to you at Astley as soon as she may. She may well be spared from Grafton, if there is a man can escort her, or even two in these troubled times, so that you may have her to bear you company in my stead. Your father is much taken up with affairs, and news reaches us from His Grace of Somerset and from my brother your uncle of Luxembourg too, of great matters which I will not set down but speak of when I am with you. Katharine and Eleanor and Martha are in good health but it would be well for them to be

*away from Calais before the heat begins. We think to send them
back to Grafton before the feast of the Salutation of Our Lady,
so I shall arrange matters when I arrive. The Lancelot is a
romance I have taken much delight in and I trust you will too,
and that it will chase away any fearful or sorry thoughts that
might otherwise breed in the idleness of your confinement. I had
the scrivener work small, that you may more easily hold the
book when you are lying in. Daughter, may God preserve you
and I pray you to be of good cheer until I may come to you.
Written in haste at Calais Saturday the next after St John ad
portam latinam.*

Jacquetta de Luxembourg de St Pol

I could not suppress the few tears that welled in my
eyes, as they seemed ready to do for so many small,
foolish causes, so near was I to my time. It was not her
words themselves, I think, or their being in English, when
she more often wrote to all us children in French for our
better education: it was the sight of her signature, big and
black in her own hand, underwriting her clerk's neat
script.

~

We had not yet heard from John when Margaret arrived
two days later.

'You are to sleep with Mal,' I said, hauling myself up
the stairs. 'I have ordered her girl to sleep in the attic.'
When we reached her bedchamber Mal began to unpack

Margaret's bags. She had brought with her almond comfits, honey from the Grafton hives, a basket of early roses, a note from Antony, a wooden sheep the size of a large kitten that my brother John had whittled for the baby, and a bundle of shirts, caps and bibs that my sisters had stitched.

'It's to be hoped your baby isn't as crooked as this cap Jacquetta's made,' said Margaret, holding it up. 'And Anne is sure it will be a girl, so she has made two smocks, instead of shirts.'

'Oh, no, I pray it is not,' I said, looking up from Antony's note. The weather had not been dry enough for much sport, he said, but he had been snaring rabbits and fishing, and reading *Épîtres du débat sur le Roman de la Rose*. He commended to me *La Cité des Dames*, by the same Christina of Pisa.

Mal shook her head and tutted. 'That's very foolish of Mistress Anne. There's no difference in the shape of it. A baby's a baby. Shirt or smock, what's in a word so long as it keeps him warm? Or her. Now, that's enough messing with good linen,' she went on, for Margaret was trying to fit Jacquetta's cap on to the wooden sheep and giggling. 'Give over, and come downstairs, for Mistress Ysa needs her rest, and I want to hear how the others go on. And have you news of the little girls at Calais?'

I was indeed very weary, and more than willing to make for my own bedchamber. 'Oh, I nearly forgot,' said Margaret, even as I put my hand to the latch. 'Our mother wrote that she has sent to Lichfield Cathedral, begging that they may lend you the girdle of St Margaret of Antioch that's there. Lambing went so well at home that she was able to offer more gold in return than she had hoped. They agreed to send it as soon as they might. There's a dragon on it, of course. I hope it may not bite the baby. Sleep well!' she cried, and ran downstairs after Mal. I could just hear Mal scolding her for speaking so lightly of such a holy thing, and of her own namesake too.

It was weeks since I had been able to lie comfortably, but the happiness of knowing Margaret was downstairs warmed me. I was just dropping off to sleep when cramp seized my guts. I came wide awake, but the cramp had faded. I reached for my rosary and began to say *Ave Maria* and *Paternoster,* hoping I might sleep again, despite the fear for John that never wholly left me. But I had not said one decade when the cramp seized me again.

Had my time come already? I wondered, as it faded. We had not yet made preparation for my lying-in. Perhaps it would pass if I lay quietly and went on with my prayers. When they were done I turned my head, and looked towards the tapestry of Melusina that my mother, as good as her word, had caused to be made and hung above my bed. Melusina in her dragon form, her ancestress and mine as the histories of France attested, strong in childbed and guardian of her young. Another cramp seized me, much worse, and I knew it was beginning.

I was quick in my time, so Mal said afterwards, but quicker is not always easier. I called Mal and Margaret, and a man was sent running to the village for Mother Goodier, the midwife. How can I speak of those next few hours? I cannot truly recall them, and yet I cannot forget them either, though what I do recall is confused by memories from later years and other childbeds. Indeed, I know of no woman that has lived through childbirth who can forget wholly, or recall truly. And of those who die shriven, should I meet them, God willing, in Heaven, I know that they will not have forgotten either. Sometimes I wonder what the saints would think, may they forgive me, to hear us discussing the curse that God in His wisdom laid upon Eve and her daughters.

By the time Mother Goodier arrived each pain seemed to seize me and crush me as if against a rock. In between I found some breath and Margaret wiped my brow with lavender water, and Mother Goodier brewed a drink of herbs over the fire for me to sip. Then just as I began to forget, to soften and doze, the pain gripped again, crushing harder and longer until I thought I must be dead, and dragged down by devils to the burning rocks of hell. And then I was cool and quiet, and in my aching drowsiness I heard an arrival in the hall below, and a clatter as Margaret ran from my bedchamber, before another pain seized me.

So fierce was this one that it seemed an age before I saw that she had returned and held something before my eyes: a strip of silk and leather, dark and stained with age, stitched with curious signs I could not read and a fat and smiling dragon. 'It's the girdle, Ysa! St Margaret's girdle. Now all will be well.'

Mal crossed herself.

'Now, mistress, we must tie it round your belly,' said Mother Goodier, bending down with a grunt to where I squatted on the stool, with my head resting on my arms where I gripped the bedpost. 'Up you get so that we may do it with reverence.'

I hauled myself up a little, and another pain took me. After that, to move again seemed impossible, but I had to do it. In the next breathing space I got my weight on to my feet and half stood. Mal raised my smock. Mother Goodier tied the girdle round, lifting my swollen breasts from where they lay on my belly. Her hands were cold, I recall. Mal let my smock fall. Another pain was due, but nothing came and suddenly I felt so tired that I had to grip the bed end harder still, or fall.

'See what Blessed Margaret can do? It won't be long now, mistress,' said Mother Goodier. 'Back on the bed with you.' I stumbled up on to it and tried to squat, but rocked forward on to my hands and knees. A pain seized me and pressed me so hard that my guts seemed near to exploding. Somewhere they were calling, praying, shouting to push, to bear down, and I did, once, then more, the pain never-ending, just the same, then more, a breath, and more still until my cries seemed to be wrenched from me by the pain itself that was tearing and splitting my guts apart and there was nothing left of me but pain and howling and then a hot slithery slipping and I collapsed on to my belly in a pool of blood and shit and heard cries that were new and small and not my own.

~

I was lying with Thomas at my breast when I heard a shout at the gate, and the tramp and shuffle of a handful of tired men and horses in the yard. Mother Goodier had forbidden me to stand out of bed until the tenth day but I tried to sit up without disturbing Tom. He began to mewl and inside his bands I could feel his little fists jerking as I rocked him quiet.

'Ysa! Ysa!' Margaret was scrambling up the stairs from the hall. 'It's John, he's home!'

By his tread I could tell how weary he was. He stood in the doorway, his brigandine loose-laced and beneath it the leather of his jack dark with sweat. 'York has won. Somerset is dead. His Grace the King is wounded, but not mortally. He is taken to London.'

'What? Oh, dear Lord Jesus! May God preserve King Henry. May God rest their souls.' I sat up, and snatched my hand from under Tom's head to cross myself with such a jerk that his hard, greedy gums wrenched at my nipple and I all but cried out.

Margaret came forward. 'I'll take him, Ysa.'

'No, he's not finished.' I lifted my breast into his

mouth again and as ever had to curl my toes and clench my hands as he bit down.

John's dark face was stiff with weariness and defeat but his smile cracked it. 'They tell me it's a son.'

'Yes,' I said. 'Margaret, please you go down and look to it that the men are given food and drink and such care as they need.' She went out as if she would rather have stayed.

Thomas sucked hard, and then as suddenly fell asleep, with his mouth still open and his head lolling on my arm. I pulled my smock to cover myself.

John came forward at last, and sat on the edge of the bed, then leant forward to kiss me. 'He's well? My son?'

'Please God, yes. And a good, lusty fellow, Mal says. We – I – thought to name him for St Thomas à Becket. But he is not yet christened. It is planned for tomorrow. We did . . . we did not think we should wait for your return. But if you dislike it . . .'

'No, Thomas is a good name. Thomas Grey. Sir Thomas Grey in time, God willing, and Lord Ferrars of Astley and Groby in the end. It's good. And you're well?'

'Yes, I pray so. I feel well enough.'

He nodded, but was silent for so long that I began to feel fearful. 'Husband, what of the King? Is he still in his wits?'

He shook his head, like a bull bothered by a fly. 'I know not. Though to have such a thing happen . . . Who knows what will come of it? York escorts him back to

London, and that's all we know.' He reached forward to touch Thomas's cheek. 'My son. It is well.' Still in sleep, Thomas's head turned so that his lips touched John's broad finger like a kiss and he made a little snuffling sound. 'York and the Earl of Warwick have His Grace the King,' John went on, as if explaining it to me, saying it again, would make him believe it to be true. 'His Grace of Somerset is dead, among many others.'

'God rest their souls,' I said. 'And may Heaven preserve the living. But how did it happen?'

'We rode south from Grafton and found the King at St Albans, holding the road to London. No more than his councillors with him, and York but half a mile or so to the east. York sent to offer submission to the King in return for Somerset surrendering himself to them, for they maintain Somerset was to blame. But when Somerset refused, they attacked. His Grace the King gave the order to spare the commons, but not the gentry.'

His words were heavy, like the tramp of troops, and quickening as if he heard again the trumpets and drums of an advance. 'Such men as we had were seasoned in France and the Scottish borders, and York's battles could not break through ours, not from the flank. Ours stood like rocks but we had too few of them. Then Warwick's archers came up past the Chequers Inn. They broke us from the front when they advanced, and we were fighting in the main street. In the end we held only the Castle Inn – do you remember it?' I nodded. We had often dined there on our way from Grafton: outside the door the street bustled with carts, mule trains and travellers, and all the world that took the London road.

John was speaking, his eyes narrowed as if he still watched for the next attack, and numbered such men as might still be gathered together to fight. 'It was not an ill position, but by then we had not even a man to bear the King's standard. I found it lying in the gutter and propped it against the inn wall. An arrow caught the King in the neck – only a flesh wound, but still – and he ran for shelter. At the last His Grace of Somerset went forth, for there was none left unwounded, and he was killed, though he killed four himself before he was brought down. He was a great man. And many others taken and held prisoner. It is given out that the King is no prisoner, but that his faithful and loyal cousin of York merely has rescued him from Somerset and other evil counsellors.'

'And that's named loyalty! But you were not hurt? Nor your father? Or the men?'

'None of ours. Joseph Carter from Grafton Mill had an arrow in the thigh, but no more than a graze.'

'That's good, him being so lately married and she with child. I would not like to think of her a widow.'

'It was not so likely. Warwick's archers shot at the lords about the King, not the commons, and they know their business. We were safe enough.'

'We must send to my father.'

'Aye, though there will be plenty carrying such news to

Calais. And with Somerset gone and York ruling the King in London, your father is like to lose his command there soon enough. York will want Calais and the garrison in the hands of his affinity. He will give it to Warwick, no doubt.' He stood up and stretched his arms above him, then winced. 'I must eat, and wash, and sleep. Who knows what may happen next? His Grace the King is not the man to hold his own against such a one as York is.'

'The Queen will strengthen his resolve, having now a son to fight for.'

'Aye. But she hates York so, and the more now, in grief for Somerset. As your father says, she has all the valour that His Grace the King lacks, but not the wisdom to temper it.'

'I know it. Husband, should we look to our own defences, here at Astley?'

'It would be wise, I think.' He stopped with his hand on the latch. 'It was said York had his son with him, Edward, Earl of March. Not much more than ten summers, he must be, but well blooded now.' He went out and closed the door behind him.

Thomas heaved a sigh. One arm twitched inside his bands, and his eyelids flickered as if he were flying a hawk in his dreams. Like a knife in my breast came the wish that he were not what I had prayed for at every Mass since at last I knew I was with child; not what I had thought to give thanks for on the morrow, when I heard the church bell ring for his christening; not what I would kneel for in gratitude before our Lady when I myself was churched. I had prayed for a son, and my prayers had been granted. Small hot tears welled into my eyes, ran down my cheeks and fell on to his brow. What would become of my son? How could he be safe in this world where even boys were brought to battle, fought, killed, and saw a king defeated and imprisoned by his own kin?

III

Antony — Prime

At least I am not chained. I have had my wrists bound only once, and how angry I was! Angry with all the ferocity and fear of seventeen. My father frowned at me and, even as I was silenced, I thought as the young do that he could not know the humiliation I suffered, in the luxury of having his knightly word accepted as parole when mine was not.

To hear the tale you would think it the stuff of boys' games, but the fear was real, and so were the wounds. When I told it to Louis he laughed as I did at the valorous folly of my boyhood, but then he stretched his hand across the tavern board and gripped my forearm hard, as if to take on to himself the hurt to my body and my pride.

Even now, with all I later learnt of Richard, Earl of Warwick, I wonder that he did what he did that night. York's idea of protecting the realm in King Henry's second madness was to give Calais into Warwick's command, but then Henry regained his wits and York was no longer Protector. He stormed back to his stronghold in Dublin, and sent his own son, Edward of March, to his cousin Warwick at Calais. There they stayed like dragons in their lair, lashing out to raid the ships that passed through the Channel laden with salt and furs and wine.

My father was ordered to Sandwich, to seize the rest of Warwick's ships in the King's name. We did it easily enough, with no blood shed worth the mention: seasoned sailors know when it's folly to put up a fight.

'In the name of the King,' I cried, in the face of one who looked to have some hot blood left in him for all he was disarmed.

'A king that's half mad, propped on his throne by a witch-woman, and his so-called son none of his own getting?'

Even a prisoner may be treated ungently when he says such things. I struck the man in the face. 'To defy an anointed king is to defy God, you blasphemous scum!' I cried. I believed it too. I still do.

'Warwick is a great man,' said my father, as we sat over a last cup of hippocras, a week later, hard by the quay in the best inn in Sandwich. Those who had been hurt in taking the ships were on the mend. The Kentish men had not risen behind us in support of Warwick, as we had feared they might, and all was quiet. My father had been shocked to find that of Warwick's five ships all were in ill repair and the *Grace Dieu* not even seaworthy, and he set the carpenters to work. We were lodged comfortably enough and dined well, which was a pleasure for my father and a comfort to my mother. We even had the time and the safety to make a small pilgrimage to Canterbury.

'But Warwick would rather squat in Calais than return and try to mend the kingdom,' he was saying. 'He will have matters on his own terms, or not at all.'

My mother rose. 'My lord – son – I am for my bed.'

I rose and bowed to her, and she kissed my brow, then curtsied to my father before he embraced her.

All was as quiet as Sandwich ever is when I rode back through the deep cold of January to my own lodging. The news of wind and tide was proclaimed by trumpets even in the small hours, and the taverns did good business with ale and wine and whores, as taverns in a great port do. But my men and I agreed that we could hear nothing untoward, only the calls of the watches we had set on each ship.

I was weary with the pleasant ache of work well done. I took a moment to scrawl a note to Elysabeth, and tied it into a bundle with presents for her boys, a copy I had made of Lull's *Booke of Knighthood and Chivalry* for Tom and a scarlet whip-top from the market place for little Dickon, to go with the next man riding to Grafton that they might send it on to Astley. The men, rolled in their cloaks about the fire of our lodging, grumbled that the light kept them awake so I snuffed my taper and knelt for my prayers in the dark.

I was deep in my first sleep when a shout burst into my dreams, and another, and blows fell upon the door. 'We're attacked! They're seizing the ships! Sir Antony! God save us, you must make haste!' I was up and pulling on my boots almost before my eyes were open, my fellows and I bumping elbows, swearing at the pain of skinning-over grazes got in the fight the week before, and fumbling with points and brigandines. There was no time to take horse – it was more urgent to arm ourselves – and we ran out, past Whitefriars and the Rope Walk to the Dover Gate, where we gathered two more men, which was all that could be spared and the gate still be held. Then we ran on down the Chain towards the quay with our swords drawn.

In the light of the inn's cressets, I saw my father standing, unarmed and in his night gown, surrounded by men bearing Warwick's badge. My mother stood beside him, dressed all by guess, a bundle on the cobbles beside her, and behind them loomed the bulk of one of the ships.

We were outnumbered but we did our best, for my father could do nothing. The enemy came to meet us with roars of *à Warwick* but our shouts for the King were soon lost in the clangour of steel. We left several wounded beyond fighting. I saw a man of theirs go down with the tendon in his knee cut, crying in French to the Virgin.

Another got a slash to his face so that he could see nothing for the blood. One of ours was killed – Joseph Carter, from Grafton Mill, rest his soul – and I got a cut on my shoulder deep enough to loosen my hold on my sword. I knew it was over even before I found a dagger at my throat.

'Save yourselves!' I cried to my men, hoarse and fearful for them, and the dagger pricked the skin of my neck. My men fled into the dark streets.

Warwick's men took no trouble to go after ours nor, as far as I could tell in the darkness, did they try to seize the town. It seemed that we Wydvils, and the ships their lord claimed as his own, were all that they desired. A hand fell on my shoulder wound. I thought the pain would brand the flesh for ever, and then I was pressed down so that my knees struck the cobbles hard.

The men about my father and mother began to urge them towards the edge of the quay. My hands were seized and bound with rope behind me.

'You scum! Scoundrels!' I tried to twist round on my knees to face my captor, but the dagger pricked my throat again. 'How dare you? How dare you? I am a sworn knight!'

'We've our orders,' said my captor, pulling me to my feet. 'Come along.'

'You must accept my parole!'

'That's as maybe,' he said.

'I'll see you hanged for this, you scum!' I stumbled on

the gangplank for I could not get my balance with my hands tied. 'You've no right to treat a sworn knight thus!'

I tried to step proudly on to the deck, lost my footing and went sprawling, striking my wounded shoulder on a barrel as I fell. Someone laughed, then another. I struggled to my knees, and found I was looking up at my father. My mother was nowhere to be seen. What had they done to her?

'Son, be still. Save your breath for when it can be of use.' He turned to the man who was even then hauling me roughly to my feet. 'Good sir, not all men learn the rules of chivalry, but you, I am sure, know them well. My son is indeed a sworn knight, and you may accept his parole in good faith. Indeed, sir, you must do so. My lord of Warwick would not expect otherwise, for he is himself as great a knight as any in the kingdom, as I well know.'

'Aye, that he is, though they say my lord of March bids fair to rival him,' said the man. 'Well, my lord, I'll take your word that your boy need not be bound.'

I could bear it no longer. 'You must take my own word, *sir*, not my—'

'My son is young,' said my father, making his voice gentle. 'We were all such hotheads once, were we not? If you would be so good as to unbind him?'

My pride would not allow me to rub my wrists where the ropes had bruised them. 'Sire,' I said to my father, ignoring the man who still stood at my shoulder, 'what of my mother?'

'She is well enough. They have not used her ill.' He contrived to smile. 'I think we are to take a little journey to Calais. She was always fond of the place, and loves a chance to use her native tongue.'

As it fell out, she had that chance for some time.

~

The mists have burnt away now. The men about me ride with closed faces, their northern voices dry and brief, speaking only of the business in hand, and little enough of that. It seems they know as well as I do what their business is. They are alert, for no man-at-arms or archer on duty is otherwise. But they are at ease, for we are in a country and among a people who have long been Richard of Gloucester's own to command. No nervous glances over their shoulders by these men, no hands on hilts, no hasty changes of plan. Just a solid troop, jog-trotting towards York at the start of a long, hot day's ride. This silent, workaday journey is a journey like any other: its route, its stopping-places, its end are all ordained.

And yet the end for me is like no other: my end, the end of my life on this earth.

Sometimes I wonder if it will be as I once seemed to see it. The day of our pilgrimage to Canterbury there was stone around me, and golden light ahead and far above. From somewhere there came singing, the notes lifting and falling among the arches. I inched my way along on my knees. Each stone rasped them more raw than the last, each pace was a trial of my strength, a test of my humility, of my patience, of my willingness to offer everything to God. Pain and humiliation, body and soul humbled together, offered at the shrine of a martyr who once offered more than I ever could, who willingly gave his whole self to a brutal death in God's service.

How little and weak was my offering by comparison: my small, young pilgrimage! The great stones smelt of ice and earth. There was incense thick and harsh, the long-dried iron of holy water on my brow and lips and naked breast, the reek of sweat. Pain and heat began to thread with the music through my mind. I reached the top of the steps, and the golden light swelled like a cloud ahead of me. I could move more quickly, make haste in my pain to the Presence, to that precious shrine that seemed almost to hang in the air before me, beckoning, flickering, ruby, ivory, sapphire and gold casing those few mortal scraps that were left to us, filling my eyes and nose with a scent that rang in my ears like bells, that drew me on and held me rapt, desiring nothing but to reach its heart, the resting place of holy Thomas, where pain and grief would be no more than a shadow, a memory of a gift that I once gave to God.

Una — Wednesday

Lionel's on the platform when my train pulls into St Albans. Izzy may not look like an artist any more, but

Lionel still looks exactly what he is: the City business-man, semi-retired only because he's made as much money as he could possibly want. Everything about him's well groomed: tweed jacket, ironed shirt and perfectly knotted tie, fine leather gloves, brogues whose polish wouldn't disgrace an off-duty cavalry officer, black hair silvering handsomely at the temples. I remember noticing how that gloss crept over him when he began working in the City, and still more after he met Sally. I'm so pleased to see him, but he makes me feel scruffy and travel-stained, though I've had time to do some washing and even iron my shirt, and a half-hour trip on a half-empty train can't do much harm.

'Journey all right?' he asks, kissing my cheek.

But I can't stop myself. 'Uncle Gareth says the workshop's got to go as well.'

'Here, let me take your bag. I know, it's such a shame. I hope you don't mind if we walk. It's not far.'

I hold on to my bag. 'I can manage, thank you. Besides, it's only a toothbrush and clean knickers. Not heavy . . . Is it really necessary to sell the workshop?' I continue, as we shoulder our way through the crowds on London Road. 'You should have seen him. I don't want to be melodramatic, but I honestly think it would be the death of him.'

'Oh, I think he's tougher than that. Though he's sorry, of course. But it does look as if it's the only way. And how about you? Have you been very busy since you got here?'

'Yes, fairly. You know what it's like.'

'You must tell me if there's anything I can do. I mean, obviously I'm not qualified for the Australian end of things. But advice . . .'

He doesn't, as Izzy did, give me a hug, but I can sense that his mind's readying itself to grapple with my business if I ask him to, and affection rushes through me. 'It's okay so far, thanks. About the Chantry: does Izzy know? I haven't spoken to her today.'

'Yes, she does.'

'She must be absolutely shattered. She lived at the Chantry longer than either of us. I always thought it was a mistake that she and Paul moved away.'

'You can't blame a man for not wanting to live with his in-laws for ever.'

'I suppose not. But is there *really* no way round it? Selling the Chantry, I mean. Never mind Izzy, what about Uncle Gareth?'

We're crossing St Peter's Street in a bright, plastic bustle of shoppers. He sighs and shakes his head. 'I've had my conveyancing specialist turning it inside-out, and it can't be done. Did you know that Sparrow's Lane is a private road?'

'I suppose so. It says so on the sign, or it always did.'

'Yes. The neighbours have persuaded the owner to block access for construction traffic. Whereas if we sell the whole property, they can use the back gate. *That* lane's a byway – public road – even though it's not tarmacked. It's all or nothing, I'm afraid.'

It sounds unarguable but I want to argue it. I didn't think I would; thought, if anything, that it would be good to shed the last scraps of my English life. But it isn't, because that means . . . shedding the last scraps of my memories of Mark.

Mark?

After seeing — what? His ghost? I can't pretend to myself any longer that it's not important, that it's all long ago. Yes, it's long ago, but it mattered too much. Things that mattered that much — that once hurt that much — don't cease to exist because years pass, because I moved to the other side of the world, because Adam and I were happy.

Somewhere inside me something stirs. Not nostalgia. Not sadness. Something small but fierce, about now, not then.

'So you're writing about the Wars of the Roses,' Lionel's saying, as we cross Chequer Street, shouldering our way through delivery men, traffic wardens and tourists making for the Abbey. 'York and Lancaster and so on. Does the battle of St Albans come into it?'

I pull myself together. 'It certainly does,' I say, 'Only it's *battles*. There were two — 1455 and 1461. The first one was — where's the market square?' Lionel waves ahead of us. 'That wasn't much more than a skirmish, but Henry VI was wounded in the neck, and captured by the Yorkists. The second one was much bloodier.'

Neatly he manoeuvres so that he's walking between me

and the road again, escorting me. The verb's irresistible, although whether it's this, or his ushering arm each time we pass a lamp-post and he stands back for me to go before him, I can't decide. Adam had good manners, but more as one thoughtful human being to another than this careful, codified male-to-female dance that is as seductively restricting as the boned and stiffened New Look frocks that Aunt Elaine so carefully cut and sewed for Izzy. Above us, plastic and steel and glass fronts are welded on to a muddle of brick and rendered buildings so that only the sideways-leaning upper windows and sagging roof-trees betray their age. There are rows of cars and parking meters, electric-lit advertisements and municipal hanging baskets, and a fine Edwardian encaustic plaque on a building society that was once the Castle Inn, recording the death of the Duke of Somerset.

A heavy lorry comes growling up Holywell Hill, each gear-change a gasp then grunt. Once, the hill was barricaded by Somerset's men, defending the King from his own cousin of York, the most powerful man in the realm. Beneath the yellow lines, the tarmac, the cobbles, the crushed stone is the very earth they tried to hold. It would make a difference how many held a bow, how many a sword, how many a pike; whether they were confident in God's help or fearful of damnation; if they were hungry, drunk or weak with terror. It mattered how sturdy their helmets and breastplates were, how strong their arms and shoulders, where they mustered and how steadfastly they stood.

What did it mean to do these things for someone you knew only as the name of your allegiance? God, or the King, or His Grace of York? To use everything that you were made of in that cause, your body and mind, your strengths and weaknesses, and know it might not be enough?

What did it mean for my father, no more than school soldiering behind him, a creator who said in a letter that he had no allegiance except to art, to find himself under fire in the deserts of Iraq and the slaughter at Coriano? That my grandfather was too old for the call-up by months but had a brother killed on the Somme, and friends dead at Vimy Ridge, the Piave river and others he could tell over like a litany? That Grandmama's brother was kicked to death for being a conchie? That Uncle Gareth never mentions Tobruk at all?

It's not, exactly, my own world, because I only see it through the grey dust of newspaper photographs and newsreel reports. But it's the backdrop to their lives and the rubble under my feet. Once I went to Mark's home, and even then there were rows of houses like broken teeth and craters full of rubble and spears of rosebay willowherb. What had he left behind after he finished work at lunchtime on Saturday? His wages, that was it. But it turned out that where he lived was no home, just a yard full of scrap and what I later worked out was stuff his drunken father thought he'd be able to patch up and sell on once he was sober. His brother, I knew, was in prison, which was something I couldn't even imagine: a real person, sort of, because he was Mark's brother, being a criminal.

A yard and a couple of rooms of half-rotted clap-board behind Rope Street, it was, almost in the looming shadow of the ships' hulls where they lay in the grey ocean of Greenland Dock. I remember my fascinated horror at the cold and food-encrusted kitchen range, the stinking earth closet at the far side of the yard, and the flea-bitten dogs I thought must be strays until I saw Mark feed them and sweep their mess out of the yard with the absent-mindedness of long habit.

'Well, thank you very much,' he said, picking up my bike from where I'd left it on the cobbles. 'Very good of you. Did Miss Butler get to finish her drawing before it rained, by the way? The one of the hens?'

'Izzy? No. But the rain stopped, so maybe she's doing it now.'

'That'd be good. She was very cross when Mrs Butler told her to come in. It's going to be good, that print.'

'Izzy always gets cross if she has to stop working.'

He smiled, at me and sort of not at me, I thought. 'Better go before it starts raining again. See you on Monday.'

'Okay,' I said.

The little door in the big gate rattled, then banged

open. A man came in and stared at me. 'What's this?' He had a local voice only sort of slurry, not like Mark's, and he smelt.

'Just something I left at work, Dad,' said Mark, quickly.

'Wages? You owe me.'

'No, just a book.' Which was a lie. I hadn't known Mark could lie.

Mark's father looked at me. 'You one of them, then?'

I nodded. I wasn't frightened, I told myself, because Mark was there, and then I saw by the way Mark had his hand in his pocket, clenched round his pay packet, that he was frightened too.

Mark's father held out his hand to me and I knew it would be very rude not to shake it, though I didn't want to. It sort of wobbled but his grip hurt. 'John Fisher. How d'you do? Want that bike? I'll give you a good price for it.'

It took me a minute to understand what he meant. And when I did, I didn't know what to do, because maybe it would be rude to refuse that too.

'Of course she wants it, Dad,' said Mark, and I was so relieved I nearly burst into tears. 'Leave her alone. How's she going to get home?'

'Only asking. Don't get anywhere in this world if you don't ask, do you, missy?'

One of the dogs was doing a mess in the corner again. Mark took the handlebars of my bike as if he was going to wheel it over the bottom bit of the gate for me, and suddenly he was between me and his father and even though I knew he was frightened I felt safe. 'Better be off or Mrs Butler'll be wondering where you've got to.'

I never went there again, and the world it was part of was slowly filled in and levelled and turned into concrete, then glass, and now heritage brick. But after he disappeared I dreamt more than once of Mark walking away, against the old backdrop of that world, silently, as people do in dreams: just one little figure in an endlessly shifting panorama of grey-faced humans, trains and signs and lamp-posts ticking past, and behind him the shards of monochrome buildings in a scarred and cratered world.

When I got home, Izzy was back lying on her front by the hen run, drawing. Obviously Aunt Elaine hadn't spotted her, because she wasn't on a rug but flat down on the wet grass. Her legs were across the path and I couldn't get my bike past.

'Izzy, can you move?'

No answer and no movement, except for her pencil, flicking in the feathers then stabbing one beady eye into the paper of her sketchbook.

'Izzy!'

Still no answer. Cross, I ran my front wheel gently into her leg. It left a grubby mark. She turned her head. 'What?'

'Can you move?'

Without another word she bent her legs up and I squeezed past, put my bike in the shed, and went in to wash my hands at the kitchen sink. Aunt Elaine was cooking. I scrubbed and scrubbed at my right hand, until the smell of Mark's father was gone, and all there was was carbolic.

'Is Izzy deaf?' I asked Aunt Elaine, while I scrubbed.

She was cutting me a piece of bread. 'No, why?'

'She never hears things when she's drawing.'

'Nor do you when you're reading. Do you want jam or butter or dripping on your bread?'

'Butter and jam,' I said, though I knew perfectly well I wouldn't get it.

'No, one or the other, you know that. And *please*. It's because you're concentrating — you on your book, Izzy on her drawing.'

'Uncle Gareth says you always used to have both. Dripping, then.'

'That was when the Press made money,' said Aunt Elaine, putting the plate of bread on the table with the jar of dripping, and going back to chopping carrots.

'But that's because it's stories,' I said, pinching a bit of carrot from the pile. 'Izzy, I mean. The stories are inside my head. I'm inside my head. You can't be inside your head when you're drawing, you have to be looking out of it.' I took another bit of carrot.

'No more stealing, or there won't be enough for the *daube*.'

'The what?'

'The stew. A French sort of stew.'

'Will I like it?'

'Yes,' Aunt Elaine said firmly, taking a jar out of the cupboard and trying to open it. 'Drat!'

Lionel came wandering in. 'Mum, where's Dad?'

'Still at the office. Homework?'

'Algebra. I've got stuck. The old boy's given us an O-level paper.'

'Uncle Gareth's in the workshop,' I said, through bread-and-dripping.

'Finish your mouthful first, child,' said Aunt Elaine. 'Lionel, can you open this jar before you go?'

He took it and struggled. When he did get the lid off his hand slipped. Juice and some dark things like pointy cherries went on the floor.

'What are those?' I asked.

'Olives, for the *daube*. I got Uncle Robert to buy them at that Polish delicatessen, for a treat, last time he went up to the St Bride's Library. Pick them up and run them under the tap, will you? They're delicious, you'll love them. And give the floor a wipe.'

I can't remember if I did like them. I suspect now that they were small and black and bitter and only the grown-ups did, and that more for nostalgia for dusty art-student holidays in out-of-the-way corners of Italy before the war than anything else. But I do remember thinking for a long time about me reading in my head, and Izzy looking out of hers, and whether it was the same thing or not.

I have to write Anthony and Elizabeth looking out from my mind, of course, establishing facts from colophons and marginalia. There are annals and account books to examine, images and emblems to decode. It's like Izzy's drawings: I can't write what's in their heads, not really, any more than she can draw what's in the hens' minds except as it shows in what their bodies actually *do*. But to make a story I need to be in my *own* head, I think vaguely, then call myself to attention because Lionel's talking again.

'So, with such an unusual property, and it being a listed building – developers are always wary of that – rather than waiting for offers to dribble in, the best option seems to be to auction the Chantry.'

'*Auction* it?'

'Yes. And the furniture and so on – anything that none of us wants. Most of the good stuff's either been distributed or sold already, of course. The Press equipment, too, if Gareth doesn't want to take it somewhere else.'

He might be discussing the dismantling of an office block. 'But . . .'

He turns towards me. 'Una, I know it's sad. But there really is no choice. I've gone over and over the figures. It's very sad, but there we are . . . Now, here's where I thought we would lunch. I hope you won't think I'm very eccentric if I keep my gloves on? A touch of eczema, you know.'

I didn't, it must be a recent thing. I only realise some-thing of what it's really about when we're settled in the restaurant and Lionel takes out a clean handkerchief. Then, discreetly below the edge of the table but unmis-takably, he polishes each piece of cutlery and even the glasses. My suspicion that something odd is going on is confirmed when we finally walk down the hill after lunch to his plump, bright white house and he unlocks a small vault's-worth of locks before disarming the burglar alarm and asking me if I'd mind very much leaving my shoes in the hall. Some of my hippier friends do this, especially the Scandinavian ones, but *Lionel*?

I say nothing about that, however, as we go in our stockinged feet into the dauntingly spotless drawing room. It smells of polish and everything gleams. The mantelpiece is full of ornaments, the paint so shiny and dustless that they stand in a pool of their own reflections: a pair of candlesticks without candles, let alone the drips of wax that Aunt Elaine never had time to scrape off, a thickly engraved invitation or two, a Dresden shepherd and shepherdess courting one another in conventional gestures from opposite ends. And in the centre is a small sculpture. It's abstract, no bigger than could be held in two cupped hands, a clean curve of metal that gleams cloudily, like a crescent moon made real. I'd like to pick it up.

'Is that one of Fergus's?' I say to Lionel. 'It's beautiful. What's it made of?'

'It's pewter, apparently. Spun pewter,' he says, but doesn't elaborate, so I imagine Fergus tucked away in a secret tower, stooped like Rumpelstiltskin over a wheel, spinning base metal into a whirl of silver moonlight.

'Picked something up in Town the other day that might interest you. It reminded me of the Chantry.' He unlocks a glass-fronted bookcase. *Le Morte Darthur* in a late-nineteenth-century art binding and wrapped like all the others in the crackling clear plastic of the antiquarian book dealer. The silvery whirl has spun my mind too. I don't open it, look at the title page, the dates, the colophon. A book's created to hold words, yet words are not what I'm thinking. It's the weight in my hand as I take it from him, the corners pressing into my other palm. I turn it over, pull off the plastic clothing, run my finger down the spine, feeling the raised bands like vertebrae and the tooled dips of title and author. Then I turn it again, open it, and furl the pages so that they tickle past my thumb, hesitating at each illustration plate, then flickering on, giving off a faint breath of paper and age. Under my palms the binding is smooth and warm and smells of beeswax. The brown calfskin is inlaid with green and amethyst leather and tooled with gold, curling round the book to suggest a lake, a sword, a grail, the colours so cleanly cut that there's scarcely a join to be felt, only the slip from one to the next under my fingers, like the swell of muscles under a man's skin.

I look up, and my cheeks are suddenly as hot as if

Lionel — my brother in all but name — knows what I'm thinking. I haven't thought much like that, not since Adam got ill. It takes me by surprise and I look down at the book again, and see that the pages have stopped flickering at a print of Sir Kay, Arthur's foster-brother and seneschal, scorning the new-come stranger he's nicknamed Beaumains for his beautiful hands. You can just see the vanishing ring on Beaumains's finger.

'It's lovely,' I say, closing it and putting it down on the table.

Instantly Lionel picks it up, pulls open a drawer and extracts a folded duster. He polishes the book and, holding it in the duster as a doctor might use surgical gloves, rewraps it in its sterile dressing and slips it back into its place. Only then does he say, 'So, what do you think of it?'

'It really is lovely,' I say. 'It's out of my period, of course, but I could tell you who to ask about it, if you wanted to know more.'

'I'm not planning to sell it on, but that would be interesting nonetheless. A collector friend of mine has one, but it's not in nearly such good condition.' He grins. 'Worth much less.'

'My big address book's in Narrow Street. I'll look some names up when I get back and give you a ring. Talking of business, what do we have to do, if this auction's got to go ahead?'

'Well, it's not quite as straightforward as you might

imagine. The Chantry's not simply Gareth's to dispose of.'

'I know I'm on the deeds.'

'Yes, and Izzy too. Under Grandpapa's will . . . He had to do it all over again when Kay . . . But it was done properly.' He smiles. 'I remember the grown-ups having a huge conference about it, and Gareth insisting that you had Kay's full share. I'd been listening at the door, and I looked out of the window and saw you sitting on the swing, and I thought how you'd no idea.'

'Did you mind?' I say, surprising myself. 'I suppose you might have got more, if he hadn't insisted.'

'No, not at all. It was purely intellectual.' He smiles. 'Besides, I knew Grandpapa was immortal. I'd just gone to the grammar, so I suppose you were about eight. Anyway, the long and the short of it is that we have to sign that we agree to the sale. And what you may not know is that I've made my share over to Fergus. A tax-avoidance measure. So as well as Gareth, you and Izzy, he has to agree. But there's no problem there: he's already agreed, in principle. He's living in York, and I've posted him the paperwork. It's easy, when it's all in the family.'

'Yes, of course,' I say, and don't add that once or twice in the last few years I've wondered what would have happened if my father hadn't died; if he'd come home to the Chantry, not to look after me as my childhood fantasies ran, but to take his place as the oldest son, the first-born, the fine artist and adored older brother. Who knows? God might know, Anthony would say, but we can't.

But there's so much before that. Brothers, yes, but uncles too. There's something beating in my mind as Lionel tells me about a scrap between the Abbey and the Town over a car park and a right of way.

> *England hath long been mad, and scarr'd herself;*
> *The brother blindly shed the brother's blood,*
> *The father rashly slaughter'd his own son,*
> *The son, compell'd, been butcher to the sire:*

Yes, it's the end of *Richard III*, when all in the kingdom – for a Tudor playwright – is set to rights. One of the things I'll be fighting against is our Shakespeare-shaped vision of the times, though he was so much nearer those times than I am. For him the War of the Cousins was a not-so-distant past that he was refashioning; old men could tell the tales, as Grandpapa told us of his father's Crimea. If you take the plays as history, then they're wrong. They lie, if you like, in the cause of a story that grips us still. So how did it look to their grandfathers themselves, not a gripping tale or a propaganda lie, but a life, as it was lived, day after month after year? That's what I want to know, the history I want to write. My refashioning is another kind of tale, I hope and believe, though my historian's conscience will always be the ruler of my storyteller's desires.

It sounds so dry, so puritanical. So dead. How can I bring them alive, yet have a clear scholarly conscience? How can I make Elizabeth and Anthony breathe? Did the stubble scratch her ankles after the Grafton harvest? How did he live through the months as a prisoner-of-war in Calais? When Edward seized the throne from Henry, what did they feel? Their mother Jacquetta was Henry's aunt by marriage, Lancastrian to the core, Queen Margaret her great friend, both French noblewomen and new, bewildered brides in this damp and chilly land. What did Jacquetta feel – do – say – when her husband announced the battle was lost, Henry and Margaret were fugitives, and the family were changing sides? And it *was* a family matter, the business of the kingdom. Family, affinity, allegiance ... These things shaped everybody's life.

I look at Lionel, who's talking about the distribution of assets, the assignment of income, and the implications for Fergus and Fay's children, if there ever are any. 'If Elaine ever has a son the problem might yet be compounded, or indeed resolved – who knows?' my grandfather wrote, years before Lionel and Izzy were born. What of my father's allegiance to 'nothing but art'? What would that have done to the Solmani Press? Craft is art made possible, I think suddenly: possible and functional. Art that feeds and clothes and houses. Would Kay and Gareth have fought over what should be done, and what could be done? At least now we're not fighting, but these things still shaped our lives. I came back to England to sign off my long-dead English life, but creeping over me is the thought that they still do shape it.

~

When Lionel escorts me to the station next day we're told there's some trouble on the St Albans line. No, I assure him, it's fine, I'll just use the alternative bus they've arranged – might as well – he's not to trouble himself. We say goodbye for now, though we'll talk again soon because there's a lot to do still about the auction; he'll let me know.

And then I clamber on to the Rail Replacement Service bus, with the other grumbling travellers, and crawl down the Great North Road towards London. Once there would have been long strings of packhorses laden with cloth, salt cod or towering bundles of flax; messengers and merchants, journeymen and prentices; a chapman with ribbons, trinkets and ballads for sale; a friar muttering a parable ready for the next market cross; a pilgrim making for Walsingham, and another with his hat cockle-shelled from Compostela; a man-at-arms and a woman with a baby on her back; beef cattle for East Cheap and geese for Poultry; a tinker's donkey festooned with pots and pans; a beggar wounded – so he says – in the late wars with France, and for a groat he'll tell of the burning of the witch Joan that was of Arc. This road's a nerve that joins London to the kingdom; where we sit in the panting, clotted traffic is a synapse, a gateway that must be guarded, or stormed, to the city that must be held, or taken. Once, twice, so many times, all these ordinary, necessary things scattered and hid at the shriek of trumpets and drums, banners slashing through the air, 'Owre kynge went forth to Normandy, With grace and myyt of chivalry' sung to the beat of hoofs and marching feet. Only they weren't going forth to Normandy but to fight their own kin.

Something aches inside my belly and it's not quite for Adam. These things are further beyond me even than he is: they inhabit me, but I've no hope of touching them.

But there are ways of dulling old wounds as well as new ones: human company is one of them, though sleep, work and alcohol are others, I think. It's not too late to ring round my English friends and fill some evenings before I leave. I remember learning how to dull wounds in my first term at university. I had to or I would have gone mad, because the old wound that I thought I was used to, that I'd hoped would skin over now I'd left home, was suddenly reopened, as raw as ever, a new wound indeed. I busied myself in libraries, archives and pubs, with historical societies and debating clubs, digging myself deeper and deeper into my work, badgering librarians, looking up references, wrestling with sentences, pouncing on ideas, following clues, and knowing always that it was better not to think of the Chantry, not to know where Mark was, not to wonder what he was doing – thinking – touching, whether he was smiling or frowning, or just concentrating absolutely on something, with that tiny whistle between his teeth.

Elysabeth – the 1st yr of the reign of King Edward the Fourth

It was in the cold of the weeks after Candlemas that I heard of John's death in the second fight at St Albans. It was like hearing of an ill prophecy fulfilled: long dreaded, yet impossible to believe. King Henry had been rescued from the Yorkist rebels, but the Earl of Warwick had escaped with no small part of his army; there would be more battles, not a doubt of it.

And John was dead. The shock gripped my bowels for hours, then the old dread in my heart chilled into fear of what might now befall the boys and me. For a day and a night I could do no more than lie abed. Grief seemed to be a sickness that had overtaken my body. I had never thought to love John as a lady would in a high romance, or in a ballad sung by a minstrel, and I had not. But we had worked together well at Astley, and lived together comfortably, and I had been fond of him as I would be of a friend or a brother. To think that I would no more know his sturdiness, his delight in the boys, the pleasures of his body . . .

Then on the third day since the news, I arose and set everything at Astley in order. I had decided I would go home to Grafton.

We met with no trouble on the road. Even when we reached Grafton I had little leisure – if you could call it that – to grieve for my husband, so heavy were the times with fear for what was happening in the West Country, in the Welsh Marches, in the north, and what might happen here because of it. Richard, Duke of York, had been killed, but his son Edward, the boy John had spoken of now grown a man with Warwick as his guide and champion, was cried king in his place. More than that, it was difficult to discover. Grafton was on the London road, but such news as we could come by left us little the wiser. One day a master cutler on the road from Oxford would stop by to tell how he had heard that Queen Marguerite had taken London again. The price he must pay for steel was risen, and the price he could get for his goods was fallen because of it. The next day a prioress warming her white hands at our fire, on her pilgrimage to Walsingham, would say that, no, the gates of London were barred against King Henry's army, and King Edward proclaimed within. In Coventry I had heard soldiers from Cornwall and Cumbria speaking their strange Welsh tongue. Now in the Northampton ale-shops you could see Kentish men and dark-faced veterans of the Calais garrison. And most damaging of all to Queen Marguerite's cause were tales of her Scots army, starving and savage since she could not pay them, ravaging barns and byres and women everywhere they went.

There were more battles. And then came the news of the fight at Towton.

Even by those first reports, it was clear that the slaughter had been like no battle before. My father was thought to have fled north with the King and Queen, and Antony was most certainly dead.

My mother's grief for the loss of her first-born son was no less for being silent, or for the news being still uncertain. My own, coming so hard upon the loss of my husband, seemed more than my flesh might bear. And still we could not be sure. It might be a false report, I told myself, but if it were, would a true one not have come by now?

It was a week before a messenger from my father brought news: he and Antony were both safe at York, and the King and Queen were fled to the Scottish king.

Our joy that Antony lived was the sharper for having thought him lost. But if it had not been one of our own men who told of my father's going to Edward of York, kneeling first in surrender and then in fealty and Antony with him, I would not have believed it.

It was my mother who was most troubled by the news. '*Mon Dieu!* I cannot think it to be right. Your father's service to the King, all for nothing. Are we just to submit to this – this *pirate* Edward, who thinks that because he has defeated the royal army he may do as he chooses with the kingdom? Everything we have worked for, gone, *pouf!* If *we* are not to stay loyal to Lancaster, who is?

What would the great Duke John say? Henry was like a son to him for – for want of his own . . . And *ma pauvre* Marguerite. I wonder how they do, hiding in the north?'

'But, madam, if my father thinks there's no hope of peace by any other means, how can he do otherwise? And it is not mere piracy. Edward of York's claim in blood is good. My noble father has not done this lightly, you may be sure.'

'That may be true,' she said, 'but I hold still that he ought not to have done it at all.'

Outside in the yard the children were shrieking. The deep cold that had gripped us through Holy Week and Eastertide had lifted, and the sun was out. 'But—' I was saying when there was a scramble of feet on the steps, and Dickon came running into the hall.

'Mamma, Mamma! Tom took my—' He caught his toe on a flagstone and fell sprawling.

He did little but bruise his knees. When he had stopped howling I made him bow to his grandmother and bid her good day. 'Now, what's amiss?'

'Tom took my hobby and—'

'Which Tom?'

'Tom Wydvil, Mamma,' he said, wiping his fat little hand under his nose and then on his skirts, leaving green smears of snot down one flank. 'Not my brother.'

'Well, can you not get it back?'

'He bigger than me! He say he my uncle and I can't

have it because we poor, and poor people can't have horses, just walking everywhere. Are we poor, madam?'

'Come here.' I sat in my father's chair by the fire and pulled him on to my lap. His gown was more darn than stuff, and not even Mal's careful stitches could make linen new when it was worn thin from neck to hem. 'Son, it is true we are not rich, but that's no business of Tom Wydvil's, were he three times your uncle.'

'Why we not rich?'

'Because I cannot get Tom's lands – our Tom, Tom Grey – I cannot get his lands back from Grandmother Ferrars. I write and send messages, and she does not answer, just takes the rents before Adam Marchant can get them. That gold is none of hers; she has her own lands. The Astley manors are Tom's in law, given to your honoured father, rest his soul. If . . .'

Tears clotted my throat until I could not speak but only press my cheek on to Dickon's head. He had his father's sturdiness though he had not yet reached his fourth summer, square and stocky with a round head and rough brown hair. He smelt of sun and snot and sugarplums.

My mother was reading my father's letter again, her mouth clamped shut. All of a sudden a weariness swept over me, and with it came the tears that seemed to stand behind my eyes all day, so easily did they spring forth when I was sad.

'Ow! You squashing me, madam,' Dickon said. I loosed

my hold on him and wiped my eyes with one hand. 'Will we get back Tom's lands?'

'I must, or we have nothing to live on. The tenants know that Tom is their landlord, as his father was before him, and Lady Ferrars takes their rent unlawfully. I must write to her yet again.'

Mal came in with a tale of a Grafton tenant on the doorstep, waving a notice of default and threatening the justices in return. I put Dickon off my knee. 'If Tom Wydvil still has your hobby, find Tom Grey. He is your brother; he must help you.'

~

It was weeks later, well past May Day, but cold and grey in a way that boded ill for the harvest, that my father and Antony came home as the church bell rang Nones. They rode into the yard with a cry and a trampling of hoofs and boots that told of a full following of men. At the noise the children came scampering from attics and stables, my mother hastened from the storerooms with her veil awry and Margaret ran out from the parlour with embroidery threads clinging to her gown. I called Mal and we set to, straightening the children's jackets and skirts, wiping the worst of the grime off with spit on a cloth and reminding the little ones of their manners. Then we went forth into the yard.

I had thought that the men would be weary, perhaps wounded, but no. They did not even ride with the stiff backs and wooden visages of men worsted in a fight. They were not defying pity, or trying to hide fear and failure. True, Wat Carter had an arm in a sling that looked like to hinder his milling for a while, and one man's cheek was slashed so deep I scarcely knew him. John from the smithy had a bandaged leg and sat pillion behind one of the squires. But my father and Antony rode easily, smiling to be home, their harness dusty from the road but clean and well cared-for.

My father raised my mother and embraced her, kissing her long and hard. Antony bowed to her, and I saw tears in both their eyes before she held out her arms to kiss him. Then my father spoke to the men of his thanks for their service, and the rewards that would come to them all, and those that were not our own servants departed.

The reward that was to come to us he told of later, sitting in the great chamber with logs piled high on the fire for all it was nearly Whitsun. Neither he nor Antony spoke of the battle but rather of other serious business, yet still he did not send the children away.

He told of the new King's dispositions of land and gold to secure new allegiances, and ensure Henry of Lancaster could get no aid from the French King. And he discussed with my mother the money that must be raised to buy the pardons for himself and Antony. But when his eye fell on Dickon or Eleanor or any of the bigger children, where Mal was keeping them quiet with sweetmeats and scraps of wood and cloth folded into shapes, he seemed to smile, as if he were glad of their presence in the chamber. Then he told us that King Edward was at Stony Stratford. My father had promised good sport, if the King cared to hunt in Salcey Forest, and a good dinner at Grafton afterwards.

For a moment we were too astonished to speak. Then, '*C'est bien, mon seigneur*,' my mother said, inclining her head unsmilingly, as if she accepted a compliment from a man she did not admire. 'We shall be ready.'

Later, sitting over the remains of the fire with Antony, I asked him, 'Did my father really invite Edward of – the King – did he really invite him in such words?'

'Indeed he did. His Grace is . . . oh, made of different mettle altogether from Henry of Lancaster.'

'He's young, of course.'

'Yes. But it's not simply his lack of years.' His eyes narrowed as if he sought to see him better. 'He's . . . He takes things lightly, or speaks as if he does. He even spoke of those months at Calais and laughed. We laughed with him, of course, and as a jest he asked my forgiveness for holding us so long, and rating me so, and calling me . . . oh, all the low names.' He smiled suddenly. 'I suppose it *was* absurd. At least, it seems so now, to us who were at Towton . . . He loves music and drink and jewels and women – scores of women, it's said.'

'Well, that is most certainly different.'

'No man could work harder by day. And to see him in battle . . .' He fell silent. I held my peace, for sometimes men speak of these things, and sometimes they keep silent, and I had learnt of John that it was not for me to judge which any man should do. 'He's tall, you know. Taller than any of those about him. We could not see — we had the snow in our faces — we could see little, until the battles turned. But always he was there. Wherever it was hardest. Wherever we thought it most likely that we might break them, there he was, holding his men together and cutting down ours as if they were no more than the corn in a field. They said he cried that God had shown his claim was just. He has taken a sun for his badge, a sun with streams . . . And when . . . But in his camp there is more wine running than in the whole of Gascony, and the clerks are hardly able to keep count of the gold that's brought, and horses and hawks, and feasting every night, though he's been about his affairs since dawn.'

'Different from K— Henry of Lancaster indeed,' I said. 'Is it true that Henry knew so little of women that the Queen's son is not of his getting?'

'Who knows?' Antony smiled a little thinly, but not, I thought, at the insult to Henry of Lancaster. 'It is said that Edward has got children of his own already. What I have seen at York . . . It would not surprise me.' He shrugged, as if to rid himself of the odour of Edward's camp, the disgust that still lingered in his nostrils.

That day we all saw each other as if through a different glass, I think. The change of our family's allegiance seemed also to have changed our eyes. I saw my brother afresh in the firelight: he had thinned and toughened in this campaign, though he still looked like quicksilver, and when he reached forward to toss another log onto the fire I saw that next to his skin he wore a hair shirt. I knew suddenly that he had always disliked excess in bodily matters, whether it be meat or wine or love. If our family's new allegiance brought us advancement then he could look high indeed for a wife and a dowry. What would he make of such a one? My brothers for the most part were much as any young man: John had a girl in the village, I knew, and my brother Edward had been beaten till he howled by my mother – my father being away on business – when one of her maids had complained he had tried to force himself on her. But Antony? I knew not. He might read of the great love of Lancelot for Guinevere and hers for him, but his own tale, surely, would be of the Holy Grail. Indeed, though I am not given to blushing, even to think of such matters in his case made me blush and look aside, so that he and I sat in silence for some time, gazing into the fire and thinking our own thoughts.

Part Two

Middle

Some there are, that by this journey of Jason understand the mystery of the philosopher's stone, called the golden fleece; to which also other superfine chymists draw the twelve labours of Hercules. Suidas thinks, that by the golden fleece was meant a book of parchment, which is of sheep's skin, and therefore called golden, because it was taught therein how other metals might be transmuted.

Sir Walter Raleigh, *The History of the World*

IV

Antony — Tierce

I thought we might skirt York. In troubled times, in
country of uncertain loyalty, I would cross the Ouse
higher up and make for the low, empty reaches of
Marston Moor before turning south. But Anderson has
no need of such discretion; ahead of us is the Minster,
and we turn neither right nor left. It shimmers in the
morning light like a vast barque carved of pearl, greater
and mightier than its harbour of walls and gate towers.

We jog through Heworth to cross the Fosse and
approach Monkgate Bar. The gatekeepers see the white-
boar badges when we are still some way off and raise the
bar so quickly that we ride straight under the arch, the echo
of our hoofbeats clattering back at us in the sudden chill.
This is Richard of Gloucester's city, his fiefdom, and there
is none who questions what right the men about me have
to do as they do.

The Minster rises to my right. There is holy sanctuary,

there, little more than two score yards away: if I had spurs and cared nothing for what or who I trampled, I could be there in a few heartbeats. But the men are close about me. I have no hope of reaching it, and who knows what they might do, even so, to those nearby to prevent me?

In the streets goodwives and shopkeepers stand back; to one or two, Anderson nods as caps are touched and curtsies bobbed. Small boys stare open-mouthed, pretty girls turn away with downcast eyes. Richard has made these people his own now, as Edward, the new King, once wooed and won his sharp-tongued Londoners, while Marguerite tried to hold the rest of the kingdom to Henry's royal, holy cause.

Now Richard of Gloucester has used his cleverness to turn on his own kin. I know – I pray – that Louis is still free, but such hope as that gives me is a small, weak thing, and on its heels comes always fear for him. But chief of my terrors, waking and sleeping, are those for my boy Ned, who is my son in all but name. When I think of his head stooped under who knows what pain my heart cramps; my breath is stopped painfully by grief, as if I have been struck a blow in the throat.

I smell the shambles before I see it, the sick-sweet stench of the gutters that no amount of water ordered by the city council can wash away, and then the cleaner smell of fresh-killed carcases as our horses shoulder through the closer throng. Our hoofbeats are deadened by blood-blotted sawdust; there is a girl ripping her knife up a skinned sheep's belly, the fleece lying like soiled snow beside her; a wizened old man tossing an ox's liver and lights into a barrel; a goodwife blowing up a pig's bladder and giving it to her still-unbreeched son for a football.

Across the far end of the street creeps a procession of priests setting forth from All Saints, and as we approach, the incense carried on the breeze cleans the air we ride through. They are bearing a reliquary shaped as a cross and wrought of ivory and silver-gilt. The heart of it is an orb of crystal so clear it shatters the sunlight that touches it, and for some uncountable seconds I cannot make out what holy thing it holds.

We cross ourselves, and one of the men enquires of the tonsured lad that rings the bell what it is. 'It is a relic of the True Cross,' says the lad proudly. Within the crystal, I can see, is indeed a shard of wood, of holy cedar wood that bore Christ's body and was stained by His blood. It is the instrument of Christ's death that He graciously and godlily accepted even in his most mortal fear. And it is the instrument of our salvation.

I will fix my thoughts on salvation, and pray for it, I vow, as we cross the Ouse bridge. For my salvation, and for Ned's.

Micklegate Bar is the strongest gate of all. Now I am leaving by it, in the company of my captors. And we entered by it so many years ago, when we rode as the staunchest Lancastrians to join Queen Marguerite and see off the Yorkist rebels for good. Duke Richard of York was already dead, killed almost under the walls of his own castle at Sandal, his second son Edmund with him, and King Henry rescued in the second fight at St Albans. My father pointed upwards to the men's heads stuck on pikes, leering down like puppets from the gate tower. They were black, not with age but with tar, the better to preserve their rictus of fear: the threat of death to the traitorous. I was nineteen, and I did not know that the wheel of Fortune would turn again so soon.

'See that one, son? Edward's father of York, and a very great man, whatever he did. Edward's brother at least was laid in the ground unbutchered. But that's what gives Edward the fire in his belly. He and Edmund were brought up together, so close in age you might call them twins, and no older than you are. He has much to avenge. When he comes north to find us, it will not be an easy fight.'

If Edward had much to avenge, then the fight at Towton was a vengeance I had not thought it possible any mortal could wreak. It was the only time, they said, that Edward gave no order to spare the commons, and forbade his men to take any prisoners for an honourable, profitable ransom. All the enemies of the House of York were to be killed.

At Tadcaster we leave the Roman road that leads to Doncaster, and turn south. The sun is hot and high now, and I pull my cap down to keep the brightness from my eyes. No more than a couple of miles' ride, and we are in

Towton village. Chickens scatter from beneath our hoofs and a glimpse of skirts shows how the women whisk themselves indoors. Beyond the huddle of cottages and alehouses the road runs level; on our left hand the heat is beginning to shimmer above the higher ground. Even the larks have fallen silent, and only a sleepy dove, calling from the trees of Carr Wood, is still awake.

How bare and high the road seemed that day, with the sky hanging like lead over the frost-hardened earth, and the becks that we could not see until we stumbled on them, so deep had they cut their way into the land. Old soldiers felt the raw wind that stung our faces and looked to the east and shook their heads. Young ones left off rubbing blisters and asked what they saw. 'Snow by the morrow,' someone said.

We were part of the vanguard, south of Towton village. Places were set, tents put up, horses untacked and watered, ale barrels broached and cannon shot stacked. Squires polished armour and checked straps and buckles, clerks scratched at lists and camp women set snares for rabbits. The men piled their fires as high as they could get wood for them and smoke began to rise. By the time I had accounted for my men and seen them settled, I could smell charring meat and fat dripping on to embers. Some was not meat but fowls, no doubt got against the rules of war. But I knew better than to ask or to tell my father. He was in command of the second battle – supporting his new young grace of Somerset – and might decide he should seek out the felons, though there were far greater matters at stake.

A shout from the London road made us leap to our feet. A straggling handful of men, a few mounted on horses whose heads hung almost to their knees. No threat to us even before we could see their badges in the failing light. A lad with more energy to waste than the rest ran to them, and ran back to bring the tale: this was what remained of our vanguard. York's men had forced through at Ferrybridge, and were even now but an hour or two away.

It was all but dark already. They would not arrive in time to attack tonight, my father said, coming out of his tent with a list of the musters who had joined us since yesterday. But we must make sure everything was in readiness.

'Edward of York has a name for quick work,' said one of the knights – Sir Nicholas Latimer, I think it was, rest his soul. He tossed another branch on to the fire. 'Did you not hear tell, my lord, how he marched the best part of six leagues in one night and won at Mortimer's Cross on the morrow?'

'And there were three suns rose,' said another, who I saw in the leap of a flame to be William Grimsby, one of the squires. 'A showing of divine favour, so he announced, being a sign of the Trinity. And the men say his victory proves it.'

We all knew that tale, but I could see my father wished

it unsaid, this night of all nights. 'We have by far the greater numbers, and the better position,' was what he said in reply, though. 'And right is on our side too. We fight not only for the House of Lancaster, but for our anointed king. Edward of York cannot claim that.' Then he sent us about our business, and it was long after dark before harness, horses and weapons were as ready as we could make them.

When the last report was in and the last order given, my father knelt to his prayers, then rolled himself in his cloak, lay down on his cot and appeared to be asleep before I had pulled off my boots. I stayed on my knees long, seeking courage, hope, grace, absolution . . . In the end I had to trust that God in his mercy had granted these things to me, though I felt nothing. Then I dragged my palliasse to the least draughty corner of the tent and lay down also, warm enough, but no nearer sleep than I would have been on the village green on Midsummer Day.

I tried to think bravely: I had years of practice with sword and lance behind me, horse-mastery, the jousts of which I had been declared victor, one or two small fights like that at Sandwich. I was a knight: I had taken my vows, and knew my trade. And I knew also that what was waiting for us beyond this night was nothing that I could imagine, nothing that I could prepare for, except in preparing my spirit for hardihood, my soul for a death that might come at any moment, and from any quarter.

Outside small noises continued; horses stamped and blew, the scrabble of a rat, the mutterings of men, the clink of a camp kettle being emptied, the sudden bray of a frightened mule that cut through the dark.

There is one way to bring sleep surely, but I did not loosen my points and slide my hand down. Not for shame, for my father's slight, slow breathing told that he slept. But this night, to seek such crude pleasure as mere distraction from thoughts of the morrow seemed as wrong as to do so when ... No, to think that was to think a blasphemy.

For the second time in as many hours I needed to piss. I rose as quietly as I might. It was dark and bitter cold, but everywhere I looked there were shadows: soldiers lying, squatting, sitting. I even saw one or two who had crept behind wagons and tents to fuck a woman. It takes some that way, I have since learnt, and I felt a stirring in me but no desire to fulfil it. One or two friends turned from their fires to raise a hand in greeting. But my spirit shrank from mortal men even as my flesh shrank from the wind. I wandered away from the fires and the snores with the frost crackling under my feet. The heath was bare, but at last I found a spinney, and pissed the few drops that my wakefulness had made unbearable.

A stick broke beneath me. To my right there was suddenly a man, snatching a knife from his belt as he leapt to his feet. 'Who goes there?' he said, his voice sharp but low, as if he yet feared to cause a general alarm.

'Peace, friend,' I said, even as I drew my dagger. 'I cry your pardon, sir, if I startled you. My name is Wydvil.' My weight was on my toes, ready.

'Mine is Mallorie,' he said. 'Wydvil . . . Of Grafton? I think your sister is married – was married – to my neighbour in Warwickshire, good Sir John Grey, rest his soul. Come and warm yourself, if you wish.'

I reckoned the Mallories I knew. 'Thomas Mallorie? Of Fenny Newbold? *Sir* Thomas?'

'The same. You have nothing to fear from me, I give you my word as a knight.' He turned away deliberately, as if to show that he knew he had nothing to fear from me either, going back to his fire and calling softly over his shoulder, 'I have some excellent sack.'

I followed like a child in search of comfort. Mallorie kicked at the logs so that they flared, and when he sat his cloak fell open for a moment before he wrapped it round himself again. Warwick's bear and ragged staff was stitched roughly to his jacket. He was the enemy, yet had said I had nothing to fear, on his word as a knight.

The wine was indeed good, and very strong.

'Aye. I have friends from my days in Gascony,' he said, grinning, the lines and hollows of his face appearing like old, carved wood in the firelight. He was blooded a lifetime ago, I recalled John Grey telling me, at Harfleur under the great King Harry, and had seen much service in France since, and the Levant too. 'Have some more.'

'I'll need a clear head for the morrow,' I said, and

wondered that I could speak as if the morrow were no more than a day's hawking.

'Oh, I fight better when I'm drunk. Just as I write better, and ride better, and make love better. Could you not sleep?' I shook my head. 'You'll grow accustomed. We all do.' He looked across at me. 'You find that hard to believe?'

'Perhaps. I know it will not be like anything I've known,' I said, and wished I had not, for in speaking of my fear I had rekindled it.

'After tomorrow, you will know. A man's knowledge. Have you good men under your command?'

'I think so. But some are from my sister's Astley lands, and I know them not so well.'

'John Grey was a handy man in a fight, but level-headed with it, and none of his father's . . . Well, a good man, anyway, and his men should know their business. I was sorry to hear that he died at St Albans. We have lost too many of his kind.' He shook his head and took a pull at the sack bottle before handing it again to me. 'None of this need have happened. Do you realise that? You young ones? Or are you spoiling for a fight, as I was when I was a lad?'

'I – I know not. Not spoiling for a fight, no. At least not I, though I could not answer for some of my fellows. But we must defend the King.'

'So you say, and no doubt believe. But look at who rules your army in truth. You fight for the Queen, and her son who is . . . shall we say, little short of a miracle?' His face cracked into something like a smile, then hardened again. 'And I must fight against the King, though he is the King who made me knight, because a great lord has hailed me out of prison to do it . . . Time was when it was the French we fought, a proper enemy. What have we come to that the knights of the realm – the great lords of England . . . that we are hacking away at each other in an English field?'

The fire had sunk to white ash, like snow, and red embers that seemed to have all the world in their hot depths. 'I don't know.'

'I'll tell you,' Mallorie said, and there were no longer enough flames for me to make out his expression. 'The great men look too much to their own grandeur, and not to their proper business of serving God first and the King after, an anointed king too holy to understand their schemes and rivalries. They care more for gold than for the worship they ought to strive for. They must have many men about them – they must scatter their badge and pay retainers far and wide – because the men they call their enemies do so too. And so on and so on, until none may go far enough away to piss without stumbling over a so-called enemy and starting a fight.' He grinned. 'As we did, excepting only the fight. Now here we are, Palm Sunday as near as makes no difference, and whoever wins, none will have won.'

'Except those who have reached Heaven.'

He waved the sack bottle. 'True. But I'd rather find a heaven on earth a few more times before then.'

'And do you? Find Heaven here?' In my thoughts flickered the golden shrine at Canterbury. For all those long months of captivity at Calais I had conjured that memory daily, calling it before my eyes as I knelt in prayer, longing for that oblivion.

'Yes – no – yes, I have found it. But not your sort of Heaven,' he said, and I wondered how he knew what Heaven was to me. 'Not even on Rhodes with the Knights Hospitaller, which is the nearest I have come to crusade. Nor the sort of Heaven men seek with the nearest wench.' He shook his head, as if impatient with himself. 'I spoke foolishly, for I do not look to find Heaven on earth again . . . I have a wife, and she is well enough. But . . . Perhaps you heard. There was a woman I loved.'

'I had heard something.' Indeed I had, though not as he spoke of it. Sir John had said that his friend Hugh Smith brought a suit against Mallorie for the taking away of his wife.

'Of Mistress Smith? No, my friends and I only helped her to escape her husband. And he would have done nothing, left to himself, for he wished to be free of her as much as she of him. 'Tis commonly done. But he has powerful friends, whom it suited to have me accused of ravishing her away . . . No. It was not she.' He was silent, staring into the fire. 'Love makes us what we are, as much as war, and both may lead us to Heaven.'

'You mean, it makes us better?'

'Better, and worse . . . Have you ever been in love?'

'No.' I did not say that I had never yet lain with a woman.

He grinned at me again and kicked a log so that the firelight brightened a little. 'Are you shocked that I should compare such a thing to Heaven?'

If I were, I was not going to admit it. 'I suppose a priest would say such a comparison is blasphemous.'

'Such a priest would know nothing of the matter.'

'We speak of the love of God, it's true. We seek it,' I said slowly. 'We seek it passionately, a priest most of all. We use the same words. And yet the loves of the flesh are so much less, and so often sinful.'

'Are they? Shall I ask you again when you know of what you speak?'

That he should insult me thus held me for a moment in surprise before my hand went to my dagger.

'No, Wydvil, keep your valour for the morrow. I mean only that you'll learn in time, as we all do. There are other heavens too, you know, waking dreams of the time when all was well in the land. Sometimes when I write of them the time passes more quickly than I seem to know. In prison there's a great need of passing the time.' He bent sideways to pick up another log, and tossed it on to the fire so that a shower of sparks rose and the flames came to life again. In the flare of light I saw that snow was falling, the flakes so small and sharp in the iron-cold air that they were like chips of ice. 'You may be able to recite every page of the *Summa Theologica*, and understand it too, but most men know only Jason and Jacob and the Good Samaritan.'

'Most men have no need of more,' I said, thinking of the snoring and shivering bodies that lay round the camp fires, then shivering myself.

'Perhaps not. But we have need of such men – ordinary men and great ones – and we must tell of these things so that they understand them. Tales, that's how it's done. Waking dreams, set down for all to read.' Suddenly a yawn swelled in my chest so powerfully that I could not smother it. 'You'll sleep now,' he said. 'Go back to your bed, and think of King Arthur and Sir Lancelot –' I rose with a stumble '– and dream of the Holy Grail.'

~

We had need of all our strength on the morrow to hold on to a dream of any kind of good. Hard to believe it now, with the sun beating down on my head and the horses half asleep under us as the road drops gently towards Saxton. Hard to believe that some men who lay down to sleep that night never woke to fight but had the snow for a gravecloth. Hard to believe that the wind and sleet drove so hard in our faces that we could not see the enemy, and our archers' arrows fell short time and again. The noise was as brutal as the press of men about me: steel and flesh, and cries for the King shrieking in our ears. So close did we fight that it seemed each army barely moved, or gained on the other. It never grew fully light, but the day crawled on. Too late did we realise that where once Cock Beck had guarded our flank, now we were turned inch by inch, and pushed back to where the ground fell away, and the men with it, tumbling helplessly down to the ice-covered rocks and bloody water. It was said the waters ran red for days. Men who could walk slipped away, those who could only crawl were left for the villagers. We who were captured in hope of ransom knelt and prayed that our knighthood would earn respect, and our estate earn safety. It was certain that the cause of Lancaster was lost.

But soon we realised that, with the battle won, Edward of York had reconciliation, not vengeance, in his mind.

'Has not God shown by this victory that there can be no hope of peace while Henry with his usurper's blood still wears the crown?' he asked my father, with a solemn face. Then he smiled. 'Sire, I have lost my great Plantagenet father, and must have men about me of worship: of courage and wisdom. There's peace and prosperity waiting for us all, had England but strong and godly government at last. You are one of the few who can give it that peace and prosperity. What say you, my lord Rivers?'

My father went to Mass and prayed for guidance, and I prayed, too, that the oath of allegiance which would secure our family would also be acceptable to God.

Edward's smiles and jokes were as potent as charms; he recalled the name of Master This or Alderman That, and took the man's arm and whispered small secrets that sounded great, and spoke of the strength and loyalty of the army that would guard the business of the kingdom. Richard was ten years younger than Edward, and he learnt in his turn of Warwick to cast such charms in his own, black-eyed way, here in the north that he held so tightly for his brother. From which of those gruff merchants now going about their business behind us in York did Richard later borrow money to secure the north from Queen Marguerite and her Scottish rabble, as he no doubt named them? Which of their curtsying wives did he bed? Which did he not?

'But thus is a kingdom secured. You understand that, surely,' Edward would say when I begged him to be more discreet himself, for his own honour, even if he cared nothing for his soul. 'To overcome our enemies, are we not urged to turn the other cheek?' And then he would slap the backside of the nearest page-boy so hard that the wine the lad bore splashed on to the rushes, and I held my peace rather than amuse him by objecting to the blasphemy.

Perhaps it is for all those times when I bent my conscience to questionable deeds for the good of the realm that I should most beg forgiveness. If it be so, then my greatest sin was one forced upon me. My joust with the Duke of Burgundy's natural son – the two greatest fighters of the age, fairly matched, as it was cried – was set forth with all the trappings of chivalry. There was a challenge and fair maids to carry it, a lady queen – Elysabeth – to champion, my company of knights and squires, men of mettle and worship. Later I remembered Louis as one such, though on so great an occasion I could spare little notice for anything but my own concerns. The bastard of Burgundy and I were indeed evenly matched, and were like to fight to the death before one of us found victory. Was it Louis who murmured to Edward that it might be best if matters were helped to a proper outcome? What good would it serve either realm if one of us died or earned dishonour by crying for quarter while still hale? But if it were possible to win for England by some less dreadful means, it would be politic. So, some happy accident? One that ensured my victory, without dishonouring Burgundy?

It was but a few minutes before the trumpets would sound. In our enclosure I looked over my horse, Belle Bête, and all our harness, as I have done a thousand times before and since. 'On such care for small things may a man's life rest,' my father used to say in the stables, when I grew impatient as boys will with buckles and thongs, the proper care of leather and iron. 'Do not trust such care to any but yourself.' When it was time to mount I saw that the trappings over Belle Bête's chest hung crookedly, and the straps at his withers were differently fastened. 'Who has done this?' I asked.

Louis came close, put his hand to the straps and turned so that none could read our words. 'My lord, it's nothing. A small adjustment.' He spoke in his Gascon tongue. 'You need have no fear. It is as His Grace the King desired.' I would rather not have looked, but it would have been dishonourable indeed to turn aside from my own responsibility, and foolish too, for if I knew not what had been done it might endanger me or my horse. Louis held my gaze, and I knew he saw my thoughts even as they ran through my mind.

Riveted to Belle Bête's breastplate, set on his nearside and angled to catch a horse in the opposing part of the chest if they met head-on, was a sturdy steel spike.

In the same breath as I saw what had been done, Louis spoke. 'Are you ready, my lord?' he said aloud, in English, and I nodded.

'It is time,' I said, and he set his hands to receive my foot that I might mount.

Burgundy's horse was killed in the first charge. It is not a rare event, a common but unlucky chance, and almost all men spoke of it thus. There were rumours, but none believed them. Next day we fought with axes, but Edward stopped the fight after half a dozen strokes that we might end alive and equal in honour.

These things must be done. I know it to be so. There is so much in ruling a kingdom for which we must then ask forgiveness: a trespass for men's good is still a trespass. When Ned was given into my care and I took him to

Ludlow, I made sure that he understood what his father knew of how a kingdom is secured. Not his father's way with others' wives, for he was mercifully late in getting an eye for a wench. But day after day I taught him how to hold men to him by force as well as favour, with secret intelligence as well as great speeches, with politic acts as well as honourable ones. I could truly write to Ysa that her boy understood these things as well as he understood his Catechism, or when to make a sword-thrust in tierce and when in quarte, or how to read a counting-book and know at once if a clerk is honest. He was clever, was my Ned, like his father and like his mother too.

Now I can hear a dove, and the faint bleating of sheep, and see how the alder trees, rising above the sweet waters of the beck, shimmer in the quiet heat.

Una – Thursday

Today the walk up from New Eltham station to the Chantry is sunny, the suburban gardens bright with well-pruned roses and bedding plants laid out by ruler. Somehow the drone of a lawnmower is as peaceful as the hum of bees in a meadow. When I reach the Chantry the trees, which in my memory are hedges no higher than my head, hold the house and workshop in thick shadow. And when Uncle Gareth leads me into the house itself, the shadows are thicker still.

'I'm afraid so much of the good stuff has gone,' he

says, 'but you must take what you like of what's left.'

I last saw the Chantry house at Aunt Elaine's funeral. Uncle Robert had died years before, and she and Uncle Gareth had been living on the ground floor for a while. When we got back from the church a handful of lodgers were in evidence round the edges of the family: earnest, pretty girls who said they were studying at the London School of Economics, and well-brought-up boys, some with paint caught in well-scrubbed fingernails, one with a packet of what I took to be cigarettes in his jacket pocket till I saw it was clarinet reeds. I remember watching Adam talking with such interest to Uncle Gareth, two craftsmen finding common ground, safe ground, real things that endured even among the mourning. Did I think much about Mark, that day? I don't think so. I grieved for Aunt Elaine, but Adam was there, so it was all right. It was sad, and sadder still when I thought of Uncle Gareth. Still, she was a good age, as everyone said over and over again. And the end had come quickly enough, as they said too: she faded fast, over a couple of weeks, but not so fast there was no time to say goodbye. When Adam and I reached the hospital, straight from the airport, she was still conscious. She smiled at me and said Adam's name, and her hand in mine, her cheek under my kiss, were feather-light, hardly there, nothing left but the essence of her self.

She died twelve hours later, and it was hard not to think that she'd been waiting to see me before she let go.

After the funeral, I remember, I was tired and chilled and when everyone had gone, and we'd helped Uncle Gareth clear up and made sure he was all right, Adam and I drove back to Narrow Street. He made us a huge pot of tea and I lit the fire, the salt in a rare piece of driftwood from the shingle below the window snapping and sparking blue. We pulled cushions off the sofa and piled them on the hearthrug, made toast and ate it so fresh and hot that melted butter ran down my wrist. I was licking it off when he came close and nipped the last corner of my toast out of my hand with his teeth, and ate it. I started to laugh, the cork-out-of-the-bottle kind of laugh that hurts but doesn't stop, as much sad as happy but still laughter, in a drunken sort of way, and he caught the infection too. By the time we stopped laughing because we were kissing too hard, my ribs were aching and I lay down on the cushions. His hand went to the buttons of my black blouse and it suddenly seemed the only possible thing to do: to make love in front of the fire, the heat flowering in our bodies after so many chilly days, our touch knowing each other as friends as much as lovers, our pleasure like coming home.

Yes, I mourned Aunt Elaine quietly and with a kind of joy for what she'd been and what she'd been to me; my mourning was simple. Whereas for Adam, . . . even after two years of it creeping ever nearer I hadn't expected the unbearable, outraged pain that flayed me in the weeks after his death. Even after two more years sometimes it still flays me, and leaves me shivering and raw for whatever cold winds of memory are passing.

I'm shivering now. The Chantry house was always shabby, but today the kitchen smells of unemptied dust-bins and stale grease. In the hall and up the stairs there are patches on the walls where pictures once were. The table I remember always having a big vase of summer flowers, or scarlet-berried rowan, or pussy-willow burst-ing into bud has gone, and where it stood is a bucket, half full of brownish water whose source is betrayed by a bubbling, peeling patch on the blue starry ceiling high above our heads.

'I've kept the dining room for an office,' Uncle Gareth's saying, as he unlocks the door, 'but I had to sell the Rennie Mackintosh table and chairs.' The browsing rabbits my father painted on to the plaster below the bay window are still there, the colours of grass and fur and beady eyes still bright because they don't get the sun, whereas the fat purple grapes and twisting vine stems round the fireplace have faded almost to nothing. It's stuffy, as if the windows haven't been open for years, and the dry office-smell of dusty files and fax machines has a damp underlay of mildew.

'Shall I open a window?' I ask.

'Yes, do.'

'You've still got the Perrault cabinet, then?'

'I hadn't the heart to get rid of of it. And Lionel said it isn't worth the embarrassing kind of sum the

Mackintosh furniture was, so that was a relief.'

I look at the cabinet and am glad. Its oak doors are a landscape of my childhood in themselves: across the four upper ones a long-forgotten great-aunt carved the tale of Beauty and the Beast, and across the bottom doors Puss strides in his boots.

'Which reminds me,' Uncle Gareth goes on. 'I've been going through the attics, and I found the plaster casts of Izzy's *Stations of the Cross*, only I can't really manage to get the boxes downstairs, and I wondered if you could give me a hand.'

'Of course.'

We go upstairs, my feet knowing how the treads turn, my hand moving along the banister rail, curving and rising round the well of the hall. The closed doors on the landing ahead seem blank and alien, the posters pinned to them as crude and loud as the rock music I heard last time.

We go up the narrow attic stairs. 'It's the end one. Mark's room,' says Gareth, and I'm suddenly skinned again. Is it the way Gareth says it, or is it me? It's as if he'll be there, reading, or mending something, just as he was whenever I had cause to tap on the door and deliver a message. And yet there were years, after he left, when it wasn't his room but someone else's.

It was about three years after he'd first started work at the Press that his father was sent to prison and he came to live with us. Of course he could stay, said Grand-mama, when Uncle Gareth asked her, and very welcome, the poor lad, whatever his father'd done. She'd have to ask something for board and lodging, but only a shilling or two.

I was eleven. I remember Mark coming back that evening, pushing his bike because it was hung with bags and parcels. What a lot of stuff, I thought. But when I tapped on the door with the clean towels Aunt Elaine had only just got dry, because it was a damp, drizzly autumn, he'd unpacked it all into neat piles on the bed, and it seemed very little for a whole life: a too-big suit and a few worn and mended shirts, some collars even worse, boots patched and repatched, washing things on the washstand, copies of *Picture Post*, some Penguins, and several other books carefully shrouded in brown paper, with the titles in neat ink capitals. If I screw up my eyes in my memory I can almost read them: Stanley Morison's *First Principles of Typography* and Fisher's *Compendium for Printers and Buyers of Printing*. No photographs, and the only pictures not his, but the ones that had been on the walls for as long as I could remember: a colour print of Manet's *The Bar at the Folies Bergères*, and the three Man Ray photograms that my father had sent from Paris and I knew – though he never said so – that Grandpapa didn't really like.

'Aunt Elaine says is there anything you need? And it's supper time.'

He took the towels from me – they were threadbare too – and looked round the room. 'I've got everything, thanks.'

'Supper's in the kitchen,' I said, leading the way downstairs, though it wasn't as if he didn't know his way round the house. He'd mended enough bits of it, one way and another. When we got there he saw the table laid and said, 'I thought the family'd be in the dining room.'

'Oh, the dining room's far too much trouble, these days,' said Aunt Elaine, taking the fish pie out of the oven. 'Move that print off the table, would you? We all just muck in together.' Lionel appeared, a bit vague and distant, the way he always was on Greek nights, and went to the sink to scrub the ink from his fingers. Mark stood there holding the print. 'You're still at school, then?' he asked Lionel.

'Yes, more's the pity.'

'Not boarding-school?'

'No, Mum and Dad don't approve of them. Grammar school. But we play rugger, so that's all right. Do you?'

'No, only soccer. Haven't played much since I left.'

'What's Izzy doing?' said Aunt Elaine, as Uncle Gareth came in from the workshop and went to the sink in his turn. 'Una, child, go and give her a shout, would you? And take that print and put it in the studio out of the way.'

I took it from Mark and went out as Uncle Gareth was asking him if he was settling in all right upstairs. The picture was round and reminded me of the big, messy flowerbed in the middle of summer. I turned it over the way everyone at home always did, even with plates before dishing up, if they thought they were interesting: *Robert Delaunay, Circular Forms, Sun and Moon, 1912–1913, Zürich Kunsthaus.* When I'd put it away I went to the bottom of the stairs and shouted up to Izzy three times. But she didn't answer, and on his way past to the kitchen Uncle Robert told me to go up and find her in her room, instead of raising the roof.

She was standing at the easel by the window and the linseed oil and turps smell was thick enough to touch, almost. 'Supper,' I said, but my voice didn't seem to get through and she didn't turn round. 'Aunt Elaine says supper.'

'All right. Coming.' She didn't even look at me then, just cleaned her brush and mixed some ultramarine and laid a streak of it in the sky of her canvas, then more. I didn't ask but it looked like Avery Hill, and she was painting the night as if it was dark searchlights, reaching down to the tiny little people on the ground. I waited another minute but I didn't dare say anything. I don't think she even noticed when I gave up and went back down and told Aunt Elaine she was coming.

The fish pie wasn't bad, though Aunt Elaine hadn't put hard-boiled eggs in it, which was the bit I really liked. Still, I got one on Sundays if the hens were laying. Mark ate his quickly, and lots of bread, as if he'd been hungry for a long time.

Izzy didn't come down till we were half-way through. She washed her hands and sat down, but you could tell she hadn't really noticed anything, not even that Mark had arrived. She was staring into space as if she could see her painting printed on the kitchen blind. Uncle Gareth was telling Aunt Elaine and Grandpapa about an illustrator he'd found, and Grandmama was scraping out the dish to find everyone at least a little bit of a second helping. Mark wasn't talking: he was looking at Izzy as if he'd never seen her before in his life.

The Stations of the Cross are piled into a couple of boxes: full-size plaster casts of the foot-square stone originals that Izzy carved. This attic seems completely dry, and they don't feel too damp, though I see a corner's crumbled off Jesus falling for the second time, and on St Veronica's cloth the image of Jesus's face has cracked. The two boxes are heavy, but they stack easily enough on to each other so, leaving Uncle Gareth to see if there's anything else he'd like a hand with while I'm here, I carry them downstairs and bump the office door gently open. To save my back I dump them on the Perrault chest rather than the floor, and with the thud a photograph falls flat on its face. I pick up the frame, but the smashed glass lies there with the photograph face down. It's another print of the same image of Mark and, still wedged into the frame, is a letter. A few lines are visible.

Dear Gareth,
I would like you to know before I tell the rest of the family that I have accepted a post in the Maintenance Department of Leyland Motor Company Ltd . . .

'Thank you, Una, my dear,' Uncle Gareth is saying, as he comes into the room, carrying a smallish painting. 'That's such a help.'

'I'm sorry, that photo fell over when I put the box down,' I say, gesturing from a safe distance.

He shifts the painting under one arm and reaches to turn the frame down on its face on top of the broken glass. 'Oh, don't worry. I'll deal with it later.' He holds out the painting. 'Here. I couldn't find anything else to carry down, but this you must have: I could never have sold it. I think you've got its pair.'

It's one of my father's oil paintings, painted, Izzy says – and she should know – just before he left New York in 1939. *Dawn at East Egg*, and Uncle Gareth's right, I've got *Evening at West Egg* on the wall of the sitting room in Sydney. Tears sting in my eyes. 'But it's yours. You brought them back from America. I remember you telling me how you smuggled them out.'

He smiles. 'Yes. Not that I had much time to worry about them with you to look after. I hadn't had much practice with little ones. But you were so good, even when you were being seasick. As long as you had Smokey Bear, you were all right. And now I'm giving this to you. They should be together.'

'Well . . . if you're sure . . . I know just where I'd put it.' I hold it out to see it better. 'There's a pair of windows, with just the right space between . . . You know, I always wondered why he didn't give them their real names. Why he used the *Gatsby* ones.'

'*The Great Gatsby* was his favourite book—'

'I never knew that.'

'Didn't you? It was. So American, that obsession with innocence corrupted. But I think it was really so that he could do what he wanted. If he didn't call them what they were on the map, he didn't have to stick to the literal truth. He could make the patterns — use the colours — that said what he wanted to say.'

'I've never thought of it like that, but it makes sense. Are you sure?'

'Well, I shan't have much room, I imagine, wherever I end up living. Take them all, if you like, the cabinet as well. I wish I could give you the rabbits.'

I take *Dawn at East Egg* to the window: the lights on the pier are caught and multiplied in the still, dark water into a necklace of jewels, and broken by the wash of an early speedboat, grey as a ghost, heading out of the bay to the open sea.

Outside the window the light trembles and I look up. Mark's standing in the garden.

No – yes – he is – it *is* Mark. Real, not a dream. Not this time.

'Mark?'

'Una?'

He's – oh, I don't know how he is, just that he's here.

'It *is* you.'

'Yes.'

I can see and hear him, but not reach to grip his hand. 'The back door's open.'

'Of course,' he says, and vanishes. For a mad moment I wonder if it's my hallucination haunting me: that I've dreamt him. Then I turn and look at Uncle Gareth.

It's as if he's dead: not moving, not breathing, and only two new purplish stains over his cheekbones tell me that he's alive.

I take his hand and I can feel his pulse lurching through the paper-thin skin inside his wrist. And I know why. I don't understand, not yet, but I know why. It's Mark.

But I say, 'You all right? You should sit down.'

He nods, follows me towards the door for a few steps, then turns away and sits down sideways on one of the cheap, not-Mackintosh chairs, and I go out into the hall and towards the back door, to find Mark.

Elysabeth — the 4th yr of the reign of King Edward the Fourth

I was mopping blood from Dickon's chin when my father rode in from Stony Stratford. It was not long after St George's Day, that I remember, for there had been a solemn feast held by the King, to which my parents and I had been bidden.

'The King comes to hunt in Whittlebury Forest tomorrow. What has the child done to himself?'

'Knocked out a tooth, sire. Only a milk tooth and it

was loose anyway, and not before time now he's breeched. There, pet, put it safe under your pillow and see what the fairies bring you. Now go and find Cook, and tell him you may have a sweetmeat for being a brave boy.' Dickon ran off through the screens and I heard him calling for Mal. 'Sire, does the King come here?'

'Yes. We meet in the forest at sunrise, and he dines here. He seems in no hurry to go north, though we hear worse tidings by the day.' He took a turn about the hall, then made for the screens. 'Where is your mother?' He stopped. 'No, I must speak first to you, Ysa. Come into the Great Chamber that we may be private.'

One of the lads was sweeping, for the recent rains had brought in much dirt. My father waited until he had ducked his head and scuttled away, but then he seemed to know not how to begin.

'Sire, does something trouble you?'

He looked at me, full of thought. I cannot forget the tale of how he died, but chiefly I remember that look: as if he chose his words, then weighed them before he spoke. 'Daughter, the King has spoken more than once of how much he esteems your company.'

'I am honoured, of course, though he has not been in it so very often, and always with many others present. He puts all to whom he speaks at ease.'

'The King is not a man who is slow to make friends, and I have seen him laugh with you more than once. And when you are absent he asks me how you do, and whether you are well. Ysa, I think he would like it if he might be in your company much more often.'

I could not mistake his meaning. But I was as shocked as if he had said he would set me to work in a brothel. I could not lie with a man who was not my husband! My sworn knight father could not dishonour himself thus, and his family. True, I was three years widowed, Tom was nine years old, and more than once my father had tried to arrange a match for me, but the times were so unsettled that a family which was one week a good ally might by the next be an enemy. Nor was my own estate much to tempt a man of worship for it was brought low by the dispute with Lady Ferrars, and my father could spare nothing to make up the difference. None of our plans for another marriage had come to anything. But how could my father think I would do this? I tucked the bloodied cloth into my sleeve with some care. Then I said, 'If he comes here tomorrow he will be in my company.'

'Daughter, you know what I would say.'

'Yes, sire, but I think . . . I think I do not wish you to say it. If it please you, my lord.'

He was silent for a moment, as if he were judging how best to persuade me. 'You do not wish to become the King's mistress?'

'No, sire. It is not an honour that I would seek.'

'Ysa, why not? It *is* an honour, for all a priest might feel obliged to deny it. For a man – a king – such as Edward Plantagenet to want you . . . And he does want you, that I know. At every meeting he speaks of your eyes and your countenance, he asks me how you do and when you will next come to his court. Think of it, Ysa. He's a fine young man, and has all the ease that his father lacked. You are lonely: widowhood is poor comfort for a young woman. And for our family it would be a means of advancement beyond all hoping. Think of it! The King is not a vengeful man. But we have not been supporters of the House of York for long enough that we can well go against him in any matter.'

'But you are on the Royal Council, sire, and Antony has his command at Alnwick, and will be well placed to win more favour with the King there. He is well married, too, and with the times more settled we may easily get good husbands for my sisters. Please do not ask this of me. We have no need of it.'

'I do not think only of the Wydvils, Ysa. What of your boys? Would you struggle for the rest of your days to keep them out of poverty and maintain the position their birth deserves? You owe them this chance, I tell you.'

'But Lord Hastings is putting my case against Lady Ferrars to the King, and by the contract Tom will marry his daughter, when he has one. All will be well, I am sure. Lord Hastings has been most kind, and you said yourself that his word may be trusted better than any other in the kingdom.'

'William Hastings is the King's greatest friend, and he

has an eye for you as well. But you could be more than a friend to the King.'

'But for how long?' How might I make him understand? 'Sire, I am five years older than the King, and a widow. He has a son, and I have two. It is said he takes a new woman every day, married or maid. For how long would he want me? I have no mind to become another of those women, or for my boys to know me as such a one. I pray you do not ask this of me.'

I might as well not have spoken. 'If you were like your sister Margaret I would not think of it. But you are clever and discreet, and when Warwick finds him a wife there is no reason that you should not keep your position in his affections. Do you not desire him? There cannot be a woman in the kingdom who does not.'

I shook my head. 'No more than I desire the sun. If I go too close I am like to be burnt.'

'There's little fear of that. He would be generous, I have no doubt, and you would be set up for life. Tom and Dickon too, and all our family. *You* would have no need of the favour of such as Hastings, and the King would be assured of *our* fidelity. You could again be mistress of your own estate. And then – afterwards – it would be easy to find you a good husband.'

'For soiled goods? The man who would marry a royal cast-off is not a husband I could esteem. I may have little enough of the world's wealth, but I have my good name, my honour as a woman. And I have Sir John's good name too. He was a worthy knight. How could I do such dishonour to him? I tell you, Father, I would rather marry a ploughman honestly than be a king's mistress.'

His mouth and hands tightened with anger, but he did not strike me; he was a knight, after all, and not a man quick with his hands. After a moment he said, 'Ysa, I had thought you wiser than this. I shall speak to your mother. Perhaps she will be able to knock some sense into you.'

'Worshipful father,' I said, and bowed my head while I shaped the right words. 'I pray you understand that I am only a woman so my honour is all the worship I have. But I *am* a woman grown and widowed, and a mother. My womanly weakness needs a husband, not a lover, though he be the highest in the land, and a husband as wise as my womanhood is foolish, and as strong as my body is weak.' I was silent, peering up from my downcast eyes, and only when I saw him smile did I venture to raise them.

'Where did you learn your cunning, Ysa?' He reached out and flicked my cheek. 'I shall speak to your mother, and you must think more on it. You understand what it would mean for us, I know you do. It is a pity that I must go again into Cambridgeshire even before he goes north. Perhaps if you know him better . . . We will speak anon.'

~

There was little ceremony about the King's arrival after the hunt. Each of the handful of nobles that rode into the yard was more plastered with mud than the last, and the King most of all. Nor did he accept my mother's offer of a chamber and hot water for washing, but glanced about him, spied the well, commanded my lord Hastings to draw a bucket of water, and pulled off his cote and his shirt. I had known him for a big man, broad-shouldered as well as tall, but I had not known till that day how well made and muscled he was. He was fair, but I thought he must often ride in his shirt and hatless, for his face was ruddy and his collarbones and breast too, so that his body looked to be made of red-gold. Under the stream of water he shook himself as fiercely as a dog, laughing at the cold and rubbing his face and arms, and when he straightened up his hair was a thick tangle of gold as dark as copper. Then he grabbed the bucket and soaked my lord Hastings with the last of the water, clothed though he was, and Hastings pretended to cuff him by way of revenge. The rest of the party then washed in their turn, though I wondered how many relished the cold water as the King did. Meanwhile, he pulled his damp shirt back on and shrugged himself into his cote. Then he ran up the steps to where I stood with my mother and Margaret, waiting to greet him.

He took my hands in both of his to raise me, and held them. 'My lady Grey, I am glad indeed to see you.' I willed myself to keep my eyes downcast and my thoughts on the courtesies proper to greeting His Grace my lord the King of England. But my father's words rang in my ears. *For a man — a king — such as Edward Plantagenet to want you . . . And he does want you, that I know.* It was true: try as I would, I could not be deaf to his low-voiced compliments, or blind to the heat of his gaze.

We were to dine in the Great Chamber, and I found myself next to him against the rules of precedence: my mother had ordered her own place removed to the far side of the table next to Lord Hastings. I could look for little help from her. Now everyone would know what was afoot: for a king, no meal is without meaning.

'This is a happy reward for a hard morning's sport, Dame Elysabeth,' the King said, when grace was done and he had been served. 'I hope you will grant me the right to call you by your name.' I made a sound he could understand as he pleased. 'Your father told me that you were here at Grafton still, but I had not dared to hope we might sit together.'

I kept my eyes fixed on my dish. It was a fast day, and I could not imagine how to swallow the collop of tench that lay there in a thick sauce. 'Did you have good sport, Your Grace?'

'We found straight away: a big buck that gave us a magnificent run. And then another, but that the hounds were too winded to catch. I am minded to hunt again tomorrow. You give us good sport here in Northampton-shire. Will I find it in Salcey Forest too, do you think?'

'My father or one of my brothers would know better than I, Your Grace.'

'You do not hunt yourself?'

'In my girlhood I was used to, Your Grace, but of late years I have not had the means, or the time.'

'A pity. It is as meet a sport for ladies' health as it is for men's. It would put colour in your cheeks: a good glow becomes a beautiful woman.'

As I had feared, and he, I thought, had intended, I instantly felt scarlet heat wash up from my breast into my face. I said, 'I marvel that Your Grace can spare the time, with so many Lancastrian rebels abroad in the north.'

The king turned away to take more sauce for the tench that he had already half eaten. For a moment I feared I had offended him. Lord Hastings caught my eye, as if pleased by my words. But the King was too quick, and saw his smile and raised eyebrows. 'So you agree with her, do you, Hastings? That I ought to forgo such knightly exercise to hunt down instead a parcel of troublemakers who fancy themselves loyal to a usurper's line?'

'Sire,' said Lord Hastings, patiently, 'you know I do, the rebellion in Yorkshire being a more grave affair than mere troublemaking. But it takes a lady of Dame Elysabeth's mettle to say it in such a manner that you hear it.' He grinned at me, and suddenly I realised that he, too, had a purpose in this conversation, and was telling me he had not forgotten his part in our contract.

'Oh, I hear Dame Elysabeth very well.' The King turned so far towards me that I could not without frank discourtesy escape his eye. 'And see her too. I'm told

Henry of Lancaster was wont to say that my good friend Rivers and the Duchess were the handsomest couple in his kingdom. I ought not to be surprised that they have sired the most beautiful children in mine, but still it astonishes me. Your brother Scales is a fine man too, and learned with it.'

'My brother Antony? Oh, sire, have you had word from him lately?'

'Nothing that your father would not also have heard.' He hesitated, then smiled. 'You must miss him.'

'How can I grudge him his man's business? He writes when he may, and often with a poem, which I may treasure, or some thoughts on philosophy. But, yes, I would have him with us.'

'You are fortunate in having such a brother.' His voice was low. 'I sometimes think there can be no friendship so close as that of siblings, when they are of an age and have been raised together.'

He said no more, but I knew that he spoke of his own brother, Edmund. As if he murmured a spell my mind's eye conjured a fair young man, not unlike him about the mouth and eyes but lacking a man's weight and strength, his skin unscarred and his brow yet smooth. A beloved brother of seventeen, his body crushed in battle far away, and his boy's neck cut.

My fears for Antony never wholly left me, any more than my fear for John had; the King's silent grief touched it and made my voice tremble just a little. 'Such a sorrow is hard to bear. And perhaps the more for those not granted time to mourn.'

He said nothing for a long time. Then I felt him stiffen his shoulders, and he beckoned a server for more wine. 'My lady Duchess—' My mother looked round from where she had been making what conversation she might with the Earl of Oxford, for he seemed to disdain my sister Margaret, sitting on his other side. 'Madam, you have a very pleasant demesne here. Perhaps we might take a turn outdoors when we can eat no more of so excellent a dinner? Perhaps even as far as the chapel. With Dame Elysabeth, if she has nothing better to do?'

With all the will in the world I could not prevent the broken meats being blessed and carried away. By now it was long after noon, and such sun as there was made the air heavy and warm. Few seemed to have much desire for honey-cakes and hippocras, though the King liked his wine as much as any man. Lord Hastings excused himself, for he had matters to look to on his own estates at Kirkby before they all rode north. As he rose from his bow to the King he winked at me, as if he trusted me to continue our contracted task. Then my father begged permission to withdraw and do business with some others of the King's party about the commission in Cambridgeshire, and within the time you might say *Paternoster* and *Ave Maria*, all that were left to take a turn outdoors were the King, a few gentlemen, my mother, Margaret and me.

The heavy air made the scents in the walled garden

seem to cling to my skin: sage and rosemary, hyssop and early lilies. The brick-laid paths of the garden were narrow and if the King chose to walk with me no other could be near. We spoke as we walked of ordinary things, of farming and grazing, of holding household and dealing with neighbours. The mill at Astley needed rebuilding, and I had some thought of working one of the farms directly when its lease was up. The King told me of the Ludlow mill where the Teme ran fast and deep, and that he was trading in wool that he might not ask the Parliament for money, but live of his own. Did I run sheep at Astley, or my father here at Grafton? From what he said on this and other things I judged him shrewd in such matters, and he listened to what I had to say with an attention I thought more than mere courtesy. Then from beyond the wall I heard squeals and running, and through the far gate burst Tom and Dickon, brandishing sticks. My heart sank, and I started forward to catch them, but they saw us just in time, and stumbled to a halt before the King. Tom, bless him, caught my eye, uncovered his head and dropped to his knee. After a puzzled look at him, Dickon knelt, but forgot to uncover. I breathed a little more easily and reached forward to pluck off his cap and push it into his hand.

'Are these your boys, Dame Elysabeth?'

'Yes, Your Grace.'

'Thomas, is it not? And the small one is Richard? Up you come, lads!' They stood, properly, and I wondered that the King remembered such little things as my sons' names. 'Oho, not so small, then! Madam, I recall William Hastings speaking to me of your Tom's inheritance. We must see what we can do about Lady Ferrars.' Out of the tail of my eye I saw Mal kneeling, scarlet in the face, and I knew that she, too, was holding her thumbs that the boys should not forget their breeding. The King must have seen my head turn, for he nodded to Mal that she might rise. 'Well, Master Thomas Grey,' he went on, 'are you minded to learn to be a faithful and true knight as your father was?'

'Yes, sire.'

'Your Grace,' I murmured.

'Yes, Your Grace.'

The King laughed. 'Well bred indeed. I think you were playing a game, and I have interrupted it, as grown-ups will. What did you play at, Dickon?'

Dickon gaped at him for a moment, then spoke readily enough. 'Please you, sire – Your Grace – we were playing Sir Ban and Sir Bors. Please you. Your Grace. Sire.'

The king laughed. 'He adds every courtesy he knows, and would offer me his missing tooth as a gift, no doubt, if the fairies had not had it. I have a son too, but Arthur is a babe compared to your lads, mistress. You must have been little more than a child yourself at their getting.'

'A little more, sire.'

He looked me full in the eye and smiled as a man will who sees pleasure ahead. Then he half turned to where my mother was several steps behind us. 'Madam, I would speak to your daughter privily. You permit it?'

She curtsied. 'My daughter is her own mistress, Your Grace.' Her French accent was very marked, and I knew that she was nervous. Margaret was gazing at us with a grin. 'Margaret, take the boys.'

The King stopped them with an outstretched hand. 'Here, one for each of you,' he said, and suddenly between his fingers were two pennies. 'Buy a toy or something, and leave your mamma to me in exchange. I'll have a care to her.' Round-eyed, my little boys took the coins with untidy bows, and pranced away from me to Margaret. Before she took their hands, she made a seizing gesture with her own to me, and grinned again. I thought, Oh, Margaret, even you?

The King walked beside me the length of the path and I could no more escape than a captive may a gaoler. At the gate he stood back, and I preceded him into the orchard.

'The blossom is very far forward this year,' was all I could think of to say, when we had walked almost full across the orchard and into the wood and he was still silent. 'My mother fears that the frosts may catch it.'

He stopped, and caught my hand so that I was pulled round to face him. 'Thank God we are alone.' He seized my other hand and I had to stiffen my arms to keep him at their length. 'Madam, I think you know why I have asked to be alone with you. I think your father has spoken of my love for you.'

'Love, Your Grace? I – I . . . He has not used that word.'

'Can you not see it in every part of me? In my eyes, my hands, my voice? Madam, I love you, and pray that you would be mine.'

I had dreaded this moment but it was no easier for my dreading. 'S-sire, you – you do me a great honour, but it is one that I do not deserve,' I managed to say, and felt him withdraw a little, though he still held both my hands. 'I – I must say no. I cannot be yours.'

'Why not? I think you cannot pretend that we are not friends, can you?'

'A humble subject may not call a great king her friend, sire, though she owes him all duty and obedience.'

He laughed and the shock of the sound made my rigid grip tremble. 'Then obey your father and your king in this, sweet Ysa – see? I know your true name. Be a dutiful daughter and subject and come to me, and we shall have such pleasure as no man and woman ever had, this day and for many a long day and night to come.'

My breath was short, as if he already crushed me in his grip. 'Sire, I beg you not to ask this of me. I am an honest lady. I was an honourable wife. I must say no.'

Then he did snatch me to him, hard against his breast, his hands like a carpenter's vice, gripping me to the bone. Even with all my strength I could not push him off. So tall and broad was he and so much bigger than John that I was almost overwhelmed. He smelt of sweat and wine and scented linen stained with a buck's blood. 'I am the sun: have they not told you? And you are the moon, with your silver-gilt hair that I could drown in if we lay together. Can you not see we were born to make merry together, as surely as the stars surround us both in the sky?'

I felt one arm tighten with a swell of muscle, and he brought his other hand round to raise my chin. I wrenched my head away so hard that my chin felt bruised from the grip of his fingers. He gripped harder, then shifted till his leg trapped mine. I began to be afraid, for there was that look in his eyes, that blind, blurred look, that means a man can think no longer of his worship or his woman but must take her wholly and at once, whether she will or no. From the meanest to the greatest of womankind, this is what we all fear.

Suddenly he let go and I all but fell. 'No, Ysa. I take no woman by force, though I desire them as I do you to the edge of madness. What can I offer you that would change your mind? You have my love already.'

I shook my head, still winded. But I did not run away, for the whole court would have known it, and I would not give them such food for gossip.

He looked down at me, frowning, for some few moments. 'Ysa, I could say, "I can make you rich, I can make your boys noble," but I think you are not a woman to be won thus. Nor by my saying what is true: that I could ruin you and them and your whole family, if I chose. If you were such a woman, to be bought or blackmailed, perhaps I would love you less.'

I almost laughed. 'My boys are dressed in rags and patches, and I cannot pay my servants. But no, sire, even for them I cannot do it.'

'Other women can. And – forgive me, but perhaps you think of them – other women have. Gentlewomen such as you, noblewomen too.'

'I know. But I cannot follow their example though they be the highest in the land.' I took a deep breath. 'I know you will not force me. You might offer me the whole world – a king's ransom – and it would still not be enough for me to shame my honour so. I have little else that I may call my own, but my soul and my body are mine. I cannot and I will not defile them with such a sin.'

'Then wed me.'

'What?'

'Be my wife.'

'Your Grace teases me. I pray you excuse me, I must go to my mother.'

He grabbed my hand as I tried to pass him. 'Ysa, I speak with all my heart, and all my mind. I love you with my whole soul and body, and I would be your husband.'

My mind was reeling, the ground beneath my feet seeming to fall away as if I were transported by Merlin to a strange land. I stared at him. At last I found some words. 'But, sire . . . you have embassies abroad to find you a wife. A princess, allies for your realm, treaties for your greater safety and glory, and that of your subjects. My lord of Warwick is in Savoy even now . . . You cannot be *married* to a subject.'

'What better wife for an English king descended of King Arthur than an Englishwoman bred of Melusina's line? The sun and moon conjoined?' He laughed, caught my hand and turned it over to kiss the palm. 'Besides, how could I treat of subsidies and armies and alliances when I can think only of you?'

I pulled my hand away. 'What of my widowhood? My years? My boys?' I bit my tongue before I could say, 'My family's late-turned allegiance?' 'How could such a one as I be married to a king?'

'Must I tell you how, Ysa? Very well, then, since you rate yourself so low.' He stepped back half a pace, as if to see me better, but I could no more have run now I had the chance than if I had truly been laid under Merlin's spell. 'You are virtuous as few other women, or you would not have denied me. You are beautiful beyond compare. You stand and walk and dance as one who already wears a crown. You are clever, and wise, and bear strong sons. How could I want for more? How may I do without you?'

I looked at him. Then he knelt, and uncovered his head. His hair had dried dark gold, and where his neck was bowed I could see the swell of muscles under his fine, fair skin, and the dark, puckered line of a sword-scratch, and the gleam of fresh sweat along the cords of his neck. The desire that I had long denied turned in my belly, so quick and hot that I thought he must feel it through the heavy air that lay between us.

'Madam, will you do me the honour of being my wife, and my queen?'

What should I have answered? I did not love him. I had not loved John, but we had been friends. This man — this king — I scarcely knew. As I had said to my father, to desire even so magnificent a man is not to love him, any more than one loves the sun, though we all turn our faces to its rays. If knowing that is wisdom, he was right to say I had it. But I had too the wisdom that said that here at my feet was a prize beyond all dreams, and that I could not — would not — refuse it.

'Ysa? What say you? You must not say me nay.'

His voice was urgent, shaking with hope and desire. Nonetheless, young men are foolish, and I would not be the victim of his folly. I put out my hand and raised him. 'Sire, you cannot kneel to a subject. You do me more honour than is proper to either of our estates, and I am silenced. I know not what to say.'

'You need only say yes.'

'Are you — forgive me, sire — are you sure? If you wish to change your mind . . . We have no witnesses.'

'I would have the whole world as witness to our betrothal, if I could. Though what my cousin Warwick will say . . . If your parents are willing, I think it might be best if none know of it until we are man and wife. But when they see you as queen, my beautiful Melusina, married on May Day, they will understand. William Hastings most of all. Oh, to see his face at the news, for he would have bedded you himself, given the chance!'

I could not but smile, and desire gripped me once again. The King saw it, and smiled back as he took my hand. A strange sound began to ring in my ears, and through it I heard him say, 'Ysa, this is no moment of madness. I have loved you long enough to know my mind. Will you consent to be married to me?'

I drew in a breath that was as deep as the hammering of my heart allowed.

'Your Grace, you do me more honour than I know how to refuse. I cannot say no.'

~

There were no stars or moon to guide us to Grafton church for Roodmas, only the light of Mal's lantern catching the whitethorn glimmering in the hedges through the still, dank air that smelt of cows and rotting wood.

'Mistress, is this wise?' Mal whispered in my ear. 'You will be so weary. You have been to confession, and you'll have a blessing like no other in the morning. You should be abed.'

'Ssh!' I said, jerking my head behind us at Margaret and my father's man that escorted us.

'Mistress Margaret talks too much to listen well. And Gregory's deaf as a post. He'd not hear the Great Sabbath if he stood in the middle of the Bel-fire itself.'

A draught brushed my cheek and a silent shadow flew by, close enough to touch. Margaret gasped, and we crossed ourselves. In the mews one of the goshawks let out a shriek of rage.

' 'Tis only an owl, Mistress Margaret,' said Gregory. 'The tawny owl that lives in the Home Wood, like as not.'

'Witches can take an owl's shape,' said Margaret, with a giggle made of fear. 'Maybe it was that woman who lives in the ruined friary. She had a black cat with blue eyes that your boys stoned, do you remember? She'll want her revenge.'

'Nonsense,' I said. 'Hurry yourselves or we'll be late. The cat lived, and I beat them both till you could hear them howling in Stony Stratford.' I caught my breath. Even the name of the town where Edward slept made my skin shiver. Or perhaps he slept not. Sure, I could not have slept this night any more than I could fly over the Home Wood, even at Roodmas, when the witches and warlocks are abroad. I had said I must go to church for the Roodmas service, though none but Mal and my mother knew why I was so wakeful, or that I meant, too, to ask Our Lady for a private blessing.

From somewhere in the wood there came a squeal, cut off dead. We stepped into the blackness under the lychgate roof. Ahead, the windows of the church were but dim gold against the dark, and the singing seemed to creep through the still air. I thought it sounded like the chanting of a spell.

I asked a hurried pardon under my breath for my blasphemy.

But what of the ones buried in the ground beneath our feet: men and women, soldiers and maidservants, ancient dames and children, and newborn babes barely blessed before they cried their last? Their bodies lay there, it was said, awaiting Judgement Day. But perhaps some unquiet souls — unshriven, dead before their time, traduced . . . perhaps such souls did walk abroad on this darkest of dark nights that comes before the dawn of May.

~

No days of preparation, no gifts or guests or great feast for us, only the wedding at the door of our own chapel, hidden in the woods, and a hasty Mass within. No procession round the parish or piping to our marriage bed, for none must know that Edward and I were made man and wife until he had spoken to my lord Warwick. Nor had we snatched many hours together since we had been betrothed, for none must think more than that the King had a new mistress hidden somewhere. Besides, he had business that I would not have kept him from if I could, raising men and arming them, cozening enemies and setting friends to work, receiving envoys and dispatching embassies.

So when we were married, we did no more than drink wine and eat sweet cakes, there in the antechamber of the chapel; my mother, Margaret — told only that morning lest she chatter – a priest sworn to silence, a boy server brought to cense and sing, and in the corner Mal, with tears in her eyes.

Then the priest and his boy took themselves off, and we walked back through the woods with every thrush and linnet and skylark in the world tossing its song to the sunrise.

The Hall was silent, but we dared not linger for the usual ceremonies. In my chamber my mother helped me undress to my smock in silent haste, unbound my hair and looped it up again with a pin or two, kissed me formally, and left with a curtsy to the King where he waited on the landing as if he were no more than his own page.

He entered, thrusting the door to behind him, and took me in his arms, my smock rumpling under his eager hands, his breath hot on my face. One big hand in the small of my back, one fumbling with his points, and his mouth greedy upon mine.

Suddenly I knew that he was not a king but a man, and not even that. He was a boy still, hasty in his desire, driven by what his body spoke of his need, with no thought for the dull aftermath when that need was fulfilled. I was his elder by but five years; I had known one man, and he many women. They were perhaps dazzled into yielding by his height, his smile, his gilded skin, his crown. But I had not yielded back in the orchard, and I would not now, for I had learnt in years of wedlock what it seemed he had not in his bachelorhood, not even from all those yielding women: how desire, held in check, feeds on itself and grows. If I could hold him back . . .

He pressed me towards the bed; I pressed my hands to his chest. 'No, my lord, not yet.'

He stopped as if I had struck him, then blinked. 'Not yet?'

'No.'

'But we are not married until I have you . . . Ysa, are you frightened? You are not a maid, but I would not frighten you.'

'No, I am no maid,' I said, and began very slowly to unlace his cote. 'And I am not frightened, except that . . . that I am bedded by a king.'

'Think not of that,' he said, 'but that you are my queen. And that we love one another.' I could not answer honestly, so instead I kissed him, then drew a little away, to run one finger from his lip, down his chin, his throat, and the warm breadth of his chest between the open edges of his cote. The hairs were like the finest goldsmith's work. He shook his head as if to clear it, and shrugged off his cote.

He in his shirt was no more clad than I in my smock and thus we were equal: man and woman, Adam and Eve.

When his gaze returned to mine I held it, then reached up and pulled the pins from my hair. It fell heavily about me with a breath of camomile and feverfew; he caught at the locks with both hands and buried his face in them so that they overflowed between his fingers. Then he let it fall and put up a hand to stroke the strands away from my face, and kissed me, not greedily now, but as if in a trance.

He raised his head, and looked towards the bed. 'You have Melusina to guard you,' he said seeing the hangings. 'Melusina the dragon, not the snake, with her wings and her double tail.'

'Yes. My mother bespoke it of the Sisters at Lincoln for my . . . my first marriage, to help get me with child.'

Even as I said the words I wished them unsaid. But he smiled. 'You are beauty itself as you are. But you must have been more beautiful still with a great belly.' He pressed a hand there. 'God willing, I will fill you with a fair prince. Would that your ancestress could know how her task is fulfilled in us, that golden sun and silver moon should unite in the *secretum secretorum*, and bring forth peace and prosperity. For you are my lady moon.'

'And you are my lord the sun,' I said, of course. I said it well: the words rang like a charm in the ever-brightening quiet, like a spell I did not know I could cast. I slid my smock off one shoulder, and slowly he reached and slipped it off the other so that it dropped to my feet.

'So fair,' he murmured, and at that I made to slip his shirt off his shoulder. The sword-cut on his neck was like a crack through the gold. He stepped back to draw his shirt over his head, then flung it to the floor. Before he could reach for me again I went towards the bed, turned and held out my hand. The linen was cool, and smelt of lavender and the bitter apples that keep it sweet.

He handed me on to the bed like a courtier, then lay down on his side next to me, so tall and broad that he seemed to stoop over me, his skin smelling of ambergris and musk. My head began to swim. He laughed and reached for me, but slowly, so that I could feel him holding his strength, his desire, in check: his eagerness was not, after all, a boy's simple ignorance. I began to move in the hot waters of my own desire and I heard him laugh again. 'See, my Melusina? You have cast your spell and I do as you will. You make me as patient as an alchemist setting his fire, watching and waiting.' My body reached for him, wanting him now as he had wanted me.

Then we were swimming together and apart, drowning in gold, and when I opened my eyes beyond his bright hair I could see Melusina with her wings wide, and her parted double-tail. Then I could see nothing at all. With a great cry he came, deep inside me, and for a heartbeat I knew that I had won — that the King was mine — before I, too, reached the secret of secrets.

V

Elysabeth — the 8th yr of the reign of King Edward the Fourth

As the highway narrowed towards Bow Bridge such was the press of horses and men-at-arms that my escort was mixed with the King's, and I found Edward himself riding no more than a head before me.

'My lady!' he cried, and reined in to ride on my nearside. 'I trust you are well. I am sorry that business has kept me from you for so many days.'

From the corner of my eye I saw our two escorts tangle, then, with a nod from the captains, range themselves properly about us. I turned to the King. 'Your Grace! Yes, I am well, and happy to see you in good health. As for business, it is only to be expected with so great an occasion to arrange.' I hesitated, but my ladies were still close about us, so I said merely, 'Yes, it is a great occasion, your sister's wedding. And yet I know you are sorry to bid the Lady Margaret farewell.'

'Aye,' was all he said. I thought of his brother Edmund,

murdered at seventeen. But that grief was long since past, or so he said and I believed. Surely he could not grieve much for a sister given to the embrace of a great duke, and no further abroad than Bruges? Charles the Bold of Burgundy was a fine, clever man by all reports, well into the years of wisdom. He had even made Edward a Knight of the Golden Fleece, the greatest order of chivalry in his gift.

'But still, to have made such a match for England's advantage, and your – our – sister's too, is no matter for sorrow,' I said.

'It is true.' He lowered his voice. 'But Margaret is not easy. I think she is afraid to leave England when –' He glanced about him, but we had reached the bridge. Only my own sister and Mal rode close by, and our voices were well cloaked by the clatter and echo of our hoofs on the stone and the rush of the Lea below us as it forced its way through the piers of the bridge. '– when we have even Sir Thomas Cooke in the Tower. He and Margaret are old friends.'

'So may they be, but Cooke is a traitor. Those men arrested named him as clearly as the rest, as helping Henry of Lancaster's cause. That he has guaranteed your sister's dowry is as nothing by comparison.'

'But it is not always easy to get a conviction when the evidence is gathered as it was in their case,' said Edward.

It was but two days after Corpus Christi and the day hot and bright, yet as if a cloud had blotted out the midsummer sun I saw a dark chamber deep in the White Tower, stone cold but for the sting of a brazier's heat. There would be the creak and grunt of machinery, the stench of burning flesh, shit on the floor, the screaming voice spewing forth names, places, plans, treason. The dry scratching of pen on sheet after sheet of paper, quiet voices demanding more – more names, more places, more treason – and yet another report sent off to the Council. Late at night the Council met, and on Sundays and other secret times, for none must know just how close we stood to open rebellion.

Edward shook his head. 'I would not have her people carry a tale into Burgundy of desperate measures in England. Or mar her happiness with fear that her dowry will not be paid, if Cooke is arraigned. She knows I cannot pay for it myself.'

'But—'

'Only until Margaret has sailed. Then he will be rearrested. I have already arranged for the commission to try them all. Your father will search Cooke's house.' He nodded towards the blur of scarlet and gold ahead, where Warwick rode as the chief member of Margaret's escort, with my brothers Antony and Edward. 'My cousin Warwick, too, is of the commission.'

'Will he do it?'

'Well, it seems wise to make him sit in judgement on such fellows.' Edward raised an eyebrow that told of more than one way I might take his words. 'He will have no truck with rebels, any more than my brother George will. And Hastings will sit with them, and the Mayor, so that London may know what treason its own may do.'

'Will an assembly of so many great men not draw attention to itself too much?'

'It cannot be helped. I must have only men I may trust to make the jury understand how this canker has spread. It will appear no more than the usual matter of *oyer et terminer*, as the clerks write it.'

Oyer et terminer. To hear and resolve was the order, though none knowing what I knew could have much hope that all would indeed be resolved, however much was heard. *Da pacem, Domine*, I prayed. *Give peace in our times, O Lord, because there is none other that fighteth for us, but only Thou.*

The road was widening now that we were past the great sprawl of the abbey mills. The walls of Stratford Abbey itself were ahead, and once more we were surrounded by men and ladies. Soon we must part, so as to enter its magnificence clad in our own, in silence and glory, as King and Queen of the land.

'And how are my little girls?' said Edward.

'Bess has a cold, sire, and with the hot weather on its way we were fearful that she was in a fever, or worse. But it does seem to be no more than a rheum, and we have kept her from Mary, though she cries for her.' My own arms ached for the want of my babies, and though it was months since I had given Mary suck, my breasts prickled as if her hungry little mouth still gaped for my milk. But

I said only, 'Mal has shortened Bess's coats, for she runs everywhere, and Westminster is nothing but cobbles to fall on when she trips on her skirts.'

'It is indeed. Would that I could be there more often, for a kiss and a sweetmeat will set most such woes to rights.' He grinned at me. 'You must tell her nurses most straitly to take care she does not knock out a tooth. We cannot have the heiress of England gap-toothed. And what use will she be when I get a son of you, if no prince in Europe will have her?' He laughed, then said, 'Ysa, I am minded to go after all with Margaret and your brothers to Margate. I would do all I may to send her off merrily, and to show the world that I have no qualms about leaving London at such a time. Meanwhile you must make haste to get the girls away from Westminster.' Then he shifted the reins into his left hand, and stretched out the right to take mine. 'If you go to Eltham, shall we meet there on my return? I shall want much comforting for the loss of my sister. And I would comfort you for the absence of your brothers.'

When he raised my hand to kiss it, I smiled at him, slowly.

~

By the time we heard that Antony had seen Margaret of York safely married at Damme and entered into Bruges with processions and pageants the like of which, it was said, had never been seen before, not even in Burgundy,

Edward had sent commissions to array the West Country. I knew that for every such public act a dozen nameless, faceless spies were sent out privily. And yet, for all that treason was creeping through his kingdom, for all that men secretly sent promises and even gold to Marguerite and the cause of Lancaster, and others watched how the wind blew, ready to turn their coats, Edward's temper in those days was hard to understand. It would do our worship no good to appear anxious, he said. We must not show that Lancaster's treason was hydra-headed, that for each man caught there seemed a hundred more to find. We must live the life of a merry court, he said, and a hard-working one: a court without a fear or a care or a debt in the world. It was good policy, and yet I thought it was more than policy that made him speak thus. When he sat at meat, with the jongleurs tumbling before him or a company of singers filling the air with a sweet new song, he would stare blindly at the shafts of dusty sunlight, pulling a manchet of bread to crumbs before calling for yet more wine. I thought a kind of accidie had crept over him, so that he would not trouble himself to do more work than was needed, though that he did do, as ever. He pored long over beautiful books, and spent more on scribes and limners than was wise. But as I watched him read, I saw in the set of his shoulders that even this pleasure was marred by the knowledge that too soon it would end.

So we played bowls on the green and threw quoits in

the dry moat. We rode out to dine in silken pavilions pitched so high on Avery Hill that, looking out over the Downs, we fancied we might see into Normandy. He would ask for his daughters and tickle them till they squealed, then were over-tired and fretful for the rest of the day. I might straighten my back from overlooking my household's accounts, and see that he had paired my sons Tom and Richard Grey with Warwick's daughters Isobel and Ann, and set them to shoot against each other at the butts. He often spoke of hunting roebuck, which was all the game that the season allowed, he would even call for horses, but as often as not would decide it was too hot, and set the dogs to race each other instead, with money on his favourite. He was seldom sober after noon; if he dined at the Palace he would shout to the band to play glees and catches that he and a squire might sing, and the ladies dance. Nor did he often arm and fight with Hastings or my brother John, or perhaps one of the Pastons. Even if I did hear the clang of steel and the grunt of men in the great court, when I looked out from my chamber window I saw that they did but play, more like bored lads in the village street than great knights and warriors on whose fighting strength the safety and peace of the realm depended. When I asked good Archbishop Thomas of Canterbury if Edward's soul was in danger he shook his head. 'The King may not – saving your presence, madam – live as quietly and godlily as the Church would wish. But he is shrewd, and wise, and when the time comes he will do his duty, and God will send him the strength he needs to make all well.'

Edward came often to my chamber at night. My sister Margaret or whichever ladies were in waiting that day would curtsy and slip away. Sometimes he liked to talk, or play chess, or drink wine, but more often he would lead me straight to bed, and I never denied him. There were times when he was so drunk I could not be sure he knew it was I whom he took. There were times when I was too weary from the business of the day to do more than lie and let him do what he would. But we knew one another's bodies and minds almost as well as we knew our own, and there were yet nights when we pleased each other well, tumbling together like new-found lovers half our age, until he came with a shout of delight that ignited my own joy.

On the nights that he came not to my bedchamber, I tried not to think of where he lay instead, or with whom. There were few women at Eltham, for the Palace is small, but it is no great ride to Deptford. Even the stews of Southwark are not so distant, and the country between is well stocked with blacksmiths' daughters and innkeepers' wives.

On one hot, stuffy night I lay for hours, feeling my sister Margaret's quiet breathing beside me, then got up from my bed. I could not bear to be closed in, for all Mal's warnings of the rheums and miasmas that the night air carried. I unlatched the casement and pushed it wide, sitting on the window-seat to breathe the cool, green air and listen to the small night sounds: the murmurs of the guard, the shift and shuffle of sleepy dogs and horses, a snore from somewhere below, the hoot of an owl. From beyond the walls came faint hoofbeats and then the call of 'Who goes there?' was answered. I heard the rumble of the gate, hoofbeats now on the wooden bridge that Edward planned to make stone, and into the court a few men rode, sitting slackly on tired horses. The yellow light from the cressets splashed across their disordered dress and faces blurred with drink and whoring. Between the King and Lord Hastings rode my son Thomas.

~

I was not surprised when my courses did not come, and then on St Mary Magdalene I woke to feel my breasts swollen and aching. The days advanced: I grew giddy with sickness once again. Many a day I went with my women to sit in the privy garden, for the sun's warmth, beating on the arbours, seemed to steady my stomach and ease the queasy aching in my bones. And if it failed, at least there were hedges to hide me when I could not forbear to spew. I was hanging over the basin my sister Margaret held, and just as I retched she began to giggle.

Having puked, I felt better. 'What is it?'

'It may be a silver bowl that was a gift from the Milanese ambassador, and you may be carrying the Prince of Wales, and I may be Lady Maltravers –' she peered into the bowl, which was shaped like a shell and bore my arms '— but puke is puke, and a baby in your belly's the same as any village brat back at Grafton.' She handed me a cloth that I might wipe my chin, and then a cup of rosemary water to rinse my mouth. I spat into the bowl, then straightened up and looked her in the eye. Even Margaret had learnt enough in the last five years to have the grace to blush. 'Your pardon, Your Grace, if I spoke too freely.'

But I could never be angry with Margaret for long, for she said what I might not, and said it with merriment that I too rarely felt. 'No, it's well, sister. Just take care none beyond my chamber hears you speak so.'

I was sicker with this baby than I had ever known. However much I rested I felt weary, yet sitting or lying down made the sickness worse, at least until I fell asleep. Even stitchery made my head swim. Never had the ruling, ordering, housing, feeding, paying and journeying of a hundred or so men and women seemed so like a labour of Hercules. In these disturbed times it had never been more urgent to husband my revenues: dower lands, customs dues, queen-gold, wardships and rents must all be looked to, and every extra groat that might be squeezed from them collected, but never had I felt so little desire to do it. It took all my strength to hear a petition or receive an embassy with the due ceremonies. Some fluent-tongued noble from Madrid or Salzburg would bow and scrape, reel forth compliments and demand friendship, and I would stare at him, wordless. When Sir Thomas Cooke appealed against the queen-gold added to his fine, I heard the plea, and forgave him, though he was a greedy, grasping man and guilty of far more — we knew as well as he did — than he had been convicted of. The King protested to me that so much more gold in my coffers might have done great good. I wrote back most reasonably, saying that since my father had perforce sacked Cooke's house for evidence, I had determined that a good name for clemency was worth more than even that much gold or covetable tapestries. But the truth was rather that I desired only to be done with the matter.

'If it is a prince, he must go to Ludlow,' said Edward one night, resting his hand on my belly. He still took me when I was with child, and took me eagerly. There are men who loathe women's bodies as if our softer flesh would poison their own man's strength, who possess us because they hate us, and to them a woman with child is most loathsome of all. Edward was not such a one. He loved my swollen belly and my heavy breasts, my rounded cheeks and hair thicker and more golden. And though the sickness rose in my throat I did not deny him, for if I had, he would have sought his pleasure elsewhere yet more often. But at these words I felt not sickness but tears rise, and had not the strength to master them.

'I know, sweeting,' he said. 'But we must have more authority there, and no charter I can give to a council will have the power over men that a Prince of Wales does. And it is meet that he be brought up in his own household and on our family lands. And he will be happy there, as I was, and Edmund too.'

'I know it must be thus. But 'tis hard to think of such a babe gone so far from me.'

He was lying behind me, and at my words he stayed his hand. 'Shall we have Antony for his governor?'

It was what I had thought myself, and an honour indeed: one I should covet for my brother. But now I had doubts. 'He is most learned and holy, it is true. And a great knight: the greatest in the kingdom, some would say, excepting only yourself.'

'Oh, I am no knight, these days, Ysa,' he said, patting his own slack belly with a laugh. 'To keep such a name uses up more hours of the day than I have to spare.'

'But would he understand a child, one no more than a babe? Would he know what is meet and what is not? I love him as much as any woman could love a brother, but sometimes I think he is like a Templar knight of old, as much ascetic as man of flesh and blood.'

'True! I tease your father that of his sons it is Antony he should have made a cleric, not Lionel. But who is better fitted to see to the education of a prince than a learned and holy uncle, whom I may trust also to rule the Marches in my stead? He knows from his own what makes a happy childhood, as all you Wydvils do. And he speaks most fondly of that daughter of his.'

'True. It is not that I do not wish it for him. Only that . . .' My voice cracked. 'Forgive me, sire.'

'Of course, my Ysa. Do not cry. There is time enough to decide.'

He did not speak of it again that night, but in comforting me for my few, slight tears, his desire was aroused. Out of respect for my weariness he asked nothing of me, and if I had protested he would have left me in peace. But I did not protest, and he took me where I lay on my side, taking his pleasure as of right, until he came. Then he kissed my neck, bade me sleep well and collapsed into his own, heavy slumber.

~

It was a girl, born but a few days before Palm Sunday, and Edward named her for his mother Cecily. It was natural enough, but I wondered if he half thought to conjure some charm over my womb, for his mother had borne four sons. Bess patted her new sister and loved to help her nurses with cloths and washing, but Mary was not yet two. One day she held out a toy bear, and when little Cecily could not take it, screamed, threw the bear and caught her on the face. Two yelling, then, and when Mary got a whipping for it Bess joined in her howls so that the chamber rang, even as the bell struck to tell me that my council awaited me. I did not think the girls heard the blessing I gave them before I hurried away; I could only hope that God did.

Now Warwick was in open rebellion, and had cozened George of Clarence to join him in restoring Henry of Lancaster to his throne. Had he promised George the crown when Henry was dead? It was not certain, though he had married his daughter Isobel to George in defiance of Edward's expressed forbidding. It was even said that Warwick, the staunch upholder – the creator, its enemies would say – of the Yorkist crown, sought an alliance with Marguerite and her son, the heir and only hope of Lancaster. Could it be true? Surely Marguerite would only treat with her sworn enemy to get her husband back his crown. What then of George's ambition?

Then Warwick captured my father and my brother John, and murdered them before the walls of Coventry. When I heard the news it was like being struck in the face by a bloodied fist. My father. My brother. A double grief.

And a double threat, so close to the Crown and to the heart of our family. I reeled, faint as much from fear as grief, so that only my hands, gripping the arms of my chair, seemed anchored in safety. The news was certain, the threat like thunder on the horizon, dark, sullen and constant, over the days that followed. I grieved as my sisters did, sorrow and fear heavy on us. And my mother grieved still more for the death of her great love and her son. But the business of the state and of my household would brook no withdrawal. None must think us weakened by even so great a loss. There was no time for private sorrow, except in the silence of the night when grief tore at my heart and banished sleep. Antony spent much time at Grafton, for he had inherited our father's title and estate, while our mother's affairs were tangled almost beyond mending with the fortunes of her first husband and the House of Lancaster.

I could not make a parade of my sorrow, but no woman who has not loved a man as tall and broad as Edward can understand the comfort I found in his arms as nowhere else. If sometimes the release of passion also released my tears for my family, he understood, for he, too, had had a father and a brother murdered. Not long after Candlemas I was with child again.

The heat came early, soon after midsummer, and at Eltham I might hear from Westminster but escape the worst. It was defensible, too, and in good order.

It was nothing new that I was sick, but I was weary with it as I had not known before. When I had respite from the business of the household, I walked round and round the courts and gardens, though even there I could not help but see yet more that wanted mending, altering, ordering. After some days of this my queasy dullness drove me further afield. My ladies trailed after me perforce, pale and sweating in the heat.

I heard one complain, and could tell even from that distance that it was Margaret Beaufort. Edmund Tudor got her boy Henry on her when she was but twelve years old, and she was a widow before she was delivered. No wonder, then, that she had neither chick nor child more, as Mal would have said, though married again long since. I could not reproach her, so my patience broke with the lot of them. 'Go back, then! I do not want you here if you can do nothing but whimper.' They hesitated. 'Go on! Go! If I have Mal, I have no need of you.'

They gathered up their skirts and backed away, hesitantly. I turned my back on them and made for the paddocks and trees beyond the stables.

'Madam,' said Mal, panting after me. She had grown stout with the years, and the ground was rough. 'Your Grace . . .'

I was among the trees at last. Deep in the thickest shade was a hillock made by the roof of the ice-house, with a coverlet of stringy, late-summer grass. I lowered myself to sit down.

'Mistress Ysa!' She clapped her hand over her mouth. 'I cry your pardon, Your Grace.'

'Oh, Mal,' I said, 'there's none to hear. I could wish it to be so more often. Pray you, sit down. To see you standing makes me feel hotter still.' She lowered herself to sit an arm's length from me. At our feet the ground fell away to the south and west, and what little wind there was seemed able to find us. Within a few minutes I felt cooler and Mal's face had calmed from puce to pink.

'Mal, is this too much for you?' I said, after a while. 'You know Hartwell is waiting for you. Not that my father's bailiff is not content to manage it as part of the Grafton lands. But I think you would like to have the managing of it yourself. And court life is – is something any woman tires of in the end.'

'One day,' she said. 'But I'll see this baby through, madam, if you're willing. And then . . . I'll not deny it would be good to be back in my own country. And I'd hear the news: there's not much gets to Grafton that doesn't cross the river.'

'That's true,' I said. Sitting among the trees as we were, with the dark green and gold of summer before me, my mind was free to go down the lane to Grafton Mill itself and over the bridge, the land rising only gently now to the neat little stone manor I had bought from my father and given to Mal so that, whatever befell our family, she might be provided for.

'Very good. I'll not deny that I would be sorry indeed to lose you just yet. But if – when – we know that all is well with this baby . . . you have earned your rest, and you shall have it.'

For a while we sat in silence, and it seemed that the breeze that stroked my cheek brought some ease with it.

Una – Thursday

In the dimness of the kitchen passage Mark is outlined against the daylight beyond. The air is thick between us and walking towards him is like pushing through water.

He is real, though: his hands are warm, their bones and muscles grip mine, and, suddenly, madly, all this – the

Chantry, the past – is real and solid too, for the first time since I came home.

Tears in my eyes and my throat, and he's giving me a brotherly squeeze of the shoulders and then he lets go and says over my head, 'Hello, Gareth.'

'Mark, my dear boy!' Uncle Gareth's voice is light and shaky. Mark goes past me into the hall, and they clasp hands. 'It's . . . It's hard to believe. I—'

'We thought you might be dead,' I say. Where has this anger come from? Mark turns his head. 'Why didn't you tell us where you were?'

'I—'

'Let's go and find a drink,' says Uncle Gareth, quickly. I turn aside to wipe my eyes discreetly. 'It's all in the workshop, Mark.' He leads the way, though the back-door latch rattles for a moment before he lifts it.

Ahead of me, Mark looks about him as we cross the garden, as curious and calm as an insurance assessor. His hair was fair and it still is because the threads that are grey are no paler than all that's still blond, and it's short and well cut above his broad shoulders. He moves easily, with a big-boned, loose-jointed confidence inside his dark sweater and very clean jeans. He was always tall: tall and fair and quiet against us little dark Pryors.

My anger's cut with a strange and different heat, zigzagging through me until I'm shivering. I'm glad when Gareth pushes a half-full glass of whisky into my hand.

'I know you're still Una Pryor,' Mark says.

How? I want to scream. *Were you watching us?* But I say, 'Yes, but I was married. His name was Adam Marchant. He was a doctor. We lived in Australia and he died two years ago.'

'I'm so sorry,' is all he says, but one of the things that was best about Mark, then, was that he always meant what he said, and said – with due kindness and tact – what he meant. He was like a good apple, I find myself thinking, as if the shock's slightly unhitched my workaday mind: one of Aunt Elaine's from the orchard, a Blenheim Orange, sharp and crunchy, straight from the tree, or a cinnamon-scented D'Arcy Spice lying in the storeroom, treasured up for Christmas.

He looks at me and says quietly, 'You all right?' and I nod, because what else can I say? Mark always did worry about you.

Always. It's a comfortable feeling, and on the heels of that comfortableness comes . . . what?

I don't know. I think confusedly that it must have a name. But looking at him now, trying to sort out the feelings that I can only know as a trickle of water down my spine, a strange shakiness in my belly, I discover only how much that I loved in Adam, I first learnt to see in Mark.

Mark, who was my past for so many years, until Adam healed all such wounds. Perhaps that's why missing Adam hurts so much, so easily. When he died, the paths of grief were already laid out for me.

And now Adam is dead. The times are suddenly reversed. Adam, whose voice I can still hear in the river-dappled rooms of my present, whose hands I can still feel pulling me towards him, is the past that Mark recalls. And Mark, who was past, is present.

'And you? Are you married?' Gareth's saying, and suddenly I miss Adam so much it's like being punched in the stomach. By the time Adam died we were beyond desire, but I loved him with my body still, because if my body could have borne what his did in his place, I would willingly have done it. Yes, it's Adam I miss, Adam I want to hold, cling to, never let go. Adam, who can make my body live.

'No. Had a partner for the best part of ten years, though, Jean. She's moved to Canada now. Her daughter I still see.' Mark's face lights up. 'Her name's Mary, though she calls herself Morgan, these days.' He looks round. 'How's the Press going? I see reviews in the Fine Press journals sometimes.'

So he hasn't left fine printing behind altogether.

'Oh, very well,' says Gareth, waving a hand at the silent presses behind him, so obviously poised to start up with the latest project. 'I'm doing a picture book, *Jason and the Golden Fleece*, which is going very well. Come and look.'

They get up and go over to the workbench, and I wonder if Mark can see in Gareth what I can so clearly: that he still touches paper as if he loves it, handles the machines like a patient groom or shepherd, judges space and proportion and form as naturally as breathing, his eyes sharp even as he shows Mark things he's already looked at himself for hours each day. How can he give it up?

And if he's angry with Mark I can't see or hear it. If he . . . What? What was Mark to him?

Mark's gaze, too, is absorbed. 'Why Plantin, not an Old Style typeface?'

'I thought originally of using Centaur,' says Gareth, going towards the shelf where he always kept the try-outs and interesting failures of the current project, and evidently still does. 'But it's too light for the blocks – it looks spindly, and then the illustrations look clumsy. Whereas Plantin has just that much more body to it. Though I was tempted to stick to Centaur, because of Cheiron being one . . .'

'Cheiron?' I ask, because I can't remember, and Mark's looking blank too.

'The centaur who brought up Jason,' says Gareth, taking some more bits and pieces from the shelf. 'His foster-father, you could say. Silly reason, really. Nothing to do with typography. But still . . . Mark, what do you think of this?'

The sun's come out, cautiously but enough to warm the air in the workshop. The oily, peppery smell of printing ink rises, and I remember going into the workshop to find Uncle Gareth that Saturday morning because I needed the dates of Marlborough's battles and he always knew that kind of thing. I could hear before I opened the door that the big Vandercook press was running, with the apprentice of the time hovering over it. Uncle Gareth was watching it the way Aunt Elaine would watch a goldfinch swinging on a teazle: absorbed but still, only his head moving a fraction to and fro in time with the press as it lolloped out the memorial reprint of the Eric Ravilious *Alphabet*. *A is for Aeroplane* danced out with *H is for Hedgehog*, and all the others, fur and clouds and telegraph wires as clear and delicate as ever, pair after pair in their work-and-tumble order, all the way to *W is for Warship* and *V is for Vole*.

I was sixteen.

Uncle Gareth looked round and saw me, and I asked my question.

'Blenheim 1704, Ramillies 1706, Oudenarde 1708, Malplaquet 1709,' he said.

I scribbled them down. 'Thanks.'

'History prep?' he asked, going over to the Arab press and treadling it. There was a crunch, it stopped, and he sighed.

'Yes. Miss Beaufort's very hot on dates. Is it not working?'

'No. It's jammed, but I can't see how. I'm going to have to take it apart, I fear.'

'Do you want me to have a look? I mean, not taking it apart.'

'Well, if you can reach to fish out whatever it is with

your nice little hands, I'd be very grateful,' he said, going to the sink in the corner to wash off the machine grease and ink. 'It's such a nuisance getting everything properly aligned again and we can't really spare the working time. I'd ask Mark to do it, but he's gone out.'

As if even the work knew its place in the scheme of things the Vandercook finished, and in the quiet I could hear the hens clucking, the scrape-scrunch of Uncle George's spade in the vegetable patch, and much further away a train whistle: the twelve thirty-seven down from London probably, with Lionel and Sally on it.

'I could look after lunch,' I said, 'or now. It's only cold ham and salad so Aunt Elaine won't mind, if you tell her it's urgent. I won't do anything drastic to it, just see if I can fiddle out whatever it is.'

So when the boy'd dealt with the finished work on the Vandercook and pulled on his jacket and left – his half-day-Saturday too – lighting a cigarette as he went, Uncle Gareth took off his apron and gave it to me. 'But be careful, now. Make sure you immobilise it; we don't want any lost fingers.' Then he tidied up the few odds and ends that the morning's work had left behind and took himself off to lunch in the house.

It must have been May or June. I know it was warm and there was no breeze to swirl dust in and mar fresh ink or disturb paper. I propped open the workshop door and went back to the Arab press. If I worked it slowly enough and found the sticking point . . .

I was sucking a blood-blister and swearing under my breath when a shadow filled the doorway. 'You all right?' said Mark.

'Pinched my finger,' I said, standing up from where I'd been crouching while I poked among the levers and springs of the press.

'D'you want me to look?' he said.

I held out the finger, and he inspected it as carefully as Uncle Robert would have: a fat, little dark-purplish lump that, as always, hurt much more than seemed reasonable. 'If you press it really hard you'll stop some of the bleeding, and then it won't be so swollen,' he said, patting my hand and giving it back. 'Pity we – you – haven't got a refrigerator. Ice'd do the trick. What were you trying to do?'

'The Arab's jammed,' I said. 'There's a screw that's fallen into the spring, down below the inkplate. I can see it and I thought I could get it out. It's either that or take it apart. But it's got itself wedged in.'

He stripped off his jacket and went to hang it over the compositor's chair. Then he crouched and peered into the innards of the press. 'Hard to see in the shadow.' He tried to reach in, but the gap was too narrow.

'Maybe if I had something thin, like a skewer,' I said. 'I'll go and get one.'

'Okay. I'll take it apart if need be. If you can't get it out. Don't drag Mr Pryor away from his dinner.'

But when I got back with a selection of Grandmama's

knitting needles and her injunction to *try* not to bend or scratch them still ringing in my ears, he wasn't in the workshop. 'Got one,' I called, but he didn't appear. Then I caught sight of the shift of his shadow against the slight light from the storeroom window and heard a soft thud, as if he'd put a stack of books on a shelf. *Beowulf* must have come back from the binder, I thought.

The Arab stood in the shadow between two of the windows, and Mark was right, you couldn't really see what you were doing. I stood up with ink on my hands and the sun on my back: what I needed was the inspection lamp from the storeroom.

When I went in Mark was leaning against one of the uprights with his back to the door. It was only after I'd gone past him and reached up to lift the lamp from its nail that I saw he had his hands over his face because he was crying.

I froze. I'd never seen a man I knew – family – really crying.

For a moment I thought he'd rather I left him, but the storeroom was so small I couldn't slip away and pretend I hadn't seen.

I put a hand up to his shoulder. 'Mark?'

He reached out and pulled me towards him as blindly as I used to reach for Smokey Bear if I half woke in the middle of a nightmare. His arm was hard, pressing me into him as if something that was inside me could help. I was so much shorter than him that his collarbone ground against my cheekbone. His breathing was heavy and uneven, as if he was trying to get control of it. I could smell tweed and Uncle Gareth's cigarettes and his own sweat, and something that I knew even then was maleness. My shoulder was pressed into his side, my chest against his ribs and my stomach against the bone of his hip.

I waited for embarrassment to grow inside me, but it didn't. I wanted to stay like that for ever.

Suddenly he let go. 'Sorry.'

I looked up at him. A piece of his hair had fallen forward on to his forehead: it was gold in the greeny, tree-filtered light from the window. 'Are you all right?' I asked, and heard it for the foolish question it was. But I felt nothing except some strange lightness where the embarrassment should have been.

'I went to see my dad,' he said.

'Oh.' What was the right thing to say?

'You know . . . you know he's out?'

'Um – yes.'

'Looks like I'll be asking your grandmama if I can go on lodging here.'

I knew that was all he could bear to say. I looked at him, at the bones of his face in the leafy light and at his eyes that were narrowed and turned aside from me. I wanted to put my hand up to his face where his own hands had been, to warm where the tears had turned cold on his cheeks.

Then he turned his gaze back to mine, blue and empty,

as if he was willing me not to say a word. And against his blank look I knew what had happened to me as clearly as if someone like God had spoken aloud: from today, if Mark hurt I'd hurt, if he laughed I'd laugh, and I'd only be happy again when he was happy too.

After a moment he said, in a nearly-ordinary voice, 'Did you get a skewer? Give you a hand, if you like. If you need it.'

The giddiness subsided, of course, over days and weeks of hiding it. Eventually it wasn't new, just part of me as the way my hair which refused to be sleek, was part of me, or my right ankle which I kept twisting at netball, or that my parents were dead and I'd never known anything about my mother. I didn't make up stories about her, though, the way they say orphans do. It was as if the stories Aunt Elaine told me about my father were enough.

Now Mark and Gareth have come back from the business end of the workshop and are sitting down again.

'So what brought you here?' I ask Mark, and my voice sounds loud and awkward from having too much behind it.

'A friend who works at the National Trust – an ex-colleague – said Lionel rang his department. He knew I'd worked here: said you were selling the house.'

'Not just the house,' I say, knowing I'm sounding brutal and deciding I don't care. 'The whole lot. Gareth and I were sorting a few things out when you arrived.'

'The whole thing? The workshop and everything?' I can't read Mark's tone, except that he's shaken.

He looks from me to Gareth, who nods, and only then says, 'Yes. I can't manage the house, and we can't apparently sell that on its own.'

'Where will you go?'

'A flat . . . something like that.'

'And the Press?' asks Mark, almost with a snap.

'I'm afraid it's . . . it's the end. I'm too old to start up again.'

'What about Izzy?'

'She's living in Highgate, cataloguing the archive. She's got her own life,' says Gareth.

Mark says nothing for a moment, but not from ease: it's as if he's thinking too much and holding it back. Then he says to me, very gently, 'And you?'

'Oh, I'm going back to Sydney,' I say. 'I'm trying to persuade Gareth to come out for a visit when everything's sorted out.'

'When does it go on the market?'

'It's going to auction, I don't know the details. Lionel's organising it all.'

'Not for a while, I guess. Takes time to publicise,' says Mark, coolly. 'Not every day a fourteenth-century chantry ruin with attached Arts and Crafts country house comes on the market.' After all, why should he be feeling anything? It was all a very long time ago, as Grandmama used to say when I asked about her brother who died in the Great War.

'Izzy's found a buyer for the archive,' I say. 'She's been

cataloguing it and so on. The university library in San Diego. So that'll be safe.'

'That's all right, then,' says Mark. 'Good to know she's looking after things.'

For a moment I think he's commending her success in finding a buyer. And then I remember how he looked at Izzy in the old days, and I know that's not it at all. He's worried about her. He cares that she's still involved with the Chantry world.

I always knew that he noticed her a different way from how he played football with Lionel or asked Uncle Gareth's advice or gave Aunt Elaine a hand with lighting the copper. But after that day in the storeroom, my eyes were suddenly sharpened. Something inside me read what he felt inside him: I recognised — what? Desire? Love? I don't know now, and I didn't then. I just knew it in him as I knew it in myself, by the way his head turned when he heard her voice; the way he remembered what she'd said about Bewick or Eric Gill from one week to the next; the way he watched as she picked up an engraving block and ran her fingers over it, feeling the end of the grain with the pad of her thumb. And I knew, too, how many nights he must have lain awake as I did, hope and hopelessness between them banishing sleep.

Gareth's asking Mark what he's doing now.

'When ... When I left ... I took that maintenance job in Preston.' He's heard what Gareth really asked, I realise, and is answering it. 'There were all sorts of takeovers and things, and I ended up running the maintenance department for Leyland Trucks. They paid for me to do courses and so on. Then it was all national-ised – got very bureaucratic. Ducked out and went with VSO to Rhodesia, it was then. Building schools and clinics.' Yes, his fair skin has the old, rubbed-gold look of long, and long-gone, sun. 'Came back in 1975. Took a while to persuade the Trust that I knew about more than breezeblocks stuck together with river mud and whitewash –' he flickers a smile at me '– but I did in the end. I was managing a mill in Northumberland when the redundancies were offered.' He looks at his watch. 'I must go. Una, have you got a car here? Can I give you a lift?'

How assured he is. When did that happen? Was it running things in Africa, or was it working his way up through the corporate idealism and unspoken snobberies that – perhaps unfairly – I assume he encountered at the Trust. Now he has a social ease to go with the physical ease he always had, the way he moved that used to make my heart turn over.

And then he says, 'May – Gareth – may I come and see you again?' and he isn't assured at all.

'Of course,' says Uncle Gareth, with plenty of warmth in his voice. 'The phone number hasn't changed, if you want to check I'll be in. Or just turn up.'

Why would I think that Uncle Gareth might be chilly? I wonder, but can't pursue the thought because Mark's asking me again if I came by car.

'No, by train. But I'm going back to Limehouse. Is that not out of your way?'

~

Mark's car is a big old estate, with a crate of tools and site boots and a hard hat in the back. We drive out of the gateway and the tick-tock of the indicator as he turns left down Sparrow's Lane seems impossibly loud in the silence that's left between us since Gareth bade us both goodbye. Everything seems more so, as if some dense, damp fog that was between me and the physical world is thinning and drifting away. Not just the sound of the indicator cutting across the ebb and flow of the engine noise. When we stop at the lights the crimson jumper of the little boy on a bike doing wheelies flares against the grey of buildings, and two old ladies gossiping are suddenly a pattern of blue-grey hair and navy coats, their faces lines and shapes. Under my thighs the car seat is thick and squashy with age and the cloth is roughly soft where I'm gripping it. The car smells of dried mud and newspapers. Inches away the bulk of Mark's shoulder is parallel to mine, warm, I can almost imagine, and moving easily as he changes gear. His hands haven't changed. I know every neat-cut nail, every curve and swell and hollow.

'How is Gareth?' says Mark. 'Silly to say, "He's aged," I know.'

'In himself, all right. Though aged, as you say. But

selling the whole Chantry . . . Putting a brave face on it, I think. He knows there isn't really a choice.'

'Yes.' He doesn't say anything more, just turns out on to Avery Hill Road. 'When do you go back to Australia?'

'Tuesday. I only managed to clear a week, just to settle everything here – selling my house and so on. Only now there's admin to do with the Chantry so it's a bit more complicated. Lionel's hoping he can get the paperwork together in time for me to sign things before I go.'

'You're selling Narrow Street?' He accelerates up the bypass towards Eltham and Blackheath.

'Yes . . . How did you . . .?'

'I do come across family news from time to time.'

'And you—' Here it comes, the anger, but it's weaker now that I've an image in my head of him, alone, working, working from nothing, with nowhere to go home to. 'You didn't think to get in touch before?'

'I . . . didn't think I'd be welcome. But now . . . I had to come back, before it went.'

'I can't quite imagine it being sold and turned into smart flats, or whatever they'll do. It's – it's always been there,' I find myself saying. 'Maybe it's selfish of me. I'm not the one trying to keep it going. It's nothing to do with me, not really. Not now.'

'Except it's where you've come from,' he says, taking me aback. It seems such an unMark thing to say. 'You all have.'

'So have you,' I say, before I know I'm going to. 'You were part of it, too.'

'I thought I was. For a while, anyway.'

'No, always. Mark, you don't know — you've no idea — how often after you left . . . every day something needed you.' My voice is cracking painfully in my throat. 'In the workshop, in the house, something that you made work and no one else could. *Every day*. Only you weren't there.'

I'm weeping properly now, properly and angrily, as if everything that's piled up inside me since Mark appeared can't be contained any longer. 'You weren't there, and it got harder and harder, no money and no help — Gareth on his own, and Izzy moving, and — and you weren't there . . . You weren't *there* . . .'

'I know I wasn't,' Mark says. I reach down to find a hanky in my bag and the car suddenly swings across a lane and to the right.

'Where are we going?'

'You'll see,' he says, and I do, the trees huge above us along Court Road, and then the scrunch of weedy gravel under the tyres as we turn into Tilt Yard Approach and Eltham Palace — Edward IV's Great Hall — appears across the moat. 'I thought you needed somewhere quiet.'

'Can we get in? Isn't it being restored?'

'Yes, but I know the administrator,' he says. 'Let's see if we can talk our way in.'

The whole building's scaffolded and shrouded in tarpaulins. The Great Hall and the art-deco country house grafted on to it are only visible through gaps: a curve of stone here and a band of brick there. The lawns are roughly cut and the shrubs are shapeless and sprawl-ing. The fog seems to have curled round me again and I can't read these things. On another day I'd be curious to see inside, to take up the offer of Mark's friend Charlie-the-administrator to show us round the restoration. Today I'm shaken enough that wandering towards the far corner of the grounds is as much as I can manage. We're among spindly trees, the grass stringy and unkempt under our feet with last year's leaves caught in it. A hump in the earth makes a good seat from where we can see north-west towards Greenwich and the Thames.

'I'm sorry,' he says at last. 'Didn't mean to upset you.'

'It's all right. Everything upsets me since Adam died. Not your fault.'

'How long were you married?'

'Fifteen years.'

'No . . . no children?'

'No,' I say, and I know that is enough for him. But I want to explain. 'It wasn't too late, but it didn't happen, and none of the alternatives appealed. It didn't matter, once we'd decided. We were happy as we were.'

He nods without saying anything and, to my relief, doesn't ask anything about the time before Adam.

'Do you? Have children, I mean?' I ask.

'No. Unless you count my step-daughter Morgan. She was seven. She never knew her father, and Jean hadn't lived with anyone before. Morgan still lives in Yorkshire.'

I think of Anthony Woodville and little Prince Edward, far away in the green hills of the Welsh Marches. Anthony must have been more his father than his real father was. 'So she grew up with you for a father?'

He smiles. 'I suppose she did. She was at college when Jean and I split up.'

I nod. There doesn't seem to be anything more to say, but it's a comfortable nothing, a silence that'll do for now. When Mark eventually speaks it's as if he's waking me up. 'How about you? How do you feel about the Chantry going?'

Another unMark thing to say, somehow. 'Me? I don't know, really . . . I suppose sad, rather. It's part of the past. And I'm worried about Uncle Gareth. But it's not present to me, not really.'

'You wouldn't move back to England?'

'No. People asked me that when Adam died. But my life's in Australia. I've got teaching and research, and all our friends . . . I come back every few years and see everyone. And there's the phone. And email, too, with my academic friends. Adam said . . . when he got ill . . . he said I must do what I wanted . . .' My voice dies. After a moment Mark's hand covers mine, and holds it, and I can go on. 'But I always knew I'd stay in Sydney.'

When I've said it safely, he moves his hand away while he seems to digest this. Then he says, 'And no one's thought of saving the Chantry?'

'How do you mean?'

'No one's thought of trying to save it? Getting funding to restore it?'

'Well, Lionel asked the National Trust, as you know, but there's no money to endow it. None of us has that kind of money, not even Lionel, I don't think, so of course they won't take it on.'

'No, I know. Just thinking aloud. But it's a historic building, being made for the Press. Even with the chapel ruined. And almost unaltered inside.' His quick smile lights. 'We might even rescue the rabbits and the starry ceiling.'

'You mean some kind of campaign?'

'Yes.'

'I . . . Sorry, it's so surprising that I'm having trouble imagining it. But people do, don't they? Someone must know how it's done. Do you?'

'Well . . . Never run one myself, but there's plenty of people who have. The first thing is getting the local council interested. It's listed, so they'll already know it has some value.'

'You sound like Lionel when you talk like that.'

'Do I?' he says, and falls silent.

'But it's an idea,' I say quickly, wondering how I've put my foot in it. 'What would be the next step?'

'Getting the rest of the family to agree. And getting the auction stopped.'

'Izzy would agree, I'm sure. I think – I get the feeling that once she was living somewhere else things, well, went a bit . . . not wrong, exactly, but—'

'She needed the Chantry.'

'Yes, she needed it.'

'We all did,' says Mark, getting to his feet, and holding a hand down to help me up. 'But don't tell Gareth. Not till we know if it's a runner.'

I think again of Gareth's photo of Mark, and the hidden letter. Such a thin memorial to Mark's life at the Chantry.

As we walk back out of the trees and cross the wooden footbridge over the moat, Mark's friend Charlie comes towards us, carrying hard hats. 'I'll be closing up soon,' he calls. 'Are you sure you wouldn't like a look first?'

'Una?'

It's too good a chance to resist. 'Well, if you're sure . . .'

The craftsmen and builders have gone for the day. 'I was involved with excavating Bermondsey Abbey in the sixties,' I say, and Charlie's eyes light up. I tell him what I remember about the dig while we walk along a wide, curving, sleek-panelled corridor that wouldn't look out of place in a grand ocean liner, and into the huge quiet of the Great Hall.

The space seems to hum against me. The windows are high in the walls and so big their stone mullions shimmer against the light, and a great hammerbeam roof of age-darkened oak lowers above and between them. Charlie says proudly it's the original. He's talking about the firebomb that came through it in 1940: the burn-marks are there, on the stones of the floor, and must be kept, for they're part of the history too. Mark's asking him about the masons' marks and carpenters' joints, and what the principle of restoration is.

'Well, in art restoration the rule is that the new work must be visible at two feet, and invisible at four,' says Charlie. 'That way you're not pretending it's real, but there's a sense of realness. Obviously here it's a bit different. We might darken a new wooden beam so it blends in with the originals, but we wouldn't falsify. No fake wormholes or smoke-marks. On the other hand, where you have to conjure up from nothing, it works better to do something completely modern, not *faux-*historical. Clean glass and steel, or whatever: something good in itself. The Courtaulds' architect in the twenties mostly knew that.'

I'm not thinking about the twenties, I'm thinking that here Elizabeth and Anthony danced, here ambassadors were given audience and wedding feasts were held, nobles drank and fenced, and the children ran riot on wet days, perhaps, with the dogs barking around them. Did they come here when Edward's sister Margaret of York had been safely married off to the Duke of Burgundy? What did it smell like, then? Velvets and flower-water? Sweet herbs and banquets? Latrines and fly-blown meat? Sweat and fear? What did it sound like? The court was famous across Europe for its music, but how did they hear it? Did it creep into Elizabeth's ears as it does mine, and make her want to laugh, and cry, and love? She wasn't in love with either of her husbands, it's a fair guess. But there's nothing — not a single whisper in a court full of her enemies — that murmurs of anyone else. Did *she* ever love someone so much that she hurt for joy, so much that it seemed beyond reason? Did she regret that she never had?

There's ancient dust gritty under my feet and outside a last, late chisel rings like a bell on the stone. If I strain my ears enough, perhaps I might hear them. If I could only peer hard enough through this time-thickened, time-thinned air, they might come before my eyes.

'Una?' Mark's voice is gentle. 'You all right?'

'I'm fine,' I say, as I see he's standing in front of me.

He takes my hand. 'Time we were going.'

'Yes. Sorry.'

'All right if we go via Charlie's office? He's got the local names and numbers who might help with the Chantry appeal. And then I'll take you home.'

Antony — Sext

It is some time after midday. Anderson spies a spinney a couple of furlongs off the road and orders a halt to rest the horses. The corn in the fields is well grown, and we ride along the rising ground of the headlands to dismount in dappled shade, like a group of friends taking their ease after a morning's coursing. One of the men leads my horse away but no man tries to hold me. They have no need, of course: I am disarmed. There is no help on its way for me, and I could no more escape on foot across these open fields than I could from an island in the sea.

So no formal watch is posted, no sentry-duty ordered. These men know each other and their trade too well. They are quiet, but for a jest or two: taking off their helmets, loosening girths, checking horse and harness, going aside to piss, eating barley bread and cheese because men must eat to do their work, watering the horses when they have cooled, but always watching. That their watch is not needed is beside the point. Still they watch, bows and horses to hand, because that is what soldiers do.

I think of my old dead friend Mallorie, leaping from his prison window and swimming the moat to gain his freedom. His peril was real enough, for none could have had faith in the justice that he would meet, when the justice who held him was the old Duke of Buckingham's friend. Old Buckingham persecuted Tom Mallorie with one trumped-up charge after another for years. I have often thought he would have lived longer without all those years in prison. At least I got his great work to press, though Caxton is as good a judge as any of which way the wind blows through Westminster, and his preface will not mention me by name.

Great men have great power, but they wield it as much according to their own temper as any shopkeeper rules his prentices or a goodwife her babes. In the business of the realm Edward had no more scruples than any other but he never harboured hatred and never let his own enmities rule his action. He understood that if a man turned his coat, he might more profitably be charmed than bludgeoned into turning it back to a Yorkist blazon. George of Clarence had his brother's charm but somewhere in a bitter, exiled childhood it turned sour, and his tenants and enemies suffered for it. And so, too, did his wife, it is said. When old Buckingham died his heir was made Elysabeth's ward and married as a child to our sister Katherine, bitterly against his will. Now this young Duke of Buckingham is Richard of Gloucester's most devoted ally.

And what of Richard of Gloucester himself? In Burgundy he was little more than a quick, clever lad serving his brother the King, and when we returned, even as I was sent west with Ned to rule in the King's name, he was sent north. He was known by report to have become a quick, clever man of firm dealing. Certain it was that Richard had his allies and his enemies, but I never heard that he did anything that was tyrannical or against most men's sense of good government. To name him as the arbiter of some dispute or as the executor of a will is common. I have done so myself, when some tenant or debtor of mine could not agree with my judgement.

Does Richard of Gloucester feel the same bitter enmity as Clarence did towards me and mine? As old

Buckingham did towards Tom Mallorie? I would not think it, were it not for what he has done.

Guilt cramps my heart: guilt that I did not see what they would do, that I lost Ned to them by a stupid trick, that I could not – did not – lift a finger to save him. The pain is real, but I would bear twice as much – bear all the pain in the world – if it would save my boy. But nothing now will do that, if Richard of Gloucester wills it otherwise.

I catch Anderson's eye. 'I would go aside to say the Office.'

He looks at me for a moment. 'Aye, my lord, very well.'

The spinney crowns the crest of an outcrop of rock and I walk towards the far edge. Here sunlight lies warm on stones, dead branches and rough grass. Beyond the rocky edge, and far below, a stream threads like tarnished silver through sour brown and green marshland. Behind me, I feel a movement and another. They are wondering if I will leap to freedom.

I will not. A body broken by such folly would be no freedom, and to seek my end by such a design would be a mortal sin. Nor would it save Ned, or help Louis if he is still at liberty. All I have left is God.

In nomine Patris, et Filii, et Spiritus Sancti . . .

I commend Ned and his kingship to God. I pray for Elysabeth, and for my two wives – one living, one dead – and for my daughter and her mother. And for Louis. Then I commend these loves, too, to God, and empty my mind of all, that it may fill with the peace and grace that God gives.

~

After uncounted time, I feel the sun on my hands and smell the peaty air. My mind's eye returns to this world. The men sit and stand at their ease, finishing their food. One goes aside to shit, another picks at his teeth. Better that I should fast, for by denying the body sustenance the spirit is freed and the power of prayer is the greater. But the day and the ride before me are yet long: to be weak with hunger would be foolish.

I walk back towards the men.

'With respect, my lord, I must ask you to eat,' says Anderson. 'We have some way yet to ride.'

I nod. He snaps his fingers at one of the men. 'Robin, meat for his lordship.'

Robin gets to his feet and fetches meat, bread and a bottle of ale from one of the saddlebags. I sit on a log, and he goes back to where he sat at the foot of a tree, and throws himself down as easily as a lad passing a hot afternoon on a riverbank. He is young, his skin reddened by the sun where his jerkin stops, and his reddish hair falling away from his brow as he leans back on his elbows. It is a long time since I have looked at a man and wanted him. It is only some trick of sun and heartsickness. I have never lain with any man, except Louis.

That I should think of such matters at such a time is

strange and sinful for my mind should be fixed on God, not on the loves of the body. But I do not love only Louis's body. It is his mind that I love most, from the day we met again by chance after many years. And now, sitting on the rough grass with my captors waiting for me to finish my meat that we may take the road again, I know that I have had no other earthly love like Louis's: not his for me, or mine for him. And now I never shall.

Perhaps I have this slow, hot ride to my death to thank for such knowing. These empty miles are a pilgrimage, a prayer; a journey void of all else but the simple knowledge of my end. And into the void God has poured this strange grace: that I may know again such love. If it is true that Louis's love for me and mine for him is but a tithe of a tithe of God's love for the meanest mortal, then how can I fear my end, when it will bring me at last to such unimaginable joy?

I rise, and nod to Anderson. I am ready to ride on.

VI

Antony — Nones

When I remember that year of exile, it is for both hunger and riches.

We had marched to Yorkshire to oppose the Lancastrian rebels. Then word reached us that the troops that were coming to reinforce us had changed their coats and declared instead for Henry. Another messenger knelt before Edward and panted that they marched hither still, but to arrest us. Young Richard of Gloucester in his boyhood valour cried that we should fight the rebels to the last man standing. His brother knew better. Many of our men had already slipped away, and Edward gave us leave to dismiss the rest back to their farms and mills, without striking so much as a blow for their king. As the men scattered we turned away and fled through the night.

We felt our way round Gainsborough in the deepest dark, and when a hungry dawn came we saw first the towers of Lincoln Cathedral, appearing against the sky like ghosts. We skirted Lincoln too, and as the dark lifted we saw how the country had changed from the green Yorkshire meadows we had left for Warwick to take unhindered. Here, dank black fields stretched to the horizon, flat as a table and seamed with innumerable ditches, mist hanging over them as if the floods were but that day retreated. Every few hundred yards a drain was cut across the road, and more than once a tired horse stumbled over one and was cursed for carelessness. We were tired, too, but could not rest: even a handful of men could be seen for miles in this empty land. We did halt once, to buy bread and meat from a farmhouse, and to rest the horses in such cover as we could find. Once in the mist we caught sight of a troop of mounted men, riding, it seemed, towards us. I thought of my own brother John and my father, trapped the year before by Warwick as they fled, and murdered on his orders without trial. At least they were shriven, and would be saved for God's justice, though denied that of the world. Then the men disappeared into the mist, and we breathed again.

The prayers for my father's soul are the same as those which I must hope for now.

We slept in a copse of pines, wrapped in cloaks and holding our horses, while the clinging damp of the mist collected on the needle-leaves above our heads and fell in heavy drops to startle us awake. At Boston, on the morrow, we looked towards the Wash and saw at once by the patched and salty mere before us that the tide was out. We must hasten to find a guide to take us across.

'May we not wait till the next low tide?' asked Hastings. 'Our horses are all but dead under us and ourselves little better.'

'That were past midnight, sir,' said the harbourmaster, shaking his head. 'You set out then, and you might as well say your prayers and ride into the quicksand and be done with the world. But so long as you're off in the next hour, you'll do. I'll get you a guide, and you get yourselves fresh horses.'

For all Edward clapped the horse chandler on the shoulder and smiled at his wife, we were told we must pay more for the horses, for the risk of the journey and the difficulty of getting them back. Nor could we quarrel with the price, because we could not hide our urgency. But at last we were mounted, and the guide with us. He was a small, dark man with a low brow and few words.

'Do you know what they say of the fenmen?' said Richard of Gloucester, sidling his horse up to mine. 'That they have webbed feet, the better to live in this marsh of theirs. Shall we make him take off his boots and show us?'

Webbed feet or no, our guide led us out across the bay at a canter, sometimes veering to avoid a deep channel but sometimes against all seeming sense making for the water and away from mud and sand. A chill, salt wind dragged at our cloaks and in the deeper water the spray reached our breeches till they clung coldly. Little was said, and we rode at our guide's command, in a body at speed where it was safe, and spreading out to pick our way when the ground began to quiver under the horses' feet. They hated it, as horses always hate uncertain ground, stepping reluctantly, balking and tossing their heads at each rivulet and green-smeared stretch of mud. We were weary; keeping strange horses together and moving on took patience and strength that none but Edward seemed still to have. He even coaxed a smile from our guide with a jest about the big sea birds and little waders that dipped and stalked about on the sand. The glow in the grey sky that was all we could see of the sun began to shift downwards, silvering the sedge and marsh grasses at the sands' rim, and casting faint, shape-changing shadows across the ground we crossed.

Suddenly a great, shrieking flock of gulls arose with a clamour of wings from the reeds to the landward side of us. Hastings's horse shied, spun and bolted. Mine gathered itself to follow, and I saw Edward's leap forward too. Then with a jab of his spurs Richard of Gloucester got himself across the King's path. The King's horse faltered, veered, and I grabbed its bridle. Once we had the King safe we looked round and saw that by the Lord's mercy Hastings's horse had made for solid ground, not the quicksands that to us looked no different. At last he wrenched its head round and returned to us at an untidy canter. We were shaken and short of breath, and sat still for a space to recover.

'Dear Lord,' the guide shouted, pointing towards the open sea. 'That tide's too quick. Hurry!' He clapped his heels to his cob and our horses, already nervous, needed no spurs to set off after him. Like a wild herd we thundered indifferently through mud and sand, looking to and fro between the treacherous ground ahead and the thin line of grey foam that slipped towards us, silent and inexorable, faster than we could ride.

By the time we sighted Lynn, the waters were up to the horses' knees, and deepening by the second so that they struggled against it.

'Well, gentlemen,' shouted Edward, 'if we drown, we may find King John's jewels on the way down, and then our troubles will be over.'

I saw Richard's mouth tighten with impatience and he jerked his head away as if the sight of his brother laughing made him angry. Hastings reached and brushed Richard's arm. 'The King knows well enough what danger we stand in, sir, but danger brings out the best in him, and the best is the courage that makes him laugh at it. Do not think him foolish. He has a better understanding than any of us.'

Richard nodded, and the waters fell away from us as the ground rose, and we gained the dry sands and saw the sturdy towers and roofs of Lynn standing at the mouth of the Ouse. If all was well – if my good cousin Haute was indeed at home, and had a ship to lend us – we were almost safe.

~

In Burgundy our hunger was not for food, for we were welcomed most kindly by the Duke's governor in Bruges and housed in the kind of luxury that no other land I know can so well supply. Rather our hunger was for peace of mind, and for riches that were not ours. Not a week went by that Edward did not send messages to his brother George of Clarence, coaxing or commanding that he might return his allegiance to his brother. He sent, too, to the enemies of Warwick, and most often of all to the Duke of Burgundy's court, publicly or secretly, to ask if the Duke was yet willing to receive us. Since the Duke's chief enmity was to his overlord the French King, we hoped he would open his arms to us. We were, after all, the enemies of France too, since France was a friend to Henry of Lancaster. But we heard nothing. The Duchess Margaret sent letters privily to her brother, but could not go openly against her new lord in this.

Meanwhile we lived in Bruges while the grey Netherlandish winter crept over us, with little to do but drink, dice and haunt the alchemists' workshops. We spent what money we could spare on furs from the Baltic, ivories from Africa and books, but it was not much, for the riches that were about us cost gold we did not have, except when kind friends and shrewd London merchants sent letters of credit to the Flemish merchants that we might borrow on their security.

The news that Elysabeth had been brought to bed of a son in Westminster Sanctuary, and a sturdy child like to survive at that, came to us when we were in exile at Bruges. It was a heavy grey day with sleet blowing in from the polders, and as always we were waiting for a reply from the Duke of Burgundy that we might lay more plans to win back the throne. The tedium of such days could rot the spirit: I was wrapped in a blanket by the fire, translating Ptolemy, Hastings was writing a letter to his man of affairs with one hand, and with the other throwing dice with young Richard of Gloucester. Edward, despairing of hearing anything from His Grace that day, had sent for his latest woman and taken her to bed. I remember that Hastings ran upstairs to his bedchamber and hammered on the door, as only he might, in right of their friendship and his office of King's Chamberlain. The roar of joy from within lifted our hearts.

'And you, my friend and my brother,' said Edward to me that evening, waving his wine-cup as if he would embrace the world, 'I shall appoint you my boy Edward's governor. Who could be more fit for such a great task than his uncle? You shall have the teaching of him, in book-learning and at arms, and thanks to your knighthood my heir shall be the greatest prince in Christendom.'

Our hopes were strengthened, though there was greater fear, too, for Elysabeth with a son was in even greater danger than before. Still we waited, and fretted, and idled away the days in Bruges. My chief joy was the books. Oh, the books! The clerks and scribes could work in three or four tongues, each glossy black letter a step, each graceful word a figure in the dance across the vellum, line after line, page after page. Then the limners would weave lapis and scarlet and gold about them, and draw the figures: saints and kings, Jason, Iseut and Melusina, ploughmen and laundrywomen, a curly-coated terrier, a bunch of grapes squeezed into a gilt and ivory cup, King Solomon's castle shimmering in the sun, the ram caught in a thicket to reprieve Isaac. One of the Merchant Venturers had a press for copying script with metal type, like that in Strasburg, though the pages it made could not compete for beauty with scriveners' and limners' work. From the best scrivener in Bruges I bought an exquisite miniature copy of the *Summa Theologica*, and had it on the tavern table beside me when a dark young man, seeing me unable to resist opening its casket and stroking the sweet new leather of the binding, asked me what book it was that I read.

He was Louis de Bretaylles, come to Bruges to offer his services to Edward, for he was a man accustomed to work in secret between old allegiances and new. When he reminded me of it I remembered him at the joust, though not a word further was spoken of that day. Why had I not seen him then as I saw him now? But then I was so newly the King's brother-in-law and the Queen's champion: I had not thought to look among my entourage for friendship. We were both older now, and wiser in telling the turns of Fortune's wheel, secrets and all.

But soon our talk turned to poetry and philosophy: he knew Christina of Pisa, and Chaucer, Aquinas and Livy. His eyes were black and his hands long-fingered, and his voice had the tang of one born speaking the *langue d'oc*, though he spoke the *langue d'oeil* well enough, English and Spanish too. And when he laughed at me that my face was still so pale-skinned, for all my years' campaigning, and began to quote Chrétien de Troyes from *The Story of the Grail* — '*Ainc mai chevalier ne conui . . .*' — I wanted to reach across the tavern board and seize him by his thin, hard shoulders, the better to kiss him long into the night. And I did kiss him so, and many nights thereafter.

My love for Louis was almost more than my soul and mind and body could bear. Sometimes I would rise in the moonlight and watch his sleeping face, his copper-coloured skin and whipcord arms, and wonder that I did not die, there, in that breath, for the love of him.

At last the Duke decided to receive Edward, and lent his support to our great enterprise. As before, I was to have the hiring and commissioning of even this tiny royal fleet. I feared that Louis and I would be parted, but he cleaved to me as I did to him. When I asked him to come to England in my train, though no longer as my squire for he was made knight himself by that time, he knelt to me and bowed his head in assent. In public he played his part perfectly, as he did so many others, though some about

Edward knew him from the past. But no man knew what Louis and I were to each other beyond comrades in arms. It was only in our private love and care that our allegiance was equal.

When we sailed from Flushing to regain Edward's crown we knew that the enterprise was as risky as any we had known. Our strength was small: His Grace of Burgundy would not spare more men or gold than what was needed to show his enemies and his wife that he espoused Edward's cause. When we sighted the Norfolk coast we sighted Warwick's ships too. Lynn was armed and readied, to defend itself and capture us, and perforce we went about and headed north.

Louis was standing in the bows, watching the dark stains that the storms ahead were casting across the face of the waters.

I touched his shoulder, and he turned his head. 'Love,' I said quietly, 'I would give you this, before we give our lives into Fortune's keeping.'

I put the calfskin bag into his palm, and he pulled the cord loose. It is a signet in the form of a ring: I bespoke it of the best goldsmith in Antwerp before we left the Low Countries. Heavy gold it is, engraved with the pilgrim's shell of Compostela, for he has made the journey twice to seek grace at the shrine of St James. On the inner face of the ring, touching his skin, is carved our private signal: Jason and his ship, threading through the clashing rocks.

He smiled and slipped it on to his finger, then embraced me as men do on the eve of battle.

'*À Dieu, mon amour,*' he murmured, for my ear alone. '*Nous nous rencontrions au ciel.*'

~

Now, after so many years, his words are fulfilled: it is indeed in Heaven, God willing, that we will meet again, and I pray God, too, that I may endure Purgatory with patience, knowing that Louis will join me there.

The afternoon light is dull and hot about us. It is not the riding that quenches all light within me and weighs my spirits with lead. I have ridden such a distance in a day many times, and we are not far now from Pontefract, the end of all these journeys. But now I must accept what I have refused to know: that no help will come. Perhaps I was foolish to half hope that it might. But the chance, if ever there was one, is gone.

I try to tell myself that it is the Devil who has seized his opportunity to cast me into sinful despair when aid may yet come. But I cannot quite believe it: this despair is born of God's truth.

Sure, my sins are manifold – as are any man's – and despair not the least of them, nor yet the most. Only true penitence can save me, that I know, and I am penitent. Yet I have never been able to think Louis's and my love sinful. It is like believing that white is black.

Perhaps I have the advantage – or the disadvantage –

of learning: I have read enough in the works of holy men such as St Aelred to know that even in his time, the time of the second Henry, true love between men was not thought sinful, and their lusts no more so, though no less so, than other men's lust for women or drink or fighting. Yet now it is preached to be a sin like few others but murder.

How will God judge me? I confessed my sin many a time, and tried to feel it to be one, as Rome and its holy men tell us it is. And yet, though their judgement changes, God's judgement – His wisdom – is unchangeable, and His love infinite. How can what Louis and I did be a sin in His eyes, when it came from the power to love that God Himself gave man?

One of the men-at-arms points ahead into the blue distance, to the cleft in the land beyond which the great rock stands, topped with the broad, high towers of Pontefract.

Una – Friday

The rain's pitting the slack surface of the river; the tide hasn't turned yet. It's lunchtime, a heavy, grey day. I slept badly after Mark dropped me home: too hot, too cold, too hot . . . And then was woken in the dark by the blare of a huge ship's horn from the river, as loud as if its bows towered above me, and I lay in a prickle of sweat with my heart thumping. But strong coffee, a shower, and a morning of telephone calls and arrangements have done the trick. I reach for the phone yet again and dial briskly.

'Isode Butler.'

'Izzy, it's Una. Listen, the most amazing thing's happened. Mark's come back.'

'Mark who?'

'Mark Fisher. He turned up at the Chantry yesterday.'

'Goodness! After all these years! How lovely. How is he? Well, I hope.'

'Fine. And – and, listen. He thinks we can save the Chantry.'

'What? How?'

'Set up some kind of trust. We were going to meet up and discuss it.'

'We?'

'Gareth, Mark and me. And Lionel. Can you come?'

'Yes, of course. When?'

'This evening at the Chantry. Lionel can get there for about six. I'm bringing food.'

'Hold on, my diary's across the room.' A clunk as she puts the receiver down on the table. I wait, and try not to remember a different, sweating dream, as dark as the ship's bulk, which looms over me still because it was of Mark.

'Una? I'm busy this afternoon. Could make it for about eight, though. Is that any good?'

'I'm sure that'll be fine. See you then.'

'Yes,' she says, and puts the phone down.

~

After the earlier rain it's turned into a beautiful after-noon, the sun lying warmly across brick and slate and even concrete, and catching my bare shoulder through the taxi window as we cross the river. On Blackheath the wide-winged mowers are out, working their way to and fro across the high green curve like galleons hull down across an ocean, so that the cut-grass scent rolls in at the taxi window.

When we reach the Chantry I'm lifting the carrier-bags of food out of the taxi's boot when Mark appears. 'Want a hand?'

'Don't worry, there isn't much. I just raided Marks & Spencer.'

He's shirtless, his chest old-gold in the sun as he approaches, pulling off heavy gardening gloves. He's caught our cousinly habits: we brush cheeks in a greeting kiss and the point of his shoulder is hard under my hand. I can smell lawnmower oil, and the scent of him that I've known almost all my life. I turn away to pay the driver and when I turn back he's picked up the bags.

'We're sitting outside,' he says. 'By the workshop.'

'Is there anywhere to sit in that jungle?'

'Been tidying up a bit.'

He has indeed: three full bin-bags squat on the fiercely shorn lawn, and when we round the bulk of the house I see rugs and a table on the patch outside the workshop where the midsummer sun lingers longest. Gareth gets up as I approach and greets me with a laugh and a hug, which seems stronger and more substantial than before. I fetch plates from the kitchen, giving them a surreptitious wash, and put out the food. The wine's still cold. Mark disappears, and reappears shirted and clean, only slightly damp round the edges. We're topping up our glasses when the deep hum of an expensive engine, then the clunk of a car door, announce Lionel.

He's wearing driving gloves and he seems pleased to see Mark, though they shake hands with the brisk neutrality of long-standing business acquaintances. Mark outlines everything Gareth, he and I have been talking about, as clearly and clear-headedly as if he were presenting to a board of directors: forming a trust to own the house, raising money to restore it and opening to the public, with an exhibition of its history, perhaps in the undercroft; using the chapel ruins as the roots of a beautiful new building to be a gallery or, more accessibly, an art and exhibition space; above all, keeping the Press going, so that the Chantry isn't a dead, didactic piece of history but a living, breathing, working world. 'And offering the chapel gallery for hire. Much easier to raise money if we can demonstrate some kind of community benefit,' he finishes.

Lionel has listened to it all without his expression changing, and only his still-gloved hands and fidgeting fingers showing signs of life. 'But would the money be forthcoming? Forgive me, Gareth, I'm playing Devil's advocate here, but with such an apparently attractive idea . . . It's easy enough to get capital grants, but running costs are different. The financial footing needs to be absolutely sound. It's not as if the Press was ever financially solid, even in its heyday before the war.'

'We managed,' says Gareth. 'It wasn't always easy, and it would never have been something to tempt the money-men, without compromising what we did beyond redemption. But that wasn't the point. And now . . . This would be a different thing altogether.'

He discussed the restoration of the chapel eagerly enough: he can remember the Courtaulds entertaining their Gainsborough Studios stars at Eltham Palace in the twenties, and the sense of a ruin living again as Eltham did has caught our imaginations, I think. But now I can't tell from his tone if the difference – the change to the Press itself – is something he welcomes or not.

'It's certainly the way things are going,' says Lionel, pulling out one of those leather note-holders and a gold pen. 'Heritage, and so on. But whether it's viable for a relatively small, unknown place like the Chantry . . . Gareth, what sort of figures are we talking about? For the restoration?'

Gareth shakes his head. 'No idea. Mark?'

'Restoring to conservation standards? Very roughly? Hundred thousand, perhaps, a hundred and fifty including consultants? Fifty thousand for the gallery?

Always cheaper to build from scratch. Then there's the fitting out. Say a quarter of a million altogether? More if there are salaries involved.'

'Thank you, Mark.' Lionel makes a note. 'Una? Anything to add?'

'Well, I won't say it's none of my business, but I certainly shouldn't have a casting vote when I'm not going to be here.' I'm not looking at him, I'm looking at Gareth, but my skin knows that his eyes are on me. 'But of course I'd like it to be saved and kept even sort of in the family. And if it was restored, I'd love to give back some of the Chantry things I've got: furniture and so on. And letters and stuff, if Uncle Gareth's idea of keeping the archive here does work.'

Mark catches my eye and smiles.

Lionel notices. 'And Mark — forgive me — how do you see your role in this? When you've only just come back?'

Mark hesitates, but more, I fancy, from picking his words than from uncertainty about what he wants to say. 'That'd be for the trustees to decide. I'll help however I can till I get another job. Needn't be any time soon. And I do know what I'm doing with projects like this.'

'You always did,' I say.

'Of course,' says Lionel. 'Well, we'd be very grateful. And the family — this putative trust — wouldn't expect you to work without remuneration.'

Uncle Gareth makes a sudden movement, as if to stop Lionel saying any more. There's a nasty little pause before

I think to say, 'Shall we have something to eat? Izzy said not to wait for her.'

There's business of plates and glasses and food but again, as if they're thin lines of light, I feel the web that nets us together. Affection, attraction, suspicion, indifference.

Love.

Grief.

As I eat I can't help but watch Mark. His plate's on the ground in front of him. Even with his knees bent up his legs cross more of the rug than any Pryor's ever would. He looks up, our eyes meet. If he'd reached out his hand – his beautiful, long-fingered hand – and actually touched my cheek I couldn't have been more shaken.

What is this heat? Memory's powerful. But this?

I was grown-up, by then, my first year at university done. Compared to many of my fellows I was sophisticated in the extreme because I knew couples who weren't married: we'd had them staying, and some were even names the more arty had heard of. My clothes were odd, but I knew every detail of the facts of life – an amazing number of the girls didn't, not really – and wasn't there something about my parents? But I'd learnt too: about girls who'd gone on hunger strike till allowed to go to university; uncles who grabbed at you when no one was looking; mothers who burnt books and other mothers who lied to fathers because you'd gone to the library again; homes that were always clean, homes that had no books, homes that had horses and parlourmaids, homes where you – the first ever – were given the parlour so you could study. I'd even found myself in dark corners with hours – well, minutes – till I had to be back in my hall, and a young man . . . I felt enough to enjoy it, and knew enough to know it didn't matter.

I knew enough, and felt enough, and still it didn't matter, because none of it was Mark.

It must have been August or September of my first long vacation. The medieval stones of Bermondsey Abbey were only just below the new skin of tarmac and paving slabs. I remember the day we uncovered a third column-base, and knew we really had discovered the cloisters. At the end of work I raced home on my bicycle, grubby and sweating, and found Mark kneeling outside the kitchen window, unblocking a drain. He squatted back on his heels and listened as I poured out what the county archaeologist had said, what Professor – what was his name? – had said, what it might mean that the spacing of the columns was . . . whatever it had measured. I could still feel the heavy brass at the end of the tape between my earth-stained fingers, and feel the grip of the postgraduate student who was holding the other end vibrating with excitement as we pulled it taut. I told Mark how we were trying to work out what it had been like, where the nuns had lived and how, these women some of whose names were known, whose births and deaths might be recorded, royal names even – it was a royal haven, founded in the twelfth century. I could – any of us on the dig could – go to the Public Records Office and find out who they were. It wouldn't be easy, but it could be done.

'Una, that's great! That you can see it now! Just under your feet.' Mark rubbed his forearm across his brow and winced. Where his hair had hidden it I saw a bruise, new and angry, with the graze barely skinning over.

I reached out my hand to touch it, I couldn't stop myself. He turned his head away, flushing red under his summer-gold skin, and went back to digging muck from the drain. 'Go on,' he said, in a muffled voice, and at the memory something stirs painfully in my throat that might almost be tears.

The chit-chat is desultory, not taking up much of my attention. Is Mark really thinking of the Chantry's past, as I am? Or is it my mind that fills this other – this Mark-shaped person sitting in the sun – with *my* moments, *my* memories, and believes them to be his? I can't know him, I can't feel what he feels or see what he sees, any more than I can read Elizabeth and Anthony in their books. I want to reach forward and shake him, push myself through the envelope of his body and find whatever's there, inside him. I want to know what he knew, what he was thinking, what I was to him then.

Because I never knew, my memories howl. What was I to you? You were glad of my help when you were mending your bike or a press, you smiled at me if I came into the workshop, you mended the latch on my window. After that day in the workshop – the day I've always thought of as the beginning – I waited to see if my heart-thumping, ringing-in-the-ears sense of your existence echoed in you. I didn't tell anyone, of course. For days and weeks and months I looked for silent signs from you, and got none.

None. I used to lie miserably on my bed and try to work it out. Everyone knew without saying that Mark adored Izzy. No one allowed themselves a more complicated or threatening verb than 'adored'. And everyone knew without saying that though he lived at the Chantry and worked for Uncle Gareth, he wasn't family, or the son of friends, or an art student changing track: no one allowed themselves a more complicated or less tactful word for him than 'local'. No one, really, talked about what he was. But he wasn't one of us, and I didn't know what the family would do, or say, if they knew I loved him, and he didn't love me. And I didn't know what Mark would do if I told him. He didn't love me, after all, but only Izzy. Perhaps he'd hate me, or be embarrassed, or try to avoid me. I couldn't have borne that. He might have left, or been told to leave, and he had nowhere to go. It would have been my fault, and I would have lost him.

I couldn't destroy what I loved most.

All that summer I hoped: a hope made up of lurches of joy at a word, a glance, a smile of Mark's, and many more plunges into tears. But slowly hopelessness began to thicken until even the good days – the days I could be near him — were greyed because joy brought with it a smothering dust of despair.

But despair couldn't smother desire. I knew enough about sex to know what I felt when Mark pulled his shirt over his head and washed under the pump in the yard, and what I felt was wonderful and frightening, and so strange. Of course I knew the facts, but I was no less in the dark about it all mentally and emotionally than my friends were. No one explained to us how wanting it addles your brain as much as his: perhaps they thought that if they didn't mention it, we wouldn't want it. Only of course we did. Even if the 'him' wasn't the one you really longed for. Nor how not wanting it was worse.

Sex started for me on the sofa in the church-hall room we'd borrowed as headquarters for the Bermondsey dig, after everyone else had gone home in the tea-time dark. It was cold, I remember, so it must have been at the end of the dig. I should have been going home myself. Aunt Elaine would chat to me over her shoulder while she made the supper, as if I was still of an age to be doing my prep at the kitchen table, and Uncle Gareth would pull a funny face and pat my shoulder. Mark would look round and smile, then turn back to the fence he was mending or the stack of books he was packing. Then Izzy's voice would call him across the garden, and I would be alone again. Perhaps it was those moments when I knew with devastating certainty that he would only ever be kind and helpful to me, that he would always go when Izzy called . . . If I made a conscious decision at all, it was because of those moments.

His name, I'm fairly sure, was Miller – Nigel Miller – and he was in his first year too, at Bristol, I think. All summer I kept feeling his gaze between my shoulder-blades. After a while I noticed that as soon as I put my hand up in the morning dig meetings to volunteer for a job, he would offer to join me. Or I'd be sitting with a mug of tea or a sandwich, thinking about Mark, and I'd look up and find Nigel staring at me. We chatted while squatting side by side, scraping earth from lumps of Norman stone, though Grandmama would have said he didn't have much conversation. But he kept looking at me, he kept saying my name even when he didn't need to, he seemed to have perfect recall of everything I'd ever said to him.

On a rare day when I went to work wearing a skirt, he asked very tentatively why I didn't more often, and was a bit surprised when I said, 'Because it gets in the way.' His attention was like an uncomfortable lamp turned on to me, making me feel hot inside my skin, and aware all the time of myself, crouching, stretching, fingers brushing carvings, sweat-damped strings of hair escaping my ponytail to stick to my cheek.

Why can I not remember his name for certain? After all, I can remember the moment on that much later day – September, it must have been – when the other diggers started leaving, grumbling that the sluicing rain showed no sign of letting up, and work was clearly done.

Only he was left. I made a fresh pot of tea. 'I don't fancy biking home in this, do you? I think I'll give it a bit longer. Do you want some tea too?' He said he did.

I sat down on the sofa with both mugs, and held his out to him.

I think I was only curious to see what would happen, though I must have known what might. I'd been at university for a year, after all. And why with him, who I'll have to think of as Nigel? There's something about the remembered smell of the gas fire and the sofa – soot and old chip papers – that tells me my reasons weren't romantic ones.

I asked him about what he would be studying next year, and gazed into his eyes while he told me. By the time he'd explained the importance of analysing eighteenth-century parliamentary division records, he was breathing heavily between sentences, red in the cheeks. I can't remember who made the first move. Remembering my twenty-year-old self, remembering the times, I doubt it was me. He was hardly a pouncer, however, so I imagine that we inched towards each other in tiny shuffles and gestures. By the time we started to kiss I had my eyes closed. It was nice, if wet. Then his tongue tried to inch between my lips and into my mouth, still tasting of tea. I wasn't sure I liked it, but then he put his arms round me and that I did like. I leant back, but I wasn't straight on the sofa, so I was already half lying, and he slid his free hand up under my sweater and found my breast.

My mind cleared enough to know this was a sort of point of no return, even if we didn't go the whole way. I opened my eyes. Nigel's were closed, and he looked as if he was going to faint. I was surprised, because I knew that 'up there' I was pretty disappointing, my bust hardly worth the stout satin and straps of a brassière. But he gasped, and pulled his other hand out from behind me, so that I couldn't help sliding further sideways until I was almost lying on the sofa. He could reach my other breast. I closed my eyes, hoping it would help, and what I thought of as the swoony feeling began to be very nice. He was warm on top of me, and he'd gone back to kissing as if it was the most important thing in the world to be doing. I started to feel as if it was too. Then suddenly he was in a tremendous hurry. I wanted to know what it was like, but I wasn't so overtaken as to forget what a friend had told me to say, or was it Izzy? I can't be sure.

'Have you got something?'

His eyes flew open, and he shook his head. 'It'll be all right. I'll come out.'

I half knew what he meant, and half knew I should say no, but I didn't. He slid my trousers off, and what I chiefly remember about the next few minutes is that one of my legs kept sliding off the sofa, and he was huffing and puffing in my ear, and it hurt, quite a lot, and then he shouted, and it seemed to be over, and I realised he hadn't come out.

The rain had eased off a little, and it was dark. When I tried to get out from under him he woke, and asked me if I was all right.

'I must go. I'm going to be late.'

'Shall I see you home?' I'll say that for Nigel Miller, if that was his name: he was well brought-up. But suddenly I absolutely couldn't bear him. I could bear myself, I thought, feeling a sort of roughness as I pulled my knickers on and then a rather distasteful stickiness. What had just happened – how I'd felt during it, and now – was quite interesting and in a way perfectly reasonable. But I couldn't feel interested and reasonable about it if Nigel was shambling alongside. That I did know.

I felt sure it must show that I was no longer a virgin. When a car overtook me as I pedalled home I thought the driver must see how different I was. There was a zebra crossing on Loampit Hill; the old lady I stopped for said, 'Thank you,' and I wondered if she knew. I was sure Aunt Elaine or Uncle Gareth would be able to tell.

I left my bike in the shed and went in by the back door. Aunt Elaine was kneeling on the kitchen floor and everything was covered with soot and coal dust: the range had gone out. And when I said hello and could I help, she said that the workshop roof had sprung a new leak and ruined several hundred pounds' worth of stock before anyone had seen. 'And you're wet through, Una pet.

Hurry upstairs and change before you catch a chill. Lionel's coming down for the night.'

I plodded up the Chantry stairs, cold and shivering, wanting nothing so much as the hot bath I couldn't have, yet feeling all the time the slight, hot roughness between my legs that told me with each step that I was utterly changed.

Mark was standing at the top of the stairs with a bucket in each hand. He must have been fetching them from the attic.

I was suddenly scarlet and prickling with sweat. I was sure he could tell — he must be able to tell. My nod and mutter about getting dry couldn't hide what I felt any more than if I'd been stark naked.

He nodded to me, and stood back to let me come upstairs before he went down. As he moved the water slopped out over the edge of one of the buckets.

I washed in cold water as best I could, and by the time I was dry and dressed supper was ready, though that was cold too because though Mark had got the range going it hadn't warmed up. I buried my gaze in my plate in dread of meeting his eye, because I didn't want him to know, not the way it had been.

But what if it had been the way I'd read about, I thought, staring at cold mutton and lettuce and bread-and-marge. Not a muddly, smelly business with a boy I didn't even specially like? The way I still knew it could be? But I knew with the certainty of youth that it could never be like that unless it was Mark.

Afterwards he went back to the workshop with Uncle Gareth to finish emptying the storeroom, and I excused myself with a plea of university work and went upstairs, so I heard Lionel arrive, laughing and swearing at the rain, but didn't go down.

I lay awake for what felt like hours. In the end I gave up, put on my dressing-gown and went downstairs to make some cocoa. The range had got going well enough to warm the kitchen, but I used the electric kettle so as not to lift the lid.

'Hello, Una.' It was Lionel. 'Missed you earlier – how are you?'

'Fine, thanks. You know, working hard.' The kettle boiled. I switched it off and poured it on to the cocoa powder in my mug. 'Did you get very wet coming up from the station?'

'Not half. Had to dig my emergency clothes out.' But even his black sweater, discreetly darned by Aunt Elaine, and rumpled flannels looked sleek somehow, I thought, and he sat on the corner of the table with a kind of self-contained ease that faintly thrilled me, his cigarette dangling from his fingers. 'I was going to have some whisky. How about some in that cocoa?'

I didn't put much in but it made the cocoa suddenly very delightful, and instead of carrying it back upstairs to drink in bed, as I'd meant to, I propped my bottom on the rail of the range and sipped it. 'Have you been talking about the Chantry?'

'No, it was too late. We're going to talk in the morning.' He got off the corner of the table and joined me against the warmth of the range. 'So how are you, Una? Properly? Feel as if we don't see much of each other, these days.' He put an arm round my shoulders and gave me a hug. 'You are all right, aren't you? University okay? Love-life not gone awry, or anything? You'd say if there was anything Sally or I could do to help, wouldn't you?'

I remember thinking, even then, how when you have to be absolutely silent about one thing you want to talk about everything else. I wanted to tell Lionel about Nigel and . . . so on. Probably I shouldn't. But as soon as I'd thought it I knew I would. A bit, anyway. He was what Grandmama called worldly. He wasn't like Izzy, who never really talked about sex, even though she was engaged to Paul and I was fairly sure they were sleeping together. Lionel wouldn't tell anyone if I asked him not to, and he wasn't old, not like Uncle Gareth . . .

Now I must say it, I told myself. Now, or I won't be able to. 'Well, there is . . . a boy.'

'Oh, good. Have I met him?'

'I don't think so. I don't think it's anything. Serious, I mean. But we . . . Well, once or twice . . .'

He turned a little, and grinned. 'And you know what you're doing? Someone's explained it all? Being sensible?'

'Oh, yes,' I said, feeling myself blushing.

'So I don't have to beat him up, or ask his intentions, or anything?'

'Oh, no.'

He stretched out a hand to the whisky bottle on the draining-board, topped up his glass, then looked at me. 'Cheers! Glad you're having some fun.' I couldn't help thinking of the chip-paper smell of the sofa and Nigel Miller's grunts, and wondering if that was what fun was supposed to be like. 'I could get Uncle Gareth to do the Victorian bit, if you want me to. If you don't want to ask him yourself?'

'No, please don't,' I said. 'It's . . . No, thank you.'

'Okay. Don't worry, I won't tell anyone. You're right. No good ever came of telling the old dears anything you don't have to. Just as long as you're having fun and being sensible.'

'I am,' I said, though I hadn't been sensible either. 'Did you know there's been a leak in the storeroom roof?' I went on, to change the subject.

'Yes,' he said. 'Nearly a thousand pounds' worth of stock they're going to have to write off, apparently. Maybe now they'll see sense and realise it's time we got rid of the old shack.'

'It isn't a shack, it's as solid as the house, Grandpapa says. It only needs patching up. Mark would have done it already if it wasn't pouring.'

'The trouble is, rain does pour. They haven't found a way of stopping it yet.'

'He's going to do it tomorrow.'

Lionel tossed off the last of his whisky. 'There's only

so much patching up that's worth doing, even if Gareth has got Mark to do it for him. I wonder what's in it for Mark, hanging around the crumbling edifice? Any ideas?' I shook my head. He put his glass down on the draining-board. 'Dammit, Una, we're more than half-way through the century, and I'm the only one who's noticed. I don't blame Grandpapa. He *is* a Victorian, after all – not surprising he's sentimental about the old place. But Uncle Gareth's a businessman. Or, at least, he's been running a business long enough. He's not going to be able to pretend it's all okay much longer. Sooner or later he'll take my side . . . Ah, well, I just do what I can. I'm off to bed. Night, Una.'

'Good night,' I said.

But I lay awake for a long time, still feeling the faint sandpaperiness between my legs, and wondering what would happen when I met Nigel in the morning.

In the event nothing happened. I'm ashamed now to think that I spent the last two weeks of the dig avoiding him. Many times he tried to catch me in private, but I couldn't look him in the eye, let alone talk to him, and I gave up volunteering for things in case he joined in. My skin crawled at the thought of his, though I knew even then that he'd done nothing much wrong except be young and inexperienced, as I was. I was also praying fervently that I wasn't in trouble. Inevitably my period was late, though it came at last, just when the dig ended. I never saw Nigel Miller again.

But night after night I dreamt of Mark. He held me and I him, and although I saw and felt the details of him that when awake I couldn't really imagine, I wasn't surprised or embarrassed. They were part of the warmth, the rightness, the unreasonable joy. Sometimes we were at home, more often we were in a place that felt entirely familiar, though I'd never seen it before. I curled my body down and down and down into his arms until I exploded, and woke panting and sweaty in the chilly dark. My eiderdown had slipped off, and dimly across my room I could see the broad, blank arrowhead of the boarded-up chantry window, but I felt as if I were still with Mark. I could almost smell his outdoors smell, leaf mould and woodsmoke and the iron-cold air off the Kentish Downs. Among my waking knowledge of his absence, the joy of sated desire lingered, so that I had to cling to both, or lose everything.

Mark's filling my glass again, and the sun's finally gone off our patch of grass when there's a crackle of gravel and a rough-sounding engine. By the time Izzy rounds the corner of the house the men are on their feet. When she takes Mark's hand he grips it, but I can't read his glance.

'So here we all are,' says Gareth, when he's kissed Izzy and we've sat down again.

'Mark, it's splendid to see you,' says Izzy. 'Una's been telling me about everything you've been up to. So nice to see you back at the Chantry. I've been looking up the post-war records. What a lot you were involved in. I'd forgotten.' She laughs and drinks wine. 'But I'm afraid I was always so taken up with my own work.'

'I know,' he says. 'Did Gareth tell you he's found the casts of *The Stations of the Cross?*'

'Yes, he did. Nice to know they're still around.' She turns to me. 'Did you know some evangelical cow in the parish tried to get the originals taken down because they weren't made by "a believer"? Can you believe it?' She reaches for the bottle and offers it round. 'Now, tell me the plan.'

We outline it again. After Lionel's professional scepticism and Mark's cool command of heritage-industry jargon, there's something very alive in her thoughtful, listening face, her narrowed eyes and the half-smile that ignites as Mark speaks of restoring wall paintings and tracking down the original furniture. Gareth catches my eye, and smiles too.

Then Mark moves on to generating income, and her smile fades, though she's still listening.

Only when he's finished does she say slowly, 'Let me get this right. You want a shop? Display boards of potted history? Tourists watching the press? *Weddings?* And to stick all the letters – the whole archive – in the cellar for anyone to poke through who wants to?'

'Any funding bids would build in the cost of converting the undercroft to the highest curatorial standards,' says Mark. 'And the warden would control access.'

'And the warden would be you?'

'I hadn't thought about it,' says Mark, blandly, but I think he's angry, as he wasn't, quite, at Lionel's insult.

'Izzy, my dear, don't be silly,' says Gareth. 'We wouldn't do anything vulgar, and we're nowhere near thinking about appointing people.'

'I can't see how you'd begin to get the money together. You know how arts funding's cut to the bone, these days.'

She said it to me, but it's Lionel who answers back: 'Well, who knows? And it would be heritage funding just as much, and that's easier to make a case for that politicians understand. No reason we shouldn't put out some feelers, gauge the interest, even get some conditional agreements.'

She ignores him. 'Una, you're the historian. You must see it wouldn't be *real*! It wouldn't be the real thing. Just plastic – a fake. A day out for coach parties. Art and craft as a tourist attraction.'

'The Press would be real enough.'

'But San Diego are expecting the archive. I should be at home finishing the catalogue now.'

'It's not signed and sealed yet,' says Lionel, making another note.

'Well, I'm sorry,' she says, getting to her feet. 'I know it's horrible, having to sell the Chantry, but doing some fake tourist attraction would be worse. The past is the real Chantry. I should know – I've read the letters, I've catalogued the prints and the little invitations and handbills and Christmas cards. This – this is *lying*, and I won't have anything to do with it. And I'm surprised you will, Uncle Gareth.' Before any of us can answer she stalks off towards the front of the house.

'Iz – wait!' calls Lionel, scrambling up and going after her.

Uncle Gareth's leaning back in his deckchair, staring at the gables and chimneys of the blank-eyed house. Mark gets up and picks up a pair of secateurs and his gloves from the grass. By the time we hear the slam of Izzy's car door and the snarl of the engine he's pruning a hedge on the far side of the lawn.

Lionel's walking back over the grass.

'Did you persuade her?' I say, as soon as he's near enough.

'I suggested there's no harm in trying to take it further. She wasn't convinced. I'm not convinced either, yet. I'll need some much more solid figures first.'

'Of course. But you think we should at least try?'

'Oh, yes. At least until we have to decide to commit ourselves to significant costs.'

Uncle Gareth turns his head to look at him. 'D'you think she'll change her mind? We can't get far, legally, if everyone doesn't agree.'

'I don't know,' says Lionel, glancing across the garden to Mark and lowering his voice. 'She said . . . She said she'd be suspicious of anything Mark suggested. That he doesn't deserve a voice, after walking out. That he just wants a job.' He looks at his watch. 'I must go – got a breakfast meeting. Don't move, Una, Gareth ... I'll do some telephoning in the morning, and let you know how it looks.'

By the time Lionel's left Mark is digging over what was once the vegetable patch, though the light's going. Uncle Gareth and I clear up the remains of the picnic and carry everything indoors out of the dew, the phrase reminding me of Aunt Elaine eyeing the bikes and blankets and cast-off gym-shoes scattered over the summer grass of my childhood.

Uncle Gareth switches on the standard lamp and peers out of the window. 'I hope Mark's all right. I'd no idea ... Well, it was rude of Lionel, but he thinks that way. Izzy, though ...'

'Perhaps ...' I'm hesitating because the thought's only just forming in my mind. 'Perhaps it's just because they haven't thought about him much, not since he left. Don't see him as he is. Whereas I ... And you ...'

He's looking at me very sharply through the slippery blue twilight. 'I know.'

And suddenly I can say it. 'You loved him, didn't you? Mark? All the time.'

He nods and then, as if he's suddenly very tired, he goes over to one of the armchairs and sits down. The other chair seems too far away so I perch on the arm of his. He moves over to make room for me, but his shoulder's pressed comfortably against my hip.

'Yes, I loved him. Oh – not in that way.'

I nod, because I know what he means.

'Though I am – I've always been – homosexual. Did you know?'

'I didn't then. I half realised later, but I didn't know how to ask, wasn't sophisticated enough. And besides, well, it seemed your business, not mine.' He's silent, and I wonder if he's going to say that he never did much about it; that for many queers in those days what was on offer by way of affairs was less attractive than getting on with the rest of life; that in the end you stopped being interested in any of it. He doesn't. But perhaps through our bodies touching he can sense something of my understanding: I sit there and will – will with fierce hope – that he can sense it.

He says, 'I loved you from the moment I saw you. Your nanny was holding you . . . nurse, she called herself. When . . . when it happened, she just took you home and went on looking after you. I think it was she who christened your bear Smokey. Anyway, there you were. It was easy. But with Mark . . . I worked with Mark. We worked together, and I loved him, and I taught him, and I wanted him to take over the Chantry because he was the only one who could keep it running as it should have been. And – and because I wanted him to have the share in it he deserved.'

A little tremor of something that's almost like joy, that might be hope, passes through me. I slide round on the chair arm so that I'm facing him. 'Well, maybe – just perhaps – maybe he will. If we can persuade the others.' He smiles, just a little, and the feeling, whatever it is, gets stronger.

And then I wonder, Why joy? Why hope? It's too intense for mere relief that Gareth and the Chantry may yet be saved. It's something to do with Mark being its saviour, with Mark having a place there again, at last.

I don't want this tremor, though. It feels as if my hold on Adam, on my love, is slipping.

'Maybe we will persuade the others,' he says, and I think how he was never one to tell you to stop hoping.

He takes my hand. 'I sometimes used to wonder what Kay would have done, if he'd lived: what having him here would have made the family into. He was so clear – so absolute – about art and craft and how life should be. Izzy reminds me of him very much, sometimes. Though you're the one who looks like him. Specially around the eyes and mouth . . . Mark's a good man. He always was.'

I wonder if he's guessed about me – if he, too, always knew – but Mark's shadow crosses the window, and there's the splash of tools cleaned under the outside tap, and then he puts his head through the still-open door and asks if I'd like a lift home again.

Elysabeth — the 11th yr of the reign of King Edward the Fourth

To lie with Edward was to be Melusina again, private in the thick gold water of the fire-lit air.

It was very late by then, with no sound but the occasional cry of a waterman crossing to the far shore and the soft slap of the river below the casement. Edward rolled aside, and his warm hand slid from my breast to my waist and over my belly. He cupped my bush as gently as any alchemist with his first precious metal.

'What did I do without you in Bruges, my beautiful Ysa?' he said, and for all it was dim in our chamber, I knew that he smiled in his drowsiness.

'I was in even worse case, without my lord.'

'You kept my son safe, nonetheless.'

'He was my first care,' I said, of course, and my smile was real, at the thought of Ned's fair head and pink fists that morning, bouncing and waving in his father's arms. Edward's eyes had been for his son, and so had mine. Yet I had wondered what he would think of me, his faithful wife. A year and a half in those gloomy little abbey chambers built not for us but for men who had abjured the world. It was sanctuary, sure enough, licensed by His Holiness himself. But some days it felt as if my eyes and brow were being carved by fear into the likeness of the grey stone that surrounded us. And then to be brought to bed in so bare a room, and the girls in the next chamber so that I all but drowned in silent screaming.

'How was it, with Ned?' he asked suddenly. 'Comfortless, my poor girl?'

My heart jumped at his knowing my thought. 'No worse than Cecily,' was all I said, however. 'And worth twice as much pain for a prince.'

He kissed my brow. 'When he is older we will do as we thought to: give him your brother Antony as his governor, and send him where we most need royal authority – the Marches, perhaps. He could live at Ludlow . . .' He said no more, and I knew he was thinking again of his own youth, hunting and dancing and jousting with his brother Edmund among those round, dark green Welsh hills. 'He looks like Arthur, I think, as well as you.'

The thought of Arthur had never troubled me much, and not at all now that I, too, had given Edward a son. Arthur's mother seemed content to live retired, and he was a pretty child who caused no trouble when he did lodge in the nursery with my children. But I would not have Edward think of him, even were it only to take his thoughts from his murdered brother, this night of all nights.

'He and Ned have their sire to thank for that. Ned's hair is red as much as gold. And he is very forward. We had the swathing bands off before he was five months old. He had his first tooth by then, too.'

'Yes, you told me so at supper.'

I was out of practice, I realised. I bit my lip and ran

the back of my fingernail along the line of his jaw. It was lean once again; the stubble of a long day glittered in the firelight, and the muscles hardened as my touch made him smile. His chest and belly, too, were as taut as once they were.

I knew he was remade from his stride that morning, when we had met at Westminster. I could hear it in the sound of his spurs striking the stone through Henry of Lancaster's dirty rushes, in his being that filled the room, in his eyes as bright as a knife and the sharp sweat of a man whose work is yet half done. He took baby Ned in his arms and kissed him; I saw more than one tear fall and darken Ned's hair. And then he raised me, kissed me long on the lips, and held me away from him the better to gaze.

For a moment his eyes lost their battle-ready narrowing and widened into the dumb, dull stare of desire. I knew it so well, and born of this knowledge was my own desire, gripping my bowels and holding his gaze with mine. If my ladies thought my tears to be womanly weakness they were right in the first, but not in the second; it was not weakness that I rejoiced in, but power. All would be well, I knew, as he raised Bess, and admired Mary's uncertain curtsy, and tickled Cecily's cheek where she sat in her nurse's arms. I had an eye to the girls, while Edward's men paid their respects to me and answered when I asked after their fortune in the interregnum. My brother Antony was to have command of the Tower, that

London might be held as Warwick approached with his army and poor silly Henry of Lancaster in his train. Likewise was high command given to Lord Hastings and young Richard, Duke of Gloucester, and all the others who had cleaved to their king in exile.

The day went on: there were miry messengers to hear, dispatches to scrawl, troops to number and wavering aldermen to cozen. And at the back of our every thought and action was war. None could doubt it: there was a great battle yet to come. Warwick came ever nearer, and there were witnesses that Marguerite and her boy had sailed from their exile in France, and would land in the West Country.

All day I saw and heard His Grace the King – my lord – numbering men and arms and roads, laughing, swearing, listening, talking, questioning, answering, planning, and all to make the most of his advantage in having reached Westminster. I spoke of what I knew, for the thick walls of the Westminster Sanctuary have their chinks, and all the while I went about my own business of the Queen's Household. Family business; the business of the kingdom.

As the blue dusk began to creep into the sky we took oars from Westminster to London. I thought of Greenwich or Eltham, not so far downriver but a world away: all sunshine and sweet airs like some enchantment hovering beyond my reach. But it was safety we needed, not enchantment, and that was best found in the grey towers of Edward's mother's house, Bayard's Castle, in the heart of the city. Behind me I heard Bess whimpering, weary and fretful with the long day. 'There, Mistress Bess, nearly there now,' said her nurse. 'There's Whitefriars and Blackfriars and Watergate and Paul's Wharf. Can you say that? Whitefriars, Blackfriars, Watergate, Paul's Wharf . . . And, look, there's Paul's itself! See the great steeple?' It was a lee tide: the oarsmen struggled against the oncoming waters and the wind and overshot by design so as to drift back to the landing-place at the foot of the castle walls.

After supper we heard Mass in the chapel, as private a *Te Deum* and prayer for future aid as the Mass and crown-wearing at Paul's that morning had been public. The clamour of the day was suddenly stilled. Edward and I knelt together, so close that his arm touched mine. A different fear crept over me. What would he think of the worry-carved lines about my eyes, my thin flesh slack with the idleness of our days in sanctuary, a tooth drawn, that scald on my arm: so many small, weary hurts to my worn body?

God knew — though Edward's confessor might not — how many women he had found to his taste among those plump Flemish maids in Bruges. And which of the dark-browed husbands of the Burgundian court had he not cuckolded? I was accustomed to put such thoughts away from me, for there was no use in indulging them. At divine service it was even a sin. I prayed for a little forgiveness, and dug my fingers into the scald on my arm, for it was still angry red, and painful enough for a penance. Then I raised my eyes to the rood screen and the nails that held Christ's bloody flesh to the carved and gilded cross of his last agony.

We were to share a bedchamber, so full was his mother's house with nobles and men, and fear of Edward's disgust grew in me as the door closed behind the last of my women, and he and I were alone. A year and a half is a long time in a woman's face — even in mine, that had brought me to a crown — and still more in her body.

He was sitting by the hearth in his shirt and an old fur robe that had proved none the worse for being shut in a chest, staring into the red heart that was all that was left of the fire's kindling. I stood in my smock in the middle of the chamber floor, suddenly afraid beyond all sense.

As if he felt my shiver he looked up. 'Mistress?'

'I—' But if I admitted my fear to him, would he see that which until now he had not seen?

He rose. 'Must you learn me again? You have not changed, not by a hair, I think. And I think I have not forgotten you.'

He had not, it was true. And I found I had not forgotten how to please him in our time apart. I knew how to yield my flesh inch by slow inch to his desire, and how to command that he please me, each finger touching where I in turn desired it.

A log slipped on the hearth and flared, and the chamber filled with light. His red-gold limbs tangled with my silver, we swam together, sliding, slipping, before, behind, between. I was Melusina again, Melusina reprieved, not bathing secret and alone but granted her freedom, my freedom, the spell broken, the wheel of Fortune halted, man and woman conjoined and reborn in the golden waters of alchemy.

Part Three

Middle

Sol and *Lune*, is nothing else, but *Red* and *White Earth*, to which Nature has perfectly joined *Argent vive*, pure, subtile, white, and Red, and so of them hath produced *Sol* and *Lune*.

Colson, *Philosophia Maturata*

VII

Antony — Vespers

Ahead, the air is still thick with heat rising from the road, though the sun is lower in the sky, striking yellow diamonds from the waters of the Aire. A cart overladen with hay is swaying across the bridge towards us and my escort draws to one side that it may clear the bridge before we move on. At the mouth of the bridge a chapel stands, half hanging over the water: a chantry, I recall, even as the bell begins to ring. I catch Anderson's eye.

He shakes his head, knowing as a good commander must what his prisoner is thinking even as I think it. I cannot give up so easily. 'Would you deny me the chance to pray for my soul?'

'The day grows late, my lord. You will have time enough for prayer when we reach Pontefract.' But we cannot cross the bridge yet, and behind us the rest of the escort hesitates.

I smile at him. 'No time can be enough for God. Sir

John, we are knights, you and I, men of worship sworn to uphold the Faith and to be merciful to all. I pray you of your knighthood to grant me the last prayer that I may ever make in this life unprisoned.' Still he hesitates. 'I have no thought of escape, only of seeking salvation. I give you my parole.'

At last he nods.

The chapel-door hinges want oil and the air within smells as much of river water as of frankincense. Anderson and three of the men cluster about me; the rest are left outside, their horses and ours that they hold dozing in the sun.

Four priests and four boys. '*Aperi, Domine, os meum ad benedicendum nomen sanctum tuum . . .*' they chant.

Open my mouth, Lord, to bless Thy holy name.

One boy looks round at our entry, open-mouthed instead in secular surprise. He is nudged to order by a virtuous fellow, but at the clank of spurs the clerks' heads turn too.

'. . . *munda quoque cor meum ab omnibus vanis . . .*' they chant, the sound wavering with a small fear. Anderson holds up both his hands in sight of the clerks, then crosses himself as I genuflect. '. . . *perversis et alienis cogitationibus.*' Two of the men stay by the door, and the singing steadies.

Cleanse also my heart from all vain, evil and distracting thoughts.

I step forward, alone, feeling my soul catch and hold to these same words, to the shape and spring of them, to the bowing of my knee, my lowered head, the pressing of my palms at my breast.

'*Sancta Maria, Mater Dei, ora pro nobis peccatoribus, nunc et in hora mortis nostrae.*'

Holy Mary, Mother of God, pray for us sinners, now and at the hour of our death.

~

Holy Mary, Mother of God, pray for me, a sinner, now and at the hour of my death.

We pray so fervently to know the hour of our death: all men's greatest fear is to die unshriven, no peace made with man, no mercy begged of God.

But it was not force that we lacked as we went about, away from Lynn to the north, and at last found a landing in Yorkshire, it was favour: this was Neville land, not Edward's own. 'Since my own brother George Clarence has proved a turncoat, what man may not?' Edward would say. 'With Warwick joining hands with Marguerite, it needs only that we fail in winning men over for Lancaster to be victorious.'

Then we slipped past Pontefract on the road south; had Warwick's brother Montague chosen to challenge us, we would have been lost. Late one night I sat alone by the fire in the cottage we had commandeered near Wakefield until Louis came in from the town. He was a good height for a Gascon, was Louis, strong and broad with bright black eyes. And yet I know no man who could make himself less visible, tucked into a corner of an alehouse, sipping a single tankard for a couple of hours, saying only a few words and those in the accent of the common sort, and listening to the drink-loosened, careless talk that tells all.

'Montague waits to see which way the wind blows,' he said, dropping the dirty cloak of his disguise on the floor and stretching like a cat. He saw my desire kindled, and smiled, his own kindling in return. 'He will not support his brother if it make him enemies among his neighbours here. If we can win enough men, all should be well.'

And we did win men over, hundreds and then thousands, most especially at Hastings's call. And in winning battles we won yet more men, for coats turned quickly when they saw that Edward of York was again more than a man, more even than a king, more royal, certainly, than poor, simple Henry of Lancaster.

Many have told tales of those days, of the turns that Fortune gave to her wheel. Soon Warwick was dead and his brother Montague too, the greatest of the Nevilles naked and despoiled both on Barnet field. I still feel the wound I suffered that day, but to see Edward holding baby Ned, kissing Elysabeth, kneeling beside her at Mass that night in his mother's house was worth a hundred times the pain. It was but a sword-cut to the thigh: men have suffered much worse and lived. Though even now, a dozen years later, when I have ridden hard it stings as sharp as a penitent's steel cilice.

And now there is scarcely any riding left to me, and little time for penitence.

Marguerite landed from France, and our army met hers at Tewkesbury. Henry's son – Edward of Lancaster, his heir, their son – was killed. He was seventeen. Ought I – ought we all – to have mourned more for him? Would I have felt more sorrow for his mother's grief – caught and caged in the Tower at last, like her husband Henry – if I had known what I have since learnt of a father's love for a son? My daughter Margaret I did love, but only because she was fair and sweet, and the image of her mother, my dearest Gwentlian. I did not watch her grow and change, teach her philosophy, kingship and the love of God, as I did Ned.

Yes, at the time Edward of Lancaster's end seemed nothing but a fortunate, politic death for which we could not but thank God, even as we commended his soul to Him.

Then from the north news came that the Neville affinity was arming again. Edward marched from the West Country to quell it. Still the Nevilles had not done with us. Warwick's bastard nephew of Fauconberg took his uncle's men of Calais, invaded and raised Kent. He marched on London and, finding the bridge guarded, went on to Kingston. There I kept them in parley while my forces mustered at the Tower, and the city men armed themselves and, after due deliberation, put their men under my command as well.

It was early morning, a week or so after St John ad Portam Latinam, I recall. The watch called that the rebel batteries were drawn up along the south bank, from Bankside to Potters Field, and that houses were afire. I ran up to the Lanthorn Tower to see what their gunners might hope to hit. A happy shot might strike the Middle Tower or the tower on the causeway. But by the grace of God, even these Calais-trained gunners would not be so lucky, and the shot would fall in the moat and cause no more harm than a wetting to anyone. But men trained under Warwick will not easily allow luck to go another's way. To the west, houses on London Bridge itself were ablaze; to the east, rebel ships were moored in the river.

Our own guns had been reported in position late last night: all might yet be well. The Constable of the Tower had ordered that the privy garden be used as a storage yard, and Elysabeth was setting her servants to stacking arrow-bundles where until yesterday had been lavender beds and lawns. Only the roses still stood, their thorns and our lack of time to dig preserving them, though now they were dimmed by the soot of the beerhouses that the rebels fired.

'No, stupid! Leave that clear,' Margaret cried, to a couple of lads who made to dump a pile of cressets by the Iron Gate as I ran down the steps from the Lanthorn Tower. 'If the cannon must be withdrawn from the city, we will mount one here to defend the gate.'

'Madam,' I called to Elysabeth, from half-way up the

stair, yet not so harshly as to awaken fear in those not bred to steadiness. 'You must take the prince and his sisters and go into the White Tower.'

'I will be of more use here, brother. There is much still to do. Margaret, fetch Ned to the White Tower, and the girls and their women.'

'Aye, madam,' Margaret called. As I reached the foot of the stair she caught at my hand and squeezed it fiercely. '*À Dieu*, brother.' Then she picked up her skirts and was gone. Elysabeth was counting the bundles of pitch-soaked arrows and the cressets that would be used to light them.

'Madam?'

She stood up and eased her back while she looked at me. She had thinned while we were in exile: so many months trapped inside Westminster Sanctuary showed in the lines about her eyes, and the thinning of the skin over her bones, but any man would still have called her beautiful. She said nothing, but I knew her of old: her silence did not mean consent, but only consideration. Truly, I thought she might dispute with me. Would she, who could command me as her subject in all things, command my obedience in this? Or could I, her brother, head of her house, commander of the King's forces, also command hers?

'Madam – Ysa – I know that you had rather fight. But your best work and your prime duty is to look to the prince, and to preserve your own person.'

A crack of cannon from the far shore startled us both, and another and another. Then our own guns began to answer the rebels, so near that the very ground beneath our feet seemed to shake.

Without another word she put her hand to my shoulder and kissed my cheek. 'Good fortune, brother. *À Dieu*, and we will meet next where God wills.'

I kissed her. For a heartbeat we were still, and in the scent of roses and crushed lavender we might have stood in the walled garden at Grafton. I looked down, and thought that she, too, recalled those days.

'*Mon seigneur!*' It was Louis's voice. I turned. '*Milord le Connétable* would have speech with you. He has word from the Mayor.'

'Tell the Constable I am with him. Sister, I must go. *À Dieu*. Heaven keep you and the children. Farewell.'

'God speed you,' she said quietly, and I hastened away.

Fauconberg's rebels shipped across the river from Kent: we watched them from the walls as they landed on the wharf by St Katharine's and marched up the Minories: well-armed, well-made Calais men, seasoned but not wearied by the last two days' fighting. It needed no panting messenger to cry that the gates on the Essex side of the city were under attack but held yet, for we could see it from the White Tower roof. We armed and mustered, and when all was ready, with Louis at my shoulder, I led the advance. Out by the Lions Gate we marched, over Tower Hill and across East Smithfield, and struck deep into Fauconberg's left flank, even as the Mayor and sheriffs charged out of Aldgate and met them head on.

Tales are told of those days. Prentices in the alehouse compare scars and shake their heads over lost friends. Goodwives tell quarrelling children to hush or the Falcon Bird will get them. Aldermen sit at their wine after a day in the counting-house, and recall how hard they fought – sword to sword, hand to hand – to hold the city, and how their knighthoods were earned not by trade but by valour, in the old, grand fashion. It was true, I saw it: Mayor and sheriffs all, fighting to hold off the looters from their shops and homes, and to keep the King of their choice on the throne, as did we all who held Edward's claim in blood to be the right one. Though for the city men, even that choice was about gold as much as blood: a deposed king cannot repay vast loans or even the interest on them, and Henry of Lancaster would have had no use for their wives, or granted any favours in return.

So they tell their tales over and over: an arming sword that once took Harfleur next did duty in a mercer's hand; a goldsmith's life saved by the saint's kerchief tucked in his brigandine; this arm wounded by a poll-axe and that sallet split in two; sooty handgunners; pipes and drums a-shrieking; valiant baggage-boys; rebels crushed when the Aldgate portcullis was dropped; rebels trapped in the gateway like fish in a barrel; rebels hunted down though it took to Mile End to do it.

No doubt the hippocras tastes sweeter for being drunk to such tales, and the women's eyes grow rounder. But I have come to think that all fighting is the same fighting, and all that the tales contrive is to hide its sameness in a semblance of difference. The names and places change, but what do we know of names and places when the alarum is sounded? On our memories it is orders and cries that are branded; the clangour of steel and braying of trumpets; the stench of sweat and shit and blood; the hot, crazed terror that masquerades as courage; the screams of a man struck in the belly; the clouding gaze of a dying boy. These are not new matters, or even great matters. They are what mortals know and, like all mortal things, they are so tiny before God that I must think Him indifferent to who dies . . . who lives . . . who reigns.

~

When Edward, victorious, entered London, he made Richard of Gloucester Constable of the Tower for he of all men, Edward knew, would not turn his coat from the colours of their great Plantagenet father of York, as their brother George had done.

On the morrow, it was given out that Henry had died of despair at the loss of his cause. His corpse was shown at Paul's, his face uncovered, that the commons would see and know it to be true. If they ran forward with kerchiefs to soak them in his blood for a holy relic, that did less harm to the realm than if the blood had stayed in his living body.

And with that the civil war, as we saw it, was ended. Edward was reconciled to his brother George, and gave him all that he asked. He forgave his marriage to Warwick's daughter Isobel, though he then allowed Richard's marriage to her sister Ann who was widowed when Edward of Lancaster died at Tewkesbury, so that the brothers fought over dead Warwick's vast lands and riches. But that was a small matter. In the business of the kingdom peace might reign at last. Edward was not best pleased that, with the realm secured, I asked permission to go on pilgrimage to Portugal and Compostela, but I had my way with the promise of doing royal business at the same time as God's work against the infidel, and that Louis, travelling in my train, would seek out intelligence that I might not.

Of that journey the chroniclers have recorded the business that was done and the realm safer for it. And our private happiness is recorded in our hearts.

When we reached England again I was made governor to the Prince of Wales, and head of his Council in the Marches. Elysabeth kissed Ned and set him on my saddle-bow, and we rode away to Ludlow, with many in attendance. Richard Grey was among them, for his mother hoped that it would be to his good to attend to his royal half-brother and the troubles of the Welsh Marches, so far away from the London taverns and the stews of Southwark.

I call Ned my boy, though in blood he is but my nephew. When Edward first promised to make me governor to the Prince of Wales I was flattered. Who would not be so? But I was a young man and knew little of the governing of children. I did not know what it may do to even a young man's heart to have a little boy of some three summers sit on his saddlebow and sob for the leaving of his mother and sisters. I did not know that my heart was changed that day, or for some months after, though I did my duty and followed the ordinances set forth by Edward for the education of his son. And then one afternoon I was standing in the outer bailey at Ludlow, looking over some ponies, for I had decreed that it was time the Prince of Wales learnt to ride.

'Sire! Sire!' I turned. Ned had escaped his nurse and was galloping over the cobbles as fast as his fat little legs would go. 'Is froggies! Come and see!'

The best-looking of the ponies was a fine little Welsh gelding. 'Trot him out,' I commanded, and the groom did so, jogging alongside. The gait was good: even, and free in action.

Ned grabbed my hand and tugged at it. 'Sire, come and see!'

'Your Grace must wait,' I said. Was there a slight halt on the offside hind? 'Canter!' I ordered the groom. No fault to be found there. 'And take him round on the other leg.' The groom pulled it round to circle the other way.

'No, not horse! Froggies! They'll go!' Ned yelled loud

enough to cause the pony to shy a little, the groom cursing as it trod on his foot. So nervous a mount would not be safe for the Prince, I thought, and yet he must learn to handle such a one in the end.

Ned's nurse came panting up. 'Your pardon, my lord. Come here at once, Your Grace! Can you not see your lord governor is busy? You show me the froggies. Come along, now.'

'No!' said Ned. 'Lord Gov'nor see.' He tugged my hand again, and I looked down. He is fair, is Ned, and was fairer still in his baby days, and his eyes as round and blue as the heavens. 'Lord Gov'nor see froggies,' he said again. 'I want *you*!'

How could I not go? The frogs were not full-grown, their leaps small and without purpose: I caught one in my hands and sent a nursemaid running for a bucket. Until she returned Ned peered into the little gap between my fingers, which was all that I dared open. In the bucket its leaps against the sides were unavailing. 'See how its back legs are long, the better to jump with?' I said to Ned. 'Like the hares we saw across the river.'

'Hares do boxing,' said Ned. 'Froggy do boxing?' He squatted down and poked at the frog, which leapt away and struck the other side of the bucket.

'No, though we might catch another and put them to each other.'

'Lord Gov'nor do it!'

But another frog was not to be caught, at which I was

glad, for I have never cared for such sport. Predator and prey is one thing, and I have hawked and hunted and gone rabbiting with as much pleasure as any other boy or man: it is the way of creation, for all creatures must eat. But to confine two creatures of the same kind close enough that they can do nothing but fight is an amusement of the crudest sort, fit only for men so base in their nature – however high their worldly degree – that they can find no joy but in destruction. My Ned would never be one such, I vowed, and I have kept my word. He has learnt to fence and dance and hunt, and though he got into mischief, as did the other children of the household, and was whipped for it, he loved his book, too.

Some days, if his tutor was absent on council business I would enter his chambers unannounced rather than send for him, the better to know how well he studied, and whether his lessons were suited to his tastes as well as to the needs of the kingdom. He and the chaplain and the two boys that studied with him would scramble to their feet and bow, and I would take up the slates and read what they had written. Ned's Latin verses were the best, and his understanding of science, his rhetoric too: it was not my love that made them seem so, but his desert. He has all Edward's cleverness, and Elysabeth's, but willingly directs his mind to philosophy and reason, while his faith is true and strong. Sometimes I watched him kneeling before the Host at Mass and my heart sang to see my boy lost so well in the love of God.

~

But not all the business of the kingdom may be so cleanly and wholeheartedly done. I have killed many men, Christian and heathen both. I have spitted Moors on my sword for the greater glory of God. I have studied where armour may be pierced, I have strengthened my arms the better to wield an axe, I have ordered men hanged for stealing a hind, or murdering a child. And then there was the great joust with Burgundy. Once, when we lay together, I asked Louis if it was he who conceived that . . . plan. He laughed and shook his head, but did not deny it.

Henry of Lancaster I did not kill. We all knew his death was necessary, though he was a king anointed by God. There could be no peace in the kingdom else. But none knew what was toward that night but Richard and Edward. Not the hour, or how the deed was done.

And yet, when my thigh wound aches like a red-hot wire in my flesh, as it does now, it is Henry's death for which I do penance, and for which I pray forgiveness.

Henry's death, and Ned's life.

Since that night I have known that it is not so hard to kill a prisoner, not even one of your own blood. Not even a king. It is not hard when you have all the keys at your belt, and at your command the watch will close their eyes, and the woman that scrubs the stone floors afterwards is deaf and mute from birth.

The bridge climbs steeply before us, the heat trapped between the parapets and rising thickly to the summit. I cannot see the far side: we ride into a translucent fire.

Una – Friday

As we pass signs to Greenland Dock and Rope Street, Mark starts talking about the first evening class he took in building maintenance, which led to diplomas in joinery and electrical engineering; a bit of teaching evening classes himself; friendships with other tutors, and the growing feeling that the real use for it all – the biggest difference he could make – was abroad. 'Not that there weren't slums enough to clear in England,' he's saying, and I know he's thinking of his father's yard. 'At least, that's how everyone saw it then: sweep it away and start again. But in Africa . . . it makes so much *more* difference. And I wanted to work outdoors.'

Rotherhithe Tunnel closed overnight for replacement of original tiling, says a series of notices, and we have to backtrack along Jamaica Road to cross the river by Tower Bridge. A gaggle of tourists reel across our path from the bars of St Katharine's Dock and take pictures of each other against the view of the Tower. The one-way system's organised by traffic-lights and signs that garland the dark, office-block canyons of the Minories, then swirl us round and down East Smithfield.

The thought of the unconvincingly clean and carefully

rusticated Victorian stone solidity of the Tower makes me ask Mark suddenly, 'Do *you* think restoring the Chantry would be a lie?'

He shakes his head. 'No. It's . . . Well, you have to tell the truth where you know it. And with the Chantry we – you – know a lot. Everything, even.'

Or nothing, I think. 'But what if you don't know the truth? I mean, if there's something I don't know about Elizabeth and Anthony. About when she saw her son Edward? About how, exactly, Anthony looked after him? And there's a lot we don't know – swathes of court and government records were destroyed in Tudor times, quite apart from the houses and monasteries and so on. I mean, I'm going to have to say all the time, "We don't know." Or "perhaps", or sometimes "It seems likely that", though then you have to go carefully, if you're not to get your colleagues laying into you in reviews. But with restoring a house you actually have to make it happen. You've got to have something to open the doors, after all. What do you do if you don't know what the handles were like?'

'You make your best guess, from what you know. From similar-date places, letters, whatever.'

'Left here . . . Okay, make it not door handles. Make it pictures, or which bedrooms who slept in, or what books would be on the shelves. It must have been a certain way, but you don't know what. Do you just leave everything bare and empty?'

He smiles. 'No. Not if you can help it. If you're just showing off the architecture it's okay. But not if you're trying to re-create a whole world. Because that would be a different kind of lie: that everything was bare. You have to make the story whole. Right here?'

'Yes, and it's there on the left.' The house is dark, the windows empty. 'Thank you so much for the lift. Have you got time for a quick drink?'

He nods, and draws up at the kerb. 'That would be good. Thank you. How's the sale going?'

'It's on the market. They're going to drop the details in for me to approve tomorrow.' I unlock the door into the chill of the house and go to switch off the alarm. 'I've realised I've actually got the weekend free. I thought I might go and do some libraries. Only preliminary stuff, but still. Do go through to the drawing room. Don't worry, there are still things to sit on, though I've organised getting rid of it all. But not till after I've gone.'

When I reach the drawing room he's standing with his back to the river. 'Is it – is it all right?' he says abruptly. 'Selling? Getting rid of everything?'

I'm suddenly enormously tired, my joints aching and the fog closing in. I have to sit down. 'Yes. It's . . . Yes, it's all right.'

'Do you want the fire?' he says, and I nod. He works out the controls for the gas without asking, casts a look at me, and then again, without asking, goes to find drinks. Only when he's put one in my hand does he say, 'You would tell me if there was anything I could do, wouldn't you?'

'Yes. Thank you. But there isn't, not really. Except about the Chantry.' I put a hand out to where he sits at the other end of the sofa. 'Mark, *do* you think it's possible? Or is it just wishful thinking, because none of us really wants to see it go? I mean, if it isn't possible, is it fair to raise Gareth's hopes?'

'I don't know. But it's not . . . it's not *stupid*. It's worth a try. Hard to know, more than that.' There's something so solid about his uncertainty, I think suddenly, if that doesn't sound odd. It's honest: an uncertainty you can rely on. It isn't odd because it's true to Mark, to what he always was.

The tremor seizes me again, hotter, more threatening, and to hide it I drink half my glass of wine. With the alcohol comes sudden clarity, like searchlights in the fog. It's about Mark at the Chantry and Mark here. It's not old, not then, it's now. I want to tell him he should run the Chantry. If he wants to. But I daren't, not after what Izzy said. Besides, what if he says no?

Suddenly I need him to say yes so much that it hurts. Need him to say he will, for Gareth, and for – for me?

No. I can't be thinking that. I won't think it. Some trick of jet-lag, or grief, or the English air of my past. I won't think it. Of course I want to show him that he ought to be at the Chantry, that he's welcome – no, more than that: that he's *necessary*. I need to make him think there's something there for him. But I won't say that, it's too close to the bone.

I drink more, and say instead, because I do actually want to know, 'What would you do, if you were restoring it? How would you do it? About the things you don't know or you can't have, because of fire regulations or whatever?'

'Best guess is all we can do. It's not the same as someone else's guess, though. Sometimes you undo past restorations and it's hard to believe what they did. Looks all wrong to us. Dare say our best guess will look just as wrong in a century or two. It's like how language changes. All the difference in the world between how Shakespeare talked, and how we do. Even when we're talking about the same things.'

'And how Walter Scott makes his Shakespeare-date people talk is different again, being half-way between then and now . . .'

'Visible at two feet, and invisible at four,' Mark's friend Charlie said. Something shifts inside me, like the pixels on a computer display, the fog lifting again so I'm seeing blocks of colour and shape: deep, bright medieval gold and scarlet and lapis-lazuli, settling into a pattern that makes sense. An astonishing sense, but still . . .

'Mark?' He's been watching the fire, sitting back against the sofa cushions, but at the sound of my voice he turns his head. 'Mark . . . I'm – I've got a couple of days, I think I said. I want to see some of Elizabeth and Anthony's places. Sheriff Hutton and Pontefract. There's not much to see at Grafton, I gather, though the church is still there. Astley, maybe . . .' I'm wittering. Concentrate, Una. 'And then there's Fergus. It's horrible, but I can't help wondering if Izzy might try to get him to . . . to see it her way. She's so angry. Maybe we should try to persuade him . . . And I don't want to do the drive on my own.'

He grins, 'Are you afraid of the ghosts?' and as if it's my own body I see his twinge of horror as he realises what he's said. 'I'm . . . so sorry.'

'No, of course not . . . Oh, Mark, don't worry. I'm used to it, really I am. This afternoon –' I'm smiling, a painful sort of smile but still '– the other afternoon wasn't how it always is, I promise. It's been two years after all. I was just a bit shaken, No, this weekend, it's only the driving. And you could persuade him so much better than I can, explain it all. Would you come with me? Share the driving? See Fergus?'

He says fiercely, 'You don't have to, you know.'

I flinch. 'Don't have to what?' It occurs to me that we're both a little bit drunk.

'Don't have to try to make it better. Join me in. I'm not family. I never was family. But it was all right, wasn't it? They didn't have to tell me to keep my hands off Izzy, or sack me, or cut my balls off. They – you – you just had to pay me.'

'Was that how it felt?' I ask, trying not to hear what he's said about Izzy.

'Oh, yes. Always. Why do you think I did so much round the house? I wasn't paid for that. But in the end . . . Haven't Lionel and Izzy made it clear enough?'

'But not Gareth.'

'No . . . not Gareth.' He gets up. 'Where's your toilet?'

I tell him, and he goes out. Winded, I lean shakily back in the corner of the sofa, and try to sort out Mark's anger into something that makes sense.

If he was so angry then, I'd no idea. Perhaps it would have helped if I'd known. Or perhaps not: I can't imagine knowing how to deal with it at nineteen.

But he never said. Just tapped on my open bedroom door when I was kneeling on the floor, packing my suitcase to go back to university after the Christmas holidays.

He had to clear his throat before he spoke, though. 'Just thought . . .' He closed the door behind him. 'Just wanted to tell you that I've got a job.'

'A job?' Something began to sting in my hands. 'You mean, not here?'

'Yeah, in Preston. Handyman for a big engineering factory that was blitzed. They're rebuilding, all landscaped and everything.'

I couldn't seem to make my voice work properly, and when he finished his speech he just stood there. I tried to say, 'I see,' but what came out was 'Why?'

'Time to move on. Stand on my own two feet.'

'But . . . But you belong here.'

He shook his head. 'No. I'm not family. Your uncle . . . your aunt's been very kind . . . and all of you. I'm very grateful.'

I stood up. 'Has — has something gone wrong? What's happened? Have you had a row with someone? Lionel? Someone in the workshop?'

'No. Nothing like that. Just, well, like I said. Time to move on.'

'But we *need* you.' I wasn't going to cry, I wasn't, but my throat hurt and I couldn't keep the roughness out of my voice.

'No, you don't. Your uncle'll find others.'

'But it's not like — it's . . . *Handyman?* It's not a career. Not like here! It's — just mowing lawns and things. *Why?*'

'You don't get it, do you? The likes of me don't have careers. We have jobs. And when one job ends, we get another.'

'But — but you're a printer. Uncle Gareth — you're his deputy. You, not anyone else.'

'I'm sorry,' said Mark. 'I'm so sorry.'

He means it, I thought, and my heart began to hammer. He's going, and I can't bear it. It mustn't happen. Think, now, Una. Think what could have done this, because then you can try to change his mind. Think quickly, because once he walks out of that door he's gone for ever. Think! What's changed that means he doesn't want to stay?

Fighting to keep my voice steady I said, 'But what

about the Press? We *do* need you. Uncle Gareth needs you. It must be nicer living here than in some horrible digs in *Preston*, of all places.' He blinked and I thought I'd touched a nerve. 'How can you go? You don't even want to. And you don't care what happens to us . . .' A horrible thought gripped me in the guts. 'Or is it Izzy? Is it because Izzy and Paul won't be living here? It is, isn't it? She's gone and you don't care about anyone else.' I'd have been shouting if I hadn't been whispering because all I could manage was not to let the tears come out. 'But she doesn't care about you. She never has and she never will. You can't have her. But what about . . . What about the rest of us? What about—'

I didn't say it. I managed not to, but it took all my strength, and I'd none left to stay standing or keep the pain in my guts pressed down. My legs gave way and I sat down on the bed and cried and cried, and I never knew if he'd guessed what I didn't say, because he just gripped my shoulder for a moment, then went out and closed the door gently behind him.

He wasn't there when I did the rounds of my own goodbyes the next day. Uncle Gareth offered me a lift to the station in the van. He said it was on his way to the binder's, though I knew it wasn't, not really.

'I wish Mark wasn't going,' I managed to say quite calmly.

'So do I,' he said. 'But he . . . he wants to make his own way in the world. That's as . . . as it should be.'

'I suppose so,' I said. Uncle Gareth, of all of us, must know why Mark was really going, but I didn't dare ask him for fear of giving myself away. 'Will . . . will you say goodbye to him for me?'

'Of course,' he said, as he pulled up in front of the station and tugged on the handbrake. Then we got out and he lifted my suitcases from the back seat for me. 'Well, Una my dear, have a good term and we'll see you at Easter.'

'I will,' I said, and gave him a hug.

He held on to me. 'Mark will be all right,' he said quietly in my ear, but very firmly. 'He's a good man. You'll see. And maybe . . . he'll be back, some day.'

And then the up train was signalled and I had to hurry. Usually Uncle Gareth would have got a platform ticket and helped me on to the train with my bags, and stayed to wave me off. But when I turned round from the ticket-office window he'd gone.

Now I know why he went, and what – perhaps – he didn't want me to see. But I still don't know why Mark left. He never gave me a reason: a solid, human need or want or fear, something I could hold and understand, argue with or soothe away. And that's what screamed and cried at me in the night, twisting and turning in my narrow bed in my college room. *Why? Does he love Izzy so much? Does he hate us so much? Does he hate me? What did we do? What did we not do? Why did he go?*

And when I wrote and told him that Grandpapa had

died, and Uncle Gareth was struggling, that the Press might not be able to keep going, that only he could save it, I got no answer.

Mark's come back from the loo and sees me reaching for the wine bottle.

'No more for me. Shouldn't be driving, really. Must go.' But he sits down on the sofa again, his long legs covering half of the hearth-rug, as Adam's used to, and his face gilded by the firelight, and my belly's suddenly gripped with longing for him to stay, for a deeper voice to disturb the thick fog of silence of my empty house, for a male body warm and breathing in my bed.

I lean forward and fill his glass. 'I can always call a cab to take you home. If ... if you *could* come with me tomorrow, I could pick you up. Or something. But ... I've been thinking. I do ... I really do think I ought to go and see Fergus. It's not the same on the phone. And you *would* explain it so much better – the Chantry and so on. You know you would. You can talk concretely about what the plans are. *You* know what needs doing. The whole thing—'

'Don't tell me – the Chantry project needs me again. How lucky I turned up.'

'No!' I say, and new understanding bursts like a firework in my head so that I grab his hand and go on before he can interrupt again. 'It's not that. You *are* the Chantry – the Solmani Press – everything. Don't you see? You're the keystone, the one thing that makes it work. Without you, it's not *going* to work. The Press will die, and the Chantry will get turned into smart flats for suburban yuppies, and Gareth will shrivel away to nothing in sheltered housing somewhere. You're the only one who can keep it alive. Come with me and persuade Fergus. Before Izzy gets to him. Please?'

He's silent, and then he slides his hand out from under mine. Is he still too angry? Should I not have mentioned Izzy? Is he going to refuse? Have I ruined everything?

'Well . . .' he says at last, and a smile breaks over his face. 'I'll do you a swap. I'll come to Sheriff Hutton and Pontefract and talk to Fergus, if we can go to Leeds as well, so I can see Morgan. I haven't seen her for ages.' He sits up so he's further away from me, but he's holding out his glass. 'Give us a bit more and then I must go home.'

Elysabeth — the 16th yr of the reign of King Edward the Fourth

True to his word, Antony wrote from Ludlow every week, that I might know always of Ned's growing and learning. He told tales of what Ned ate and drank, what he said and sang, how he learnt to pray and fight and dance, and these did ease the ache in my arms for the absence of my boy. As Edward had promised, it eased my sorrow, too, that to have a Plantagenet Prince of Wales living in the western Marches — and him and his council governed by so great a man as Antony, Earl Rivers — did as much for the security of the realm as half a thousand men-at-arms.

His Grace the Prince is already able to spell out the tale of Jason and the Golden Fleece, and I have promised him that when we next travel to London he may see the workshop where his book was made. For to one of his tender years, a press will command his interest better than a clerk bent over a scriptorium desk, however much gold and lapis the latter may lavish on the page. Even this very morning, the prince's great love of the tale led him to defy his tutor, for Master Gwilym tells me that he stamped his foot when told it was time for practice at the quintain, and demanded that he be let finish the tale, for he had not yet come to the dragon's teeth . . .

I had read this far when Margaret entered. 'Madam, if we are to reach the Archbishop's mint at the hour appointed by the King, we must make haste. And it is cold outside, you'll need your furs.' I tucked the letter into my gown, and rose. Great things for the betterment of the realm were promised through the mysteries of science, and since such things must be paid for, I had resolved to see for myself what might be done.

When I reached the mint, Edward was already there, and Archbishop Neville was as full of hospitality and self-importance as his brother Warwick had been, although with an ecclesiastical tinge of humility before God if before no other. The workshop was warm: I loosened my furs, and gave my hand to the man who knelt already before Edward. He was some years older than any of us, and his head was properly bowed, but his eyes, I saw, looked sideways to where a vessel filled with water steamed above a little brazier of charcoal.

'Your Grace,' George Neville was saying, 'this man has studied alchemical science with the great Ripley himself, and at Peterhouse, and learnt what Ripley will not let be written down. We have every hope – God willing – that this will prove what we have so long searched for.'

'Ah, Master Wintersett, good day to you,' said Edward, waving him towards the workbench. There were jars labelled *argent vive* and *lupus metallorum*, vials of liquids blue and gold and deep brown, and glass vessels with beaks and spouts, more like creatures than a dish or a bottle. 'Tell us more of what you will do. I think I met your brother once – or your cousin, perhaps. Does he not have lands adjoining mine in the West Riding?'

'Aye, Your Grace,' was all Master Wintersett said, heaving himself to his feet. 'Now, to the matter in hand. I would – that is, Your Grace, though I have all the resources of my lord archbishop's mint,' George Neville smiled like an innkeeper, 'if you permit, I think that one of your old nobles, and from your own hand, will provide the best matter for transmutation yet.'

'So you alchemists don't care for my new angel coins?' Edward said, snapping his fingers for a page. The lad was one of my son Thomas's bastards, I recall, that had been named Grey for his grandfather, and he came forward, struggling with the strings of a purse, his frown so like my brother John's – dead at the hands of the Nevilles – that I felt winded.

Edward took the purse from him, and brought out a handful of nobles.

I remember the weight of an old noble in my hand, can still feel it in my palm, heavy with gold, as I can still feel the weight of my babies in my arms, and Edward's body pressing into mine.

'As to that, we all know what stability and good fortune the recoinage brought,' George Neville said hastily to Edward, but with a bow to me, 'even as the same year brought Her Grace the Queen to her throne. May I ask if my lord Hastings is to join us?'

I looked sharply at him, but he was all deferential smiles.

'We performed our own alchemy, did we not?' said Edward. 'More golden angels were made than nobles had been melted down.'

'Indeed!' said Neville.

Wintersett shook his head. 'True alchemy is more than melting gold. Even as the sinful human spirit is refined in holy fire,' he glanced at George Neville, who nodded as one wise man to another, 'so we alchemists refine base matter that it, too, may become the purest gold. And the touch of an anointed king . . .' He took the noble from Edward with a bow, and set it in a great stone mortar. 'Now, the first stage . . .'

From a flask he poured mercury – slippery, bright and dark – then from another vinegar, with a whiff of the kitchen, and finally salt in white crystals so clean they seemed to glow in the lamplight. He bent over the mortar and began to work the mixture.

He spoke quickly and in a low tone, as if he were more accustomed to talk to an apprentice, or another alchemist, than to a king and his court. 'This is the *nigredo* – the base matter. Ripley boiled this for a day and a night before straining it in linen, but I have found that if I use regulus of antimony, and a little arsenic, the precipitate is almost . . .' When it was ground to a slurry he poured it into a glass and set it in the little bath of boiling water. I needed to know of this work, but I had never troubled to learn enough of the simple matters, and now could not understand that of which he spoke. Margaret was rapt, following every word, even taking out her tablets to write down the substances that they spoke of: *albedo* and *rubedo*, the *opus circulatorium*, the *solve et coagula*. Edward, too, seemed to know more of these matters than I had thought. Of course, Antony had said alchemy was much discussed at Bruges and studied at the University of Leuven.

'No, no, Your Grace, the peacock displaying is the sign that the design is *nearly* accomplished,' Wintersett was saying. 'Has not your royal self been shown on the history rolls as the Feathered King, triumphant? The *dragon* is as mercury: great power for good, and just as great for ill.' The air was thickening with the fumes of ground gold and arsenic. 'It must be poured quickly, and the vessel shaken with the other hand . . .'. The room was tilting about me. I stiffened my back, and bit my tongue as I did when sickness threatened during an audience. It took all my power to stay standing, to keep my face and hands in some semblance of attention. When at last the mixture was set aside to cool, before the secret, final stage that even a king may not see, I knew not if new gold had been made, or only dross.

We had need of the gold. Edward's great invasion of France to reclaim the lands King Harry won would cost the kingdom more than it could spare, and the royal exchequer too. He returned with no blood shed, a match with the Dauphin for Bess when she was of an age to marry, and a pension for himself, but no blood meant no glory like that of the fifth Henry. Neither Parliament nor the great merchants would willingly pay yet more in taxes after that.

And not all the new gold that the alchemists promised us seemed likely to satisfy George of Clarence, or the old gold snatched from Warwick's widow, or the blood of my father and brother, or even Jason's fleece itself. Nothing but the gold of his brother's crown would do. At last even Edward's power of forgiveness was worn to shreds.

Richard of Gloucester was in the north, ruling in Edward's name. But George of Clarence was no anointed king. There was no need this time for the Tower keys to be put into such very safe hands, or the watch commanded to close its eyes. When Parliament was called in the new year His Grace George, Duke of Clarence, was arraigned on a charge of treason, tried by his peers and condemned.

But Edward would not sign the death warrant. I thought of his next brother Edmund that he had loved so well. I thought of my sons: Thomas and Richard Grey, grown men famous in the lists, Ned far away with Antony and learning to be a king, little Dickon still clinging to my skirts, and baby George, safe with God. All brothers to one another, these my boys: flesh of my flesh, brothers of the whole and the half-blood. I knew the warrant must be signed, and yet knew that Edward could no more set his hand to the deed than I could have plucked baby George from my breast and dashed his brains out.

I was not there when Dame Cecily Neville came from Baynard's Castle, and knelt before Edward, her first-born son, to plead for her third son's life. But she of all women had made Edward what he was. All that she won was his word that George of Clarence might be put to death privily, and in the manner of his own choosing.

I could not help but think of myself in her place. Lord God! I prayed. Defend my sons from such enmities, and me from choosing between them, from having to take sides. I comforted myself that my own son Richard Grey had no desire for the weight of duty and power that came to his brother Thomas along with his marquessate. Neither had he the capacity to discharge them well, and Edward knew it: he never gave but where he got good service in return. Richard Grey whored and drank and, though it grieved me to hear of it, he had grown up at court and learnt its ways, and I could spare little time from the business of the household to change them. But what of my little boys? What of Dickon? Would he grow up to hate his brother Ned, the king-to-be, as George of Clarence did Edward? To demand yet more riches and power, though he had not earned them? To turn at last to treason? Dickon did visit his brother at Ludlow, and Ned came to London: when Edward went to France he was here for many months as Keeper of the Realm. But my younger boys could not share their boyhood as Thomas and Richard Grey had done at Astley, or Edward and Edmund once did, growing up at Ludlow. Not only more years but also the training of a king stood between them.

I had last seen Ned at Ludlow, some months since. I did not take Dickon with me as I had planned, for he was sick, but I was sorry for it. Ned knelt to me and I raised him, and found him well grown for his eight years, his hair still pale gold and his face a little leaner and more tanned from his knightly exercises in these long, warm days. He was proud to show me his skill at the quintain and when I asked how his studies went, even prouder of his translation of Horace. At my bidding he read a few sentences, and if he stumbled once or twice, it was only from shyness, not ignorance. Antony smiled: he knew the reason for my forbearance.

For four days we sat in meetings of the Prince's Council, heard petitions, and gave banquets to reward those men that had earned them and some who had not. When I saw Ned sitting at the head of the council table, my heart turned over. He listened carefully as we discussed the granting of market charters, a report from Ireland, two parishes that would not mend their bridges, and a commission of *oyer et terminer*. An innocent man had been killed by those hunting a band of outlaws that were said to have done murder, and there was some talk of this death being not an honest error but part of a feud that stretched back to the days of Glyn Dwr. Such matters feed unrest and must be ended. When a widow knelt and petitioned for aid in getting her only cow back from her son-in-law, Ned heard her out not with his father's jests and kindly words but with the grave courtesy of Antony's training. When she had stumbled to the end of her tale he raised her and thanked her. 'Mistress Griffith, you shall have justice,' he said carefully. 'The secretary of my council will see to it. Go now with him and you have my word that all will be well.'

On the fifth day Antony decreed a holiday.

The austringer and cadger were mounted as well as the men-at-arms and the rest, for we were to make a day of it and dine on the ground wherever we found ourselves at noon. 'Such a lack of ceremony will do you no disworship,' said Antony. 'And it is good to show Ned that even his royal mother has no need of it.' We rode out from the castle gate and round by Dinham to cross the river. As we left the lee of the castle walls and began to pick our way down the hill the breeze caught us and two of the hawks bated and cried. 'Do you remember my Juno?' Antony asked me.

'I thought you would die for joy of her.'

Ned looked round, 'Who was Juno, sire?'

'A hawk I had when I was a little older than you are now. A goshawk. When you are older and stronger in the arm, you may have one.'

His words recalled to my mind a small commission from Edward. 'Brother, is the country hereabouts open enough for falconry? The King is minded to give Ned a gift of a bird, and would send his own man to the next fair at Valkenswaard to buy it.' We were jogging over the bridge, and our path wound up the cliffs: the tops were thickly wooded. I turned to Ned. 'Son, would it be happiness, or disappointment, to have a falcon that you might not fly within half a day's ride?'

He seemed in want of an answer, and at last said, 'Madam, I am grateful to my royal father for the thought, but I – I care not for the sport as my brothers do.' I stared at him, and as if he read my thoughts he glanced at Antony and said, 'Of course I have learnt what I must know. But . . .'

On another day I would have enquired further, but there was a crack in his voice, and I would not for the world spoil our holiday. I held my peace and, as the path reached the level ground above, spurred my horse into a canter. Ned was eager to follow, and we rode through the woods knee to knee with the rest behind us.

~

That was a happy time, and as the year went on I had more and more often to turn to those memories before I could sleep. Clarence's treason was clear: he had even tried to accuse my mother of witchcraft in procuring my marriage. But still Edward would not sign the warrant.

By Twelfth Night the world seemed made of ice. The greatest logs heaped high and burning day and night could not soften the bitter cold that had settled on us, and the Candlemas processions were a penance indeed. In the second week of Lent the lords, longing for the warmth of good coal fires that might not be lit till they had done Parliament's business, made a petition that the sentence they had passed be executed.

It was late, hours past Compline, and the wind getting up after the hard, still frost of the day. I dismissed my secretary and went to my bedchamber. I was too tired for the usual gossip with my women and ladies, with which we unwound our day and made ready for the night, and though I took up Antony's new work, the *Morale Proverbes of Christyne*, to read while they worked, I could not have told what I read. I stood and let my ladies do as they would, and they heard my silence and held their peace. This way and that they turned me, unlacing, unbuckling, unpinning my hair, unhooking my bodice, untying my points, rolling down my stockings, and all with the due bows and kneelings. When I was bare of all but smock and nightcap they wrapped me in my thickest night gown, mink and velvet with a hood, and still I needed a shawl against the draughts. I sat down and they washed my hands: I had seen the water steaming in its jug not five minutes before, and yet it was all but cold. They cleaned my teeth and took down the hood to comb the crimps out of my hair. Then Margaret began to plait it – over right, over left, over right, over left – hissing a catch softly between her teeth for none but me to hear, like a stable-boy grooming a horse. Her fingers worked their way down my back, and as she reached my waist I stood as I always did, that she might reach the end without grovelling on the cold floor. We did not stint our prayers, though I must hope that Our Saviour forgave the speed at which I said them; perhaps the cold that struck through to our bones was penance enough in return.

When they had warmed the bed, and put me in it, then taken my night gown and drawn the bed hangings I dismissed all of them but Margaret. I lay back on the pillows, with the piled furs and blankets heavy on me, and draughts yet found their way in. Margaret trimmed the lamp that burnt on the mantelpiece all night, got in beside me, and soon by the softening of her body I knew that she slept.

But as so often these days I was too tired to sleep. The aches of the day and my years came and went and came again. Unwelcome thoughts nipped at me like the thin draughts that were as sharp as needles on my face. I curled down beneath the covers but found I could not breathe. I must write to my neighbour at Barnwood Manor, Sir William Stonor, who had been seen hunting on my land. Yet he was a good man and neighbour who must not be angered to the point of forswearing his allegiance. Mal had written that her pension had been late in the paying, so did that mean that others were too? I must find out. The bed was too hot, the air too cold, my body awkward and aching. How long was it since Edward had come to me? Not since New Year? I did not think so, for with Parliament summoned and men of worship come from across the land to sit at Westminster, business pressed in upon both our households, and on the courts and the exchequer too. Truly not since New Year? So many weeks? Perhaps I should not be surprised. I was older than he, and my body too lean these days for beauty and worn with childbearing. Though the songs and tales still called me beautiful, I no longer felt myself so: how, then, could he?

The coldest air yet caught at my breast, and I heard the creak of wood. I sat up, and peered out at the window curtains: they shifted constantly, as if the shutters were not closed. I thought to wake Margaret, but she was snoring and I had not the heart to do it. I slid myself out of bed and down to the floor, my feet striking matting as cold as cathedral stone. One New Year's Day, long ago at Grafton, I had tugged off my glove and put my hand through the ice and into the millpond, for John had wagered Antony that he would not swim across it, and as the oldest I would not be done out of my share of valorous deeds. Tonight the cold struck my skin like those same shards of ice. My night gown hung on a chair across the room, as far away as the window was, for no one would think that I might need to get to it myself. To fetch it would take longer than the cold was worth. I went to the window in nothing but my smock.

Sure enough, the shutters were not latched, and the wind had driven them apart.

Across the courtyard, a light still showed in the King's apartments. That was nothing new. I pushed the shutters to, latched them, and lapped the curtains over each other again. Even if Edward were drinking or whoring, he was doing business too, for Hastings and my sons were companions in all three. It was nothing new. But this night, of all nights . . .

I all but ran back to bed, and climbed in. My icy feet met Margaret's warm ones: I pulled them away, but could not forbear to press as close to her warmth as I could without touching her.

'What is it?' she said, her voice muffled by furs.

'The shutters were not latched.'

'Oh,' she said. Then, like the seals we used to see in the waves off Walsingham, she raised her head and looked at me. 'I could have done that. Are you ill?'

'No.'

'Then what?'

'I am wakeful, nothing more.' Still she looked. 'You know how it is with me, sister. Go back to sleep.'

She shook her head, and touched my cold arm with her warm hand. 'Did you look out of the window? Did you see something?'

'Nothing but . . . There are still lights in the King's apartments.'

'And you are anxious?'

'Sister, it is said that he has signed the warrant tonight.'

She nodded but said nothing, and I knew suddenly that there were no words – no songs, no stories, no sayings – for what had been done. Perhaps not even prayers, perhaps only *Pater noster . . . dimitte nobis debita nostra.*

Our Father . . . Forgive us our trespasses . . . even as we do not forgive those who trespass against us, but rather kill them by Act of Parliament. I could not stop my thought before I thought it. I had to ask pardon for my blasphemy.

Margaret said, 'You could send to him. Ask if he—'

I sat up. 'If he what? If he regrets what he has done? How could he? But if he does . . .'

'Well, just send to him, then. Say that you have him
in your thoughts, that you are his faithful wife, that you
love and honour him as your lord. You need say nothing
more.'

But it was many years since we had sent to each other
with such words. Many a messenger went between us, but
the words they carried were always of business to be done.
Our lives were all business, even to when we would dine,
or whether a child was sick, or what saint's feast fell on
which day of the week. Even to the getting of children
itself.

'If you do not wish to wake one of the men, I can go,'
said my sister.

'Wander around the palace in your smock? That you
will not!'

'I shall have my night gown. Why not? What harm can
it do?'

'Your good name . . .'

'Stuff! Once you had more force of mind than that.'

I sat up again. 'And so I have. Enough to care for your
good name, with my lord Maltravers away. I shall go.'

'*You?*'

'Yes,' I said, pushing back the furs.

'If you do not care to send me, or one of the women,
then send one of the watch at your door. I will write for
you, if you would not have a clerk know what you wish
to say.'

'No.' It was as if the frost tingled in my veins as it used

to at Grafton, calling me out to ride across the fields, cheeks red and nose nipped with cold. I could not bear to sit in my chamber, waiting in the dark for Margaret's return.

I stood up. 'I shall go. I am the Queen, and that is my will. None will question it.'

'But – but what if . . .'

She was right. If Edward were not alone, it would be an insult to me that the whole palace would know of by the morning. 'You may come with me, and ask if His Grace will receive you. I shall be hooded: they will not think that it might be the Queen. And if he receives you, I shall enter too.'

Sleepy guards looked up and saw us pass, Margaret leading the way with a nod to them, and my face hooded. Icy air whistled along the passages and snatched at our night gowns as if we stood on a heath. Through the King's presence chamber, where pages and men-at-arms slept restlessly about the fire, through his great chamber, and his privy chamber, to his bedchamber door. When the guard opened it to bear Margaret's message, the light from within spread across the floor at our feet and seemed to warm it.

Edward was sitting by the fire with a night gown cast over shirt and hose, with Hastings and the page Grey – my oldest grandson, though I only acknowledged him privily – in attendance. I could not see that they had been dicing or singing, or doing anything but drink. They looked round as we entered, then rose. As I curtsied, I put back my hood.

'Madam,' said Hastings, astonished. His bow, though not steady, went full to the prescribed depth.

'Go to bed, William,' said Edward, coming forward to raise me, but dropping my hand as soon as I stood. 'Boy, escort my lady Maltravers to her chamber.'

They went out and he waved to me to sit, but stayed standing. He towered over me, the great bulk of him wrapped in velvet and gold, his eyes small and bright in the flesh of his face.

He said at last, 'What brings you, Ysa?'

'I . . .' I began, but could not go forward. All I could think of was that which I must not speak of, unless he did so first.

'Are you wakeful?'

'No more than any night.'

'So why did you come? In this cold, alone.'

'I was not alone, I had my sister with me. I came because . . .' From somewhere close by came a giggle. The sound was like a blow in the face.

'No, Ysa, that is not what you think.'

'No?'

'No . . . Oh, for God's sake, you know how it is with me! If it *were* a woman of mine, it would still mean nothing, and you know it!'

I pressed down my hurt.

He turned away. 'Besides, it's no woman, it's young

Hatton's catamite. Will you drink Rhenish? Or would you have me call for a different wine?'

'No, no. A little Rhenish, if you please, my lord.'

He filled two cups, and handed one to me. He did not pick up his own, but held out his right hand to me, palm up. 'And do you know what this hand has done?'

'Yes.'

'Say it!'

'It has signed the warrant,' I said.

'Of what?'

'The lawful warrant of execution of the sentence that His Grace the Duke of Clarence be put to death.'

'Of my brother. I have killed my brother.'

'You had no choice.'

'Oh, but I had, Ysa. I could have chosen as I chose before.' He turned away, then drank deep, staring into the fire.

'You chose to trust him and he betrayed you, time and time again.' The Rhenish was beginning to warm my cheeks, but my hands were chill. I held them to the fire. 'Many men – many kings – would not have done so much. You gave him everything he wanted, and still he did as he did. The time had come to finish it. Now it is finished.'

He spoke low, as if to the infernal depths of the fire. 'Perhaps if Edmund had not been killed . . .'

'Perhaps. Who is to say? We cannot know what might have been.'

He raised his head. 'By God, you're like your brother Antony when you speak thus. Are you a philosopher now, Ysa?'

'No, indeed I am not.'

He smiled. 'I think you were born to be a queen.' He poured us both more wine. 'Did you know it when you were a little girl?'

'No. I knew my fate would be as it first appeared: to be the wife of some good knight.' I drank. The Rhenish smelt of flowers. 'And so I was. Though sometimes my father would jest that my mother might indeed have been a queen by her first husband, were it not for—' I stopped, but contrived to hold my face in the likeness of jesting.

He was not deceived. 'Were it not for Henry?'

I was silent.

'So I am twice a murderer?'

'No!' I cried. 'These matters must be ended, by whatever means is best. Finished. Sometimes it is in battle. Sometimes it is . . . otherwise. Great matters – the business of a kingdom, a man's business, and a man's end . . .' I got up from my chair and moved towards him, slowly enough to hold his gaze. 'And you are a man, sire. A man, and more.' I put my hand up to his cheek. It was full and slack these days, cracked with sun and cold, stained with drinking. But it was still gold as well as red that glittered harshly along his jaw, and in his neck and collarbone the muscles were thick under my fingers. I saw his eyes arrested, and rejoiced even as I turned my head so that the candlelight might catch my cheek and the lock of hair that had escaped my cap and fallen on my breast. 'A man, and a king.'

He took my hand from his cheek and kissed the palm. 'In this light you might be Lady Grey again, and I a lad, crazed with desire.'

I pressed closer to him. 'If I were Lady Grey, I would not be here.'

'Would you not?' he said, smiling as he smiled at my maids, my women, my ladies, my brothers' wives.

I mastered my anger. 'You know I would not.'

He gripped me to him and his fingers bit hard into the thin flesh of my waist. 'No, you would not. But you are here, and I want you.'

He was hurting me, but I pressed my mouth to his. He tasted stale, of Rhenish and weariness. Then he pulled away and said, 'You are not frightened to kiss a murderer?'

'You are no murderer, sire, so I will kiss you.' I made to kiss him again, but still he pulled away.

'Ysa, I am sorry. I am but poor company this night. Shall I call a boy to escort you to your apartments?'

I felt near to tears, but they would not help me, or him. I steadied myself. 'Sire, I would not trouble you for the world if you are sad or weary. But I think you ought not to be alone tonight, and if you wish, I can bear you company. There is no need of more.'

After a moment he pulled me into his arms, resting his

chin on the top of my head and letting out a great sigh. 'Yes, I am weary, Ysa, and you too, I think. But with you I can hope to sleep as I have not these many days.'

I took his hand, and with my other snuffed all the candles but one between finger and thumb. 'Then come to bed, husband.'

He let me lead him, meek as a lamb, and when we were in bed put his arms round me as a child hugs a much-loved poppet. I kissed his brow but said nothing, and lay watching the light from the fire painting the chamber dark red.

I thought that perhaps he slept. Then suddenly he spoke into the night. 'They asked his will as to the manner of his death. My brother jested that his will was to be drowned in a butt of good sweet wine.'

The watch called three o'clock.

He pushed himself up on his elbow so that cold air clutched at me. 'It is done.'

'Oh, love.' I raised myself a little to kiss him. 'Then you may sleep at last.'

'Ysa, my brother is dead. I have caused him to be killed. How can I ever sleep again?'

'He was confessed and shriven,' I said. 'He was lawfully condemned. Now he is at rest, more than he ever was in life.'

Edward turned towards me. 'Aye, that he is.' He smiled. 'He is at rest . . . Oh, wife, I love you.'

He bent his head and kissed me, and suddenly it was

as if we were young again, his mouth hungry for me and my body arching with desire.

We knew each other so well. It is not a thing that one forgets, and in remembering each other, we could forget ourselves, and the world. Only the arts of desire were in our minds and our bones and bodies fitted together as well as they had ever done. And our souls too, I thought, in my heat, like two lutenists, twisting their song together and apart and together again. Was that not why he still wished for me on such a night, not the score of others, younger and sweeter, that he might have had?

We were hot amid the velvet and furs of his bed, and the linen clung to the sweat on his broad back. His eyes were glazed with desire, and when he pushed me on to my belly I laughed again.

A hoarse cry sounded without the window. I felt Edward start, every muscle alert and his heart racing. Then frosty air bore in the sound of the guard: tramping boots, sergeants calling, the clattering of arms. For a moment I thought that all would yet be well. And then I knew it would not. His desire was gone.

He pulled himself off me and lay face down.

I reached to touch the back of his neck. 'Love—'

He shook his head as if my fingers were a fly that bothered him hardly at all. 'We should leave one another alone, Ysa. I am no lad, and nor — with no discourtesy — are you a lass, to be tumbling together without a care in the world. We should have done with love. You should go back to your children, and I to my counting-house, and think no more of such things.'

Then he turned his back to me and pulled the covers over his shoulder, as one who will go to sleep.

What comfort could I give him, if my body were not comfort enough? Had I been a fool to think he still desired me, though we were ten years married, and had got eight children together? My body could no longer drive all sorrow and fret away for him, as once it had, leaving only desire. What words could I utter to comfort him instead? His women no doubt babbled flattery while he cuckolded their husbands or took their maidenheads. But I could not shape such falsehoods, for on my lips he would know them for what they were, and they would not reach him in his despair, any more than the pretty piping of a cabin boy will save a great ship from sinking.

I turned away from him and buried myself among the icy linen at the furthest edge of the bed that he might not feel the tremors that forced hot tears up into my throat and spilt them on to the pillow.

'Ysa?'

If I spoke, I would sob till dawn.

'Ysa, do you weep?'

I nodded. I felt the bed sway under me, and then his chest pressed to my back. He put his arms round me, and gathered me in to him. I was wholly held in his warmth, in the depths of his flesh.

He kissed the corner of my jaw, and I felt my tremors stilled by his warmth.

'Sweet, do not weep. We have done great things, you and I. We have made a kingdom rich and peaceful. We have rid ourselves of our enemies. And you –' gently he turned me towards him '– you have borne three fine heirs to the kingdom, and raised daughters almost as beautiful as you that all Europe wants for wives. Where would I be without my queen?'

I smiled, though the tears were still cold in the corners of my eyes. He kissed me on the mouth and I clung to him, so that the kiss went on even to the quickening of my desire, and his. All cleverness, all cozening had drained from me with my tears. He moved to the middle of the bed and drew me with him. For a moment my cheek touched his pillow: it was still wet with his own weeping.

We employed no arts of desire now. We held each other face to face and kissed, and when at last he took me and I him, it seemed that our love was plain and sweet and good.

VIII

Antony — Compline

Ned was three years old when we went to Ludlow. He had Ysa's pale gold hair, and the promise of his father's great height in his long-fingered little hands that gripped the reins above mine as best they might. He is twelve years old now, almost a man. But even in his earliest years none could see him, still less hear him speak so wisely of weighty matters, and not think him the scion of his great father, of the blood of the Mortimers, even as the Rolls show it, even to King Arthur himself and thence to the great Brutus. At least, thus do the scribes and astrologers tell it, and the common people credit them, and look upon their monarch with wonder.

Louis and I could not always be together, for all men of worship must look to their affairs and those of the world. Nor were we inclined to give the world food for its malice by making a public show of what was our private love. After our pilgrimage Louis owed his estates in

Gascony much care and Edward still had a use for him in missions when secrecy was most needed. As for me, even without the care of Ned at Ludlow, and the ruling of the Welsh Marches, I had much to do in England about my own and the King's affairs. And thus it was for some years: we would spend a few weeks together, then many months apart, so that we grew accustomed, and parted as long-standing lovers do, with much sorrow in our hearts, but with little said and that of little things, for the great matters needed no words.

~

When the King's messengers arrived at Ludlow, mud-spattered and weary, it was as if they must tell us that the sun were snuffed out. 'My lord, the King is dead. God save the King!'

For the beat of a heart I would not believe them. But the Council seal on the letters they held out told that they spoke truth.

'May God have mercy on his soul!' I knelt, bared my head, bowed it before God and crossed myself. A scuffle of men and spurs told me that the others followed my lead.

For a moment I held Edward's soul up to God, for if he had indeed a great need of forgiveness, who on this earth had earned it more hardly?

Then I rose and turned to Richard Grey. 'Nephew, where is the Prince? Or, I should say, the King?'

'With his confessor, Uncle. I saw them go out into the herb garden.'

'Let no man speak of this, or go to him, till I have told him the news.'

It was but two days after St Gregory, and the wind that blew in over the Marches from Wales had little of the warmth of spring in it. For a moment I stood in the shadow of Mortimer's Tower and watched Ned where he pranced between the rue and rosemary bushes. He spoke, Sir Peter answered, and they both laughed: Ned's a boy's laugh, light and easy.

This, then, was what nearly thirteen years of Elysabeth's care and ten of mine, of our teaching, of our love, had come to. Such as he was – such a king as he would become – was of God's and our making.

But I hesitated. Although God would not give Ned kingship at his crowning for some weeks yet, when I spoke, my boy would know himself to be Edward, by the grace of God King of England and France and Lord of Ireland, the fifth since the Conquest of that name. And try as I must – for the business of the kingdom waited on it – I could not bring myself to step forward and tell him what he had become. He is tall, it is true, but his body is a boy's, lightly built, malleable, his bones yet fragile and his skin still thin. How heavy is the mantle that his father, in dying too soon, cast upon his son's small shoulders? Ned's hands are still so slender that in the sunlight you might fancy you could see the bones beneath the blue veins that thread through his white skin.

Anger gripped me then, as it grips me now, three months later, with the walls of Pontefract dark above me against the evening sun.

Edward knew well the weight of kingship, and never once regretted it. But Edward was a man, as strong and quick and clever as any in the world, and he chose his destiny for himself. Even so, when he had won it – when he had no enemies left to fight, but only daughters to sell – he let pleasure and profit, not philosophy, rule him. He grew high in flesh and slack, the bright gold of him tarnished. It was as if to govern a peaceful kingdom well – for so he did – was not enough for him. He spent his strength on women's bodies, drowned his quickness in wine, wasted his cleverness in choosing silks and sauces. Why did he not heed the wisdom of the ages and his doctors, and moderate his life? Had he but cared as much for his body's health as for his kingdom's, not given in to his flesh's demand for pleasure, then it need not have fallen out as it has. To say that it is God's will is true enough, but we are in part masters of our fate, for God has given us that mastery. And Edward was more master of his fate than most, for he was subject to no man. How dared he yield to the desires of the flesh, I raged, and leave my boy to bear the weight of a crown that is surely too heavy for a child's neck?

It was a heavy weight indeed. Yet all would be well, I hoped and prayed, for Ned was wise and learned beyond his years. Richard of Gloucester would make as able and shrewd a Protector as a kingdom could hope for. Then there was Elysabeth and her son Thomas Grey, Hastings, and all the men of the Council, holy men and noble men all. Such enmities as they held for one another would not hurt Ned, for which of them did not have the kingdom's good at heart? All would be well, I prayed, and believed.

I stood for one more moment, watching my boy in the last, laughing air of his boyhood.

Then I stepped forward.

Ned and Sir Peter turned and began to stroll towards me.

'Sire,' called Ned, 'have you heard? There's a band of mummers come to the town. May I command that they should come to the castle?'

'Your Grace, I have not yet given you your penance,' said Sir Peter. On another day I would have reproved Ned. But not on this day.

'Your pardon, Sir Peter,' I said. And then to Ned, 'Sire, your father the King is dead. By God's grace, long may you live and reign.'

I knelt before him, and Sir Peter did too.

Ned stood, spellbound.

Then he held out his hand for me to kiss as if it did not belong to him any more, but to some stranger who had come to inhabit his body.

~

Elysabeth wrote publicly of the decision of Edward's executors, of whom she was the chief. Though a full army would be an escort proper to the estate of the new king as he progressed to his capital, she wrote, she was mindful of Hastings's advice: so great a show of force might inflame the embers of Lancastrian hate, most especially since our road from Ludlow to London must pass through Warwickshire and all but under the walls of Warwick's castle at Coventry. So we were to muster but two thousand men: Richard of Gloucester would meet us on the road from York, and join his forces to ours for the entry into London.

Privily, Elysabeth wrote that all seemed to be well, and that she would be joyful indeed to see her Ned. Dickon too, though she had told him that his big brother would have little time for play when he arrived. The exchequer was full, and Edward had done his best to set matters in order as he lay dying: he had commanded Thomas Grey and Hastings to be reconciled for the good of the realm. If Elysabeth knew that one cause of her son's enmity for her husband's closest friend was not only land and rivalry for the favour of the King but also for the favour of Elizabeth Shore, who had once been the most beloved mistress of Edward himself, she did not write of it. Nor did she write a great deal of her own grief, save that she had no hours to spare for her sorrow, through press of the business of the realm. Whether this were true I could not tell from her secretary's neat hand. I knew that she must grieve, for she had come to love Edward beyond the politic love that any queen must declare for her king. But to know truly what lay in her heart, I must wait until I reached London, and we could be private, for she did not readily speak of such matters in the presence of her household. In the meantime, I could only hope that Margaret and our other sisters would comfort her.

It took some weeks to muster the men and make all ready for our progress, for I decided to disband the household rather than bear the cost of maintaining it: we would not be keeping so many men and arms – such royal state – again. To my joy Louis arrived, and paid homage to Ned, who smiled on him, for Louis was just such a bold-seeming knight as a boy will admire. Nonetheless, we had to make safe the Marches we were leaving behind us. Then there was fit lodging for ourselves to be arranged for the road ahead, and billets for the men. Nor could we hope to be in London in time for St George's Day, so we must wait to celebrate it in Ludlow with particular ceremony. But we left on the following day, and were rewarded for the delay with better weather. The road was long, but the sun shone, and we had hawks and dogs with us, so that we were not without amusement when time permitted. I desired to show Ned that all pleasure need not be put aside now that he was king. He knew well how hard his father had worked, but too many of Edward's pleasures had not been ones that I could speak of to a boy of his years.

Two thousand men cannot move fast, still less so when they have the arms and goods of a prince's household to carry with them. We whiled away the miles in talking of the coronation, of his council, of what gifts and dispensations it would be proper to his state to make, and what would most surely secure the realm.

'Your mother will best advise you on these matters. She knows well what can be spared of rents and duties, and who deserves them most.'

'Will my uncle Gloucester not also advise me?'

'Certainly, and you will do as he advises. But until you are crowned he is Protector of the realm, and he will be much taken up with affairs of state. Besides, from his long ruling of the north, he knows less well what is toward with the London merchants, for example, and the contracts to supply the household.'

'I understand,' said Ned, and I thought that he did.

We rode through the steep green hills and red earth of the Welsh Marches and into the more open land round Hereford. The fields were just beginning to haze with green and ewes heavy with wool butted their sturdy lambs away impatiently. I pointed them out. 'There is your private wealth, sire, and England's too. Your father has left you well provided for.'

We came to Stony Stratford on the last day of April, Ned sagging in the saddle with weariness when he thought himself unseen. 'This was your great father's favourite hunting lodge,' I said. 'And it was here that he lodged when he was married to your lady mother.' As we approached we saw a man riding to greet us, bearing Richard of Gloucester's boar badge. Their Graces of Buckingham and Gloucester were arrived in Northampton already, he said, and begged that when I had settled the King and his train into his lodging, and myself in mine at Northampton, I would dine with them.

As many stayed at Stony Stratford as there was lodging, and among them was Louis, for we take care that no man shall know us for lovers beyond that love that any man may have for a true comrade in arms. And it was politic, too, I said to him, as I made ready to ride back to Northampton. I would know what was talked of among the new King's retinue. When all was in order I left Richard Grey to guard Ned, jointly with my cousin Haute, and Vaughan, that loved Ned like his own son and had long been his faithful servant.

I have seen Rome, and Lisbon, and Paris, but when I was a boy Northampton looked to me as grand as I imagined London to be, and the road to it from Grafton an Appian Way of promise. I smiled as we reached my lodging in the high street: one of three inns, all meet for the custom of the nobility and gentry, said the bowing landlord, though his inn, he trusted, was the best appointed. Their Graces were housed in the inns on either side.

That night at Northampton we dined, and drank a little but not too much, and used each other courteously, making plans for the progress of the King and the coronation. I had not long since begged Richard of Gloucester to arbitrate in a dispute with one of my tenants, and we spoke of that and other business of our private estates. He has a quick mind for such matters, and an instinct for what is both fair and politic. At dawn I rose and made ready to go to Ned: we were but a day's ride from London.

But the doors of my lodging were barred from the outside, and the men that held me prisoner were Richard of Gloucester's.

~

They say that each man destroys the thing he loves the most. Through my agency Ned is destroyed, for though he lives, he is alone, and I cannot hope that he will ever be crowned. Day after day and night after night in the chill quiet of Sheriff Hutton I have known that it was my own failure, and no other, that Ned was taken from my guardianship. By comparison with that, my own death is as naught.

And yet, wherein did I fail? Where — at what moment — did I decide wrongly? To this day I do not know. Sometimes I have thought that it would be easier to bear if I could comfort myself that we had fought Richard of Gloucester and been defeated in battle, that Ned was torn from my hold. I did mistrust Buckingham, for he hated all Wydvils, including his wife. But Richard was in command, a prince of the blood royal, and I did not know Richard for an enemy. He was my fellow in faithfulness to the memory of his brother, and in care for our new king. If he cleaved more to Hastings, and took his part in Hastings's enmity for my nephew Thomas Grey and my brothers, it was no more than the usual matter of disputes over land tenure, precedence and women.

I destroyed my boy because I trusted a man I had no reason not to trust: a sworn knight, an honourable ruler, the most faithful brother of our late king.

~

Men pray that they will know the hour of their death. You might say I knew it then, and but for the wild dreams of hope that overcome me in moments of despair, and make my despair worse when they flee again, I have known it ever since.

We were outnumbered and but lightly armed, for the main body of our force was with the new King. When they unbarred the doors, I was arrested in the Protector's name, on a charge of attempting to rule the realm and the King, of plotting the destruction of the blood royal: the Protector himself. I argued my case: I was the King's legal guardian by Edward's own appointment; Gloucester was not yet confirmed Protector; I had done no plotting, but only fulfilled the late King's charge as best I might.

To no avail. I can still feel the hand of the captain

on my shoulder; hear the scrape of my sword as I unsheathed it and gave it up at his request; see Richard of Gloucester's eyes as black as a lake in the dark while he listened courteously to my reasoning.

'The King is safe in His Grace of Buckingham's care,' he said at last, with a shake of his head. He stands very still, does Richard of Gloucester, but when he moves at last, he is quick and sharp. 'He will be taken to London as arranged, with all due ceremony. But I cannot allow any men guilty of plotting against the blood royal to go free, however much *undeserved* favour my late brother granted them. Not even if they are men of the cloth like your brother Lionel.'

I was taken aback. Here, new-minted, was his brother Clarence's envy. Had Richard only been more politic in hiding a bitterness that was yet the same?

I suppressed my scorn for his rancorous words. 'I tell you again, and plainly, and swear it on the most Holy Cross: I have made no plots, nor have my affinity. Such favour as I have been granted is nothing to what the late King most properly gave to those of his own blood. And what I have, I have certainly earned, as has my sister, Her Grace the Queen. Those of our family whose service to the King has been more modest have had no more than modest advancement.'

'And your nephew, the Queen's son? When did he earn the right to enter the Tower and seize the treasure there?'

'Thomas Grey? *If* he has done so, it will be by a

commission of the Council's, of which he is a member. If there is some misunderstanding it may be put right in a moment when I reach London.'

'You will not reach London. Richard Grey, Haute and Vaughan are all arrested. You will be taken to separate custody in the north, that the King and the realm and the blood royal may be safe.'

Then he turned away, and vaulted on to his horse unaided, as he always did, though he was small and ill-made, and took the road to Stony Stratford. My only comfort was that as I mounted, unarmed and set about with many well-armed men, I looked at the sky, the clouds, and towards the west. 'I hope it will not rain,' I said to my captors.

'Aye, my lord,' was all they vouchsafed, but it was as well they were taciturn, for a qualm of hope had seized me. To the west dark clouds were massing, but also, down Alley Yard, I had seen Louis. He made no sign that might have betrayed him or me, and even as I turned my head away that my gaze might not draw others' to him, he vanished.

We were brought north with a politic haste, each of us guarded by a body of men, so that we might not speak or even signal to each other. My cousin Haute and good old Vaughan were to ride straight to Pontefract; Richard felt no need to prison them so deep in his own fiefdom. Our roads parted at Doncaster, for Richard would not chance our being imprisoned together. I was bound for Sheriff

Hutton, but I was permitted to embrace Richard Grey before he set off on the long road to Middleham. Each of us prayed for Ned's safety, and promised to get word to Elysabeth and Thomas Grey if we might. His body pressed to mine, and I felt his hand slip inside my jerkin, inside my very shirt. Then he was led away.

For the last long hours of the ride I did not dare seek what Richard Grey had given me, though I could feel it, tucked inside the linen of my shirt, a tiny penance where it pressed my hair shirt just that more hardly into my flesh.

Sheriff Hutton stands high and lonely in those wide Marches. In the failing light it was dark indeed. When at last the door of my cell was closed and bolted, and I was alone, I undid my jerkin.

Richard Grey had given me Louis's Jason ring. It lay heavily in my hand, and though it could give little hope, it gave much comfort, for I knew even then that I had little time left to me, and that after two score years my life's journey was almost at an end.

Little time, indeed, and all of it needed to prepare my soul for death. Yet I have spent hours and days of my captivity trying to understand Richard of Gloucester; trying to understand how I could have misjudged him so; trying to understand what he will do with Ned. When I heard that Elysabeth had gone into sanctuary at Westminster on that same first day of May, and young Dickon with her, I was glad. If Dickon was safe, then so, too, was Ned, for Richard was shrewd enough to know there was then nothing to be gained by harming him.

Yes, that is how I failed. I should have seen Richard for what he is: the same breeding as his brothers. George of Clarence would have killed his brother and taken his crown could he have done it. Even Edward did not scruple at the last to kill a cousin and anointed king, then his own brother, to keep himself safe. What Richard of Gloucester has done should be no surprise. He will not rest till he has everything in his grasp, and he thinks that we Wydvils are of the same mettle. He must hold land, and ships, and gold, and women, and the person of the King so that we cannot. It is beyond his imagining that Elysabeth and I want nothing but Ned and the kingdom's good, no more than our just deserts for our great labour in the service of the King, and peace among the guardians of the realm.

Now I am brought to Pontefract in my turn. A horse slips and stumbles on the cobbles as we turn into the Castle Garth. Its rider curses, and slashes his whip across its neck. The drawbridge echoes under our hoofs, there is the clang of bolts, and almost silently the gates begin to open. This strange pilgrimage — one hot day's journey, and my whole earthly life — is almost at an end.

Una — Saturday

The car-hire office is a City company round the corner. Adam and I used it so much, rather than keeping a second car, that we ended up having an account with them as if we were a company. We went on using it when we visited from Australia.

'Good morning. I rang earlier. I'd like to hire a small car for the weekend.'

'What's the account number, please?'

I flip the pages of my England Admin notebook and find it. The assistant clacks away on her computer. 'That's in the name of a Dr Adam Marchant?'

'I'm the other driver.' I show my licence. 'Una Pryor.'

More clacking. 'That's fine, Professor Pryor. We have a complimentary upgrade for you this morning,' she says, which I know means they've run out of small cars. A printer squawks, I sign things, and when I say I'd like to pay now rather than put it on the account, as I'm going abroad, she smiles, and waves my card away. 'That's all right, Professor Pryor. Dr Marchant left a credit on the account last time he was here. There's nothing to pay. Enjoy your weekend.'

A small grief prickles in my throat, but the car Adam's already paid for is as solid as a great ship that's just slipped its anchor, the engine a deep hum in the carpeted hush inside, so that soon I'm all right again. I head west through London towards Mark. When I pull up outside his flat in Ealing, and he gets in and closes the passenger door, it seems to embrace him in his turn. I pull away from the kerb.

~

At Grafton there's not much to see: a handful of houses clustered about a Y-fork off the Northampton to Stony Stratford road. There's nothing left of the manor that Elizabeth and Anthony knew, and the church, which they did, is locked, the instructions for getting hold of the key foundering on churchwardens who've gone out for the day. We stand by the porch and wonder what to do. A sign points along a lane and down the hill to Ashton and Hartwell.

'What good names,' I say. 'Hartwell. Ashton. They sound as if they mean something. Where's the map? Is the river that way?'

'Yes,' says Mark, showing me. 'First the canal — that wouldn't have been there — then the river and, look, there's a mill. Fancy a leg-stretch?'

'Yes.' I'm looking at the map. 'I suppose the railway wouldn't have been there either.'

'But it's the lie of the land that dictates them, and the old main road.'

'And the MI, look, over there by Salcey Forest. And that's the east-coast main line heading for the north, I'm sure. All within a couple of miles of each other. The arteries of the kingdom.' The road is an old one, sunk between deep banks. 'I wonder what it was like, the village. Not so different, maybe. Still fields and trees. Smaller fields and the lanes muddier. A pig in each garden. It must be very quiet at night even now.'

'Except for the owls,' says Mark. 'Ever heard a rabbit that's been caught by one?'

'Witches' familiars . . . I suppose there's no reason not to put that sort of thing into the book: what people would have believed. But I can't know what *they* would have believed, Elizabeth and Anthony. They would have been pretty sophisticated. But I don't *know*. You can't *tell*. I can't *say*. Not really.'

He's been looking at me hard, and now he smiles. 'Oh, Una, I know. You never do know. Doesn't mean it isn't worth trying, though.'

We walk as far as the canal, then wander back up the hill. As we reach the car I say, 'Just so I don't put my foot in it with Morgan, why did you and Jean split up?'

'She found someone else,' he says. 'Usual thing. It was bad at the time, but it hadn't been good for a while. We had about ten great years, and then . . . Well, people change, don't they? Mostly it was just recognising it was over. And Mary – Morgan – she got over it. I worried about her when Jean emigrated to Canada. But I think she's okay.'

I nod but don't say anything because he's made the story sound so finished. I start the car. I'm glad he found someone in the end, I realise, though there was a time when it would have hurt almost beyond bearing to know it. But how little I know, really, about his life. He gives so little away.

'So, where next on our pilgrimage?' he says.

Pilgrimage, I think, as the road dips down and away from the Grafton crossroads and towards Northampton. *Pilgrimage*. It was so important. It might be Jerusalem, and the heat and danger were the sacrifice you were making to God. It might be what we'd call a crusade, murdering the infidel or converting them at the point of a sword: your own grace bought with the souls of others. It might be walking with a crowd of goodwives along the cold, salty road to Walsingham. Or Canterbury, full of miraculous stories, the building more vast than any you'd ever known, the gold and ivory and jewels of the shrine beyond imagining, while the great arches seemed to stretch up into the clouds of incense.

But you might have a pilgrimage to a shrine in the next town, the same town where on another day you went to buy a pig and hear the latest news, and you might take no more than a day to do it. If the same journey could be, or not be, a pilgrimage, *how* you went must have been important too. The actual steps, the movement of your body, the songs you sang and the prayers you prayed, the images you held before your eyes.

I must have spoken, because Mark turns his head and raises an eyebrow.

'I was thinking about pilgrimages,' I say. 'About the

travelling being as important as where you were going to.'

'D'you remember what Izzy said about her *Stations of the Cross?*'

'No.'

'In an interview she did for one of the fine-art magazines. She said, "For me, it's about the right image for each moment. But I must remember that for the believers it's just as much about what happens in between." ' He speaks slowly, as if her words have been some kind of talisman for him. 'Una, what happened to Izzy?'

The loss in his voice makes me ache for him, and I don't have to ask what he means: I've asked myself often enough. 'I've never been sure. It wasn't that she wasn't good enough, not when she was in her twenties. And Paul was proud of her then. But he didn't want to live at the Chantry, and you can't blame him, I suppose. And when Fay was born it was hard. They didn't have much money, and she had no one to help, which she would have if they'd been at the Chantry. It was hard for her to get the commissions, and Paul . . . Well, he's not a bad bloke, but I don't think he understood how Izzy needed fuelling. How she needed everyone talking art and printing round her. How she couldn't work in a vacuum, and look after Fay, and drop everything to make sure supper was on the table when he got in from the office. Away from the Chantry and without the work – commissions – she was out of the loop . . . But why that should make her so against the restoration I don't know . . .'

At Astley there's even less to see. The landscape is flatter and less rolling than in Northamptonshire, and less satisfyingly rural too, the fields wedged between light-industrial overspill from Coventry and Birmingham. When Elizabeth was its lady Astley Castle was a fortified manor house, but now there's only a burnt-out, privately owned brick shell of Victorian battlements that we can't reach and can only just see from the churchyard. And this church, too, is locked.

'D'you want to track down the key?'

'No,' I say. 'I'll have to see it some day, but let's not bother now. If we're meeting Morgan at four-ish we ought to get going.'

We head back to the motorway and, with the driving easy, the same questions start to beat in my mind again.

How much did he love Izzy? Could I have made him love me, as I did him? Why did he leave?

How can questions I've asked myself so many times, for so many years, still ring so loudly in my head?

Because ring they did. Yes, I tried to bury myself in libraries and archives, the deep trench-digging of my doctorate work, the academic papers, the meetings and seminars, the conference speeches, the new appointments and departmental committees, but nothing stopped my ears. Then, before long, I found a way that did silence the ringing in my head, for a day, or a night, or a week.

A smile just that little bit longer than good manners across the lecture hall should allow, an eye-meet at a dull drinks party to welcome a new professor, the academic gossip spun out late into the evening in the bar of the conference hotel.

It was fun to think about how I should dress, speak, move and touch, to talk of type-foundries and colophons, watermarks and printers' patrons, and all the time watch a man's hands, the tilt of his head, the way his mouth moved as he spoke, the way his fingers brushed mine as he put more drinks on the table. It was fun that could fill my head and then my body, that bright, dumb spark in a man's eye that made my skin shiver in response. And we were away from home, after all, it was only a week, and the sun was shining on the Venice canals, or the moon was rising from behind the Rockies, or the coal fire in my rooms was so glowing that it shut out the grey cold and the Lancashire rain, and wrapped us in warmth.

But when he'd gone – whichever he was – when we weren't together, new questions rang in my head.

Shall we . . . ? Can you . . . ? Do you . . . ?

My need for answers about the man – whichever man – was newer and sharper, a tinnitus of desire, than the dull bass note of my longing for Mark, and it was a new, sharp struggle to ignore it.

I'd sit and sweat in my office or my rooms, trying not to reach for the telephone, striding from desk to bookshelves and back so that I wouldn't stride out of the room altogether, leave my own work and go and find him at his, or in his favourite pub, or at his home, whatever the risk.

And there always was a risk: risk seemed as necessary to my desire as the man's intelligence or his body. A risk bred of some impediment professional or personal, to put it no more crudely than that. What I told myself I wanted from him – loved in him – was never his to give, at least not freely or publicly. Though I refused to see it like that until Izzy, uncharacteristically brutal, pointed it out. I was crying over the latest, and she had her arm round me. But what she said was, 'I think you look for people where there's something in the way, Una. I think you need it to be like that.'

It was true, though I refused to know it, and if it was safe to weep on anyone's shoulder, I wept for the unfairness of other people's lives.

I met Adam at a party, and talked to him because I couldn't be seen talking to my host, whose wife was there too. And suddenly there was no risk, no impediment, only Adam.

Then I could allow myself to know that Izzy was right, and I'd lost fifteen years to loves that weren't loves, to men with only half a heart to give me, to tears and sometimes guilt and always loneliness because, without letting myself know it, I knew they wouldn't want more than half of me, and that half was all I had to give. The other half was Mark's.

And then I met Adam, and loved him with all my heart.

Fifteen years. I think about lying in bed with Adam
and talking about everything under the sun, my head on
his shoulder or his on mine; or laughing ourselves sick
over some silly cartoon or the latest idiocy of the latest
health minister; or coming half awake as he collapsed
into bed from a call and snuggled up to me as if my
warmth made everything right; or me sitting up late into
the night over a paper for some journal, while he brought
me hot whisky and lemon and asked how it was going.
He'd read where I'd got to while I drank the whisky and
watched the little frown between his eyebrows, and then
he'd ask the one thing that made my argument fall into
place. Before the eyes of my mind the pattern I'd been
struggling with for hours would sort itself out, and the
pleasure of that was the same as my pleasure in the way
his smile went up more at one corner than the other. It
was as if my mind and my heart and my body could at
last feel the same, be the same, live and love in the same
place.

And now Mark, who I thought was long past, is
present. He's here beside me and I've known since he
stood, silhouetted, against the midsummer light in the
Chantry garden, that what I loved in Adam, I first learnt
to love in Mark. So where's Adam now?

I don't know. Mark, sitting across the car from me, his
long legs stretched out and his hands at rest, seems
impossibly, bafflingly substantial. How dare he stand
between me and Adam? How dare he block my access to

that easy love, which I refuse to know can no longer be reciprocal, the love I'm still sending into a void, because not sending it is worse?

I can't bear it. It's unbearable, as remembering Adam so clearly was not, and a hot tear slides quietly from the corner of my eye and falls on to my jacket, a small, clean stain.

'You all right?' says Mark, and I wonder how I could have felt so angry a moment ago when I know so well the weight and gentleness of his voice.

I nod. 'A bit tired. Not too bad.'

'Do you want to stop? Have a rest? Tea?'

'No, it's okay. I'd rather keep driving. It's not much further. Did you say we'd meet Morgan in the market?'

'Yes. She's got a jewellery stall. She said come and find her there.'

We roll on up the motorway, out of the plump, low Midlands towards a bigger and rougher landscape of hills and moors and deep-carved river valleys. There are signs to the junction at Ferrybridge and I think of young Anthony seeing his beaten fellows limping back from there, waiting on Towton moor for the battle that would certainly come and the death that might. It didn't, not for him. And then, half a lifetime later, he rode back over that old life, retracing himself from Sheriff Hutton to Pontefract, knowing that this time he was, certainly, going to die. We know that they told him, and we know the journey need have taken no more than a day, so near midsummer: a long, hot, single day.

But I can't think what he thought as he rode, or feel what he felt. He was a man of – no, not *piety*, that's too smug and narrow a word, and *faith* too weak. He had a belief that's hard for us to feel, perhaps impossible: a structure of absolute certainty that transcended faith, a knowledge as much part of him as his own bones, clothed in words and rituals that had clad him since the chrisom-cloth first wrapped him, since he was borne to church, to be baptised with holy water to bless him, and salt to scare away the Devil.

I'm very tired, and deeply shaken, and it suddenly seems unbearable, too, that I can't know Anthony, that I can't read his books, talk to him, walk beside him, look into his eyes, touch his hand. Perhaps if I try hard enough, perhaps if I imagine completely . . . I try to feel him riding at my shoulder, but he isn't there.

~

Pontefract Market fills the whole of Micklegate with people and goods: pyramids of oranges, freezer packs of chicken thighs, videos and CDs, and cheap T-shirts swinging in the breeze. The far end is filled with crafts and tourist-catchers: old prints, sweaters hand-knitted in colours like muddied jewels, unlikely-sounding jams with gingham tops.

Morgan's sitting down, with a tray of work-in-progress on her lap: silver wire, clasps, beads and miniature pliers. She has dark-golden skin with shimmering purple eye makeup and dark red lipstick, and her long, wiry black hair's tied up with a rubber band and clumped into dreadlocks. There's a vague air of richly jewelled alternativeness about her, but without the mind-body-spirit accessories, except for big silver earrings, one a lightning bolt, the other a broadsword. She's a bit taller than me, looks around twenty-five, and is very pleased indeed to see Mark.

He envelops her in a hug, then holds her away from him to inspect her properly. 'You're looking well.'

'Yeah, not too bad. Yourself?'

'Can't complain. Now, this is Una – Una Pryor. Una, Morgan Fisher.'

'How do you do, Morgan?'

'Hi,' she says. 'I remember Mark talking about you.'

'Goodness!' I say brightly.

A couple approach and start to admire her stock, and it is indeed admirable: on one black-velvet-covered side of the stall lie necklaces of suns, nose studs of moons, and a Melusine in her dragon form. On the white silk side are delicate, dangling earrings of green and blue glass that looks like rainwater, silver stars and enamelled leaves, and another Melusine, this time in her double-tailed sea-serpent guise. There are neat little notices, hand-written in gold and silver ink, about all the earring fittings being sterling silver, and credit cards accepted, and how hallmarking works.

'Looks like you'll be busy for a while,' I say, as the couple pay for a ram's head pendant for him and a lightning-bolt brooch for her, and their place is taken by a round-eyed girl still clutching the consent form for ear-piercing and fingering her own bright pink lobes with awe. She starts to inspect the stars.

'Morgan, would you mind if I went to the castle?' I say. 'Sorry to be unfriendly. But it's important and I've never seen it.'

'Of course I don't mind,' she says simply. 'That's what you came for, isn't it?'

'Mark?'

'Yes, all right. Morgan, love, we won't be long.'

'Take your time,' she says. 'I'm not going anywhere.'

Mark and I walk up Castle Chain in silence and the market has scarcely petered out before we enter the barbican. Above us the castle walls are thick; even in ruins the towers are massive, the entrance broad, the scale formidable. This is a great administrative centre and the big map on a signboard shows it: there are lodgings for a king and others for a queen, as well as for clerks, comptrollers and justices. There are stables and armouries for hundreds of men, counting-houses, bread ovens, wine and ale cellars, magazines for gunpowder and cannon-balls, space for tourneys and jousts, gardens for food and medicine and gardens for pleasure, even a bowling green.

'He must have known what it meant, being brought to Pontefract.'

'Who? What did it mean?'

'Anthony. That he was brought here after all those months hidden away at Sheriff Hutton. You see, Richard III seized power. Well, he wasn't Richard III then, he was Richard, Duke of Gloucester, youngest brother of Edward IV, who'd just died.' I never know how much history people will know: is it more condescending to explain too much, or not to explain enough?

But Mark's just listening as we walk into the chill between the gatehouse towers, and come out into the inner bailey. 'So Richard of Gloucester was uncle to the new boy-king, Edward. Anthony was Elizabeth's brother, so Edward's uncle on the other side, and *he* was his guardian. He was bringing Edward to London to be crowned, and Richard met them at Northampton, and took control of Edward, arrested Anthony and sent him to Sheriff Hutton. Sheriff Hutton was Richard's private castle, if you like. His personal stronghold, miles from anywhere, just the castle and a village to supply it. I haven't been there, but you can see from the maps and the records. And a few weeks later they told him he was going to be executed, and brought him here. But this is quite different.' I wave a hand ahead of us. 'It's an official place, a government castle, if you like. Richard didn't have to hide Anthony away any more. He was secure: he'd got everyone who mattered to support him. He *was* the government. Not young Edward. He was safely put away in the royal apartments in the Tower, and then he was moved to smaller ones . . . Richard III was crowned the day after Anthony died . . . I wonder what Anthony was thinking on that ride from Sheriff Hutton. He must have known what Pontefract meant, mustn't he?'

The inner bailey's vast, ringed by the roots of walls and the stumps of towers, with the keep lowering over it from its motte. More information boards tell of butteries, pantries, chapels, and draw impressions of what was once here. And yet it's all impossibly other, impossibly strange: we're estranged from it. Perhaps it's just as well I'm only writing about their books and their accounts, what the annals say and what the ruins show.

There's bright new gravel on the ground, and we're standing under the stony, vaulted remains of a building labelled as the brewhouse and steward's lodging. 'I want to know what really happened to those people. What it meant to them.'

As I say 'them', our eyes lock, and then he looks away. I'm sure he's thinking not of Elizabeth and Anthony but of the Chantry, as I am. There, the clean earth-damp of the undercroft; the tang of bramble jelly cooling and dripping in the scullery; turps and linseed oil from the studio; warm wood under your bare feet where the sun had been lying on the stairs all morning; shaving soap and Pears in the bathroom; the dry dustiness and the raw wood of the handrail as you run up the attic stairs to call Mark for something . . . A hundred thousand moments – memories – as fleeting, as transparent, as a scrap of gauze tossed to the wind, which nonetheless can take over your body and senses as completely as hate, or fear, or love.

'Shall we walk round the walls?' says Mark, and we do, but still I'm thinking of the Chantry: the rhubarb smell outside the back door; the creaking clucking of the hens; the dance-beat clamour of the press. The sharp, warm smell of Mark's skin as we bent, side by side, over it and watched the latest section of *Gulliver's Travels* appear: the ghost of Aristotle 'stooping much and making use of a staff', then Gulliver and Alexander the Great trying to understand each other's Greek, conjured by ink and iron and wood.

These things fill my mind's eye and my body's memory; by comparison the hard yellow stone under my feet, the municipal gravel, the leisure-clad tourists and warning signs of steep drops and dangerous masonry are nothing.

'Do you want to see any more?' says Mark, as we descend from the walls and stand once more in the outer bailey.

I want to smell and feel Anthony's past, but I can't. 'No, let's not bother. He's not here.'

'What do you mean?'

'Anthony. He isn't here.' Something akin to grief, a wisp of what I've known for Adam, catches me in the throat. 'I can't find him.'

He looks at me. 'Did you think you would?'

'My grandfather's still at the Chantry.'

'But he . . . We knew him there. And the house is still there.'

'But so is this. Sort of.' What does it matter that I can't find Anthony? I turn away, back towards the entrance. 'Oh, well. I'm still glad we came. And the shop will have booklets and things. I'll be interested to see what line they take on Anthony. Up here they're still Richard of Gloucester's supporters. They won't have him responsible for the death of the Princes in the Tower.'

'What? After five hundred years?'

'Oh, yes. And even though I don't agree – I don't think the evidence supports it – we should be grateful. Nothing like a really good controversy to get the historians digging away, amateurs and professionals, finding new records, testing the old assumptions. In fact—'

'Una.' He puts his hand on my arm. My heart starts to thud. He's smiling. 'Sssh. Morgan would say, "Mourning is allowed too, you know." '

'I know it is,' I say, and only then wonder which mourning he means.

~

After we've helped Morgan take down her stall and pack her stock into the boot of the car, it seems natural to go to the pub. It's full of other market people as well as locals and a tourist or two. We squeeze ourselves round a small table; on another day I'd enjoy seeing a proper pub properly full, but today's taken its toll and I'm very tired.

My bones ache. Mark goes to buy the drinks. Morgan looks tired too, and with a better cause.

'Are you working tomorrow? Doing another market?' I ask.

'Not a market. Got ten days off from work, too,' she says. 'I was owed some holiday.'

'So you have another job, as well as the jewellery?'

'I'm a carer. I work in a old people's home. Living in, some of the time.'

'Are you going away?'

'No. I'm saving up to go and see Mum in the summer. I'll probably just chill, build up some stock and see friends and things.'

I could ask if she wants to come with us, I think. Mark would be pleased, surely. And then I wonder whether I would, and why I want her. However nice she is – and I'm beginning to like her a lot – she'd inevitably be in the way.

In the way of what?

'Did you make your earrings?'

'D'you know, I came out in such a hurry I don't know what I put on? I don't wear earrings at work.' She touches the lightning bolt. 'Oh, yes, this is mine. It's called Thor.'

'You give them names?'

'Well, I do for myself. I'd get confused otherwise. When I'm doing a market I have to keep track of what I sell: two Excaliburs, a Sun and Moon, and three Merlin's Globes. Or whatever. Only when it's cold my fingers don't write properly and when I get home I have to guess. But the King Arthur things always go well, them and the dragons. I'm always trying to think of new ones.'

'Have you read *The Once and Future King*?'

'Yeah!' she says, her eyes lighting up. 'My mum gave it me after we went to see *The Sword in the Stone*. I don't think she knew how weird the whole thing is, though. I was only about twelve. And it was sad, in a bitter sort of way. I remember I wasn't expecting that, the bitterness.'

Mark returns with the drinks and sits down next to Morgan. 'How's your mother? And Keith?' he asks her.

'She's all right. He had a heart-attack and they paid for me to go over at Christmas, but he's okay now. The snow was unbelievable.'

'Give her my regards when you're next in touch.'

Is that what marriage or partnership, and its ending, becomes? A polite nothing? Then I remember Adam's call when he heard my key in the lock, my heart contracting each time he walked away through passport control and turned back to smile at the last minute, the smell of the back of his neck or his wrist when we lay curled together in bed.

No, marriage does not always come down to polite formulae. What, then, is it that burns in my belly when I look at Mark? The anger squirms again, only it's not at him, it's at me, at this flare of desire, which blots out Adam and casts our love into darkness.

Desire. I should recognise it for what it is. No

good pretending. Some trick of fatigue or grief or delayed shock or affection. Desire. No less but no more. Definitely no more.

Morgan drinks the top off her pint of lager. 'So what are you up to, Mark? Still working for the National Trust?'

'Took voluntary redundancy. Looking about me. Only . . .' He glances at me, and I nod. 'Just a possibility. Una's family's house might be being restored. I might be helping with that.'

She looks at me. 'Oh, yes, I remember. At the – the Chapel?'

'The Chantry,' says Mark.

'I remember Mark used to talk about all of you. Was it the whole family, all living together?' Morgan asks. She sounds as if she really wants to know.

'Yes. My grandparents, my uncles and my aunt Elaine. My parents were dead, so they were my guardians. And my cousins Izzy – Isode – and Lionel.' Anxiety twinges in me about what, if anything, Izzy might be saying to Fergus. 'And always other people, too, like Mark helping to run the Press, or friends staying, or refugees – lots of those after the war. My Uncle Gareth still runs the Press, but it looked as if he was going to have to sell it. But now, with Mark on board . . . But it's early days.'

'Sounds great, all those people. It was just Mum and me, mostly. Till Mark came along.' She smiles at him, her face and voice unshadowed by anything unsaid but contradictory. Whatever happened then doesn't seem to have left any pain, any twisting internal unhappiness, any store of silent . . . anything. 'What's — what's the name? Isolda?'

'Isode. It's from Thomas Malory, *The Morte Darthur*. We all are.' Her eyes light up, so I go on. 'Kay, my father, and Elaine, and Gareth who still runs it. Izzy's Isode, her daughter's Fay and Lionel's son is Fergus. I'm the only one who doesn't belong,' I say, and feel something prickle against my skin, as if Mark has suddenly moved. 'It's still Arthurian. Una is from Spenser's *The Faerie Queene*.' Morgan opens her mouth and I know what she's going to say. 'And you are, too, aren't you, Morgan?'

'Yeah, I thought she was cool . . . It must make you feel that all that stuff's so near. Not Arthurian stuff, but having grandparents, the history. The house — did you say it was a bomb demolished the medieval bit? Was that the Second World War?'

'Yes,' says Mark.

She shakes her head. 'I kind of can't imagine it. I mean, you see all the stuff on the TV, and movies. Probably more than they — you — ever saw then. But it's . . . in the streets you know. People you know. Some of the older ones where I work, they've got amazing memories, even when they've no idea what day it is. There's one old lady did nursing in the *First* World War, in the trenches and stuff. We had a hundredth birthday party for her not so long ago, and she's all there. Remember that series on the

TV – *Testament of Youth*? She says they got it all wrong.'

Laughing, I stand up to fetch more drinks. 'Heaven help anyone trying to re-create the past with eyes as sharp as hers watching.'

'So, this pilgrimage you're on,' Morgan says when I come back. 'Is it to do with your work?' I explain, briefly but as clearly as I can, since she says she didn't do medieval things in history at school. She nods, then says, 'But the pilgrimage thing—'

'That's Mark's word for it. I suppose it's quite suitable, really, though it makes it sound a bit grand. I could look a lot of it up, rather than doing all this driving. But it is . . . Feeling the distances between the places does help, specially with Anthony.'

'Bit like Zen walking, I suppose.'

'Like what?' I say.

'I thought that was motorcycle maintenance,' says Mark.

'It's a sort of meditation,' she says, smiling at his amusement, though his implied cynicism – if that was what it was – doesn't touch her. 'You walk somewhere, but you do it noticing everything about getting there.'

'You mean the scenery? Birdsong? The wind?' I ask.

'Yes, but even more your body. If you do it properly it's like you observe your heel touching the ground, then rolling on to the ball of your foot and off the ground again, and the other foot doing the other half of the cycle, and the way your arms and hands move, and how your shoulders feel, and so on. It's about existing in that movement, but you're still going somewhere, not like when you're meditating sitting still and where you're going's only in your head.'

And as she speaks, as if she's given me the vision I was denied in the car and at the castle, Anthony is present in me: his body absorbing the movement of his horse, the creak of saddles, the clink of bits and swords, the dust in his nose and the scent of hot, worn leather, and always, part of his bodily existence, the knowledge that where he was going was death.

Later, when Morgan goes to the loo, I can tell Mark's longing to ask me what I think of her. 'She's lovely,' I say, and he looks delighted. 'Is there a boyfriend?'

'Not at the moment.'

'It's a shame we've got to move on tomorrow.' I say no more, and am tickled by my cunning as I watch the idea come to him before I continue: 'Otherwise you could spend a bit more time with her.'

'We could . . . No.'

'What? See if she wants to come with us?'

'Well – yes.'

'Why not? It would be fun.' It would also be safer for me, but I don't say that, try not even to think it. Safer for what?

'You sure? Don't want to hijack your pilgrimage. Don't want to derail our plans.'

'Well, they're your plans too, and just as much yours to

derail . . . No, seriously, it's fine. What's the use of a pilgrimage if you don't include everything?'

'Everything?'

'Well, if you're trying to understand what happened . . .' I say, which is odd, because that's not why we're doing this trip, after all.

'Morgan isn't part of what happened,' he says.

'No, not directly. But you are, and she's part of you.'

He doesn't answer me, but not as if he's lost for words, more as if he's too busy digesting what I've said, and what I haven't.

The pub's Saturday-evening full by now, loud and smoky. When he asks Morgan if she'd be free tomorrow for a day trip to York and Sheriff Hutton, she's straightforwardly pleased and accepts at once. Only when it's too late does it occur to me that our meeting with Fergus, set up as a friendly aunt-drops-by-before-she-leaves-England visit, could get distinctly tricky. And with Morgan there . . . I can't imagine her being embarrassed by anything, somehow, but she's definitely not part of the Chantry, the family disagreements or even fights.

And then I realise that the straightforwardness, the honesty, the lack of subtext to what she says and thinks will mean that she won't be hurt or embarrassed if I suggest that she goes elsewhere while we discuss it. She won't mind, she'll take it at face value. How wonderful to be able to say and hear things so simply!

It's arranged. We'll pick Morgan up first thing in the

morning – 'Sorry to drag you out of bed so early on a Sunday,' I say.

'Oh, I'm used to it. Besides, it makes sense,' she says.

We decide on a dull motel, which is cheap, predictable and convenient for collecting Morgan. I go in, leaving Mark waiting by the car to unload the bags if they have a vacancy. 'Is that a double room, then?' says the receptionist.

'N-no. Thank you. Two singles,' I say, my skin suddenly burning.

'Would you like them next to each other? I've got a couple on the third floor.'

'Yes, please,' I say, because to refuse is to say it matters, and I won't say that, even though my body's shouting it. Thank God Mark wasn't at my side. And if he had been, what would I have done? What would I have wanted to do? Adam, where are you?

I sign the credit-card slip and fail to hear the information about dinner and breakfast at the restaurant next door, drink and snack machines on the landing. There's apparently no lounge or any neutral space, just floors of rooms. Then I go to the window and wave the two keys at him, and he lifts our luggage from the boot, locks the car and shoulders through the door into the lobby.

'I'm so tired I hurt,' I say, as we stand outside our respective rooms. 'All the driving and – and so on. Shall we just eat in the restaurant?'

'Why not?' he says. 'D'you want a rest, or shall we meet in ten minutes?'

'Ten minutes. If I lie down, I might not get up again,'

For a moment, he looks worriedly at me, then nods, and turns away to unlock his door.

It's not a restaurant but a roadhouse pub. Over tough steak and chips we talk desultorily about tomorrow's plans. 'Morgan won't mind us discussing business for a bit with Fergus, will she?' I say.

'Course not. She knows it's complicated. Besides, she's not one to be offended.'

'No, bless her,' I say, and the talk turns to other things.

It's only when we've paid the bill and are walking back across the car park towards the motel that he says, 'I nearly walked out on them, you know.'

This is what doctors call the hand-on-the-door moment, I think with sudden clarity. 'On who? Jean and Morgan?'

'Mary, she was then. Yes. I – Jean had a new job, very busy, meeting new people. And Morgan was going to college and . . . they just didn't seem to need me. It got worse and worse. Rows and things. We kept getting across each other. They didn't want me, I thought. So I said I'd go.'

'But you didn't.'

'No. But we didn't really talk about it, though Morgan knew. And it wasn't long after that I discovered about Jean and Keith. They didn't try to hide it much. I think she wanted me to know, in a way.'

'But she's forgiven you? Morgan has, surely, hasn't she?'

'Yes. I've — I've even forgiven myself. Almost. But I wish I hadn't said anything. It did damage, I know; it hurt Jean, and maybe that's why . . . But I thought I was doing the right thing.'

I wonder whether to ask him if he does, after all, want a cup of coffee in one or other of our rooms, but hand-on-the-door moments are just that, Adam used to say. People say things then because they have their hand on an escape route. If you cut that off, they stop talking.

And, besides, I don't trust myself to be that neutral, compassionate or even uninterested doctor. There are questions rising from somewhere inside me to sit painfully in my throat. *Is that what you thought you were doing to us?* I want to ask him. *The right thing? To me? Walking out? And why was it different with Jean? Did you love her more?*

But I can't say it: I'm so tired that my body's smarting with old pain rubbed raw and new, and I flinch from what might happen if I did. So many years' silence isn't easily or safely broken.

We've reached our rooms. His silence makes me hurt. 'You can't *know* that that was what did it — made Jean . . . look somewhere else. Maybe it wasn't. And, besides, you didn't leave, did you? You stayed.'

Mark holds out a hand to me, palm down, the way you do when you want to touch someone just a little, at a safe distance. 'Yes, I stayed . . .' Our eyes meet, but not with the heat of our shared past and present as they did at the castle. He looks tired and a little sad. Maybe he feels I'm a safe distance away from him, safe enough to say these things, to ask for just a little help. His hand cups the back of mine for a moment.

The touch of him is like an ache and I long for more, as if only his whole body will assuage my hopeless exhaustion. And he feels it too. I can tell in the way his hand opens to grasp mine completely, in the heat of his palm and the grip of his fingers. We stand for a long moment, and my heart begins to slam in my chest. Adam, where are you?

I haven't said it aloud but almost as if I had, he seems to withdraw into himself. Then he stoops, and brushes my cheek with his lips. 'Good night, Una. Sleep well.'

'Good night, Mark.'

Then we turn and unlock our separate rooms, and go to bed alone.

Elysabeth — the 1st yr of the reign of King Edward the Fifth

They called me froward that I would not heed the Council. They called me a sorceress, and that woman of Edward's too, Mistress Shore, at which I would have laughed if by the same man I had not heard that my lord Hastings was arrested in the council chamber and killed within the hour. They said that Prince Richard, Duke of York — my little Dickon — had no right to sanctuary for he had done no wrong, and his brother the King had need of young company in the royal apartments of the Tower while he made ready for his coronation.

With Antony a prisoner and Hastings dead, the two men on the Council that had the most care and love for Edward's children were gone. The great and honest men left to govern had no other power than Richard's by which to do the business of the realm. Yet, much though I heeded their concern that my refusal set the people against them, I would not give up Dickon.

They called me Medea, destroying my children's liberty to avenge my enemies. But Edward was no Jason, and how could I be destroying the things I loved best in the world, my own two youngest sons yet living? I would not be beaten: point by point I argued my case. I said that sanctuary protects the innocent as much as the guilty and that they might rather bring Ned here to Westminster if he was in want of diversion and a mother's care. They put forth no argument that I did not refute.

The better to change my mind, they surrounded the sanctuary buildings at Westminster so tightly with Richard of Gloucester's men-at-arms that they could have broken in at a word. From every window we could see them, and they us. To break sanctuary is a terrible thing. But I could not be sure that Richard of Gloucester would not give such a word. Tewkesbury Abbey was not a chartered sanctuary, but many men still thought ill of Edward that after the battle he had dragged his enemies from it, and had them headed in the marketplace. And Richard had learnt from his brother in so many things.

I knew on what errand they came that day, yet still I was glad to see good old Archbishop Thomas of Canterbury when he entered the Abbot's hall with other lords of the Council. He was a big man, Thomas, comfortable-looking in his cardinal's scarlet, with a broad face that creased easily into smiles. Many times after yet another council meeting that had ended in shouting and the threat of challenges, he had come to my private apartments, and sat by the fire, and spoken calmly of how these squabbles could be smoothed over. Then we would pray, and I would kneel to him for his blessing, and that night sleep would come to me more easily.

It was but a week before the eve of St John. Mummers were to come, if they could be persuaded to do nothing that would offend on this consecrated ground, and I had promised Dickon and the little girls that they might go up on to the roof to see the bonfires. I stood on the dais of the Abbot's hall, holding Dickon by the hand, Bess and Cecily in waiting on me. Had all gone well, they would both have been wed by now, safe in the care of their husbands. I was married to John Grey and a mother at their age. My beautiful Mary had been in her grave a year, but it seemed to me that she hovered between her sisters as she had in life. Was my son Richard Grey dead too, deep in the dark towers of Middleham? And what of Thomas Grey? When we heard of Antony being taken, he vanished to safety in Brittany, as we hoped, but we had heard nothing to be sure.

I banished such thoughts and stiffened my back, and listened as Thomas of Canterbury set forth the Council's arguments yet again, that I should give up Dickon. At his words I felt weariness flood in where I would not allow terror to dwell. But there could be no rest for me until we were safe. I saw impatience grow on their faces for they could not make arguments that I could not crush, and they had no other lawful means of gaining my boy. I drew myself to my full height, and raised my voice to fill the room.

'My lords, I ask your pardon. It is not womanish fear or frowardness that makes me refuse your request, but a mother's proper care for her children. Did I fear to send my son Edward away to Ludlow when he was Prince of Wales, though but a babe? No, for it was for the good of the realm. But there is no good to be had by taking Richard, Duke of York, from my care, and much ill. The law allows no man to have custody of one by whose death he may benefit, be he Protector or any lesser man. I call only upon the laws of man and nature. You who have the well-being of my sons at heart will understand, I know. I know, too, that whatever his — his insults to me, which I will not repeat for scorn of them, the Protector would not do his soul so much harm as to threaten holy sanctuary. Therefore I thank you for your courtesy, my lords, and I bid you good day.'

There was a rustle among them, as if they would step closer and argue harder, for all I knew that they had no arguments left. Sure, I would be sorry if these good men wished me ill, most especially Thomas of Canterbury, and they certainly did not wish me well. But that would not make me change my mind.

Then Thomas stepped forward. He was not smiling, but looked very kindly on us. For a moment he put his hand on Dickon's head; he bowed under the blessing.

'Madam, we have dealt long and happily together, you and I, since I crowned you and anointed you so many years ago, here at Westminster. I give you my word that you need have no fear for your son. You cannot think that we of the Council would deceive you, or that we are so lacking in wit as to let the Protector deceive us.' He held up his hand. 'I, Thomas Cantabriensis, Cardinal Archbishop, pledge my body and soul before God that your son, Prince Richard, will be safe both in his life and in his proper estate as Prince of the Realm and Duke of York. Amen.'

There was silence in the hall. Outside there came the sound of marching and the clatter of steel brought to attention. Were they, perhaps, mustering in greater numbers, waiting for the word to burst through the gate? Would they strike out at any man, priest or monk or valiant sanctuary boy, who dared oppose them? Would men, holy men, even God Himself, say that I had holy blood on my hands for being the cause of such a terrible thing?

I turned away, still holding Dickon's hand, that I might see more clearly what I must do. I could trust Thomas of Canterbury, that I knew. Edward had trusted him for all the years of his reign, and never been betrayed as others had betrayed him. I could have faith in the kindness of his heart, and the holiness of his soul, and the shrewdness of his worldly wisdom. I could have faith in his pledge.

But it was so hard. Ned I loved, but it was Antony who saw him every day. Dickon was my little boy, and since my baby George was taken by God, he was my only son still to hang on my skirts, and hold my hand, and show me a book or a catapult or a cut knee, as once Thomas and Richard did all those years ago among the apple trees and cornfields of Grafton.

I knelt down to hold Dickon, and could not forbear to weep, though I smiled as best I might. 'Son, you must go with the Archbishop, and he will take you to your brother. You may play and sing and read tales together, and be happy. When he is crowned, we will be together again.'

He gazed at me gravely, darker than Ned, with something of my mother in his long French nose, and the quickness with which he looked at the great men now standing silently at the other end of the hall. He had a rheum, and his upper lip was still rough and red. 'Madam, I want to see my brother, but I do not want to leave you and my sisters.'

'I know, my darling.' I took out my kerchief and wiped his nose. 'But it is for the best, and you will like to see Ned. And it will not be for long. A few weeks, at the most, and you have often been away from your sisters for that long. And you will be at the Tower. You may play Uncle Antony killing the rebels. There will be men there who defended it and can tell you many tales.'

As I spoke I saw his face brighten. 'I shall like that. Please you, madam, tell Anne and Katherine they may play with my knights, but only till I want them again. And Bridgie may have my toy dog. Now I shall soon be ten years old, I shall have no need of him.'

I drew him into my arms again. '*Au revoir*, my darling. We will be together soon. And give my love and humble duty to your brother. Remember that he is your king now, and pay him all proper observances. God bless you both.'

He nodded. I rose, took his hand and led him to Thomas of Canterbury.

'Madam, you are acting most wisely and well,' said Thomas. 'The Council commends your wisdom, and is pleased that you have heeded it.' He took Dickon's hand. 'Come, sir.'

'You have pledged your soul and body,' I said to him. 'Do not forget it.'

'I could no more do so than I could anoint any other king than your elder son,' he said.

Behind me, I heard a sob, muffled hastily, and then another. I could not go to comfort the girls, for if I did

I would break too. The lords of the Council might think I had placed my trust in their honour; I would not let them think they had crushed me.

I stood without moving while they made their bows and kissed my hand, and I watched as Thomas of Canterbury led my son out of the hall and out of sanctuary, and all the other lords followed after him.

IX

Antony — the Eve of St John

So near midsummer, so far to the north, the light takes an age to die. The yellow sun clings to the towers of Pontefract, so that they glow like dirty gold, and touches the roof of the chapel, though the bailey, where a few men lounge about their business, is deeply shadowed. The stones still breathe the day's heat. I have said the Office and now there is a whole night to pass. I have asked for a priest, but there is none can be here until dawn. I made my will before I began this last pilgrimage, but I must write to Elysabeth, and to my wife.

Behind me, I hear the iron shutter over the grating in the door open and close, and the bolts drawn back. Like everything of Richard of Gloucester's ordering, they are well oiled and quiet. A servant enters, carrying the ink and paper I have asked for, and a flask of wine.

'Thank you.'

'It's nowt.' A boy's voice, half growl, half squeak.

'You are no gaoler.'

'Just helping out, sir. Your pardon, my lord, I should say,' says the lad. 'I serve the Constable, Sir John, but he's away south.'

'Ah.' The light has slipped from the roof of the chapel. I turn to look fully at him. He is dark and small, not like Ned in the least. 'What's your name?'

'Stephen, sir. Stephen Fairhurst.'

I reach for the flask, but my hands are shaking as they have not for years, not since my first battle, my first joust, my first woman. Not since Louis.

'If it please you . . . shall I pour the wine, my lord?'

There is no scorn in his voice. Perhaps he has not seen. 'Yes, thank you.' The wine smells of sun and I pick up the cup to breathe it more deeply. I could get drunk tonight: I would not be the first. But how then could I comfort Richard Grey on the morrow, or pray with a whole mind, or greet my death, and my God, as I should? No, I will not get drunk.

The lad is staring at me. He is not a child, nor yet a man.

Suddenly it comes to me: he has been told I am his enemy. Does he not know that even an enemy's hands may shake? I have known that ever since I stumbled through the trees at Towton and met Mallorie.

'Shall I pour some more?'

I hold out my cup. Now he does know. 'It's quiet, this evening,' is all I say, however.

'Most of the men are gone south, my lord. His Grace sent for them.'

'Indeed.' He is older than Ned, perhaps fourteen or fifteen. 'You were not sent with them?'

'No. Though why not, I don't know. My master said as he must leave the castle well garrisoned. But I'm not a man-at-arms, only a page, and besides, there's nowt happens here and all to do in London, they say. I would I were there . . .' He recollects himself, and ducks an untidy bow. 'Beg pardon, my lord.'

'Stay for a cup of wine.'

'I – thank you, my lord.' He glances at the door behind him. 'But—'

'Have it closed, if you like. You may call for it to be opened. Just for a little while? There's a cup there, on the floor by the bed.' He ducks his head again, goes to the door, calls with careful ease that my lord has asked him to bear him company, and pushes the door to. Then the bolts slide home.

'Get the cup, and pull up that other stool.'

Stephen does so, but sits uneasily on the edge, and drinks with small, nervous gulps. I watch him. Only when he has drunk at least half of it do I ask, 'So, you come from hereabouts?'

'No, I'm from Sheriff Hutton. My father was a tanner, but he died at Tewkesbury. My mother's – friend, he got me the place here. He said there'd be ways of getting on, lords and such, all going about His Grace's affairs. But mostly there's nowt to do, and when there is it's not me that's chosen. I stand there, and some other man's preferred. There's only tenants and cottagers for the garrison now, and they care for nowt except being dragged away from hay making. How can I make my way in the world, shut up in this place all the year round?'

His voice rises from proper humility to natural indignation, and then he blushes.

I drink. Is it thus with all boys? I, too, wanted to conquer the world, though more of it was offered me than a widow of Sheriff Hutton may give her son. 'And that's what you want? To make your way?'

'Aye, that I do.'

Outside the quiet is still hot. 'But a man may also have enough of making his way. Once I was so weary of the world that I went on crusade.' His face lights up. 'I said that I had rather serve God by gutting Moors in Portugal than stay in England to feast and dance and scheme. The King was not best pleased.' He stares at me. He can never have spoken to one who was the King's friend. I could as well be speaking of King Arthur or King Agamemnon. 'Edward forgave me, of course. He always forgave everyone, even his brother George. And when I returned, he gave me his son, the Prince of Wales. He charged me to . . .'

I cannot speak. I look away and drink a little more, and he does not break the silence. 'It's quiet tonight,' I say, when I can command my voice again.

'Aye,' says Stephen.

I am repeating myself. Does time roll over as in an hourglass, the same sand as before? When will God decide to break the glass, and shake the souls out, the better to pass judgement on them?

'And I went on pilgrimage to Rome, and to Compostela . . .' The thought that has been nagging at the edge of my mind suddenly takes shape. 'It's quiet. Is there no hammering, or is it that the sound does not travel?'

'No hammering?'

'Although . . . I must recognise that my end is not a public act. Why should Richard of Gloucester order a scaffold?'

That I should name his penultimate lord thus makes him blush scarlet, as my talking of the King did not. 'I – I don't know. I'm – I'm sorry, my lord.'

I touch his hand. 'A rhetorical question. No need for an answer.'

He smiles, relieved perhaps that he has not offended me. 'More wine, my lord?' I am shaking more than I had bargained for. I wave my hand, and he pours.

I drink, drink again, set the cup down. 'But a priest is ordered for – for the morning?'

Stephen clears his throat, then says hoarsely, 'Of course, my lord. Sir John would have done it anyway, but His Grace most especially ordered it in one of his dispatches. He is a man of God.'

'So it is said. It is his desire to hold all earthly power

that—' I stop. 'Never mind . . . I must write some letters.'

'Will I go then, my lord?'

'No. Stay.'

There is no man that I may trust with a message: I must set what I would say down on paper, and any who would break a seal may read it – though any man might have listened to what I have said to my wife any time these ten years, and found nothing worth the hearing. What would have come to me had the marriage to the King of Scotland's sister that was proposed not foundered among the raids and bloodshed of the Borders? God knows: I cannot calculate such things.

Madam, I greet you well and send you God's blessing and mine.

Kind words, for though I have never loved her, yet she has been a good wife who brought a good portion, and I have a husband's duty to her well-being of mind as well as body. I pray that the provisions I have made for her in my will are honoured when I am gone.

When the letter is finished, I give it to him. 'Will you see that it is sent? If you are able to wait, I should be grateful. I have only one more to write.'

'Aye, my lord.'

The light is fading fast now. I pick up flint and steel but my hands are still shaking. Without a word Stephen takes them from me, lights the tinder and thence a taper.

I long to write to Louis, and I must not. It was through me that Ned was lost. I could not bear to think that it might be by my act that Louis were captured.

The candle flame buds and brightens as I write to Elysabeth.

~

At last I have done. And yet I wish that I had not: to end this letter is to end something for ever. Through the window seeps night air, and what little I can see of the sky is like black velvet. I am very cold. The boy has sat quiet for all this time. Most boys cannot sit still for two minutes together, though perforce I schooled Ned in the bearing proper to a king. But this lad Stephen has a still thoughtfulness about him, which bears me company without troubling my spirit.

They tell me Richard of Gloucester will be acclaimed king tomorrow. If I cared for it, I would take it as a measure of his fear of me that he will not do so unlawful, so treasonous a deed until I am dead. But if it is a thing decided, then the law or the commons will not prevent him, any more than they have prevented him ordering my death, though the Council itself could find no grounds for arraigning me of treason. How do you fight a great man who will do as he wishes, though the rule of law says him nay? Perhaps it will always be thus while kings need great men to rule for them.

If Richard is to be proclaimed king, then my boy is lost. Richard knows better than most how easy it is to kill a king, when you have the keys of the Tower in your hand and the watch have been told to look the other way.

I am very cold. I fold my letter to Elysabeth, then take the candle and hold it aslant, putting the sealing wax to it. A heartbeat, and red falls in perfect drops on to the sallow parchment, pools into a great round, as wet and glossy as blood. The seal presses down, red lapping the brass. A breath, and up: a pilgrim's scallop shell lies there, hard, and cooling fast.

Without a word the boy picks it up and puts it with the other, then says, 'Will you take more wine, my lord? It'd warm you.'

'No, I thank you.'

'Will I fetch a blanket?'

'Yes, if you please.'

He wraps it round my shoulders. It is rough and heavy, and still I shiver. I cannot sit up all night. I have done so many a time, to pray or to make ready for battle. But I must not risk weakness of body or mind on the morrow.

The watch calls and changes. I know not how many hours I have, only that this midsummer dawn will come soon enough.

'Perhaps I should sleep now. Will you ask that I am roused when the priest arrives?' I take my rosary from the table; it is cold and heavy in my hand, for only prayer warms it.

'Aye, my lord,' says Stephen, his eyes on the click and fall of the gold beads.

I sit on the edge of the bed. 'I could never sleep before a battle,' I say, and in the candlelight I can see that he is wondering how it feels to know there will be a battle on the morrow. I wrap the blanket tightly round myself and lie down, facing the chamber.

'Shall I snuff the light?'

'No. Leave it.'

My eyes are half closed. Stephen moves quietly, slowly, putting the cups and half-empty wine jug on the tray. At length he goes to the door and raises his hand, but falters. Perhaps he thinks that I sleep, and does not wish to wake me by knocking loud to gain his freedom.

'Would you stay?' I hardly know I have spoken. It might have been a thought, not a voice. But no, he hears, and turns back.

'My lord?'

'Please, bear me company.'

So he does, and calls a message to the guards, who grunt assent.

'Take more wine, give me some, and sit down,' I say, pulling myself up a little. Stephen pours into both cups and gives one into my hands, before sitting at the table with the other. I drink, then lie down again.

If I can but think of Jason, at the end of his travels, killed by the beam of his own ship *Argos*, that was called *Dodona* for being the gift of the gods... If I can but think of him, and know that all that comes to me is God's will likewise, then I may face death with the fortitude proper to a man.

But sleep does not come. I lie and think of Stephen.

Does he know why I have asked him to stay? What can he know, truly, of what I know? He has probably never slept alone in a bed before, never faced a battle, never read a poem, never travelled further than York. He must learn: he must understand what he is yearning for.

'When I was first taken, I thought they would make away with me privily. I feared that I would not know the hour of my death.' He is staring at me. 'I tried to keep my soul in readiness for the end. I prayed all day, and every time I heard the bolts drawn back I would pray harder, *Deo, in mano tuo.* It was weeks before I realised that it would not be thus. For an hour or two I hoped. And then I understood that I would still die, and that how I died no longer mattered . . .' I am wide awake. 'You see —' I reach for my wine cup '— I saw that if my death need not be secret, it was because Richard of Gloucester did not fear revenge — knew Edward would never be king. And so I knew that N— that Edward must be quite in Richard's grasp . . . If despair is a sin, I have sinned more since then than I have in all my years in the world.'

A drop of wine runs from the corner of my mouth and falls on to the pillow. I wipe it away. 'And today I learnt how right I was to fear for Edward. Did they tell you that Richard has thrust him aside?' Stephen is silent. It must be for his allegiance's sake; he is Richard's man, after all, wears his boar badge as well as his own master's, as so many do. Or maybe he does not understand. 'I would have wished they had kept it from me, except that there are still a few hours left to pray for Edward. Not for his rule, now. For his life.'

The blanket is falling away, and the cold air breaking through. I pull it up. 'I taught him all I could. He learnt of God and the saints, history, good government, the rule of men, jousting, singing, the chase . . .'

But these foolish things are more painful than any high matter. I must not let myself think them. 'Bring me my book of hours. There, on the table.'

He puts it into my hand and I pull myself upright and open it. 'Bring the candle closer, lad.' But the darkness in the chamber seems to smother the light, and I cannot make out the words. 'My eyes are cloudy . . . Are you lettered? In Latin?'

'Aye, a little, my lord.'

'Come closer, and read me something.' I turn the pages, which are soft with study and handling. 'There, the *Oratio ad sanctissimam Trinitatem*.'

He takes the book and looks at it. I had no time at Northampton, and this little book is all I could bring with me. I can see the lad is disappointed, in the book and its small, rough woodcuts, and in me as its possessor. 'It's a printed book. There are hundreds the same, made by a press, a machine, and sold for a shilling or two. You could have many yourself, full of prayers and tales and great deeds. Not just a missal.' I see his face, and laugh. 'I know. Most boys do not care for book-learning. Even

Ned had to be tempted to his desk, when the sun was out over the Teme and he had a new horse to try.'

'Ned?'

'My boy.' I say no more. After a moment he squats on the floor, studying the pages.

The air is thick and chill. He reads slowly, as if he must push the words through it. '*Pater aeterne! rogo te per vitam et mortem acerbissimam delectissimi Filii tuii . . .*'

These are sounds I have had in my ears all my life, words I have always known, and he almost knows too. They roll from the black-clotted page to his eye, over his tongue, spoken to the air, hanging there like incense.

'. . . *miserere mei nunc et in hora mortis meae. Amen.*'

'Amen,' I say. He stays sitting on the floor by me. 'Do you understand it?'

'Not exactly, my lord.'

I put out my hand, and touch his shoulder. He is warm. 'Let me see . . . "Eternal Father, I ask Thee by the life, and death – bitter death – of thy most beloved Son, and by Thy infinite goodness . . . mercifully grant that in Thy grace I may live and die." ' Under my hand, I feel the shock run through him. After a moment, I can go on. ' "Most benign – most kind – Jesus, I ask Thee by Thy love of Thy Father, who – who always embraced Thee . . . and by Thy last word – when Thou wast hanging on the cross – which didst commend Thy spirit to the Father – receive my spirit at my life's end. Holy Spirit, enkindle perfect charity in me and strengthen my spirit with it until I . . . I leave this life. O most holy Trinity, one God, have mercy on me now and in the hour of my death. Amen." '

The candlelight is waxy yellow on his face, picking out the jet in his hair and eyes. He is small and alive, and his hair under my hand is rough and springy, like heather on a hillside where you might lie under a summer sun. But what of my boy – my Ned – my son?

'I should have guessed what Richard would do. I should! But I thought he would work through the Council. Through the court. I was ready for that. But not . . . not for what he did.'

He half turns to me, and looks up. His look is my undoing.

'He has my boy.'

I can hold back my grief no longer. Under it I bow my head to my knees, and then it presses on me so greatly that I can no longer stay upright, and fall on to my side with my face to the wall, weeping for the end of my world, and for the world that will go on afterwards.

~

After a long time I feel Stephen's arm about my back, a slight touch, then a firmer one when I do not shake it off, gripping my shoulder. It brings me back, and I realise my shirt has fallen open. The inside of his wrist rasps on my hair shirt, and he starts.

'It will not hurt you,' I say. 'The hairs are too fine to

cut the skin, they cut your conscience only. They clothe a man in repentance.'

'Do you have need of repentance, my lord?'

'All men must repent, for we are all sinful, since the fall of Adam,' I say, like a dutiful schoolboy. It is not enough, though: if I speak of such things, at such a time, it should be wholeheartedly, to the glory of God.

I cannot. I am too weary, and too afraid.

Yes, afraid.

No man will speak of fear before a battle except to a dear friend, lest he be scorned. A captain may not speak of fear at all, lest the chill of it steal through his men. But now? What may I do to drown my fear, with no clangour of battle in my ears, no glory to hope for, no blood on my hands, no great and dreadful moments when it is kill or be killed?

I must sleep.

To go sleepless for prayer and fasting is to discipline the body's desires, and so to free the soul to love God.

To go sleepless for mortal love is a joy so great it is beyond joy, and beyond pain.

To go sleepless for fear is weakness that will lead to weakness on the morrow.

I cannot sleep.

I am shivering, and I know that he feels it. I must sleep . . . I *must*.

'Will you lie with me, Stephen, that I do not sleep alone? I do not think . . .'

'Aye, my lord.'

His weight is slight: the ropes of the bed bear down only a little, and the straw in the palliasse creaks. I shift myself further towards the wall. And then behind me comes his warmth, his grubby boy's smell, his breath on my neck, and his arms once more about my shoulders. He says nothing, but holds me. He is warm and my breath eases, then my body with it.

'Sire?'

'Yes?'

'I have hidden your letters in my jerkin, my lord. God willing, I will carry them safely.'

'Thank you.' I pull the blanket up round us both, and the Jason ring knocks my jaw. Soon I shall be with God and shall have no need of it. Nor could I be sure that so fine and large a piece of gold would not tempt a poor man in Richard's service. I pull it off. 'Will you take this too, and give it with the letter to my sister Elysabeth?'

He takes it from me, and I feel his hand dive again into his jerkin. 'Aye, my lord. I swear by the saints I will do as you ask, though it cost me my life.'

His ardent voice conjures tears in my eyes. 'No, that is too great a cost for any boy. But if you can do it safely, you will have my very great thanks.'

Without my ring, that was Louis's, it is as if I have at last relinquished everything that ties me to this world.

All is quiet. Sleep hovers over me. I am wearied unto death with all that mortals must know: weary with fear, weary with grief, weary with talking and planning and fighting, and weary with the old wound in my thigh, and the new wound in my heart: that I have destroyed Ned.

~

It is the feast of the Salutation of the Blessed Virgin. From inside the door of the Constable Tower the garrison's sallets below me are ranks of steel cobbles, their faces invisible. It is dawn-cold, yet their brigandines are stained with weeks of sweat. No tabards, though, no standards to hang limp in the still air. There is no one here except Richard of Gloucester's affinity, and they do not need reminding. The presented arms waver, for all the best men, Stephen told me, are gone south. These tenants and cottagers are held in by the castle walls, ranged to order round the the headsman's block, bound by their contract, their allegiance.

Standing over the Deputy Constable is Sir James Tyrell. I might have known he would be here, for he has ever been Richard's most trusted man. He is here to see his master's command obeyed. If there is need of other, more secret work—

I will not think it. I have commended Ned's soul to God, and trust in Him as I may trust in no man. I can do no more for Ned. And now I must do the same for my own soul.

I have seen many men executed, by the rope, or the axe, or the fire that cleanses heresy from the world. Some curse, some struggle and cry against the hangman's grip, some scream of their innocence, or their guilt, as the flames begin to sear. Most shit themselves. I will not – I *will not* – betray myself thus. Besides, I am going to God. Who could feel fear or sorrow, knowing what I know?

A hand pushes me in the back: my guards are impatient. Stephen is nowhere to be seen. When I woke at the slamming back of bolts that heralded the priest, he was gone.

The morning light is sharp. I blink and drop my rosary. The flesh feels naked where Louis's ring has lodged on my finger these last weeks. The priest picks my rosary up and pushes it back into my hand, and I touch St Augustine and St Bridget and our Holy Mother, the small, dull beads between them as small and dull as we are to God, yet part of the circle too.

'*Dulcissime Jesu Christe, si ultimum verbum tuum in cruce . . .*'

'Where are my friends?'

'They're dead,' says the guard. 'All three.' And, yes, in the corner of the bailey there is a cart, with rough sacking tossed over it and blotched with blood.

Elysabeth's boy, Richard Grey, is dead. I sent him a scarlet whip-top from Sandwich, the day we were captured by Warwick's men. Once I met him, stale-drunk, outside a whorehouse in Southwark. 'You will not tell my mother?' he said. He was no more than Stephen's age. Stephen has a widowed mother with no love or care in her life but him: Richard's mother was a queen. She loved him very much, but she had too much, too many, to care for besides.

My cousin Haute is dead, who stood on the shore at Lynn as we stumbled up from the sands, and called that he had a ship, that the master would sail on trust that he would be paid in the end, that Edward and all of us were saved.

Sir Thomas Vaughan is dead: Ned's chamberlain, who loved Ned as his son, and carved him Jason's ship and all the Argonauts to sail on the millpond at Ludlow, and wept as we rode north.

They are dead. We shall meet again soon. And I shall see Louis when God grants that I may.

'*Profiscere, anima christiana, de hoc mundo . . .*'

I walk forward. I will not hesitate, or stumble. I will not.

It is an axe, of course. I was not tried by my peers, as is my right. Nor am I granted that final right, the last rites of knighthood, that I be killed with our own, our honourable steel. No matter. Even such honour is a thing of the world.

'*Deus misericors, Deus clemens, Deus qui secundum multitudinem miserationum tuarum peccata paenitentium deles . . .*'

I am to be killed. I will — I can — in no wise seek to prevent it.

Thin ranks of men. A block, brightly bloodstained. I see it, but my vision is hazed with prayers.

'*. . . sanctus Joseph, morientium Patronus dulcissimus, in magna spem te erigat . . .*'

I look up. The sky still arches above me. Somewhere beyond it, beyond all possibility of imagining, judgement awaits. I walk forward to the block. The men stand silent. The man in the leather apron is speaking: I nod, for I do forgive him as we all hope to be forgiven, each of us, for what we have done in our lord's service.

'. . . *contemplationis divinae delcedine potiaris in saecula saeculorum*.'

Something moves. Down the steps from the keep, across the bailey, walks Stephen. He does not pass the line of men. But as I reach the block, he moves again, pulling off his cap. He bends his knee to me, and bows his head.

'*In manus tua, Domine, commendo spiritum meum*.'

I kneel before the block, and fix my mind's eye on God. It is finished. It will begin.

'*Jesu, Jesu, Jesu*.'

Una — Sunday

The road gets narrower, turns off, then on another, smaller lane we wind downhill and up between oak and beech, until Mark tells me to turn yet again, on to a rough track whose farm gate has been open so long that brambles have lashed it to the hedge. Over our heads the trees tangle and the big car curtsies and sways along the track for what seems like an eternity, our progress marked only by stones and sudden hollows, and occasionally a scattering of birds shouting the alarm at our approach.

A small hand-painted sign announces Friary Cottage. The track leads to a large clearing and fades immediately to nothing. At the far side of the clearing is Morgan's house: a small, red-brick, slate-roofed cottage like a child's drawing, standing at the junction of wood and field. It has dormer windows, like raised eyebrows, smears of green where a gutter's overflowed, a trickle of blue smoke from one of its four chimney pots, and the front door is propped open with a large stone. A black Labrador bounds from the woods with a token bark.

I get out to stretch my legs and greet Morgan, and am promptly butted in the small of the back. At my yelp Mark laughs, the dog barks again, and I turn, and find myself being butted in the stomach instead, by a dark brown donkey.

'Oh, that's Neddy, don't mind him,' says Morgan, bending to catch the dog by the scruff of the neck. 'Quiet, Beth! Neddy's terribly nosy, but if you rub his ears he'll love you for ever.'

I do as I'm told, and find them surprisingly muscular and warm, with miraculously soft fur. He has no head-collar or rope. 'Does he run free?'

'Oh, yes. The chickens too, only I haven't let them out this morning as I'm not going to be here. The only fences are to keep Neddy off the vegetables. He was found abandoned and I said I'd look after him. Come in while I get my stuff.' A big rosemary bush covered with blue flowers and happy bees hangs half across the doorway. Neddy disputes our right to enter, but Mark gives him a shove and he dips his heavy head and ambles away.

'Can I use your loo?'

'Yes, just through the kitchen and out the back door. It's on the right.'

The kitchen has an ancient bottled-gas stove, a Formica table with an oil lamp on it and a scatter of jewellery tools and materials, a tiled fireplace laid ready with raw-smelling coal, and a beautiful inlaid Queen Anne wall clock tocking away in the corner, showing the phases of the moon and the movement of the sun through the zodiac. As I head out of the back door and find the privy, a black shadow of a cat with blue eyes slips past my legs and away like warm smoke.

'How are we going to handle talking to Fergus?' I ask Mark, while Morgan locks the cottage with the dog inside and the donkey outside.

'D'you reckon Izzy will have rung him?' he asks.

'I don't know. Lionel said he'd be talking to him. I have the feeling they talk quite often. They obviously get on.'

'Wouldn't have thought Lionel was the type to be chummy with his son, somehow. Though I suppose Fergus isn't on his territory.'

'You mean living in York?' I say, wilfully misunderstanding him because the relationship of fathers and sons isn't easy to discuss with Mark.

'No. Being an artist, not a banker. No competition.'

I think of Lionel, running small and fast and strong down a rugby pitch; sitting in the Chantry kitchen in his brand new City suit, bowler on the table, arguing that the Press wasn't profitable and never could be; sitting in St Albans and talking about the copy of Malory worth less than his. 'I suppose he *is* competitive,' I agree, but keep to myself my fear that he'll want the Chantry to be his project. 'But territorial?'

'Always was,' says Mark, and there's an edge to his voice. 'Anyway, you'd better do most of the talking, being family. Ah, here she comes.'

Morgan opens the back door and settles into her seat. 'All sorted out. I made Malkin a cat door last year: it didn't work whether I shut her in or out. You can't shut cats anywhere . . . This is great, by the way. Thank you for taking me along.'

The sign to Towton flashes past, the bridge that carries the road to it a mere flicker over our heads, and then we swoop off the trunk road to trundle through the suburbs of York. Micklegate Bar looms before us against a thinly grey sky; we turn left round the outside of the walls and past the station. The road threads casually through the city walls and gates, back again and over the Ouse. Ahead of us the Minster lies at anchor with the smaller buildings clustering about it, and our road skirts them at a respectful distance. Anthony would have been taken straight through the city, I realise, riding under escort through streets where cars are now forbidden. Did he want to stop at the Minster for Mass, or for private prayer? But they wouldn't have let him. It was a sanctuary, after all, a consecrated place of safety, and they wouldn't have dared drag him from it, even in Richard of Gloucester's fiefdom. To the right Monkgate Bar stands, the road from Sheriff Hutton almost a tunnel through it, so deep and thick is the stone it's built of. We're making the same journey as Anthony, I realise, only backwards, from Pontefract to Sheriff Hutton. Our pilgrimage is to recover the past. His was a ride towards some kind of future, which he, I suppose, believed to be eternity.

We cross over the Fosse towards Heworth.

Fergus lives in a neat loop of 1930s houses with a blob of well-mown grass in the centre, each garden neater and more flowery than the last, except his, which has a long-haired lawn and a certain accidental beauty about the way the neglected shrubs pile themselves against each other. It's such a backwater that he heard the car, it seems, because as we park he comes out on to the doorstep. He must be twenty-five or six, I think, taller than Lionel, with Sally's fine-grained Celtic wiriness to go with his dark Pryor colouring.

'Hello, Aunt Una. You found it all right?'

We hug. 'I don't think you ever met Mark, did you?' I ask, though I know perfectly well he can't have. His birth was one of those pieces of family news that even after nine and a half years I longed to tell Mark.

They shake hands, and Mark introduces Morgan.

'Shall we go through to the kitchen? I'll put the kettle on,' Fergus says.

'Don't bother with "Aunt",' I say, over my shoulder. As we go past I can see that the two main rooms have been knocked together and Fergus is using them as his studio: I glimpse sheets of metal and machine tools standing on a bare-boards floor, and the wall I can see is a thick patchwork of sketches, postcards and pictures torn from magazines. The kitchen also has bare floorboards, and cupboards that have been hand-painted a colour that reminds me of a collared dove's breast feathers.

'Did you knock the rooms together?' I ask him.

'Yes. The neighbours disapprove, of course. Not the knocking-through, the machines and things. Though the front garden's their biggest trial.'

He's grinning cheerfully, so I don't try to hide my puzzlement. 'What made you move here?'

'I was living with someone and we needed more space. It was — it was her kind of place. Dad said it was a good investment. And it's a good size. Only it . . . She decided she couldn't hold her own against the sculpture in the end.' After a moment he shrugs and says, 'I sometimes think I ought to move, but I can't be bothered. I've got used to being here, I guess.' He flips the kettle on and raises his voice. 'So, what do you do, Morgan?'

'I make jewellery, and I'm a care assistant,' she says, and the way his gaze sharpens makes me realise they're much of an age. Amused and touched, I half listen to their talk of burnishing and annealing and the properties of titanium, and try to work out my approach to Fergus.

'. . . needs to be really stable,' he's saying.

'I could lend you my jig,' she says. 'It'll take just about any gauge of wire.'

'Could you spare it?' He pours the kettle into the cafetière.

'Sure. I don't use it much.' She grins at him. 'Would you do a swap? Show me how to use your lathe some time?'

I hold my breath, because asking an artist if you can use their tools — as opposed to offering your own — is rather like asking if you can borrow someone's best-beloved suit or kitchen knife. Will Fergus feel obliged to say yes? Will Morgan mind if he doesn't? And then I realise two things simultaneously: that Morgan won't mind if he says no, and that he's not going to say no to that or to just about anything else she might suggest.

Smiling, I glance at Mark. He isn't smiling, just watching Fergus with a slight frown.

'So, Aunt— sorry, Una,' says Fergus, bringing the coffee to the table. He looks round, and Morgan already has a clutch of four mugs by the handles.

'These ones?'

'Yes, thanks. Una, Dad sort of explained, but tell me properly what this restoring-the-Chantry business is about. How *is* Uncle Gareth, by the way? Just grab sugar and milk, everyone.'

'Shall I go away?' asks Morgan, taking her coffee from him. 'Family stuff and all. Fergus, would you mind me having a nose round your studio?'

She's slipping out of the kitchen door before anyone can answer, and the three of us sit down at the kitchen table. I set out, as even-handedly as I can, the situation, the problem, the possibilities, the obstacles. The only obstacle I don't mention is Izzy.

'And Dad says he doesn't think it's possible unless we can raise lots of money?'

'Well, we all think that. But we can't even *try* unless we all agree it's something we want to do. Everyone who owns the house.'

'There needs to be some kind of trust before we can start trying to persuade organisations that it's serious,' says Mark.

'And of us all, Mark's the best qualified to work out what it's likely to involve, in money and work, and he's the one with the contacts,' I say, then realise what I've said.

But Fergus doesn't say, 'But Mark's not family,' though that would be understandable. He just nods. 'And I've got a vote.'

'Apparently you've got Lionel's share.'

'Yes, he reminded me. I'd forgotten.' The telephone warbles. 'Excuse me . . . Fergus Pryor . . . Oh, hello, Aunt Izzy, how are you? How nice to hear from you.' Remembering my last conversation with Izzy I try to catch Mark's eye, where he's sitting across the table from me, but he's staring into space as people do when they're listening to a conversation behind them. 'Yes, she's here . . .' Fergus is saying. 'Yes, we are . . . But . . . Why not? . . . Yes, I do understand what she's suggesting, but I don't see— Okay, hold on.' He holds out the receiver to me. 'She wants to talk to you.'

I take the receiver. 'Izzy? It's Una.'

'Una, what on earth's going on?'

'I needed to do some research, and then I realised it was my last chance to see Fergus before I go home,' I say, which is true, if disingenuous.

'But you've been discussing the Chantry.'

'Yes, as it happens.'

'I really don't think it's wise to take it any further,' she says, her voice dropping so suddenly, by an octave and several decibels, that I can tell she's forcing herself to sound reasonable. 'Fergus isn't in a position to make the right judgement, after all. He hardly knows the place. It's not as if he's ever lived there.'

'Well, he owns quite a chunk of it . . .' I say, and can feel myself losing my temper in turn. 'Izzy, we've had this conversation before. Can it not wait till we get back to London?'

'*We?* Is Mark there?'

'Yes. He wanted to see his step-daughter in Leeds. Do you want to talk to him?'

'No, it's none of his business what goes on in the family. I'm really just ringing as a courtesy to tell Fergus

I've finished the inventory, and I've instructed shippers to take the archive to San Diego. But you'll do to tell. It's booked in to go on Wednesday. Can you pass the message on? I can give you the details before you fly. A copy of the bill of lading if you like. Goodbye, Una.' The line goes dead with a clatter.

Winded, I put the receiver down and tell Fergus and Mark about the shippers.

'Why doesn't Aunt Izzy want the Chantry restored?' says Fergus. 'She's the one who wrote the book. You'd think she'd be pleased.'

'I think . . .' I arrange my words carefully. 'As far as I understand her, she doesn't think restoring the Chantry is the important thing, that it's the documents that matter. And she's — she's worried they won't be safe at the Chantry. Though, of course, we wouldn't dream of keeping them there unless we could have proper archival storage.'

'It must matter to Great Uncle Gareth, if he's going to lose his workplace. And his home, come to that. I mean, I know he's old, but you'd still mind, wouldn't you?' says Fergus, reminding me of Morgan and her old lady. 'And, anyway, it's such a great idea. Though a lot of work. I suppose it comes down to how much we want it, really, doesn't it?'

'Well, I want it, but it's not my call. I'll be in Australia in a few days' time.'

I can feel Mark's eyes on me, and when I turn my head to meet them, heat creeps up my cheek.

'Can't you get that thing you do to stop something quickly?' says Fergus.

'An injunction,' says Mark.

'Even if we do,' I say, swallowing the cold dregs of my coffee, 'if Izzy doesn't want to help, long term it's going to be next to impossible to get the restoration off the ground.'

'Can't do much till Monday anyway,' says Mark.

'No, but thanks so much for bothering to come and explain it,' says Fergus, getting up. 'Dad's so brisk. I mean, he always makes lots of sense, but it's money sense. I don't think . . . Well, he doesn't talk about the other kinds of sense.' He opens the kitchen door. 'Must let poor Morgan out of purdah. I'll give Dad a ring later.'

In the studio Morgan's holding a small sculpture of burnished golden metal to the light from the window: a series of roundels assembled at odd angles, so that they seem to shift and gleam, at once irresistible to my gaze and impossible to see.

'That's lovely,' I say. 'Is it one of yours, Fergus? It reminds me of the moon your father's got. The one in spun pewter? I thought that was beautiful.'

'They're a pair. This is brass, though. Should be silver and gold, of course.'

'Oh, I don't know. Brass is incredibly enduring. And there's something wonderfully human about pewter.'

Fergus smiles, then says to Morgan, 'I ought to give him this one as well. They ought to be together.'

'That would be good,' she says, and hands the sun to Mark.

He holds it, turning it this way and that, and I watch his movements because they have the confident care of this small work of art that reminds me of Adam's care of human bodies. Mark looks up, and I'm scarlet again, the heat running down my neck and breasts and into my core. Then as I watch, and know he's seen, he looks down again for a moment, then across to Fergus and Morgan. Is it my own quickening, or just my wishful thinking, that I seem to see approval, now, in how he regards them? Side by side, Morgan's deep gold, jewelled looks make Fergus's dark hair and eyes appear engraved on silver.

When I suggest that although I need to go to Sheriff Hutton there's no need for Morgan to come if she doesn't fancy it — we can pick her up on the way back — Mark raises no objection. Nor does he suggest that he, too, stays behind.

'So, is that the last stop on your pilgrimage?' asks Fergus.

'Yes. Unless you count the journey home. Not that London is my home, these days.'

'I've always wondered about that,' he says, to my surprise. 'Going home after a pilgrimage. Must have been such an anticlimax.'

'Depends whether you think the shrine was the most important thing, though,' says Morgan. 'Or the process of getting there.'

'If you get the process right in sculpture –' says Fergus '– this your jacket, Una? – I think you always reach the goal. Even if it's not the goal you set out for.'

Morgan nods. 'Sometimes I think the more surprised I am, the better it turns out to be when I stand back. But only sometimes.'

Fergus says, 'You know, one of the things I always think when I'm reading books about artists is how *unlikely* it all sounds – I mean compared to when you're in the studio with the plaster bandage hot and wet in your hands and a maquette that won't stand up and five minutes to get it right before it goes wrong and dries that way for ever. I'm not sure art historians understand the *doing* of it. Even if they read letters and things. When you're doing it you don't think, I want this to be a new stage in my developing sense of spatial form. You think, How can I get the bloody thing to stand up, or would it work better lying down anyway?'

I laugh. 'But you do think that later, don't you? About spatial form?'

'Yes, of course. When I'm teaching or having an argument with another artist. And certainly if I was writing my memoirs.' He laughs. 'Though other people see things that I haven't sometimes. They fit it into a story I didn't know it was part of. But at the time, no. And yet . . . what's more real, more interesting? More true, even? That moment, all plastery? Or where it fits in a story you didn't even know about then, but can see so clearly when you look back? It's like Heisenberg said about quantum mechanics.'

'Who?' says Morgan.

'Heisenberg, the atom-bomb man. The uncertainty principle. The more accurately you measure the position of something at a particular moment, the less accurately you can measure where it's going: the velocity – the trajectory. At least, that's roughly it. My father could tell you more.'

'Could he?'

'He's good at that sort of thing,' says Fergus, smiling at her.

~

We could take the trunk road, I see, peering at the map Mark's holding, but that's new. I can only guess the route that Anthony's escort would have taken him, but I do my best. Halfway along Monk Stray I tell Mark to turn left, and we run north alongside the Fosse, through Huntington, Haxby Landing, Towthorpe, Strensall Common, where red military signs point into deep woods, Strensall itself, lying in the curve of the Fosse with the railway slashing through. Over the Fosse and down on to Haxby Moor. The country's flatter than the big-boned hills and valleys round Grafton, marshy and low-lying, the fields greeny-gold, threaded with streams and dotted with copses of dark-green high-summer trees. It's hawking country, I think, as the road lifts over a little bridge where the Fosse has curled round again to cross our path before splitting in two. A bird rises from Whitecarr Beck at our left: a big heron in his wedding-guest grey, wings unhurried, heading west.

With a glance at Mark, who seems to understand, I stop the car so we can watch him. What was it like to fly a hawk after such a bird? To unhood a goshawk and feel her suddenly alert on your fist, head turning, wings easing at the shoulder. To brace yourself to put her up and feel the grip of her talons on your glove shift, tighten, thrust down, let go? To strain your eyes after her? Regina might have been her name, or perhaps Juno, for you had a classical education. Juno, yes, a gift from your father to his eldest son, the most glorious, heart-stopping gift you'd ever received. Your eyes dazzled so you could hardly see her, you feared suddenly she'd gone for ever beyond mortal gaze. But no: she stooped from the sky like a thunderbolt and the heron was twisting and struggling in her grip. By the time you caught up with her the heron was dead, and you, Anthony, had taken your first quarry.

Our heron's still flying west. The crack in the clouds has widened and gleams of sun are catching a willow-tree top, a spangle of raindrops caught in a spider's web, the rough velvet of the meadow.

The moment's over: I know it, and I can feel it, too, in how Mark suddenly shifts in his seat. As if he senses my attention he looks sideways and smiles at me, and my skin's doused with heat.

I start the car again, pull away, and before we've found speech there's Sheriff Hutton, the castle towers on the higher ground far ahead of us, tall and hard and jagged, like mailed fists smashed on to the land. Four towers: the four corners of the keep, I realise, as we get nearer, still holding the ground they always did, though what joined them's mostly gone and their windows no longer watch for friends and enemies but hang above us sightlessly.

~

There's nowhere in the big, tidy village where we could avoid the castle's presence even if we wanted to. It lowers over everything, and the post office, when we go in for water and a packet of biscuits, has several booklets about its history, alongside the notices of traffic-calming consultations and the Sheriff Hutton Players in *Sleeping Beauty*.

'Are you going to the castle? It's privately owned, you can't go in, but you can walk all the way round,' says the shopkeeper, coming out from behind the post-office counter to serve us. 'That'll be six pound twenty, with the booklets. And the church is worth a visit too. Beautiful old tombs and the like, and flowers.'

A wide drive leads up from the road to the castle. There's a farmhouse and a cluster of outhouses built among its ruins. From somewhere in a clutch of trees there's the crack of a shotgun and a cloud of rooks rises, cawing. 'No Entry,' says the notice on the way into the yard, and the official route turns away from it to the right and left, through wicket gates and round the flank of the castle mound. The paths are English Heritage-functional, the red-brick farm buildings among the ruins turn their shoulders on the towering crags of stonework behind and between them. To the left there's a stand of dark-blue ornamental conifers, and a Japanese-style pergola in orange creosote standing naked on tidy lawns. This isn't the world I had in my mind, not the fierce, ruined power that we saw in the distance, the castle imposed by a high-stomached earl on wild Marcher lands.

We turn through the right-hand gate, widdershins, as if we're trying to cast a spell.

The path widens a little. Mark catches me up and our hands brush, but we don't speak. Willow trees loom over us, and beyond them a single spar of stonework, several storeys high, as pale and grey as a ghost. Then, closer, lower walls that hint at chambers beyond, and a lancet window. Around them is a thicket of briars and brambles, stems as long as whips and barbed with thorns, as if the castle has slept for a hundred years.

The path leads out into the open, where the castle mound spreads wide and low. Here, from further away, we can see much more. There are more windows, enough for comfort and almost too many for defence, scraps of ornamental battlements, coats of arms carved above a grand doorway. Tufts of greenery grow on the tops of the towers, and a couple of small trees look rather forlorn in the wide space that must once have been levelled to make the killing field.

No shiny noticeboards here, no competent line-drawing reconstructions that remind me of my childhood history books. Here are only fields and fences and crumbling stone. What's left is just that: leavings. After the lead's been stripped from the roof, the timbers taken to build a barn or burn Guy Fawkes, the good dressed stone carted away for some squire's new house, what remains is only what's too stubborn to be easily used again.

We walk up the slope to get as close as we can, lean on the fence and look into what I think would have been the inner bailey. I tell Mark about how George, Duke of Clarence's children were kept here, prisoners of their blood, because they had a better right to the throne than Richard III, Duke of Gloucester himself. Later Elizabeth's daughter Bess was sent here too, it was said because the rumours about her and her uncle became too loud and reached the ears of his cancer-ridden wife.

'Pity we can't get in,' says Mark.

'Yes,' I say, gazing up at the tower. Here, if anywhere, Anthony should be: the echo of the slam of a door, the clank and stench of a bucket, a wisp of candlesmoke, the shadow of a bent head cast on a stone wall as he writes.

To Elizabeth, perhaps, newly widowed, brought full circle back to her old condition, alone.

Mark's watching me, and this time there's no mistaking what's in his gaze. I meet it, hold it, try to see through it to Adam because otherwise Adam's lost to me.

'Una, can I tell you something?'

I nod.

'Let's sit down,' he says. So we walk down the killing field and sit across from each other on a picnic bench that has two sides, one watching the castle, one looking out over the fields. What is this? Into my blank surprise all sorts of things project themselves: illness, bad news, a girlfriend, or that . . . that he – that he's . . . Silly idea that he's going to say something about us, because there isn't an us, whatever I've seen in his eyes. That's just – that's just what Adam rescued me from. I must hold on to Adam.

'I . . . I want to tell you why I left the Chantry,' he says.

Something's beginning to ring in my ears. 'That would be . . . That would be good.'

'You see, I'd got this idea for *The Iliad* and *The Odyssey*. Licensing a translation. Would have been a big outlay, but Penguin had done well with theirs. Seemed to me we'd find buyers for a really fine edition with a good translation. And because he'd had a proper education – Latin and Greek and everything – I asked Lionel about it. About which were the good translations of Homer. And he said . . . Una, love, are you sure you want to hear this?'

'Yes,' I say, then realise what he's called me. But he's speaking again, quickly, as if he's held this in for years and years, and now it must come out.

415

'He told me some names of good versions. People who might do a new one. And then he asked me if I'd said anything to Gareth. I said no, not yet. Then he ... Then he laughed and said, "Well, don't worry, he's not going to say no, is he? Not to his heir-apparent. Gareth refuse to print the story of Achilles and Patroclus? Not for his blue-eyed boy. Not an ... an old queer like Gareth."'

He stumbles on the words, and their offensiveness stings my ears, but I don't know what to say. I've no clue to what Mark is feeling now, or what he felt then.

His hands are clenched on his knees, as if he's driving himself on. 'I – I ... I'd thought Gareth just ... I'd no idea ... We didn't know much in those days, did we? I mean, I knew what Lionel meant, of course. But Gareth ... He – I'd thought of him as an uncle. Sort of a father ...'

Sort of a father. Suddenly I want to cry. 'I did too. He was to me. And he said ... That's how he saw you, he told me. As – as the only person who could carry the Press on. Oh, Mark, I'd no idea. I thought it was what I said.'

'What *you* said?'

'About Izzy.'

'What?'

'I thought it was me, saying you didn't care about anyone except Izzy. When you went. And she didn't care about you ... And then you didn't answer my letter, when I asked you to come back. When Grandpapa died. You didn't answer, and I thought ...'

He's silent for a moment. Then he reaches and takes my hand. 'No, I know. I should've. I'm sorry. I – I was in such a muddle . . . But in your letter you said so much. Told me all about it. Your grandfather'd died, and the business was failing. It was . . . But I couldn't go back. Everything I'd learnt from Gareth – everything we'd talked about – was poisoned. Even though he'd never said anything. Because of what Lionel said. Oh, not because Gareth was a man, not in the end, though then, well, I wasn't sophisticated, like Lionel and Sally, just a Bermondsey boy. But I couldn't remember Gareth cleanly. It . . . All his care. All his teaching me. It meant something different. Not what I'd thought. Not what I relied on. I think it was because I wasn't there any more: I just remembered the things I *couldn't* join in with. The talk and the art and everything . . . I didn't belong. I wasn't family. And Izzy had left . . .' I must have moved or something, because his hand tightens, gripping mine so it almost hurts. 'No, not that. It was just knowing how empty the Chantry was without her – without a real artist. Like your father was, by all accounts. Nothing else mattering. I did have a crush on her when I was younger, it's true, but I grew out of that long before, years before she married Paul. It was you were my friend.'

The lines of his face are deeply carved, his eyes shadowed and the lids heavy. I put my hand to his cheek and hope he can't feel the pulse, like a drum-beat, in my wrist.

He takes my hand from his cheek and holds it. 'I'm sorry, Una. I could've told you all this in London. Should've.'

'Isn't that what happens with pilgrimages, though? That you end up where you started?'

With his other hand he gestures at the jagged castle towers. 'It's a long way from New Eltham. And I couldn't ever tell Gareth what I told you. Not face to face, anyway.'

'No, I can see that. But I meant where you started in yourself . . . the things you've always had . . . The—' it's difficult for me to say, dangerous and yet necessary '– the feelings you've had.' He says nothing, but he's still holding my hand. I raise it, and kiss his fingers where they curl round mine. The skin's warm, the bones and tendons clearly defined under my lips. 'Thank you for trying to save the Chantry.'

He pulls his hand away. 'Didn't, though, did I? I didn't come back, and the chances are it's still going to be sold. We're not going to raise the money, you know.' He starts to get up from the bench. 'Let's go home.'

'Mark! Look at me!' He's standing now, very tall and half turned away. It feels like my last chance, but I don't know what to say. 'You tried to save it – us – everything. That time, with your plans for the Homer. This time, with the trust. You did something about it. You're doing something now.' I get up too, disentangling myself from the bench and stumbling on the rough grass in my hurry to get between him and the road. 'Listen! You — you tried then, and you're trying now. Trying is enough. You can't do everything.' He doesn't move. I remember how he was always there, running a press, doing a late delivery, mending a light switch, persuading the van to start. Even if he was in his room, not officially working, he always seemed to know if something needed doing and there he was, offering to take the spanner or hold the other end of the shelf and saying, 'Would you like a hand?' And it seemed to me then that it always worked, whatever it was, as soon as he set his hand to it. 'You did more than anyone else for the Press. And — and everything. All of us. The whole Chantry.'

He still won't look at me. 'But it was your family, not mine. Perhaps that's why I failed.'

I grab his arm and try to pull him round. 'Is that what you think? That you failed?'

He nods, slipping his arm out of my hold. 'They say everyone destroys what they love most, don't they? Maybe I've destroyed the Press. Certainly haven't saved it.'

Suddenly I see it all, as if the sun's come up. 'Destroyed it? I've never heard such rubbish in my life.'

He shakes his head and moves away, towards the path.

'Mark! Stop! The only thing that nearly destroyed the Press is post-war economics, only it didn't, not quite.' I go after him, raising my voice and not caring if anyone will hear. 'The only thing that *might* yet destroy the Chantry is Izzy.'

'Well, that's her right, you could say,' he says over his shoulder, and his voice is dull and cold. 'Nothing to do with me.'

'But it's *your* right to try to save it. If you want to. None of the rest of us can, not without you. It's you who would make it possible.' He's still far away, but at last he stops and looks round at me, really properly. 'You're necessary. And this time . . . This time everyone knows it.'

He's too far away. I can't see what he's thinking. Then he says, 'There are people I know. Things I can do.'

I nod, but something in the way he's still holding my gaze tells me that his mind's beginning to thaw, so I keep silent.

He says slowly, 'It could work, you know. It could be good.'

Relief begins to shake in my stomach. 'Yes. I think it could.'

'Got to get the money together first.'

'As you say, you know people. And Lionel's good at money. But — but not the other stuff.'

'No.'

'We won't know unless we try.'

'Well . . .' He takes a step towards me. 'I'll . . . If you think . . .'

'I do think. And trying is enough.'

He sort of smiles. 'We could have a bloody good try, all together.'

'Yes, we could,' I say, and he comes closer and takes my

hands, both of them, as if it's some sort of pledge. Something releases inside me and he's filling my sight, blotting out everything else, so that even as I return the pressure of his fingers I'm crying, I'm gasping, I'm fighting for Adam.

Mark holds me. I can't speak or even see much. 'It's all right, Una. Cry if you want to. It's all right . . .'

He holds me so that I don't even think that it's his arms, that it's not Adam, just that I'm safe.

I don't know how long it is, but at last I can hear rooks cawing and smell the peaty wind coming to us over the fields.

'Do you want to go?' he says gently, loosening his hold, so I can pull a tissue from my jeans pocket, but not letting go.

I give my nose a last wipe. 'I'm fine. Thank you . . . I'm just so glad you'll do it. Shall we go and find the church? I like the sound of the tombs.'

Elysabeth — the 1st yr of the Reign of King Richard the Third

I had no hope, yet hope would not die. How could I hope, when all reports told of my boys' servants dismissed? How could I believe they lived, when the word was they were not seen even at the Tower windows seeking a breeze that might thin the stench of London's heat? How could I *not* believe them dead, who had known what the sons of York had done to Henry of Lancaster, or their own George of Clarence? Thus did I try to kill all hope that my boys still lived.

But it would not die, not mine, or my girls'.

'My uncle Clarence's children are kept close for fear of their royal blood,' Bess said once. 'Perhaps Ned and Dickon are but kept closer still. At Middleham or Sheriff Hutton. We would not hear reports from there. Ned was ever a good boy who would do as he was told. He would not plot, or try to escape.'

How could he plot? I would think. He is but a child. But I said nothing.

Antony and my son Richard Grey I mourned with tears and prayers, and bitter anger too for, though I had agreed to a poor escort in bringing Ned to London, it was they who lost my Ned to our enemy. And had they not lost him, Dickon might yet be safe as well. But I was bitterly angry with myself also. Had I not given Dickon up, as surely as a mother who leaves her babe naked in the woods, when I could have kept him safe? Sometimes I thought my grief and rage and fear would tear me in two along the scars of sorrow for my husband John, for my father, my brother John, for Edward, for my babies Mary and George.

They are with God. But for Ned and little Dickon I could not bring myself to say, '*Requiescat in pacem.*' Whatever they suffered, I could not hold them. I could not even know. And I had delivered them to that suffering. But I would not believe them killed; I must believe them alive, imprisoned, fearful at every hour for their lives, perhaps, but living still.

Sometimes the turn of Cecily's head would make the light fall across her face so that it might have been Ned who stood by the window, singing a catch under his breath. Sometimes when I held Katherine on my knee, patting better from a tumble or telling my mother's tale of *Le petit chaperon rouge*, the smell of her neck and her small warmth in my arms made me seem to be holding Dickon.

'And what do you think the little girl did when she saw it was a wolf in her grandmother's bed?'

'Tied him up,' said Katherine.

'That's right. She was a clever little girl,' I said, holding her close.

But Katherine wriggled off my knee and left my arms empty. 'Where's Dickon? He want his knights back to kill the wolf.'

'Dickon's safe with Ned,' I said. 'God will look after them.'

'When will we see them?' Anne asked, as she had asked so often before. 'Are they truly safe?'

Anne was eight by then, not a child for much longer, and lies now would serve her ill. 'I know not. I pray so. We must all pray,' I said, but could say no more.

But as the yellowing leaves dropped under the weight of the autumn rains, as sleet slashed past the windows and the lamps must be lit before a stitch could be set, she ceased to ask.

Even by day there was little enough to keep my fears and my crazed hopes at bay. I had no household. We lived on the Abbot's charity, even for food and firing, and the girls squabbled and fought for idleness and lack of bodily exercise. I would not let them fall into lethargy, though, and every morning they set to on their lessons: law, and accounting, and the ruling of a household. Even their stitchery was practical, for their linen must be mended. Bess was translating *Le Chanson de Roland* into Italian, and Cecily had vowed to learn by heart Antony's *Dictes and Sayings of the Philosophers* in memory of her uncle. Anne cared little for her book, and had to be bribed and beaten to learn even a few pages of *The Life of St Francis*, though I had thought the tales of the animals he tamed would delight her. Katherine cared more for swords than needles but a knight we met in the sanctuary garden – taking refuge on account of what crime I did not ask – taught her a sword dance, and she would sit with her hornbook long enough if I said she might get the swords out afterwards. Baby Bridget was slow to speak, and must be helped to learn her prayers. In the afternoon we danced, or played at shuttlecock or bowls, or anything that stretched their limbs, made them laugh and leap, and brought a glow to their cheeks. In the evening we played at cards and chess. At prayers we prayed for them, but I could not bring myself to say *Nunc Dimittis*.

Cramped and confined as we were, if one sickened we all did: an ague or a quinsy throat quickly overtook us all, slack as our bodies were with enforced idleness. Idleness bred fears in my mind, too. What would become of the girls if I were to die? And whether I lived or died, who would protect them? Who would marry them honourably? Failing her brothers, my beautiful Bess was the true heiress of England and Cecily after her, and both were of an age and more to be married. Bess was our hope, and that was her greatest danger. Would she be a pawn as Warwick's girls had been, the weight of their father's ambition all but drowning them? Be brought to bed like Isobel on a tossing ship barred from harbour and the child die? Forced into marriage to seal the bond between enemies, as her sister Ann was to Queen Marguerite's boy? Most men think Isobel was poisoned and not by the woman that was hanged for it but by her husband, George of Clarence. And now Ann, we heard even in sanctuary, was mortally sick and Richard Gloucester urgent to be free of his wife that he might marry some great princess now that he called himself king.

And in Bess I saw another danger too: in how she moved, in the way she hid in a corner to read yet again of Lancelot and Guinevere, in how she watched a new novice in the Abbey garden or the urgent gaze of a messenger, in some small gestures when she thought I slept. She was eager for the pleasures of her marriage bed. I could read her thoughts, the heat that burnt in her, the flesh that yearned for a man's hand, because these things I once knew so well in myself. So many marriage plans we had made for her when her father was alive: she knew her value, and that of her maidenhead. But now, with no hope of marriage, how could I be sure her desires might not prove too strong for her virtue? We were cabined, dull, so weary of each other that even the air of our chambers was stale with boredom: a new face quickened our spirits for an hour or a day. I could see how to Bess – full of a woman's desire but with no hunting or merry-making to still it, no flirting to relieve it – the blush of a stammering novice or the bow and smile of a gentleman messenger was like strong wine. There was little that could happen in secret, so little privacy had any of us, but even a rumour that she was not chaste, creeping out into the court at Westminster and beyond, could do infinite harm to our cause.

So it was not only to make us safe that I began to lay our plans, it was also to give my girls a reason to be patient. And we could lay plans in sanctuary, for none could prevent Margaret Beaufort's doctor visiting me. We were careful, but messages came and went: offers of help, counsel, small steps towards safety and freedom. By this route I heard, at last, that my son Thomas Grey and brother Edward were safe in Brittany, with Margaret's son Henry Tudor. There was much to arrange, and much to hope for.

But by night there was nothing to ease my terrors. Often I took Bess or Cecily into my bed, that I might find the strength to stop my tears and even take some comfort in their young scent and the quiet of their breathing. But still I would lie listening to the soldiers stamping and calling beyond the sanctuary walls. Each unaccustomed sound — shouts, a horse ridden hard, the rumble of wheels — made me lie rigid, straining my ears for what might be toward. To be the cause of such a desecration would be a crime, a sin it would be hard to bear. Even silence, when I expected the watch to be calling, made me sweat, for Richard might choose to seize us by stealth, rather than make a public show of strength against mere women. But they would not kill us, surely. Even Richard of Gloucester could not do such a deed, could he? And yet, even so must Antony have thought, on the long, hard road to Sheriff Hutton. Would we be forced to take the same road?

And when at last my weariness was stronger than my fears, the nightmares began. Like black-winged demons they showed me what the day denied: the manner of my boys' dying. Night after night I heard their cries, knew their choking in my own throat — blood, wine or bitter cloths — felt their arms clutch for mine, and be dragged away.

It was a relief to wake, even with sore eyes and aching flesh, though by day the night's terrors still hovered in the dark edges of my mind. And even by daylight fear and grief for my boys lay in my heart, as heavy as lead. The days wore on, and we lived almost as straitly as if we were indeed in prison.

Still, we planned. It was my sweet, smiling baby Bridget who found the lucky bean in the Twelfth Night cake, and sat clapping her hands with her paper crown awry as her sisters danced. On the morrow the first part of my plan was accomplished, when we heard that on Christmas Day in Rouen, my old friend Margaret Beaufort's boy Henry Tudor, Earl of Richmond, had been betrothed to Bess. For all that Richard of Gloucester – for I would not call him king – had declared my marriage to Edward void, and my children bastards, the last of the Lancasters would marry the heiress of York. The invasion would take time to plan, but it would come.

On the day after that I woke, and knew that I must act as if my boys were indeed dead, and Bess the rightful Queen of England.

She nodded. 'If you . . . think it best, madam, so be it. I wish we had not come to this.'

'I know. But wishing will not bring them back from . . . wherever they are. We must work as we can.' I wiped my eyes. 'Besides, when your brother was born, you hit Mal when she said you were no longer Princess of Wales.'

She smiled. 'Did I? I had forgotten. It will be good to be in the world again. Sometimes I hate this place so much that it's as if I'm being smothered. I want to scream, but my gorge rises until I could not.'

'We cannot help your brothers now. But I will not leave until I know it is safe. Not if we must stay here till Doomsday.'

She sighed and, after a moment, turned away to the window. Snow lay on the sill, but she forced open the casement and let in a draught of icy air, which made the flames of the fire shiver. I did not reprove her. How often had I opened a window, just so that I might believe our cage not made all of iron?

Not so much iron as steel. Always, beyond the walls, we could hear and see the soldiers, waiting for us: the clang of pikes, the tramp of boots and clatter of arms, the call of the sentries, day and night. Time and again Richard sent envoys to argue that we should leave sanctuary. The only future for my girls lay in the world, that I knew, but there was no safety for them there. Time and again I refused, until he swore an oath before the bishops, lords and commons that I and my daughters would be safe, that he would protect them and provide for them. And then I could perhaps trust that Richard would not willingly endanger his soul or his throne by breaking such an oath, for he was a man of faith as Edward was: it was not he, fool that I had been, who had sworn that my boys would be safe.

Enough, I told myself. I must work for my girls, find them not just an unmarried girl's place in the world but a husband and a secure estate, the means to live comfortably, even perhaps a measure of happiness.

And for me? If I could but know they were provided for, I no longer cared for my own state. I was too weary to wish much for myself: grief for my boys ran in my veins like a wasting sickness, yet I could not wish it gone, for to do so would be to wish them dead. I had no hope for them, I chose to act as if they were dead, yet I could not let hope die.

~

So it was that one morning we walked of our own free will from sanctuary, through the Abbey gardens towards the gate. I would not show my fears, and Bess and Cecily must not either, I had warned them; we must behave fittingly for what we were, the greatest ladies in the kingdom.

It must be so, yet the solemn oaths and assurances, the letters and messages, all the good sense and reason had not been able to still my fears. Was I delivering my girls to our enemies, even as I had delivered Dickon thus? The March wind was no colder than my fears, and I shivered.

The porter stepped forward to let us out: I stopped to thank him and give him gold, for I would let no man say we were less than royal, not even the least of those who had once been my subjects. Then he opened the gate, and we saw what lay beyond.

A small relief from fear rushed through me: all but a handful of the soldiers were gone, and those who remained were not guards, but mounted and formed into an escort. 'Enough for safety, few enough for speed,' Edward would have said, and the memory stung. As we walked out into the world the wind caught at our shabby cloaks and buffeted our faces so that Bridget began to cry. Katherine stared at the hunting dogs, pedlars and hurrying squires for she scarcely remembered such things. Bess picked up Bridget and gave her a sweetmeat.

There was only one man waiting by the horses who was not a soldier.

'Master Nesfield?

He sketched a bow. 'Dame Elysabeth, well met. I trust you will not find our journey too wearisome.'

I forbore to quarrel with the form of his address but looked directly at him. I needed to know how straitly we were to be kept, and in knowing that would learn much else. 'I have not been told where we are bound. Why not?'

He did not answer me, but said merely, 'Only as far as my manor of Heytredsbury. It will be my care to make sure that you and your daughters are comfortable in my custody.'

My courage rose: as I recalled, Heytredsbury was indeed only a manor, no fearful castle where we might be hidden. But it was a long way to Wiltshire, three days' journey or more, and we were none of us fit for such a ride.

'My younger daughters are in poor health. They will need to rest.'

He gestured behind him. 'As you can see, they may travel in this litter. My orders are to reach Heytredsbury as quickly as we may, and for that it is necessary to ride. You need have no fear: the horses are ridden by trusty men.' I had to bite my tongue not to ask him what danger he thought to avoid by forcing us to travel quickly. It would not be politic to quarrel with our keeper, and yet it was hard, for we were in custody as we had not been in sanctuary. Now we were confined by Richard of Gloucester's order, not by our own free choice.

We rode along Petty France. For all my anger and fear, my spirits rose to see the road stretching before us, and to be mounted on a horse beneath a wide sky. Once Westminster was behind us I could see primroses, pale as sunlight, tucked into the grass beneath the hedgerows as we approached Knight's Bridge. But we were prisoners no less, though differently from the prisoners we had been in sanctuary. To judge by his tight-closed mouth and the silence of the men who rode with us, Nesfield would not be a gaoler who took his duty lightly. No matter: I could hold my peace, for I knew that Henry of Richmond, too, bided his time, and planned for the future.

~

At Michaelmas Bess and Cecily were ordered to court. Nesfield allowed us to come to the gate to bid them farewell, though without much ceremony. It was cold, and Bess was impatient to be off, and after we had embraced, and they put up behind the grooms, I gripped the little girls' hands because I could not hold my big girls to me any more. What manner of farewell was this? Had I judged right that they would be safe? Men swear oaths before God and man: who can tell which will be broken until they are? God send I have done right, I prayed. God keep them safe and send them health and happiness.

'Madam, you're hurting me,' said Anne, tugging her hand away.

'Your pardon,' I said. The horses had vanished round a bend in the lane, and only by the faint jingle of steel did I know that they were not long gone. 'Go in, now. It's too cold for little girls.'

As the days passed, thick with the tedium of a household that was not mine, and that heard no news that was not censored, I could only pray that Bess and Cecily would be safe, and trust that even Richard would not forswear his oath. My brother Edward wrote that Richard needed the respect of the great men before whom he had sworn more than he needed Bess and her sisters dead, and I had to be content with that assurance. And the younger girls stayed with me.

The first hard frost came just before Martinmas. Nesfield's secretary brought me a letter from Bess and I sat on the settle beside the fire to read it. It had been unsealed, of course, and read too, I had to assume. There was nothing that reached us unexamined.

From the farmyard came a scream as long and shrill as any human soul's. Bridget burst into tears, and Anne dropped her embroidery hoop on the floor.

'It's only the pigs,' I said, as my woman went to comfort Bridget with a sugarplum. 'Pick your work up, Anne.'

'I don't like it,' said Anne.

'It must happen, or what shall we do for meat, all winter long? It's quickly over.'

'Sausages!' shouted Katherine. 'Madam, may I go and watch?'

'No. Hush.'

'But there'll be blood! Lots of it.'

'No. Be quiet, daughter. That's no sight for a princess.'

Another squeal came. Bridget looked up but did not begin to cry again. She took the sugarplum from her mouth, stared at it, as if to judge its power to keep her safe, and popped it back in. In her stead Anne began to cry. 'The poor p-pigs. It must hurt them so.'

'Block your ears,' I said. 'What can't be mended can always be endured.'

'It doesn't work, madam. It never does. I hear it still, like a nightmare.'

I know too well what you can hear in a nightmare. 'Come here, then, and bury your ears in my lap.'

I stroked her head, and began Bess's letter once more. There was nothing in it to trouble the most censorious gaoler. She began in the proper form, recommending herself to me, but then her news outran her care to write a neat hand: everyone at court was very kind, and she had three new gowns; they had held a competition among the maids as to whose hair was the longest – Aunt Buckingham the judge – and Cecily had won by three handspans. The King had spoken most kindly to them both, though the Queen was sick again and had not left her bed for a fortnight past. In fact, the King had danced with Bess twice last evening, and made her promise to dance again with him when next they met. Could I arrange for her silver girdle with the turquoises to be sent? It would look well with her new blue gown. And her Cicero too, please, she thought she had left it in her bedchamber. She had not studied as much as I had recommended, but had promised at confession to amend this as soon as she might. Next time she would send presents for the girls, if I could let her have a few shillings, for all her money was gone on cards.

As well as my eyes would permit I searched her words for a sign that she did not think of Richard of Gloucester as king in her rightful place, nor yet Ann Neville as his queen. Had she written with Nesfield's secretary in mind, or was her pleasure real? She deserved the pleasure, my good and clever Bess – if I could but be sure that she knew what was her true desert, and cleaved to the knowledge even as she danced with her usurper.

My woman still dandled Bridget, so I asked her to set pen, ink and paper on the table at my elbow that I might write to Bess myself.

I had only just begun when Nesfield's secretary entered. 'A Dame Peters has called. My master permits you to receive her. Is it your pleasure to do so?'

Mal! My dearest Mal, come all the way from Hartwell! Rounder than ever for the cloaks and scarves she had wrapped herself in, and rosy-cheeked from the frost, she stumped into the room, and when I had raised her from the small curtsy that was all her rheumatics allowed, we embraced. In her arms, though my sorrows and fears were beyond her power to amend, for one strange moment it was as if I had no more to trouble me than a cut knee and an unlearnt lesson, and Mal the craft to mend them both. But even Mal had not such craft.

She saw the tears I could not hide, and nodded to my woman to take the girls away. 'I'll come and see you in a while, my sweets. Off you go.'

'Can we go and see the pigs being butchered?' I heard Katherine beg, as they went out. 'Please? Please? They're all killed, now, so Anne needn't be such a cry-baby.'

'Your brother Master Edward was just the same,' said Mal, loosening her wrappings and casting her cloak on the window-seat. 'A pity she'll not be Admiral of the Fleet like her uncle, for I warrant she'd do well . . .' She sat down beside me. 'And how keep you, madam?'

I had to shake my head, but mastered myself at last. 'Well enough. Bess and Cecily are at court, did you know?'

'Now that I did know. With your brother Sir Richard – the new Lord Rivers, I *should* say – with him at Grafton so much, even quietly, the news gets there. And as I promised you, there's not much that doesn't cross the valley to Hartwell after. And is she well, Lady Bess?'

'So she says. I would I knew more of how she does.'

'She'll do well enough. Your sister Mistress Margaret — my lady Arundel, I *should* say — she'll have an eye to them. It'll not be your girls getting a court belly, whoever else does. And from all I hear His Grace of Gloucester's court is sober and godly, like himself, and his lady too.'

'So he would have us think. And poor Ann Neville mortally sick. She was not made for such a great position, I think, usurped or no. Warwick crushed everything out of her before ever she was married. And then she lost her own boy, Edward. But who knows what Richard of Gloucester really is?'

She sighed. 'And there's no hope?'

A great lump of grief rose in my throat. 'How can I hope? And how can I not? . . . Oh, Mal, every day I go from one to the other until my belly heaves with it. I'm frightened, now we're not in sanctuary, and yet it's better for I cannot see . . . I cannot see Dickon as I could at Westminster. And Ned . . . Oh, Ned . . .'

She drew me into her arms and let me weep unhindered, uncajoled, but comforted, as I had not wept since the day I had vowed to act as if they were lost for ever.

I shall never reach the end of my grief for my boys: it is unfathomable. But from near enough to it, deep in the well of my sorrow, I cried out, 'I cannot recall Ned's face. Or his voice. Or his smiles. I have nothing of him to remember. Antony had it all, and Antony lost him, and Antony is gone.'

Then Mal wept too, for Antony had ever held the chief place in her heart, and two winters had not served to still her grief, any more than they had mine.

At last I was too weary to weep any longer, but half lay against the cushions on the settle. Mal sat with her arms about me, staring into the fire. When my woman entered with comfits and sweet wine I could command myself well enough to eat and drink, then asked for the children. Mal had never seen Bridget, and knew the others scarcely more, and she had brought presents for them all.

They did me credit, thanking Mal prettily enough. Then Anne showed Katherine how to whip her top, though I had to frown at her before she would open the chapbook of the story of St Martin that Mal had brought her. Bridget patted the little wooden horse and cart but then just sat and looked at it, not trying to play. After a while Mal scooped her up and carried her to the window to catch what light there was. Then she gave her a kiss, set her down before her toy, and came back to where I sat.

'More than sixty years I've been on this earth,' she said quietly to me, 'and I've never seen a child with eyes like Lady Bridget's that learnt her book. Did you say she's sickly?'

'Yes, though it's not her chest or her belly. The doctors say her heart murmurs. But she's happy enough, always laughing. Do you remember the rages my poor George used to fall into?'

'Aye, God rest his soul. He'll not be raging where he is now. But Lady Bridget is a sweet soul, that I can tell, and always will be. You may find she's best off with the holy sisters when she's older. They'll care for her, and St Bridget will guard her as her own, for she is that, bless her. She'll learn enough before then, with her sisters to play with her.'

'I think I could not bear to lose another.'

'You'll not be losing her. Mistress Ysa, only looking after her in the best way you may. Just as God looks after all those he has in his keeping.'

I wept again then, but quietly.

It was past Nones, but Nesfield would not let Mal lodge with us. 'No matter,' said Mal. 'The sisters at Warminster have a guesthouse; my head ploughman's niece is but lately taken on there as a novice. It's no distance with rested horses, and my man knows the road.'

So we parted, with many promises to Heaven and each other to meet again, whether better times came to us all, or no.

Part Four

End

All joy and sorrow for the happiness or calamity of others is produced by an act of the imagination, that realises the event, however fictitious, or approximates it, however remote, by placing us, for a time, in the condition of him whose fortune we contemplate; so that we feel, while the deception lasts, whatever emotions would be excited by the same good or evil happening to ourselves.

Dr Johnson, *The Rambler*, Saturday, 13 October 1750

X

In the church of St Helen and the Holy Cross Mark lays a hand on the boy's tomb. The figure's worn, the praying hands lost and the feet too, the stone face smoothed almost to nothing in the cool morning light. But the proportions are a boy's, and the long, heavy gown and elaborate cap, the high Gothic mouldings of the base, all breathe the grandeur and wealth of his small life. 'Edward of Middleham,' Mark reads. 'He must have been important.'

'He was. He was Richard of Gloucester's son, his only heir. He died when Richard had been king for less than a year, of a fever, I think. A political disaster too, of course, to lose your heir — for the Prince of Wales to die. His parents were shattered. His mother died a year later.'

'Losing a child.'

'Yes.'

It's not even sure that this is his tomb, I read, despite

the hopeful local labels. And yet someone's present, as they weren't at the castle: a man and a woman mourning a child. It's not Elizabeth, not Anthony, who mourn this child: they've never stood where we stand and this is the home and the sorrow of their enemies. And yet somehow, in this air scented with long-dead candle-smoke, the cold and ancient stone, the bitter spice of myrrh . . . somehow they invade my senses and my mind and bring Anthony before me like an opium dream of the heart, and Elizabeth too, for losing a child is losing a child: a grief unfathomable.

Behind us the latch of the church door clacks, footsteps sound and the swish of a cassock. A woman dressed thus is still a novelty. She's carrying a stack of old books and newer booklets and has a square, sensible face. Only when we catch her eye does she come over.

'It's beautiful, isn't it? Amazing to think of it being so old.'

'And they don't know for sure who it is?' I ask.

'So I'm told. I haven't really had a chance to catch up with the history yet. Goodness knows, there's enough of it, somewhere like this, but what with the school and all the work in the parish and the diocesan projects . . . York's not the glamorous time-capsule the tourists think it is. Are you just visiting?'

'Sort of, though it's also professional. I'm a historian.'

'You might be interested in these, then,' she says, nodding at the pile of books in her arms. 'My husband's been working his way through the books my predecessor left behind, and he said these two should go in the safe. Would you like a quick look before I lock them up? My name's Anne, by the way. Anne Stewart. I'm the rector, as you'll no doubt have deduced from the collar.'

I smile and thank her with the automatic but non-committal warmth I use for non-professional helpfulness, and she unlocks the vestry, and takes us in.

The bindings are mid-eighteenth-century calf, thick and smooth and in remarkably good condition. The first book turns out to be contemporaneous with its binding: *The History of Tom Jones, a Foundling*. A racy read for an eighteenth-century clergyman, I'd have thought. I show it to Mark.

'Could he have thought it really was a history?' he says. 'They'd only just invented novels.'

'Or an improving tract,' says Anne Stewart, stacking Series Three Communion booklets briskly on a shelf, next to worn but gaudily illustrated Ladybird *Stories from the Holy Land* and *The Good Samaritan*. 'Like all those awful Victorian moral tales. Do sit down, by the way.'

'Nothing very moral about Tom Jones. At least, not in the Victorian sense,' I say, perching on a schoolroom chair tucked into a corner. I flip carefully through the pages: it's printed by Foulis in Glasgow, which is as I'd expect. 'It's a nice, workaday edition, and a good binding. May I see the other?'

It looks much the same on the outside, but it isn't the

same at all inside. No businesslike product of the clattering presses of the Enlightenment, this. Here is a mixture
of pages, papers, sizes, typefaces. There's no real title
page, only a printed list of the contents, the printer given
as Peter Small of York, MDCLXVII. It starts, ortho-
doxly enough, with the sermons and prayers of Lancelot
Andrewes in a good Plantin, though the type was worn:
his Jacobean words lilt steadily across the page.

> *Seeing the text is of seasons, it would not be out of season itself.*
> *And though it be never out of season to speak of Christ, yet even*
> *Christ hath His seasons. Your time is always, saith He, so is*
> *not Mine; I have My seasons.*

Then there's a *History of the Parish of Sheriff Hutton incorporating*
also the parishes of Lilling, Whenby, Cornborough, Stittenham and
Flaxton, their Notable Inhabitants and Memorable Events, as recorded
by the Reverend Isaac Ferguson esq. MA DD, late of Magdalene
College Cambridge, to celebrate the restoration of King Charles II. A
rather roughly cut van Dyck fount. I run my eye down a
page or two, and it's clear why *A History of Tom Jones* was the
better seller. Anne Stewart emerges from a deep cupboard
and sees my faint grin. She looks over my shoulder as she
goes past behind me with a whiff of mothballs and brass
polish. 'Is that handwriting? Strange, in a proper book.'

I look down at where my careless page-turning has
brought me to. 'Oh, it's quite common at this date.
Printers sent their books out in the sheets, and they were

bound and sold locally. So you could get your local binders to put together anything that you wanted kept together: essays, recipes, letters, whatever. You get all sorts of stuff mixed up.'

It's a good late-sixteenth-century hand, not the court hand of clerks, my paleographic colleagues would say, but the italic style of an educated man or woman, accustomed to write a good deal. The black strokes jog across the page with no more force or flourish than necessary, as if the writer was old, and could spare little time for more than was needed to tell the tale.

What follows was kept to the day of his death by my great-great-uncle George Ferguson esq. sometime Rector of this Parish of Sheriff Hutton, as am I in my turn in the eighth year of the Reign of King Charles, in this year of Our Lord MDCXXXIII. Though distant kin on the distaff side to Ann Nevil, wife of King Richard III, whose family had been lords of Sheriff Hutton since the days of the first King Richard that was called Cœur de Lion he was so well-beloved of his parishoners for the holiness of his life and the wisdom of his words that all trusted in him and sought his counsel, whatever their allegiance in the War of the Cousins that was only ended by the uniting of the houses of York and Lancaster under the late King Henry Tudor.

'Is it authentic?' says Mark, putting a hand on my shoulder to peer at the page.

'I don't know. You'd need to test the paper and so on to be sure. But everything fits: the binding, the handwriting, the dates. On the face of it . . .'

I turn the page. The next is in a much older hand, though fluent enough in its still-Gothic style, the spelling more variant, the words and their ordering more foreign to the eye.

> *In Nomine Patris Dei. This letter being brought to me George Ferguson Rector of Sheriff Hutton by one Stephen Fairhurst late of this parish, he desired me firstly to copy it and then seal it again with mine own seal and mark, that the most gracious lady* [scratched out] *that will God willing read it shall know that the seal was broken of no malice or malfeasance but for her sake and the sake of her brother* [scratched out] *the most wise and learned nobleman that ever met his end at the hands of his enemies, so that whatsoever befall the true letter at the hands of said enemies, there might be a copy extant that in better times could yet reach her. When I had done copying he departed for London and I pray to God that he meet with nowt on the road that hinders him in the execution of his purpose. Gloria Patri et Filio et Spiritui Sancto. Sicut erat in principio et nunc et semper. Written at Sheriff Hutton the fourth day after the Nativity of John the Baptist.*

And then, in the same hand, but more carefully, as if the writer took care to observe words and spellings that were not his own:

Most gracious madam, my Queen and sister, I recommend me humbly to you, and give you God's blessing and mine. I shall entrust this letter to the boy that waits on me this night which is my last on earth. His name is Stephen Fairhurst and if this reach you by his hand it may have been at some danger to himself. I pray you see that he be rewarded in as much as it lies in your power to do it.

I must first tell that your son Sir Richard Grey, being brought here to Pontefract with our cousin Haute when I was held at Sheriff Hutton, lives, and is held here still. I am told he is well enough, although the Constable will not suffer me to speak with him nor yet send word. But alas, madam, he is to die on the morrow, even as I am. God willing, I shall be granted time to speak words to him of comfort and good cheer. To meet steadfastly all that life in this world may inflict on us is the first duty and virtue of a man.

They tell me that you have taken Sanctuary: may God and His Saints keep you safe and Prince Richard with you, and also the girls. You know as well as I that while Dickon lives in safety Ned is safe also. I pray each day that Ned is well and merry, for he has been as a son to me and I love him as any father would. There may yet be a means of restoring him to his throne: our brother Edward and your son Thomas will advise you, also His Grace of Canterbury. And though my lord Hastings has long been opposed to our family in matters of interest and governance; he is a man of great honour and loves the King's children as well as he loves his own. And should it never happen that Ned is crowned, you may comfort yourself that, though a king has more than common men's power to do good in the world, it is not easy to do it, and yet keep his soul truly fixed on God. May God's will be done in this as in all things.

You must look first to Ned's safety and your own and that of your other children, but if you hear of aught ill befalling my most beloved daughter Margaret, or my wife, and if it is in your power to amend it, you will have my great thanks. Touching my Will, I have appointed honourable men to execute it, praying Richard Gloucester to look that all is done aright, for though to my great grief he has Ned in his power and may take his Crown, he has ever looked to the late King as his example in the proper despatch of affairs. I have been well treated here and at Sheriff Hutton, suffering no insult but that I am deprived of my liberty and now my life. A priest will attend me shortly, and I shall die confessed and shriven. I trust in God that the one I loved best in all the world will follow me into His care. I comfort myself that there is nothing in this sorrowful world that I can wish for more than I wish for what lies beyond death.

O Elysabeth, my greatest grief is that I did not foresee what would come. May God forgive me, for I cannot forgive myself. I did not know Richard Gloucester for what he was, did not guard Ned as I should have guarded him. My most dear sister, I pray your forgiveness too, though it is beyond my desert. How can I hope for it when I have failed in the greatest charge you and my lord the late King ever laid on me? How can I forgive myself, knowing that Ned may not be able to forgive me? I have lost to our enemies your most

*beloved son, who is the son of my heart also. That I did not
look for betrayal from such a quarter cannot earn me your
pardon, nor is my own penance in death enough. I can only
entreat humbly and lowly that you pardon me out of love,
even as I have loved you as long and as well as any man
may love his sister and his queen. I pray for forgiveness at
every Office, and find it not in my own heart. My poor and
only comfort is that in this, as in all other things, it is the
fate of mortals to fall short of God, who forgives all.*

*I shall not know if you have pardoned me. I can only
hope that you do. I go to my death in the hope of resurrection
in the world to come. Almighty Jesu have you and yours in
his safe keeping, most beloved sister, and God send you such
health and happiness as the world can provide, knowing that
it is but a grain of sand, by comparison to the joy of
Heaven which by God's grace awaits us all. Written at
Pontefract on the eve of the Nativity of John the Baptist and
knowing the hour of my death.*

Antony Rivers

Not a ghost, an opium-dream: a vision so real my
mind does not trouble to tell me it is not.

Something touches my shoulder. 'Una, are you all
right?' says Mark.

'May I copy this?' I say to Anne Stewart, as I pull
notebook and pencil out of my bag. My hands are
trembling and I drop both on the floor.

'Not in pen,' she says quickly. I straighten up. 'Oh,
you've got a pencil. Yes, of course. But why don't you both

come over to the rectory and you can do it there? It's much warmer, and my husband's probably got the kettle on.'

~

'He never knew,' I say to Mark. We're sitting on a rug on the grass by the great stump of a windmill, just off the road to Thornton-le-Clay. Around us the country stretches away without a soul or an animal in sight, just trees and fields the greeny-grey of unripe wheat, and a small breeze, under a pale grey sky as flat and bright as the fields. 'He never knew if she got the letter or not . . . Or if Ned was safe.'

'Ned?'

'Edward, Prince of Wales. "May God forgive me, for I cannot." His son, as near as made no difference. Anthony never knew if Ned forgave him.'

After a long time Mark says, 'What are you going to do about the letter?'

Somehow I find a neutral, scholarly voice. 'Well the diocesan archivist is the proper person, as Anne's husband said. But I've got the copy and there's no reason I shouldn't use it. If I were a young, hungry history post-doc, I'd think I was made, professionally speaking.'

'But you're not.'

'What?'

'A young, hungry history – what did you say?'

'Post-doc. Someone who's done their PhD and is trying to make a career.'

'Is it relevant? I mean, to your book about Anthony and Elizabeth's books?'

With a shock I realise it hasn't occurred to me to ask myself the question. 'Of course it's not relevant, except in the general way. He doesn't mention his own books in the letter, though the will refers to them. If he wrote anything in prison, the way Walter Raleigh wrote his *History of the World*, or Malory wrote *Le Morte Darthur*, we don't know about it. The letter's not even an autograph, though a contemporaneous copy's much more convincing than a later one. If it *is* a copy of something that once existed. It might even turn out to be a fake – a game – a wish-fulfilment by some Woodville supporter up here in Richard's fiefdom. But I wish it was relevant. To me, I mean. Because it's him, isn't it?' I can hear the longing of the opium addict in my voice. 'It's him the way a will isn't. His voice, not just his business.'

'Should you be writing a biography?'

I'm dumbstruck. It hasn't occurred to me. I stare out to where the broken spars of the castle are black against the sky. 'I don't know. It's not my field. Some people would be rather shocked. Academic historians despise biographers, much of the time.'

'But you don't.'

'No, not at all. But it's not what I do. I do books.' I don't know where my sigh comes from. 'I want to do people, but it's so difficult. You're trying to write something whole, where things make sense, where they're certain, and you can't. Not with people like that. There's too much you can't know. It's all *if* and *perhaps* and *maybe he thought* and *maybe she remembered*, and the last two are pretty dubious, in scholarly terms. At least balance sheets and watermarks actually exist.'

'Just have to wait and see when you've got all the material, won't you?' says Mark. 'Like a survey of a building I'm involved with restoring. Then you'll know how best to set it out. Whether it's best guess, or clean glass and steel, as Charlie said.'

'Yes, I suppose I shall,' I say slowly.

I'm so aware of Mark's presence on the other half of the rug that I feel him bracing himself to say something before he speaks. Then he says, 'Could you forgive me for leaving? Some day?'

The breeze brushes over us and the leaves show their pale undersides like a wheeling flock of birds. 'Yes,' I say, because I find I have. I've forgiven Mark.

'I'm glad.'

The silence is enormous. It's a vast space where my anger was, and now, just ... isn't. Perhaps it's this pilgrimage. Or perhaps it's as Anthony would say: forgiveness is not an act of will, it's God-given, a grace we can only pray for.

But when Mark turns and smiles down at me, as if it were my own body not his I can feel the easing of something in him. My heart turns over and I can't pretend it hasn't happened: I can't pretend any longer that

I don't want him, and I can't pretend he doesn't know.

Would Adam forgive me for desiring Mark?

The thin cloud above us is breaking into wisps and scraps and the breeze is freshening. Mark looks up at the sky. 'Are you cold?'

'No, I'm fine.'

'Had enough of these sandwiches?'

'Yes, thanks.'

I realise I'm very tired, though why I don't know, and then a voice in my head that sounds like Morgan's says, 'If you're tired, lie down,' so I do, as simple as that, with the wool of the rug tickling my cheek. We borrowed it from Fergus, and it smells faintly of oil paint.

I could lie here for ever, I think, smelling the grass and the wind. Mark's leaning back propped on his elbows, idly watching the breeze brushing the wheat from dark to light again, like a hand brushing velvet. Yes, I could stay here for ever, with Mark, not speaking, just being.

Only I can't stay another night, must go back to London, back to Australia, back to where I can best hold on to Adam. But for the first time since I set off from Sydney I wish I could. I want to see the castle with the bare daylight waning or the moon-cast shadows showing me what wasn't there before.

Am I silly – childish – to want to see that shadow bowed over this letter, to hear the scrape of quill on paper, the stamp of horses and the clatter of arms? To smell the resin of hot sealing wax, the sweet dryness of a snuffed candle, even, yes, the stench of a prison, the dirty straw and bucket of soil, the fear . . . Is it silly, if it means being able to touch his world, and tell his story as I believe it?

Believing stories is what children do, and I'm not a child.

I trust in God that the one I loved best in all the world will follow me into His care.

Who was that? We know so little, except that it was probably neither of his wives. There was Gwentlian, the mother of his child, or the child Margaret herself: we know he did love her. It might not even have been in England but Rome or Portugal. It might not even have been a woman.

Even if somewhere there's a letter, a poem, a chronicle that tells me, I shan't know, not really. Not *know*, as you know your own hands, or your child's face, or your lover's body. I can't write how he paces out his cell, four paces wide and six deep, the walls of pale grey stone and the sky beyond the window. I can't say that he sits in his cell remembering the weight and grip of a goshawk on his arm, or the scrambling, bloody stab and slash in the dark at Sandwich and the ropes cutting shame into his wrists as they were herded below decks and realised with a terrible hollow fear that they were bound for their enemy's stronghold at Calais. I can't say that he looked up from his book in a Flemish tavern, and saw a young man with skin the colour of copper, and loved him and lay with him, touching each gloss and flaw, the thick muscle close under fine, hard skin, the broad fighter's hands, thigh pressed to thigh and arms that grip, bodies as taut as an archer's bow, seizing each other.

I'm woken by Mark gently touching my shoulder. 'Una, we should go. It's getting late, and we've got a long way to drive.'

Elysabeth — the 6th yr of the reign of King Henry the Seventh

I sleep better, these days, than I have for many a year, but still, as all my life, I wake early. This morning, St John's Day, that was the eve of my brother Antony's death not so many years since, I stood watching the sun rise over the Thames, and listening to the last notes of Matins from the chapel across the Abbey garden. When the sun had risen in glory, I turned away.

I am no prisoner, but live here in right of my royal widowhood, and it is enough for me. And I have realised that a chamber such as this is all that my life requires. Four paces wide, and six deep, the same on both sides, and another chamber beyond it where I and my woman sleep. I know, because I paced them out when I first came to Bermondsey, to see what of my goods would fit to my new life. Four well-made walls of pale grey stone and a window high enough to admit God's light and air. Bermondsey Abbey is a great house and generously endowed: every beam is massive and well seasoned, every stone well carved and dressed, and the chapel glows with gold and fine work. Here I have all that a soul and body require: meat and bread, a roof and a fire to warm my thin old bones, holy Mass and private prayer. The sun and the moon shed light for me and I have my book of hours and an image of St Bridget painted on ivory, as perfect as a jewel. And I have my books. Here, at my hand, is the wisdom of St Thomas Aquinas and Antony's translation of Christina of Pisa, my book of the *Hours of the Guardian Angel*, tales of St Nicholas and of Iseut and Tristan, and the songs of love and beauty and despair that were sung at the courts of the great Queen Aliénor who came from Aquitaine.

I do not have the letter that Antony wrote the night before he died. I took it and the ring from the lad's frozen hand and gave him meat and gold and set him to warm himself at the fire, for autumn had come early to Westminster that year, and the stone walls of sanctuary breathe cold. He told me what he could of Antony's end, and when he had gone I read the letter, over and over again, till the words were written on my heart. Then, because I dared not keep it, I held the paper to the flames, and it flared and burnt away to nothing, and into my bodice, next to my heart, I put his ring.

It was nearly two years before Henry Tudor sailed from the Seine and landed in Wales, but that day did come, and then came the news that Richard of Gloucester was dead. We heard it at Heytredsbury, and did not trouble to hide our rejoicing from Nesfield.

I was still much about King Henry's court when we first heard that a rebellion was formed on a boy they cried as Richard, Duke of York, younger son of the late King Edward IV. At the news my heart was joyful, then sick. I knew it to be false, yet my spirit craved the consolation that it was true: that though Ned was lost, Dickon did live and breathe. For an hour or two I hoped, though hope for Dickon meant I must fear for Bess and the King and baby Arthur, my grandson. Then the men who pulled the lad's strings changed their tale: this was George of Clarence's boy, they cried. But I knew — we all knew — that *he* lives at the Tower, a prisoner of Henry Tudor as surely as my boys ever were prisoners there.

It was nothing, though it took a battle at Stoke to show it for the nothing it was.

Yes, I have my books, and they comfort me, and make me smile and laugh, or ponder great things, or breathe with those lovers who thought the world well lost, so greatly did they love. But sometimes I can do nothing but sit at my window and look over the rooftops to the river and beyond it to the Tower. I know not if it is my sons' grave, but it is all the grave I can imagine.

When there is nothing left, there is always prayer. Each bead and image on my rosary stands for a prayer that helps to fill the void.

My daughters visit me, and I do go to court. But I find there so little that I wish to find, excepting only my grandchildren, and the courtiers court not me, the Queen Consort's Mother, but Margaret Beaufort, the King's Mother. I have known her all my days, and I do not wonder at it. But it leaves little business for me, who was wont to have the business of a kingdom to look to, and what business I had about my own estate wearied me as it has never wearied me since my first days at Astley. So I have given up my dowry lands to Bess in return for a pension from the King, and with them I have given up all that tied me to this world and tangled me in the web of interest and obligation, power and treachery. On the eve of Bess's coronation, I watched the ceremonial barges sail upriver from Greenwich to the Tower, and prayed that she might know all the happiness and none of the sorrow that I have known.

That was two years ago. Now I am sitting in the window with my work untouched on my lap, looking across the river, which lies like grey, crumpled silk about the Tower walls.

A lay-sister enters. 'So please you, Your Grace, one Master Jason is in the visitors' parlour, and craves an audience.'

This is puzzling: I know of no such man. But I learnt of Edward many years since that he or I may forget many a man who will never forget meeting us. So I summon my woman, and go down to the parlour.

A small man, Master Jason, I see, peering through the glass which is let into the door of the visitors' parlour that no religious might be accused of secret or unholy dealings with those still in the world. This man is certainly still in the world, though plainly dressed and dark; you may see a dozen such in any street in London and swear you saw none. He uncovers his head as I enter, but before he kneels to me he looks keenly into my eyes as if to be sure that I am the one he seeks. When I raise him I find him taller than I had thought, and broader, strong in the arm and with a light in his dark eyes that I suddenly know.

'You are—'

He raises a hand and I am silenced. I turn to my woman. 'You may go.'

'Madam—' she says.

'I am not a religious and Master Jason has private business with me. You may watch through the glass if you prefer,' I add, for I have no wish for idle gossip, however ill-founded, about this visit.

'Aye, Madam, if you wish it.'

When the door is shut behind her I say, in French, 'You must forgive my lack of ceremony, and that I speak French, not the Gascon tongue. But you are nonetheless welcome, Monseigneur le Chevalier de Bretaylles.'

'Madame, I see no lack of ceremony in such royal discretion. I pray you excuse my directness, but I have little time and must come to the point. I think you know that your brother was the man I loved most in the world.'

'I know it,' I say, and though it is eight years since Antony was killed, I must swallow hard to keep my tears in check, for the love I bore my brother is very like to that which such close comrades in arms bear each other, and to hear de Bretaylles speak of his awakes my own. There were times when it seemed that Antony was more faithful in my service and constant in his love for me than was Edward or any other man, even as I was in my love and care for him. This man before me must have tasted some of that same constancy in the face of the world's battles.

If Louis de Bretaylles feels his own grief rise, I cannot see it. After a moment he says, 'I must tell you that when Antony was taken I was with the Prince, your son, at Stony Stratford. I . . . Prince Edward had many good men about him, not least your son Sir Richard Grey, and I pray you will not think me a coward that I judged it better to be free, and do what I might in secret, than make yet one more prisoner to be buried in the Duke of Gloucester's fiefdom.'

'No, indeed, and I am glad to know that you were not taken.'

'*Mais oui, madame.* I regret that I have not been able to come to you before, but in such uncertain times any man who is known about the court for secret work is regarded with suspicion. Only when I heard news of King Henry's great victory over the pretender at Stoke, and that he was truly safe, did I judge it safe for me, too.'

'You were wise. You must know that so dangerous did the King judge the times that he even imprisoned my son

Thomas, though my brother Edward fought in the King's name and was wounded.'

'I had heard. But, Madame, I have little time, and I must tell my tale.'

'Of course.'

'When I saw there was nothing I could do during the new King Edward's journey to London I rode ahead. But soon I knew there was little to be done either in overthrowing Prince Richard. He had too tight a grip on men and arms, and still tighter once he was crowned. I knew – I knew my lord Rivers was dead . . . I stayed in London, listening and watching for news of the Princes, your sons.' I nod, and swallow again. 'Nor did I dare come to you at Westminster, for many there would know me for myself. I set myself up as a Milanese, a teacher of swordfighting, and made a name for myself also as a frequenter of the alehouses in Smithfield and the Hounds' Ditch.'

He seems at a loss how to go on, and then my heart begins to pound. 'And . . . ?'

He nods. 'I could do nothing for the Princes except stay where I might hear it, if there was a whisper to be heard. It was two days after Ascension Day. I met a man in a tavern, better not to say which, or name him. I thought I knew his face from the court of the Duke of Brittany, and I was right: he had but lately sailed from Brest. Thinking that he might have news of who had collected about Henry Tudor, as he was then, at Rennes, I called for wine. I think he was lonely, and happy to speak in French. This man knew little of any plans, but he suddenly began to speak of what had brought him to London. Not exactly, you understand. He would not at first tell me what his own commission was. But he spoke of secret doings about the Tower, of meeting Richard of Gloucester's man Sir James Tyrell. He told me that it was not thought safe for King Richard's crown that the Princes were known to be alive.'

'And . . .' I must know, yet I feared to know, even as a man fears his death but fears still more not to know the hour of it. 'And this meeting? What was decided?'

'Everything. On the day we met – he was in his cups by then – he told me . . . Ah, Madame, would you have me go on?'

His voice is gentle and it breaks through my guard. 'Yes, I must know, I must! Anything is better than this torment, anything! You must tell me.'

'He said that now King Richard was safe.'

'Ah, God have mercy!'

'But, Madame, it is not quite . . . That is not the whole story. He told me . . . that he had borne a message from Rennes – you understand?' I nod. 'From Rennes, yes, with gold for Sir Richard Tyrell, and a message, that – Rennes would also find it safer if your sons were not known to be alive. And the gold was to make doubly sure it were done, and done soon . . . and done mercifully.'

I am overwhelmed with sorrow so strong I cannot stand.

Louis de Bretaylles is kneeling before me where I sit, gripping my hands as if only thus can he be sure that I will hear his tale. 'Madame, thus was it done: mercifully. It was the eve of Ascension Day, and that was the reason given for sending their confessor to them that evening. They confessed, were shriven and blessed. Then together they slept, on that holy eve, and knew nothing until they woke and found themselves with God.'

I am weeping still, though not for long: so much grief have I known that I have learnt to stop my tears quickly when I must.

'Madame, forgive me. I have stayed too long for your safety or mine. You must know that their mortal remains are safe, and decently interred within the Tower, although I know not where. Forgive me, I must be gone.'

'Of course. Monsieur, you have all – all my gratitude, to the end of my days. And I know . . . you pray for my brother's soul, even as I do.'

'*Oui, Madame*,' he says, and now I can hear his grief in his voice.

'Excuse me,' I say, and turn away. When I turn back he has pulled on his cloak and taken up his hat. 'I have something that was his. He sent it . . . with a letter that he wrote on the eve of his death. He asked my forgiveness for what had happened, and now . . . May I consider you his representative on earth, and give you this, in token of my gratitude?'

I hold out Antony's ring, heavy in my palm and warm

from my heart's blood. The pilgrim's cockleshell gleams, then the little ship inside catches the light too, and I remember the sobriquet Louis de Bretaylles used. 'I think you know this ring.'

He takes it from me with a bow, and presses it to his lips. 'Madame . . .' He clears his throat. 'Your brother gave it to me many years since. It was a token of our friendship, and of the journeys we made together. When I saw what was toward at Stony Stratford I contrived to give it to your son Sir Richard Grey. Sir Richard — you will, I think, like to know that he, too, was most coura- geous in the face of such force . . . And he must have done as I hoped in giving the ring privily to Antony . . . It . . . I am more grateful to have it than I have words to express.'

'No more words, then, Monseigneur. There is no more to say, I think, though much to pray for. You will have my thanks for all eternity. Farewell, and à Dieu.'

He bids me farewell with all courtesy, and yet, by the time the door is open and my woman is in the room, he has shrunk to the ordinary Master Jason, and by the few words that he says before he takes his leave you might think he had never travelled further afield than Deptford.

I withdraw from the parlour, go to my chamber and weep.

After many hours the black, bitter stone that has been lodged in my heart for so many years begins to soften, as if my hot new grief is an alchemist's fire.

~

I have decided to trust what Louis de Bretaylles has told me: not only that my sons are dead but as to the manner of their dying. But tonight I do not sleep, or even lie in my bed, though my woman pleads with me till I send her away. I sit at my window with the casement open to whatever bad airs choose to enter: it is no matter. I sit and feel the emptiness next to my heart where Antony's ring was hidden until this day, and look through the night at where my boys died, and where they lie.

I think, too, of my son Richard Grey and weep for him, that in his last days he did this small service, which he cannot know brought comfort to three people.

But my thoughts and tears cannot long stay away from Ned and Dickon. To know their fate is such a new sorrow, and such a comfort, that I can hardly bear to believe it. Sometimes as the night draws on I think I do not deserve such comfort, for it was I who gave up Dickon to his fate. Sometimes I wonder if Louis de Bretaylles spoke truth. But I *must* believe. Slowly, as the night wears on hour by hour, marked by each bell that rings in the heavy air, and each night-watchman's and sentry's cry of 'Who goes there?' . . .

Slowly, by God's grace, I do believe.

The darkness is lifting: to the east, down the river, the land is rimmed with grey the colour of pearl. Below, in the Abbey grounds, I hear the sharp shuffle and murmur of the lay-sisters rising to go about their tasks in the garden, the kitchen, the orchard. The silence of the holy sisters calls me to join them. The latch rises: my woman is coming to help me dress, though it is an hour or more till Prime. Even with plain old gowns and no more headdress than a widow's hood it takes time, for we are both old, and my bones ache, and there is little flesh on them. I move slowly.

But I have been granted God's grace in this: the pain and weariness of my body keeps me in mind of the pain and weariness of this whole world, racked as it is by the endless turning of Fortune's wheel. This is God's mercy, for there may be mercy even in the death of hope: He did bring me news, so that my days and nights might be quiet at last. And His still greater mercy is that each of these quiet days brings me nearer to my death, happy in the knowledge that in Heaven all weariness is banished, all life is joy, and there, at last, I shall see my boys.

Una — Sunday

We picked Morgan up from Heworth, and Fergus waved us off, knee deep in his gently rebellious garden. When we dropped Morgan home, even though the midsummer light still stretched before us we didn't linger after the hugs and farewells. Morgan whistled Beth out of the way as the car bumped over the grass. Threading our way through the lanes towards the motorway I suddenly saw how Morgan makes sense of what Fergus has inherited from the Chantry: how in her, art and craft are underpinned by the ordinary family business of food and talk and fondness, which has been lost to us – to Izzy, and Lionel, and Mark, and me – since we were scattered.

Driving at night is a bit like being in limbo: all you can see is what's lit as you go past, and the small patch ahead that your own lights illuminate. The noise of road and wind is mesmerising: I hear Uncle Gareth's voice reading me a bedtime story, his voice low and rumbly. My fingers fiddled illicitly with the fraying hole in the silk of my rosy eiderdown, and Smokey Bear snuggled up against my side. Something about days being like a string of beads but travelling days belonging to a different string. But what book was that from? I can't remember, but it's true, and I think suddenly of a rosary.

No slow stations on our pilgrimage now: the motorway roars straight past Nottingham and Derby, Leicester, Northampton, St Albans, and into a diversion that's traffic-clotted even though it's gone eleven o'clock, so that we crawl round to enter London by way of Barnet and Highgate. Mark and I don't talk much. There's nothing more, for now, to be said about Izzy, though on Monday there'll be a lot before I fly.

What still needs to be said about Mark and me is also going to have to wait till the morning. And Adam.

It's nearly midnight when we roll off the end of the A1 and into a queue of panting cars at Archway. 'You must be so tired,' says Mark. 'Why don't you drive straight to Limehouse, and I'll get a cab home from there? Ealing's out of your way.'

'Well, if you're sure . . . I am tired, I must admit.'

In Limehouse I draw up outside my house and pull on the handbrake, and he lays his hand over mine. 'Well driven.'

'Come in. We'll call a cab, and have a drink while you wait for it.'

I unlock the front door and we go into the same chilly emptiness that was waiting for me when I arrived from Australia. The alarm shows that it's past midnight. It's Monday. I've been in England exactly a week, and tomorrow evening I'm flying home to Sydney. Will the emptiness be there too?

The difference is that Mark's here, behind me, tall and warm as he follows me into the house, his voice filling the emptiness and his hands dealing competently with bag and baggage: his by the front door, mine at the foot of the stairs.

In the kitchen I turn on lots of lights, switch on the hot water and heating, find bottle and corkscrew and give them to Mark. The cab-company phone number's in my England Admin notebook, which has buried itself somewhere in my overnight bag. When I straighten up and turn to go back into the kitchen he hasn't poured the wine, he's just standing there in the brilliant light, watching me.

Suddenly I want him so badly it's like being punched in the gut. I want his mouth, his hands, his weight on me, the smell and touch and taste of him filling my mind and my body and my bed. Before I can ask myself why now, before I can remember anything, or forget it, I say, 'Would you like to stay the night?'

He might not want to . . . That's silly, he does want to. I've seen that heat in enough men's eyes.

But he still might say no. Maybe he's not sure what kind of stay-the-night I mean. I should have waited till we were comfortable, till we'd had a drink, till later, till never. My heart's banging in my chest and he hasn't answered me. If he does . . . He's protecting himself, or me, or he's thinking of some other comforting reason that won't expose me or him to humiliation. Because I can feel humiliation crawling up from my belly, over the skin of my chest and up into my face till my head hums with it.

He puts the bottle and the corkscrew very carefully on the side, comes over to me and takes my hands, holding me at a distance.

'Una, are you sure?' Which relieves one of my fears.

I nod.

He draws me closer, bends his head and kisses me. 'I'd like that very much.'

His touch washes away the rest of my fears. We take the wine upstairs to the drawing room and light the fire, though it doesn't seem chilly at all. I'm wide awake from the driving, but not tired, it seems, and neither is he; we're curled close together on the sofa and I'm feeling the fire warm on my face, and watching it gild his. This time it's not about comfort, it's more than comfort: I'm more alive with each shift and tautening of his muscles under my hands, his touch on my neck, shoulder, waist, his mouth and tongue flickering against my skin, the faint salt-sweat taste of him and the scratch of hair against my cheek.

When I want more of his skin against mine I uncurl and stand up, holding out my hand. He stands up too, and we go quite quietly and simply upstairs to my bedroom.

There's light coming in from the river, watery scraps of brightness and no need for more, or less, no need to draw the curtains and shut it out.

His shirt's already unbuttoned. I pull it free and slide it off his shoulders and then while I fumble with his belt buckle he catches my hands and pulls my top up over my head. How easy it is! Even the silly fiddling with zips and hooks, even the ridiculousness of socks: we're easy with each other, with everything about desire, about each other's body and our own. We take our time, relishing each button, each crease of skin, each rumple of cloth pushed aside, each delicate revelation: the soft skin on the inside of my elbows that his tongue finds, the dip under each of his ribs where the muscles turn inwards, his tiny groan when I nip the dark flesh at the base of his thumb, my gasp when he brushes each of my breasts, then cups them, their weight and heat filling his hands, his gaze blurred.

Would it have been like this then? If I'd had this, my heart's desire, when I first fell in love with him? Or would it have been as young love is: awkward, embarrassed, urgent, clumsy? Secret, it would have been, almost defiant. Would we have given in to our need even so, and grabbed for each other as the young do? It's maturity that's wise enough to savour every lick and kiss and shiver.

Do I want it now so much because I've wanted it so long? So keenly that my body cries out to seize him now and drag him into me till we both explode, because I couldn't seize him then? Is this . . . Is this an ending, not a beginning? And if it is, does it matter? I'm alone in the world, and in myself. May I not take my pleasures where I find them, even in ending?

'Professor Una Pryor,' he says softly, slowly, stretching the syllables, relishing them, and relishing me, too. The breath hisses out between his teeth in a way that makes me want him desperately: the only thing I want, the only thing that matters. 'You always were wonderful, Una Pryor . . .'

Is this an ending for him, too? Is his relish not for me but for himself, that he's finally taking possession – the ultimate kind of possession – of what my family denied him for so long? Is *that* why he wants me?

Is *that* why he wants me? The chill of this thought shrinks down on to me. The heat in my belly shrivels. I'm closed and cold and I have to force myself not to roll aside.

Mark sees, or feels, or both. His hands leave me, he moves away. 'You all right? Cold?'

'A bit.'

'Here,' he says, 'let's get under the covers.'

But when I've rolled aside and he's pulled the duvet up and over both of us, I don't turn into his arms, I can't bring myself to. It would be like letting him take possession of my soul.

I feel his hesitation, his uncertainty like a shiver between my shoulder-blades. Then he lies down behind me and puts his arms round me.

'It's all right. We don't have to, not if you don't want to.'

'I . . .' I try to start, but what can I say?

'Is it Adam?'

I nod because I can't lie out loud, and besides, if I speak I'll cry. And then the tiredness hits me again and, worse, the miles of road, the driving and the talking: Gareth's eyes looking at the end of his working life; the jagged spars and shadows of Sheriff Hutton; Anthony, whom I'll never know; Elizabeth, who knew my widow's grief better than I know it myself; and Adam, who owned my heart though not my soul, and whose heart I own still.

'Would you like me to go?' says Mark, very gently, after a long time.

'I'm sorry.'

'It's okay. I understand.' He slides away from me, and only when he's dressed does he crouch beside the bed so that he's looking me in the eyes. 'But are you sure you're okay? I could stay downstairs, if you don't want to be alone in the house.'

'No, I'll be all right. I just need to sleep.'

'Of course.' He reaches out and strokes my hair, just once, then leans forward to kiss my forehead before he leaves. 'Sleep well.' By the time I hear the front door close I'm sinking into sleep.

~

In the middle of the night I wake, burning and sweaty, and get up to go to the bathroom. On the landing, just outside my room, are my bags. Mark must have carried them silently upstairs and set them down before he left. *Are you all right?* he said. He was doing what he could, even right to the end. I suppose it is the end, I think stupidly, but grief is so tiring. I sleep.

~

When I wake again it's midday light that spills into the room in bright shards. I stretch, and feel the stiffness in me soften and warm, then remember.

So it was an ending, it seems, an ending of sorts, anyway. This soft, sad lead in my belly is so familiar I don't even have to ask what it is.

Still, I'll take it easy, get up slowly, I think. The

technique, too, is familiar. Perhaps go to one of the new-old pubs that do lunch or even just for supper, take it gently after my busy few days. That's it. I've had a busy few days, that's all. Later I'll ring Gareth: arrange to see him tomorrow to say goodbye. I haven't got much to pack. Perhaps I'll indulge myself with a taxi to the airport.

I have a long, hot bath, and unpack my small bag from our little trip. Not many clean clothes left, but enough for today: jeans and a sweater. I tidy up, put some washing on. It's three by the time I'm drinking coffee and eating toast, and I think I'm fully awake, but the phone ringing makes me jump almost out of my skin. I pick up the receiver. Perhaps it's . . . 'Hello?'

'Una? Lionel.' His voice buffets me. 'You've heard from Izzy?'

I try to shake my brain into some kind of sense. 'She rang when we were at Fergus's. She said she's arranged the shipping. I knew she was anti the whole thing, but I'd no idea she'd do this.'

'I don't think any of us had,' he said. 'Anyway, don't panic, Fergus rang me later — said how nice it was to see you and Mark, by the way, and Mark's step-daughter. What's her name?'

'Morgan. Yes, we had a lovely visit. I thought he seemed very well.'

'Got his balance better now, I think. Morgan, goodness, the things they call themselves, these days.' I forbear to point out that our family's names aren't exactly ordinary. 'Anyway, we can get an injunction tomorrow on the grounds that ownership's disputed.'

'Oh, good, well done. Have you told her? But I hate thinking of this kind of war.'

'I know. Family businesses can get messy,' says Lionel, and I'm awake enough now to be able to tell that though he'd rather Izzy wasn't on the other side, he's quite enjoying the prospect of a fight. 'But an injunction's only temporary. And if she decides to fight it'll get very expensive, which is silly, when we could spend the money on working out this plan for the Chantry properly. Besides, discretion's the better part of valour in these things, isn't it, don't you think? When it's family?'

'Undoubtedly,' I say, and am amused to find myself slipping into his style.

'Quite. So I've been doing a bit of ringing round in the last few days. Anyway, I tracked down a publishing acquaintance who works for Hesperium Press – you know, Hesperium, the big liberal-arts college in Maine?'

'Yes, I've lectured there. Big design faculty. Excellent bibliographic archive.'

'That's the one. Very well endowed. Turned out he was over here on business for the Press. I asked him and Izzy for drinks this lunchtime. Champagne, all the trimmings. Anyway, as I hoped, he's offered her a commission to write a book about the restoration of the Chantry, and she's agreed.'

'Oh!' I say, too astonished to work out the implications.

He chuckles, and I realise he is — he definitely is — enjoying this. He never once laughed while I was visiting him. 'I pointed out to Izzy that the book's only worth writing if the Chantry's as fully restored as possible. Everything any of us has going home. *Everything*. Including the things she wants to sell to San Diego.'

I start to laugh too, because this I do understand. 'Lionel, you're a genius!'

'Well, she's only agreed in principle, but I'm sure it's all right. No advance, of course, and he couldn't commit himself to details, said he wasn't allowed to do back-of-an-envelope costings, these days. But it'll be a handsome affair, they always do a good job, especially for what they'd consider one of their own. Nothing less than the best for William Pryor and the Solmani Press. And the royalties split between Izzy and the Chantry Trust. That's symbolic, more than anything. I don't suppose it'll be serious money.'

'That's not the point, though, is it? And having that bit of publicity will encourage the fundraising.'

'Quite. So I don't think we need worry about Izzy.'

'You said she's only agreed in principle, though.'

'Yes, but I've known my dear older sister for half a century. She won't change her mind.'

I think of her absolute certainty about her work. 'No, you're right.' Now that what he's said is beginning to sink in I'm shaking slightly with shock and relief. 'You're brilliant, Lionel. Have you told Mark?'

'I tried to ring him, but he's out. At least, I only got the answering-machine. Do you want to?'

Everything comes back to me properly, like being winded in the throat. 'No . . . No, you do it. I'm horribly busy. You try later. He – you'd explain it so much better.'

'Yes, of course. Listen, Una, if I don't see you before you fly, have a good journey.'

'I will,' I say. 'Don't know when I'll be back, I'm afraid.'

'No, I know. Though I'm thinking of getting my computer at home hitched up to do electronic mail. Do you have it at the university?'

'Yes. That would be good. Let me know. And lots of love.'

'And to you. Goodbye, Una.'

'Goodbye, Lionel. Good luck with all the Chantry stuff.'

~

In the event I can only arrange to see Uncle Gareth on my way to the airport on Tuesday afternoon. 'I've booked you a taxi for later,' he says, giving me a hug. 'And I've boxed up *Dawn at East Egg*, though you'd better take it as hand-luggage if you can. I never trust those baggage handlers. But come in and tell me how Fergus is, and all the places you saw. I've never been to Sheriff Hutton, though I know York.'

'Fergus was very well, as far as I could tell. A bit shaken by the Izzy stuff.'

'I know. I think we all are. But . . . but it does sound as if it's going to be all right.' He's saying cheerful things, but he sounds so tired and sad. 'I could never have forgiven myself if my not wanting to lose the Press made a rift between you all.'

'But it's as Lionel said, family businesses are like that,' I say quickly, following him into the workshop and sitting down in one of the armchairs. 'You've said yourself that you wondered sometimes what it would have been like if my father had been alive.'

'I know. Family things . . . Towton, I remember, 1471, isn't it? Your father . . . dear Kay. Who knows? You're very like him, you know, Una. Specially about the eyes and nose.'

'I know. But it's always nice to be reminded. Except that I always think of you as my father.'

'Oh, Una,' he says, rather shakily. 'That's – good. Yes. Well. You and Mark . . .' His voice trails off.

And then I know what I must do, though not how to say it. It's dangerous, but I'll probably never see Mark again, or not for years. It won't matter by then. And I can trust Uncle Gareth. He'll do what's best with what I suddenly know I'm going to tell him.

'Uncle Gareth, Mark said . . . While we were away, Mark said . . . He said about why he left. And stayed away. Because I think he wanted to finish things properly.

An ending. We were talking about endings...' I hadn't known I was going to put it like that and my voice stumbles. I'm avoiding Uncle Gareth's eye. 'I – I think ending things... ending things properly is important too... Though I suppose it's his... private thing, really. But I'd like to tell you.'

His gaze sharpens. I have wondered if he knows what I'm going to say, but if he does I think he'd say so, to spare us both embarrassment. But he doesn't, he just says, 'He didn't tell you in confidence, did he, Una? Because if he did you shouldn't...'

'No, no, he didn't. I wouldn't dream of it if... In fact he sort of said he wished he could have told you. He said, "I couldn't tell him, not face to face."'

'Fair enough,' he says.

So I go on. As nearly as I can, I quote Mark's words so that I'm faithful to them, and Lionel's, too, because it's easier than recasting such words as my own, though they're shocking still, said to Gareth's gentle, thoughtful face. 'And – and it had never occurred to him, not till then. Mark – he wasn't very old,' I say, and try not to sound pleading. 'None of us was.'

Gareth sits very still for a long time. 'I suppose I should have known, or guessed, and said something to make it clear that... that I loved him because he was the nearest thing I've ever had to a son. Maybe I hoped no one would think anything else, if I didn't say anything. You know how people were about queers.'

'Maybe he was so shocked because he – he loved you so much. "Gareth was the nearest thing I ever had to a father," he said.'

Tears start to roll down his face, stumbling in the creases of his age and running again. He pulls a handkerchief out of his trouser pocket and mops his eyes, and I don't say anything because I've never seen him cry before, not even at Aunt Elaine's funeral, but I do lean forward and take his hand, and we sit like that for a long time.

At last, when he's blown his nose and stuffed his handkerchief back, I say, 'Should I not have told you?'

'No,' he says. 'I'm glad you did.' He doesn't say anything more, and I keep quiet. After a while he says, 'Shall you come for the opening?' with a half-grin that means I must know he wasn't born yesterday, that many another plan to save the Press has come to nothing.

'Of course.' But I wonder if I'll be able to face it. I don't know, I can't tell. Everything that's happened . . . I want to go home and I'm about to start crying, but I mustn't, not even in front of Uncle Gareth, not when it's like this, not after what I told him.

The distant crunch of gravel, and a car hoots. 'That'll be your cab,' he says. We both get up and I turn away as if to pick up my bags, so that I can brush my sleeve across my eyes. 'Oh dear, it's sad to see you go. You and Mark . . . Yes . . . He . . . But never mind. Who knows what will happen?'

'Who knows, indeed? I still want you to come out to stay in Sydney and get some sun. My birthday party, too. I've got so much out there I want to show you.'

'We'll see,' he says, and I know he's thinking he's too old. 'And *bon voyage*, dear Una.'

~

Summer holidays seem to have started early this year, and the check-in desks at Heathrow are thick with travellers. I'm flying home into winter, of course, grey and cold, but that's all right. And home without Adam is . . . just how it is.

But my skin still feels sore with knowing the emptiness waiting for me.

I fish a book out of my shoulder-bag. 'We know little about Elizabeth's childhood and upbringing, not even the exact date of her birth . . .' I read, and sigh the exasperated sigh of the academic balked of the most elementary facts.

'That boring?' says Mark, close to my shoulder.

I drop the book. He picks it up and gives it back to me. 'What are you doing here?' I say, when I've recovered.

'Gareth rang me. I thought if I could get here while you were checking in, I'd be able to find you. He said you told him what – what I told you.'

I turn full on to him, because this matters so much. 'Was I wrong? Should I not have? I'm sorry if . . .'

'No, you weren't wrong. I'd have said if I didn't want

you to. We talked. We might not have, otherwise. I came because I wanted to say thank you for making it happen.'

'Did you . . . Sorry, it's none of my business, but you sorted it out? With Gareth?'

He nods, but then it's my turn to check in and there's a fuss about whether *Dawn at East Egg* is too big for hand-luggage, though it isn't because Gareth's been too clever for that: it slots in and out of the size-testing frame with millimetres to spare. I'm worried Mark will go, because he's said what he needed to, but he doesn't.

'Coffee?' he says. 'Or do you need to go straight through?'

'Coffee would be nice,' I say, my heart giving a kind of lollop for some reason, though I refuse to think it's embarrassment. My head's starting to feel light and buzzy. 'They won't call the flight for ages yet, and in the next twenty-four hours there'll be quite enough time to stare at departure-lounge walls of one sort and another.'

He sort of laughs and we start to make our way through the terminal. It's a limbo-world, constantly moving and always the same; none of it touches me. We go up some stairs, Mark moving clumsily, without his usual craftsman's concision and ease. We find a corner of a coffee bar that is neither crowded nor dirty and I'm making some silly remark about hoping Customs don't ask to see documentation for my father's picture, it not being that valuable or him that famous, when Mark puts his hand over mine and grips hard. I stop dead.

'Yes, I did sort it out with Gareth,' he says, and then is silent, his gaze withdrawn as if he's still hearing the conversation. 'But, Una, he said something else.'

'What?' My heart starts to thud as if his hand's squeezing it directly.

'He — he said you said something . . . about ending properly.'

'Yes — yes, we did. About . . . I was trying to explain *why* you told me about you leaving the Press. So he wouldn't think I was just giving away a confidence.'

'I know. You wouldn't. But — but . . . I'm sorry, tell me if it's none of my business. I've been thinking about Sunday night. It's all I've thought about since . . . And Gareth said he wondered . . . Did you . . . I understand that for you — it's . . . Was it about ending for you? About the Chantry? About leaving England? About Adam, above all? I know that . . . But I hope you'll forgive me if I say . . . An ending, like you said. For you. But it's not an ending for me. And I've realised that I . . . I . . .' He stops.

I have no words, nothing to say, nothing that could possibly keep up with the feelings that are pouring through me. Everything I've been afraid of seems to be happening. I don't know how to stop it. I don't know if I want to stop it. I look away, because looking at Mark's eyes, at his mouth, at his beautiful hands, which are trembling as much as mine are, makes my mind slip its moorings.

Mark clears his throat. 'I . . . I don't think I should say

what I'd like to say,' he says, and when I can't help looking up, the way he's watching me reminds me suddenly of Morgan. 'Such a lot has happened. And Adam, still. So . . . so I won't say it. Not yet. But if . . . I'm sure we'll be in touch over the Chantry. But if I found myself in Australia in the next few months, could I come and see you?'

Inside me, everything stills. Good manners would say yes. My fear for myself – for Adam – would say no.

But what I loved in Adam, I first learnt to love in Mark. If Mark does come to see me . . . then whatever happens, I can still hold on to Adam. There is no battle. He'll always be there . . . whatever happens.

I smile at Mark, though I think he can see I'm nearly crying with relief. 'I'd like that, dear Mark. I'd like that very much.'

~

When the aeroplane's engines have settled from a shriek to a roar and the seatbelt lights are switched off, I stand up to open the luggage locker above my head. I so nearly missed the plane that my belongings are in a muddle, and I get a dirty look from my neighbour, as if I've caused quite enough trouble to my fellow passengers already. I dig in my bag and eventually find a notebook, then a pen, and a photocopy of Mancini's account of Richard III's *coup d'état*. Before I do, I bark my knuckles on wood. On the crate he handmade to fit *Dawn at East Egg* so exactly, Uncle Gareth has written 'Property of Professor Una

Pryor', his writing as always black and beautiful, and now on the crate a grand statement, visible to all. Only it's not my property, not exactly. On the other hand, it's not Gareth's either, according to my legal inheritance. But who would know that, except me?

I sit down and arrange my books on the tray-table as well as I can. Even my work has changed, though it's got no easier. Can I do it? *Can* I?

It isn't that I don't know what happened. With patience it's possible to leave few stones unturned, though even now there may be more scraps to be ferreted out, or stumbled on as we did the letter, more connections to see, more conclusions to reach. The gaps you have to bridge do get smaller.

But bridging gaps isn't what I want to do, not any more. 'You have to make it whole,' said Mark.

Perhaps I've found some kind of answer, some way of telling the truth in the blanks between the facts where, till now, there's been nothing. A way that is neither truth nor falsehood but is whole. But do I dare? There are no authorities for this, no references and precedents and peer-reviewed journals; no familiar track with familiar rules. My only authority is what I choose to write. The freedom's frightening, the track, such as it is, is strange: Narrow Street, East Smithfield and the Chantry, St Albans and Grafton, from Astley to Pontefract and York and thence to Sheriff Hutton, and a letter that was there all the time . . .

I know the journey has a beginning, a middle and an end, that it is whole, but Anthony and Elizabeth could not. To them it was a pilgrimage: the past was past, the future unknown. All they had was the moment.

At each moment – each station of the cross – they're no more beyond my reach than Adam is. But there's only one way to reach them, I've been thinking, slowly and uncertainly since yesterday: only one way. I must dare to do it this way, because otherwise I'll never reach them.

Gareth said, 'I think it was really so that he could do what he wanted . . . he didn't have to stick to the literal truth. He could make the patterns – use the colours – that said what he wanted to say.'

Will what I write be my words or theirs? My life or theirs? It won't be history's. 'Visible at two feet, and invisible at four', said Mark's friend Charlie, at Eltham Palace.

And where should I begin? At the beginning, as Izzy begins her story of the Solmani Press? Or at the moment when, after exile and despair, God amended all?

I think of Mark, and the emptiness that awaits me in Sydney seems warmer and more bearable, because it won't be for ever.

I'll start, I realise, with Elizabeth, no longer a child, riding home, knowing that awaiting her was a new life and a new place in the world.

Elysabeth, she signed herself, but I must find her voice, and give it to her. Slowly, I begin to write . . .

The road home to Grafton was always a merry one. That it was the custom of families of our degree to send their children away, the better to learn the skills and lessons proper to their estate, did not make my childhood's exile from Grafton to Groby any easier. Sir Edward Grey of Groby was kindly enough, but his wife Lady Ferrars was not. Besides, what girl of seven or eight would not miss her home and her sisters? Nor is the promise of a good marriage much comfort to such a child. When my sister Margaret joined me at Groby, it was better, and as I grew older I learnt discretion, so that Lady Ferrars could find no fault with my words or my duties, still less in my seeming submission to her in all things . . .

That year we lay for a night at Harborough, for Sir Edward Grey's man who rode home with us from Groby said that with the snow threatening as it was, it would be folly to press on further and perhaps find ourselves stranded at nightfall.

Historical Note

To my mind bibliographies and lists of sources are out of place in a work of fiction, but the Heisenberg principle applies to historical novelists as well as to historians. In plotting the position of Elizabeth and Anthony Woodville at certain moments in their lives, I know that I may have left readers wondering about the trajectory of their story. So here it is.

Elizabeth (Elysabeth) Woodville was probably born in 1437, and Anthony (Antony) four years later. Their mother, Jacquetta of Luxembourg, had first been married to John, Duke of Bedford, who ruled as regent for his nephew, the boy-king Henry VI, and wore himself out trying to hold on to England's vast possessions in France. Their father, Sir Richard Woodville (Wydvil), had been the late duke's seneschal, or deputy, in Normandy: his and the widowed Duchess Jacquetta's elopement caused a court scandal. They were soon forgiven, became active in royal service, and had sixteen children. Richard held various commands, most notably at Calais, and Jacquetta was a lady-in-waiting to her fellow Frenchwoman Queen Margaret (Marguerite), daughter of the King of Anjou. Margaret was strong-minded and perforce became politically active, for Henry VI was gentle and pious, and wholly incapable of controlling a ruling class that no longer had England's traditional claims to France as a safe outlet for their rivalries.

The Woodville family seat was at Grafton in Northamptonshire, and at some time around 1452 Elizabeth was married to Sir John Grey, the eldest son of a knightly family based a little further north at Groby, just outside Northampton. They probably lived at Astley in Warwickshire, and she bore two sons, Thomas (Tom) and Richard (Dickon in the first half of the novel) Grey. Anthony, meanwhile, following in his father's footsteps, became well known as a successful soldier and performer in the joust. He married an heiress, Elizabeth, Lady Scales, and became Lord Scales in right of his wife. The Woodvilles and Greys were staunch supporters of Henry VI and the Lancastrian royal line. But in 1454 Henry VI succumbed to what seems to have been catatonic schizophrenia. His cousin Richard, Duke of York, who had a better claim in blood to the throne, was made Regent, with *his* own cousin Richard Neville, Earl of Warwick, as his chief supporter. During this time Margaret of Anjou gave birth to a son, Edward of Lancaster, Prince of Wales. When Henry VI recovered his wits, Richard, Duke of York, resigned the regency, but claimed and won the right to be Henry's heir in place of the baby Edward of Lancaster. Refusing to accept the disinheriting of her son, Margaret drew even more on the support of her ally the Duke of Somerset, and the nation's political rivalries were polarised: supporters of the House of York or of the House of Lancaster.

Through the twists and turns of what became known as the War of the Cousins the Woodvilles and the Greys supported Henry VI. Sir John Grey was killed at the Second Battle of St Albans in 1461 leaving Elizabeth a widow with two young sons. Richard, Duke of York, was killed in battle in 1460, and his eighteen-year-old son Edward inherited his claim. At the battle of Towton in 1461 Henry and Margaret's army was annihilated. Along with many others the Woodvilles switched sides to the victorious young Edward. Henry was captured and imprisoned in the Tower of London, Edward was crowned as Edward IV, and Richard and Anthony Woodville were soon active in royal service.

In 1464 Edward IV fell in love with Elizabeth Woodville and they were married in secret. He was twenty-two, and she twenty-seven. In the next five years she bore him three daughters: Elizabeth (Bess), Mary and Cecily. Her father was raised to the peerage as Earl Rivers, and he and all her brothers were prominent in royal service, while her sisters made a series of advantageous marriages. Inevitably there were tensions between the different factions at court, including that of the Woodvilles. It was accepted that the King's family would benefit from grants of land and power (the two being more or less synonymous at this date) as well as wealthy marriages. But Elizabeth was the first English-born queen consort, and there was no precedent for the proper treatment of a queen's family, and such a large one at that. Elizabeth's son Thomas Grey was made Marquess of Dorset, and in due course was given a place on the Royal Council and some political importance, while her younger son Sir Richard Grey did little in royal service and received correspondingly little reward.

Anthony became the courtier *par excellence*, finding time for literary and philosophical study even while he was engaged in political, diplomatic and military service, as well as running the complicated business affairs of any man of property. He was England's champion at a famous joust with the champion of Burgundy, an event of political as much as chivalric importance. One of his squires at this tournament was a member of the Gascon gentry named Louis de Bretaylles, who was in English service at the time. Years later Louis is also known to have been of Anthony's party on a diplomatic and religious mission to Portugal and to Santiago de Compostela in Spain.

By 1469 Edward was growing ever more independent of the Earl of Warwick's judgement, and Warwick began to intrigue with Edward's younger brother George, Duke of Clarence, and then with his erstwhile enemy the exiled Queen Margaret. The upshot was a series of treasonous rebellions, and when Edward realised that even his supporters could not be relied on, he fled with Anthony and others to Bruges in Flanders, then part of the domain of the Duke of Burgundy, who was lately married to Edward's sister, Margaret of York. Elizabeth and Anthony's father, Earl Rivers, was killed by Warwick's faction along with his son, their brother John. Elizabeth fled with her daughters into sanctuary at Westminster, where she gave birth to a son, Edward (Ned), styled from birth Prince of Wales. It seems likely that it was in exile that Anthony translated from the French an anthology of the *Dicts and Sayings of the Philosophers*, while it is fairly certain that it was in Bruges that he met Caxton, who had set up a printing press there. In 1470 Edward invaded England, giving command of the Tower of London to Anthony, and in a series of battles defeated Margaret of Anjou's forces. Her son and Henry's heir, Edward of Lancaster, was killed in battle, as was Warwick, while Henry died at the Tower in mysterious circumstances. The line of Lancaster, founded by the usurping Henry IV, seemed extinct, the only male remaining being Henry Tudor, Earl of Richmond, who traced his royal blood through his mother Margaret Beaufort, not his father Edmund Tudor, and lived a fugitive life in Wales and Brittany.

The toddler Edward, Prince of Wales, was sent to

Ludlow, one of the York family's principal castles, to endow the council that ruled the often troublesome Welsh Marches with royal authority. Anthony was appointed head of the Prince's Council, his guardian and governor and, although he travelled a great deal on his own and royal affairs, spent much of the rest of his life at Ludlow. His *Dicts and Sayings of the Philosophers* was the first book that Caxton printed in England after his own, and he and Elizabeth became noted patrons of Caxton's press. Elizabeth, meanwhile, gave birth to more children: Margaret who died at eight months old; Richard (little Dickon in the second half of the novel who, as second son of the King, was immediately made Duke of York; Anne; George who died before the age of two; Katherine; and Bridget. Elizabeth's second daughter Mary died in 1482 aged fifteen. In 1475, when Edward invaded France in support of the traditional claim of English monarchs to the French throne, he made Elizabeth an executor of his will, and guardian of the Prince of Wales.

A crisis in 1478, when George, Duke of Clarence, attacked Elizabeth and her mother Jacquetta with accusations of witchcraft, finally exhausted Edward's patience with his traitorous brother, and he was tried by his peers and condemned to death. Meanwhile their youngest brother, Richard, Duke of Gloucester, was ruling the north of England in the King's name, as Anthony was the west. At one stage, as part of an alliance with Scotland, it was proposed that Anthony should marry the sister of the Scottish king, as his wife had died in 1473. Anglo-Scottish relations cooled soon afterwards, and nothing came of it. He later married Mary FitzLewes, a young and well-connected heiress, but his only known child is Margaret Stradling, whose mother Gwentlian Stradling was a member of an important Welsh gentry family.

In 1483, at the age of only forty-one, Edward IV died. His will appointed Elizabeth as his chief executor, and she also had a seat on the Royal Council. His only surviving brother Richard, Duke of Gloucester, was to be appointed Protector until his twelve-year-old son Edward attained his majority, which by custom might only be a few years hence. Arrangements were made for Anthony to bring Edward from Ludlow to London for his coronation. At Northampton on 30 April 1483 Richard and the Duke of Buckingham met them as agreed, but arrested Anthony, then Elizabeth's son Sir Richard Grey, took control of the new King and his escort, and sent Anthony to Richard's castle at Sheriff Hutton.

On hearing this news Elizabeth again took sanctuary at Westminster with her five daughters and youngest son, Richard, Duke of York. Her eldest son, Thomas Grey, escaped to France, while her brother Edward Woodville, Admiral of the Fleet, held ships in King Edward's name but eventually escaped to France as well. Their brother Lionel Woodville, as Bishop of Salisbury, was relatively safe. The sanctuary was surrounded by troops, and

Elizabeth could no longer take part in the Royal Council's affairs as they ran the country with Richard, Duke of Gloucester as Protector, and arranged the coronation of her son. At last she gave in to pressure from the Council, and in May allowed young Richard to join his brother Edward in the royal apartments at the Tower.

Eight weeks after his arrest Anthony was moved to Pontefract, where he and Richard Grey were executed on 25 June 1483, then buried uncoffined in a common grave at a nearby monastery. Anthony was forty-one. Richard, Duke of Gloucester, was proclaimed king on the following day. From that time the boys, Edward V, and his brother Richard, Duke of York, were seen less and less and their servants were reduced drastically in number: the last sighting of them is recorded as being in July of that year. The evidence suggests that rumours of their deaths spread quite quickly, although it will never be known for certain what happened to them, when they died or by whose hand.

Elizabeth and her daughters probably left sanctuary some time in March 1484 and entered the custody of Richard III, although where they lived is not known. Later that year she allowed her two oldest living daughters, Elizabeth of York, as she was known, and Cecily, to go to Richard's court, while the three youngest stayed with her. Since the disappearance of her brothers, Elizabeth of York had a strong claim to be Queen of

England in her own right. After some months the girls were sent to Sheriff Hutton, where George, Duke of Clarence's children had long been kept. Meanwhile the exiled Lancastrian Earl of Richmond, Henry Tudor, laid his own claim to the throne, and undertook to marry Elizabeth of York when he had succeeded in his claim.

Henry's second attempt to invade England, in August 1485, was successful, and at the battle of Bosworth Richard III was killed.

Only when he had been safely crowned King of England did Henry marry Elizabeth of York and have her crowned as his consort. Elizabeth Woodville, as Queen Dowager and the Queen's Mother, had an assured place at court but in practice was very much subordinate to Margaret Beaufort, as the King's Mother. In 1487 Elizabeth retired to the traditional royal retreat of the Abbey of Bermondsey, giving up her personal estates and assets to her daughter, as was traditional, and accepting in return a pension from Henry. She died at Bermondsey on 8 June 1492, at the age of fifty-five, and was buried with Edward in the Chapel Royal he had built at Windsor.

Acknowledgements

A Secret Alchemy was written as part of a PhD in Creative Writing at Goldsmiths College, University of London, and I would like to thank Maura Dooley and all the staff and students there for their help and support.

EMMA DARWIN

The Mathematics of Love

'Convincing and involving . . . a book to lose yourself in'
Daily Mail

'This sweeping tale of nineteenth-century war and courtship and twentieth-century teenage rebellion has a real flavour of its own that will grip you to the end . . . An accomplished, vividly realised debut' *Marie Claire*

It is 1819 and Stephen Fairhurst wants only to forget the horrors of Waterloo and remember the great and secret love he lost. But, despite his friendship with the clever Lucy Durward, he cannot tell her about the darkness in his past.

In the summer of 1976 the teenaged Anna, hot, bored, and lonely in the Suffolk countryside, becomes entangled in two men's lives: Theo, a photographer in exile, and the forgotten Stephen Fairhurst.

Acclaimed, gripping and extraordinarily moving, *The Mathematics of Love* is one of the most powerful novels you will ever read of war and suffering, the heat of passion and the redemptive power of love.

'A beautifully written, intelligent book . . . as historically graphic and passionately romantic as Sebastian Faulks's *Birdsong*' *Waterstone's Books Quarterly*

'A daring debut novel . . . Emma Darwin's prose is golden and convincing. Addictive' *Daily Express*

'The reader is spellbound . . . electrifying' *Independent*

978 0 7553 3064 5

headline
review

You can buy any of these other
Headline Review titles from your bookshop
or *direct from the publisher*.

FREE P&P AND UK DELIVERY
(Overseas and Ireland £3.50 per book)

The Mathematics of Love	Emma Darwin	£7.99
My Latest Grievance	Elinor Lipman	£7.99
Foolish Mortals	Jennifer Johnston	£7.99
An Accomplished Woman	Jude Morgan	£7.99
The Good Thief	Hannah Tinti	£7.99
The Infinite Wisdom of Harriet Rose	Diana Janney	£7.99
The Red Carpet	Lavanya Sankaran	£7.99
Passion	Jude Morgan	£7.99

TO ORDER SIMPLY CALL THIS NUMBER

01235 400 414

or visit our website: www.headline.co.uk

Prices and availability subject to change without notice.